Sue Moorcroft

THE *SUNDAY TIMES* BESTSELLER

Summer
at the
French Café

avon.

Published by AVON
A division of HarperCollins*Publishers* Ltd
1 London Bridge Street
London SE1 9GF

www.harpercollins.co.uk

HarperCollins*Publishers*
1st Floor, Watermarque Building, Ringsend Road
Dublin 4, Ireland

A Paperback Original 2022
1
First published in Great Britain by HarperCollins*Publishers* 2022

A catalogue copy of this book is available from the British Library.

ISBN: 978-0-00-852564-4

Typeset in Sabon LT Std by Palimpsest Book Production Limited, Falkirk, Stirlingshire
Printed and bound in UK using 100% Renewable Electricity at CPI Group (UK) Ltd

MIX
Paper from
responsible sources
FSC™ C007454

Acknowledgements

Thank you for reading *Summer at the French Café* and I hope you enjoy it. Readers are everything to an author, and if there's one aspect of online life that I love, it's being able to hear from you. I'm around on Twitter, Facebook and Instagram, have a blog, a website and a newsletter. Join me wherever you can!

You might also like to check out Team Sue Moorcroft – find it on www.suemoorcroft.com. Thanks to its members for helping me choose character or place names and for shouting about my books far and wide.

I'm fortunate to live close to Wicksteed Park in England. I walk there often, enjoying it in all seasons and moods and noticing how others use the space. Some love the rides, others the playthings, the lake activities and the wild walks, or just find it a lovely route to work and school. I'm always grateful to the park's benefactor and its trustees for giving this amazing facility to the public. When it occurred to me what a gorgeous setting it would make for a book, my imagination transplanted it – with a couple of additions – to Alsace, my favourite region of France, to be Parc Lemmel.

The circumstances of Solly losing his teaching job were created for me by my son Paul Matthews and my agent's sister, Madeleine Marjoram. My thanks to them for lending authenticity.

Thanks to my brother Trevor Moorcroft for his enduring willingness to find me just the right material to read. It makes research so easy.

I'm grateful to fellow author Mark West for being my early reader and treating me to his usual pithy commentary – which I think he enjoys writing as much as I enjoy reading.

Thanks to Pia Fenton (who writes as Christina Courtenay) and Myra Kersner (Maggie Sullivan) for their constant friendship, support, and the Sunday-evening WhatsApp calls. I'm blessed to have many author friends and I value every single one.

I wouldn't be bringing you this book if not for: my awesome agent, Juliet Pickering, and all at Blake Friedmann Literary Agency; and my wonderful publishers, the team at Avon HarperCollins. Massive thanks to them and to the many publishing houses that release my novels around the world. It's a delight every time.

Lastly, gratitude to and appreciation of the fabulous book bloggers and bookstagrammers who invite me onto their sites or review my books, utilising their creativity to spread the joy of reading. And if you've enjoyed *Summer at the French Café*, a review from you will be equally welcome! Thank you.

To
Margaret James

When I was a member of the Romantic Novelists'
Association's New Writers' Scheme, author and
columnist Margaret was its co-ordinator. I've never
forgotten her kind encouragement or how generous she
was with her time. When now I say to newer authors
'never give up' or 'don't make enemies', I'm simply
passing on a little of her great advice to me.

Chapter One

Kat halted in the act of sliding two novels into a crisp paper bag for a waiting customer as a dark-haired man sauntered into the book café, hands in pockets, a large backpack dangling from his shoulder. What on earth was Jakey doing here, in Livres et Café? He'd been staying with her in her small apartment since last Wednesday, but this morning she'd almost been made late for work by them saying their goodbyes. He wasn't meant to return for eleven days.

Jakey grinned as he caught her astonished gaze. Ignoring the wicked twinkle in his brown eyes, she switched her attention back to her customer. 'That's seventeen euros ninety, please.'

The woman, a sunburned Brit with a beautiful Welsh lilt, produced her payment card. 'Friends said we must visit Parc Lemmel because it has something for everyone,' she confided. 'My kids are on the rollercoaster and my husband's rowing on the lake.' She leaned forward eagerly. 'And for me, there's this lovely shopping arcade and your bookshop selling English novels. My husband bought me an e-reader because he said my paperbacks weigh down the suitcases, but I like proper books.'

'Me, too,' Kat agreed because, as the manager of a book café, she wasn't about to admit to the Kindle lurking in her bag in the office. She dropped into her routine tourist-friendly patter as she tapped the buttons of the card machine and turned it towards the woman. 'And I completely agree about Parc Lemmel. I'm so lucky my bosses rent these premises and I get to work in this gorgeous place. Eastern France's borders with Belgium, Luxemburg, Germany, Switzerland and Italy bring in loads of tourists, especially with Strasbourg being only seven or eight miles away, and the River Rhine not much further than that.'

Looking impressed, the woman fumbled with a pair of glasses before squinting at the screen, giving Kat a moment to glance back at Jakey, who was still hovering in the background. His thick, dark hair flopped forward, and he waggled one suggestive eyebrow, making Kat's cheeks heat.

She held out the bag to her customer. 'Thank you. Enjoy your new books.'

The lady wandered away to peruse the pastries in the café section, where assistant manager Danielle was serving. Jakey glanced at his watch and lifted the eyebrow again. Reading his unspoken message, Kat turned to a nearby assistant tidying the small selection of Italian-language books. 'Justine, can you serve for five minutes, please?'

'*Oui.*' Justine jumped up, brown ponytail swinging. When she caught sight of Jakey she grinned knowingly, then turned to the next customer, beginning in French but switching to English when the elderly gentleman placed an English-language history of Alsace on the counter. The region's rich history of belonging alternately to France and Germany meant local history books sold well.

Kat headed for the back area with a discreet gesture for Jakey to follow. The moment she opened the office door, her dog Angelique leapt from her bed with a joyful, 'Woof!' and whirled into a waggy canine welcome dance.

'*Oui, oui*, Angelique,' cried Jakey, laughing, but also holding out a discouraging hand to prevent Angelique from jumping up and sullying his clothes with her rust-coloured hairs. 'I love you, too, but I have only ten minutes and I wish to spend them with your gorgeous owner.' Jakey's rolling French accent caressed the English words. He spoke English well, having spent several years in the UK, and Kat spoke French well, having lived in France for over eight years, so they alternated between the two.

Kat, who never minded Angelique jumping up because it saved her bending down to pat her, gave the foxy-looking dog a consolatory ear-rub, then said, 'Bed!' and clicked her fingers towards the cushiony oval with 'Kat's Dog' embroidered on it. Angelique's tail drooped as she gazed at Kat to check she meant it, then she plodded across the room to flop down with a disappointed sigh.

Jakey dropped his backpack to the floor and then reached for Kat. She stepped into his embrace, curling her arms around his neck. 'It's not even five in the afternoon,' she said. 'Shouldn't you be at the circuit?' At this time on a Sunday, she'd expected Jakey to be engaged with his job in the world of kart racing, which was what had brought him to Alsace from his base in Rennes in Brittany. Though she had little interest in motorsport, she understood he coached and managed up-and-coming young karters who hoped to move on to more senior racing categories. After something he called 'debriefs' with the drivers and their

3

attendant parent at the local kart track, Jakey was scheduled to embark on the long train journey back to Rennes this evening. For the following week he'd be office-based at the sports management company that employed him, before beginning the cycle again.

Kat couldn't believe that karters as young as ten might need a coach-manager, but why else would Jakey travel the breadth of France to work with such hotshots? It sounded exciting to nurture young talent and 'scout' new drivers, but Kat much preferred her own job in a book café in the middle of wonderful Parc Lemmel where, as well as the rides and lakes, there was everything from formal gardens to vast green areas. Her younger brother Solly had just come to work in the park, too, and she was guiltily aware that she so far hadn't devoted much time to helping him settle in, having spent the past five days wrapped up in Jakey.

Jakey kissed her, his mouth hot and hard. 'The sessions were cut short because of a safety issue with a barrier. I jumped on the tram to Muntsheim to take a few minutes with my lover before going to the train station.'

'You're taking the tram in and out of the city to snatch just a few moments?' Kat let her head tilt to the side so he could nibble a spot on her neck that sent sparks arcing through her. 'You can't stay tonight?'

'I wish I could.' His hands roved down to cup her buttocks. 'But I cannot miss the Monday meetings I have arranged. I will not bore you. I know motorsport makes you want to fall asleep.'

She laughed, then switched to a scolding, 'Jakey!' as his warm hand slipped up her red polo shirt and deftly unclipped her bra.

'We have time,' he murmured, cupping a breast.

4

Infatuated Kat might be, but a quickie when a staff member might walk in was very much not her style. She clapped a firm hand over his. 'I have to return to work.' Then, when his face darkened, 'We'd embarrass Angelique, anyway.'

Angelique took the sound of her name as an invitation to leap from her doggy bed and rejoin them, wagging her tail and bouncing on her hind legs, smiling her most ingratiating doggy smile.

'Damn the dog, and damn the work,' Jakey grumbled, reluctantly allowing Kat to fish his hand out of her clothing.

'You wouldn't stop work if I suddenly appeared at the kart track,' she pointed out, reaching behind her back to refasten her bra before straightening her shirt.

'*Non, c'est vrai*,' he agreed firmly. 'Never do that. You would distract me.'

Kat had zero wishes to visit the kart track, so didn't argue. Clothing rearranged, she indulged in more kisses and then escorted Jakey decorously back into the sales area, suspecting that her cheeks were pink after his attentions when she caught Justine and Danielle's knowing looks. Crossing the indoor café section, she took him through the doorway to the outdoor seating. June had just begun, and the full complement of tables and parasols were set out. Above them, the summer sky was dotted with clouds like white stuffing bursting from a huge blue mattress.

'Kat!' a man's voice called from one of the outdoor tables.

Recognising the familiar voice, she glanced around to see a grinning young man seated beneath a dark green parasol. 'Hi, Solly!' Then, to Jakey, 'That's my brother . . . well, half-brother. I told you he arrived last week for a working holiday. I haven't got used to him being around, as we've lived in different countries for the past eight years.' Grasping Jakey's hand, she towed him towards a table, which, she realised, Solly was sharing with another man wearing the same green park staff uniform as him.

Solly stuck out his hand for Jakey to shake. 'So you're Jakey, who my sister's seeing? Jakey's a funny name for a Frenchman, isn't it?'

'It's Jacques, really, but when I worked in England someone mispronounced it "Jakes" and it ended up as Jakey.' Discreetly, Jakey checked his watch. 'I'm very sorry to leave as soon as we have met but I must take the tram quickly, to catch my train. Excuse me.' He gave Kat's fingers a last squeeze and hurried away, backpack bobbing. Kat watched his handsome head as he threaded through the milling visitors in front of the park shopping area. Her heart was still pattering after the snatched moments in her office. A dating app had brought them together a few months ago and before long Jakey had begun to arrange his work schedule to take his rest days in Strasbourg . . . or, more precisely, in Kat's apartment in the village of Kirchhoffen, just outside Strasbourg. Their time together was filled with laughter and lovemaking, but Jakey's schedule ensured her time to herself, too, which was the best of both worlds, in her view.

She wasn't sure that this whirlwind romance was going to come to anything, partly because half the time there was geographical distance between them. Also, Kat didn't give her heart easily. There had been a couple of proper relationships in her life – one at uni and one here in France – but neither time had she thought, *This is the one*.

'This is Noah, who I'm sharing staff accommodation with,' came Solly's voice, reclaiming Kat's attention. 'But he's on the lakeside staff, not gardens and grounds like me.'

Hastily remembering her manners, she turned with a welcoming smile. 'Hello, Noah. Are you new at Parc Lemmel, too?' She addressed him in English as Solly had already mentioned he'd been allocated accommodation to share with 'this older guy,' who'd lived in France since childhood but was originally from near Edinburgh. Kat wouldn't have termed Noah 'older' as he appeared to be around her own age of thirty-seven, but the perspective was different for a twenty-five-year-old like her brother.

Compared to Solly's round features, Noah's face was dominated by stubble and cheekbones, golden-brown hair curling above very blue eyes. His smile was slow and gentle. 'I arrived the week before Solly, so I was able to snaffle the biggest bedroom.' There was still a good Scottish burr to his spoken English.

'He did,' Solly agreed with mock indignation.

Kat was glad to see her brother already on sufficiently good terms with his housemate to allow this jokey exchange but when Danielle came out and began clearing nearby tables, she remembered there was plenty of work to be done, even this late in the afternoon. 'I'd better get on. Have you finished work for today?'

Solly nodded. 'We just stopped for coffee and cake to fortify us for the long slog home.' He grinned because the staff quarters were an exceedingly short 'slog' away. They were old, caravan-like aluminium park homes, which had been moved up behind the shopping arcade when supplanted at their previous lakeside positions by smart new wooden holiday cabins. Kat had checked this new home of Solly's before he'd arrived from England. Though showing signs of wear, it was

7

hooked up to mains services and contained two bedrooms, a shower room, kitchen and living area.

After clearing Solly and Noah's cups and plates, Kat went back inside. The queue at the book till had disappeared and there was only one customer at the café counter, who Danielle was serving with peppermint tea, while Justine wiped empty tables. Few cakes remained in the glass-fronted cabinet at this point in the day and Kat swerved around it to deposit her crocks through the hatch to the kitchen, ready to be stacked in the dishwasher. 'I'll cash out when we close,' she called over her shoulder to Danielle. 'I think we've had a good day considering it's only early June.' When the summer was so young, the rides and shops would close at five. Come July and August, they'd stay open to eight p.m. all week long to give tourists plenty of time to part with their holiday euros. The summer months were the pot of gold for Livres et Café, when the bookshelves were firmly orientated to British, Italian and German tourists, and Kat wouldn't increase the stock of French-language books until November or even December.

Her customer served, Danielle's brown bob swung as she used tongs to transfer the last few slices of cake to a tray so she could clean the cabinet's interior. She sighed. 'It's strange not to work with Reeny and Graham anymore.'

Owners Reeny and Graham were absent not because they were heading for retirement, though they were both in their sixties, but because Reeny was seriously ill, a fact that hung over them all like a grey cloud.

At the thought of her friend fighting so hard against her illness, Kat had to swallow a sudden lump in her throat. 'Hodgkin lymphoma sounds horrible and chemo and radiotherapy are gruelling. Poor Reeny – she's so weak it's no wonder Graham's sick with worry. Then, with his mum developing heart trouble back in the UK . . . well, you can see why they've left Livres et Café in our hands.'

As Reeny kept being hit by infections that necessitated postponing chemo cycles, she was often too vulnerable for visitors, so Kat kept up with her via FaceTime. Even if Reeny was too fatigued for a chat of more than a few minutes, she'd summon the strength to ask Kat if she was finding time for writing or how things were going with Jakey. Illness had robbed Reeny of much, but not her warm, caring nature.

It was Graham Kat emailed or phoned on business matters but she knew the best way she could help him at this awful time was to run the book café and otherwise keep out of his thinning hair. As well as Justine, she'd recruited three other part-time assistants for the summer – Romain, Antoine and Pierre – to work alongside herself and Danielle, and felt she had everything in hand for the busiest months. Far from minding the added responsibility, Kat was delighted to step up because Reeny and Graham had been kind to her from the moment they met, seven years ago.

Then, Kat had still been a journalist. With no close ties to the UK, she'd gone freelance, wandering Europe, writing travel features and website content. Then she'd reached Alsace and fallen in love with its colourful timbered buildings along the many tributaries of the Rhine. Drifting into the town of Muntsheim, she'd spotted two of her favourite things on sale together – food and books – and gone into the book café, then called Le Café Littéraire Anglais. When she saw they had a summer job on offer – just when she needed to boost her bank account – it seemed as if the stars had aligned. Reeny and Graham, the UK ex-pat owners, had been overwhelmingly welcoming, so much so that they even housed her in their pool house for a few months, and soon her employment became permanent. Danielle joined a couple of years later, to complete the team. Last year, Reeny and Graham had transferred their business to its current prized position within the town's busy tourist park, renaming it Livres et Café – not grammatical to the French eye, but easily translated by tourists – and increasing their stock to include books in Italian and German.

Everyone had been jumping for joy . . . until Reeny's diagnosis brought them crashing back to earth.

The sound of the door opening disturbed Kat's thoughts and she looked up to see Solly's co-worker Noah enter, his blue eyes homing in on the shelves of books, a frown digging a line between his brows. Diffidently, he said, 'I could use a book that takes my mind off things.'

Kat didn't tell him they were closing, instead crossing to a display of the summer's bestsellers and touching the moody red cover of a paperback. 'This is a good escapist read – the characters time-travel to the Viking age. Nothing like slipping back a millennium or so to forget the day-to-day.' She moved on to another book. Its cover was black with accents of blue. 'Or domestic noir's popular.'

He rolled his eyes. 'We all get enough domestic agony. I'll take your recommendation.' He took down a copy of the Viking book, paid with a card bearing the name N M Toleman, smiled and said, 'Bye,' as he left.

Justine and Danielle cleared the outside chairs and tables and brought them inside. Kat cashed out the tills and headed for the office, Angelique bouncing to her feet the moment she set eyes on her owner.

Kat laughed. 'You know the cash drawers mean it's

nearly time to leave, don't you? Let me get to the safe, then.'

Finally, she was able to say goodnight to her colleagues and lock the front door behind them. Next, she wrestled the excited Angelique onto her lead, grabbed her bag and stepped out through the back door into a balmy summer evening filled with birdsong. After locking up, she freed her dark, curly hair from its topknot to let the wind rake through it.

Kat usually walked Angelique in the park before and after work. Though Angelique got company throughout the day from whoever had business in the office, Kat tried to give her a lunchtime outing, too – usually past the formal knot garden and down to the biggest lake where swans, ducks, geese and coots coexisted serenely alongside humans in rowboats and kayaks. The midday treat was tricky on Danielle's day off as either Danielle or Kat had to be present whenever Livres et Café was open, but a few days ago Solly had offered to give Angelique a lunchtime run when Kat couldn't.

She paused, enjoying the warmth that small act of kindness kindled in her, and the novel pleasure of having her brother nearby. They'd shared their father's home at weekends until Solly turned six but then Kat had gone to university and struck out alone, rarely returning. She wasn't entirely sure why Solly had suddenly decided to use the working holiday visa scheme to come to France. He'd been sailing through his year as a newly qualified teacher in the UK . . . until he wasn't. So far, his only explanation for this had been, 'Didn't work out.' Kat hadn't broached the subject with their dad Howard as Solly's mum Irina would no doubt have taken exception, had she found out. Irina wasn't the wicked stepmother of fairytales but neither was she the friendly, welcoming variety, and she'd always been ultra-protective of her son, apparently unconcerned if Kat was sidelined in the process.

With a pang, Kat thought of her own mum, Joanne, picturing her long dark hair with the fringe that never quite lay flat. After Howard had left home to form a new family with Irina and Solly, Joanne had eventually married Geoffrey, a quiet, serious man who'd probably felt safe and restful after Howard. Kat had lived with her mum and Geoffrey on weekdays and Howard and Irina on weekends. Big-hearted Joanne had welcomed Geoffrey's young children, Amber and Jade, and when their own mum had been tragically killed on the road, she'd devoted herself to helping them through their grief – leaving Kat feeling sidelined there, too. Joanne had passed away during what was supposed to have been a routine medical procedure when Kat was in her twenties and Geoffrey had taken his kids off to live in Canada. Apparently, he'd been too sunk in his own grief for it to occur to him that he could be there for Kat as Joanne had once comforted his children when they lost their mum.

Kat should *definitely* make more of Solly while he was in France, she decided. It was a shame he didn't speak better French, because then he could have worked at Livres et Café. Luckily, working as a park groundsman needed no great language skill, and Kat had been able to smooth the way to her brother joining the workforce.

She set off through the trees, using her pass to open the gate bearing the words: *Accès réservé au personnel*. Solly's park home – or Solly and Noah's, she supposed – was a minty shade of green with darker green stripes and four metal steps leading up to the door. She strolled down the gravelled track towards it, Angelique trotting alongside with her nose to the ground, looking a lot like a fox. While the dog's bent ears twitched as if listening to the trees tossing their heads in the breeze, Kat studied the nests built in the topmost branches and tried to recall whether folklore said this was a sign of a good summer.

Then a man in park uniform sitting statue-still on a bench caught her attention.

His arms were stretched along the bench's top rail, legs crossed at the ankles while he stared fixedly at a spot on the patchy grass. Low sunlight picked out strands of gold in his hair. Beside him on the bench lay a white paper bag, out of which peeped a book. Kat knew it was about Vikings and time travel . . . because the man was Noah.

He seemed totally unaware of Kat's approach, and her steps slowed. There was something about the blank desolation in his expression that made it hard for her to stroll on by. 'Hi again, Noah,' she called softly.

Noah blinked, his gaze focusing so slowly on her face that she wondered for a shocked instant whether he'd taken something. Then his eyes cleared. 'Sorry, didn't see you. Miles away,' he mumbled. He managed a smile, as if gradually pulling his thoughts together. 'Nice dog.'

Angelique flattened her ears, looking pleased.

'She is,' Kat said fondly, thinking Noah had a nice smile – calmly confident, but kind at the same time. 'I made the mistake of following a local rescue centre on Twitter and when they put Angelique up as needing a new home, I sort of fell for her.' She laughed. 'She was so frightened of everything when I first got her that I called her "Scaredycat". Then I realised that might bruise her dignity, so I use her real name of Angelique.'

He leaned forward to hold out a hand and Angelique dashed forward to meet it with her wet, black nose. He

13

said gravely, 'If someone's naturally anxious, you do have to be careful not to damage their self-esteem.'

Kat laughed. 'True. I probably ought to have renamed her "Superdog".'

His blue eyes twinkled. 'Are you looking for your brother, by the way? He's gone into town for a beer with a few of the park crowd.'

'Oh, right, thanks. Glad he's making friends. We'll just finish our walk, in that case.' They said their goodbyes, then Kat set off again, hair blowing in the evening breeze, wondering what on earth had put that sad expression on Noah's face and why he was sitting alone rather than joining his colleagues for a drink.

And if he wanted a book to provide an escapist read, shouldn't he actually pick it up and read it? Letting it sit next to him on the bench didn't seem to be doing the trick.

It was the middle of the night when Kat was yanked from sleep by a phone call. She'd expected Jakey to text, as he usually did, to grumble about the long journey home and changing trains in Paris but had fallen asleep before anything arrived.

She fumbled for the handset, guided by its illuminated screen. Drowsily, she answered, 'Hello?' then, in case the call was to take place in French, '*Oui, allo?*'

A pause. Then a female voice spoke, the accent French but the words English. 'Is that Jakey's girlfriend?'

Kat woke up properly, reaching out to switch on the lamp, its pool of light spreading over her peacock blue duvet cover and the geometric-pattern rug, picking up the lights in Angelique's eyes as she lifted her head from her bed by the door. 'Is he all right?' she demanded, her heart giving an unpleasant thump. Her bedside clock told her it was past two a.m.

'Yes, yes. I did not mean to worry you,' the female voice said soothingly. 'I'm one of Jakey's colleagues and I cannot locate him. Is he with you, perhaps? I apologise for being so cheeky as to ask you.'

Kat relaxed onto her pillows, her heart returning to its normal rhythm. 'It's OK. No, he's not here. He was at the track today and then he was to head back to Rennes.' She didn't feel the need to mention the ten-minute tryst in her office. She glanced at the clock again. 'Why do you need to talk to him at this hour?'

'At the track?' the female voice asked on a note of curiosity, without commenting on the time.

'Yes, near Strasbourg – as usual,' Kat answered briefly, feeling irritable that once Jakey's colleague had established he wasn't with her, she hadn't simply apologised before ending the call.

As if reading Kat's thoughts, the woman said, 'Sorry to have disturbed you,' and then the line went dead.

In the silence, Angelique yawned and turned around on her bed before resettling. Kat was about to switch off the light when her hand paused in mid-air. How had a colleague of Jakey's got Kat's phone number? He'd certainly never mentioned that he'd listed her as a contact with his employer, which would have been polite, especially if colleagues might be searching for him during the night.

This conundrum, and the fact that Jakey still hadn't texted, stopped her drifting back to sleep.

It could be as simple as him getting home and forgetting to send her a message before putting his phone on silent.

But what if something had happened?

15

Chapter Two

Mondays and Tuesdays were often Kat's time off but this week Danielle had requested them. At least a busy Monday at work would take Kat's mind off worrying about Jakey, she thought. He was still out of contact and the more she worried over the call in the middle of the night, the odder it seemed.

She opened the wooden shutters at the windows of the apartment before giving Angelique breakfast. She'd overdone the 'Kat's Dog' humour when she fetched Angelique from the rescue centre twenty months ago. It was lettered on the dog's purple bowls and her dog beds here and at the office. The silly joke sat badly with Kat's present baffled, uneasy mood and the drained feeling that went with tossing and turning half the night.

Usually, Kat was very happy at 1 La Maison Blanche in the prettily named Rue du Printemps. Her apartment was the ground floor of what had once been an impressively large family home and had high ceilings and tall windows. The bathroom was small but the kitchen spacious. She'd filled the rooms with an eclectic mix of furniture from an auction room and a charity shop in Muntsheim, painting several pieces a pleasing green called *vert palatino*.

Her landlords, M and Mme Picard, lived in the topmost apartment, often to be seen enjoying their retirement on one of the pretty balconies between dormer windows – the front balcony if they wanted to watch the world go by and the back if they fancied overlooking the garden that went with Kat's apartment. They chatted with Kat when they met, but that wasn't often.

The erstwhile front garden of La Maison Blanche was now a gravel drive where Kat parked her yellow Citröen Cactus alongside the white Peugeot of the men who lived on the middle floor. Kat didn't know the men. She'd tried to speak to them once in French but they'd answered in Alsatian – the dialect of Alsace, not barking like dogs. According to M Picard, they didn't like Brits and thought Brexit had been an excellent idea.

Kirchhoffen was filled with properties as pretty as La Maison Blanche. Walls painted blue, white, red, tan or yellow, some with shutters or window boxes frothing with summer flowers, the houses radiated from around the boulangerie, patisserie, *salon de thé*, mini market, post office, restaurant and a white church with a steeple like a very pointed witch's hat. The village also had its own park, including a wood with a stream where big otter-like rodents called coypu lived, trailing long tails behind them as they swam busily through water the colour of tea.

Now, with Angelique following her closely, Kat collected tea, yoghurt and fruit before stepping out through the bi-fold doors to sit on the garden bench with a breakfast she didn't really want, the sun warm on her bare knees beneath the hem of her shorts. The garden included a lawn

– luckily M and Mme Picard's grandson cut it for her as part of her rental agreement – a patio and the wild-ish sort of flowerbeds where everything jumbled together.

She finished her yoghurt and gave the empty pot to Angelique to lick out. 'I hope Jakey's all right,' she told the dog, examining her apple dispiritedly before biting into its crisp flesh.

Angelique peeped at her as she curled her tongue to get to the bottom of the pot.

'He's probably just broken his phone.' She thought for a moment. 'Maybe he's emailed me from his laptop.' She clutched the apple in one hand as she took out her phone with the other and checked. Nothing. She opened an email to *Jakey.Marsaud@gmail.fr* and tapped in, *Everything OK? Just checking as you're not answering texts or calls. xxxx* It was his private email address, but she didn't have his work one. She didn't know the name of his organisation, in fact, because Jakey usually referred to it as simply, 'the agency I work for'. He was bound by a privacy agreement, especially when it came to clients under the age of eighteen, he'd explained. Perhaps she ought to have contact details for him other than his phone number and private email in future, though.

Angelique abandoned a now thoroughly licked yoghurt pot and sat down to wait politely for the apple core, brown eyes gleaming and eartips flopped. Kat tossed her all the remaining apple, watching her crunch her way through it. Then she drank her tea before gathering everything and returning indoors to finish getting ready, Angelique dogging her footsteps in case Kat forgot her.

The book café was due to open at ten but it wasn't even nine when Kat used her pass to open the entrance barrier of the park. As vehicles had to travel at walking

18

pace within Parc Lemmel, it took a further few minutes to reach the parking area behind Livres et Café and then let Angelique out. She allowed the waggy canine to run loose because there wouldn't be many people around until the attractions opened, and the local schoolchildren who cut across the park on the way to the town's lycée technologique or the collège would have been and gone, as school began at eight-thirty. Many would return here for their long lunch break, eating at the park tables, drinking iced tea or pamplemousse – grapefruit juice – or buying from one of the cafés. The great park was used by an enormous number of people.

Kat tried to relax her shoulders as she strolled across the vivid green grass, FaceTiming Reeny as she walked, understanding the restrictions of serious illness and how cheering a glimpse of the park could be.

'Hello, dear,' said Reeny, when her pale face topped with a silver fringe popped onto the screen.

'Morning,' replied Kat cheerfully, putting aside her worries for the duration of the call. 'Look where I am.' She reversed the camera so Reeny could see the carousel and the chair-plane ride, from which members of park staff were pulling off grey tarpaulins to reveal fairground colours of yellow, red, blue, silver and gold. Behind towered a contorted turquoise slide, all ready for people to whiz down.

'Oh, how lovely of you to take me on your morning walk! And look, we're coming up to the old teacup ride,' marvelled Reeny with a creaky laugh. After the teacup ride came the red or blue cars that ran on rails, a few other junior rides and then the free area of slides, swings, seesaws and climbing frames.

Still chatting, Kat turned the camera around again so

19

she and Reeny could see each other as she made her way downhill towards the lake, where the goslings, ducklings, cygnets and whatever baby coots were called were half-grown now. Angelique ranged around with her nose to the ground, giving the swans and geese a wide berth, having learned all about their hissing and flapping. By previous agreement, Kat didn't pester Reeny with health enquiries, but she did say, 'Things aren't the same without you. I'd never have stayed in Alsace if you hadn't let me live in your pool house at first.'

'Our gain,' answered Reeny, eyes twinkling. 'Who else could we have trusted to look after Livres et Café? It's not too much for you, is it? You're looking anxious.'

Dawdling while Angelique sniffed, Kat decided not to share her worries about Jakey, who Reeny had never even met. 'I was thinking about how I ended up in Alsace, earlier,' she went on. 'One minute I was alone, scraping a living writing travel pieces, and the next I was part of your happy team, selling books and cakes.' Then, noticing that Reeny was looking tired already, winked. 'But I'd better get off to work now. My bosses are right slave drivers.'

That at least made Reeny laugh before they ended the call. Not knowing who to worry about first – Reeny or Jakey – Kat whistled, and when Angelique didn't come, she turned and saw the dog had paused, paw lifted and ears up as she inspected a man in park uniform who was perusing one of the boards bearing a brightly illustrated map of the park, his hair stirring in the breeze. Recognising Noah and remembering he'd only been working at the park a week longer than Solly, Kat veered off course to come up beside him. 'Are you lost?'

He turned, smiling when he saw her. 'My boss asked

me to go to the park office but I can't remember where it is.'

'Not where it says on the map,' she explained cheerfully. 'It's being refurbished so has been temporarily relocated to opposite Livres et Café. Shall we walk up together?'

'That would be great.' He lingered for another admiring perusal of the map. 'This is quite a place. Three lakes, woodland, gardens, the shops and cafés.'

She agreed. 'Two cafés belong to Parc Lemmel itself but there's enough business for us as well.' She drew a circle on the map with one finger, outlining a large area further along the park where the larger rides had been cunningly slotted in the middle of a go-kart track – the ordinary kind of karts, not the racers that Jakey dealt with. 'Have you been on the rollercoaster yet? It isn't big, but it's deadly.'

'With that recommendation, I might try it.' He fell into step beside her, and they began up the slope towards what was noted on the map as 'Le Centre', where the book café stood in a row of red-fronted shops that sold toys, pottery, glass artwork, sweets, T-shirts, souvenirs and general tourist-trap merchandise. Kiosks sold tickets and wristbands and petunia-filled baskets dangled from ornate green lampposts.

As someone who'd worked in this magical place for a year, Kat felt obliged to share her knowledge. 'At the end of Le Centre there's an exhibit about the park, and how rich local industrialist Charles Lemmel left it to the town. There are sepia photos of nineteenth-century men in suits and top hats and women in high-waisted dresses and big bonnets. It's fun to compare then with now. For instance, the formal gardens are still in the original layout, but the shops have taken the place of a pavilion.'

'I'll take a look,' he answered politely. He'd shortened his stride to match hers, his hands in his pockets.

She checked the time and whistled again for a dawdling Angelique. The baked goods delivery would arrive soon. 'Solly says you've lived in France since you were a child,' she tried, giving him a more open subject to go at because it seemed odd to march along together in silence.

'That's right.' Then, just when she was about to give up on trying to converse with him, he unbent. 'Mum was left a property in the Dordogne and so my parents converted it into a small hotel. They're retired and travel a lot, but I still live in the region, in a town called Castillon-la-Bataille, right on the river. I've done a lot of water sports there, which is why they've put me on the boats and stuff at the lake.'

Kat didn't say what she was thinking – that it was funny to say you 'still live' in the Dordogne when you demonstrably lived in an old holiday home with other park staff – as it might send him into retreat after he'd just strung four sentences together. 'You're here for a change of scene?' she asked.

He shrugged. 'Something like that.'

It seemed they were in danger of falling back into silence now they'd climbed the long, grassy slope, a patchwork of greens created by bright sunlight and the shade cast by clouds. As they passed the gardens, almost at Le Centre, she offered, 'I travelled through the Dordogne, about eight years ago.' The subject of her journeys through Europe before she settled in France lasted them until they reached the office, where she was able to say, 'Here you go. It's just through the door and up the stairs,' and lift a hand in farewell, mind already turning to the day ahead.

'Thanks for steering me to the right place,' Noah called

after her. Then, just before he stepped through the door he added, 'She really is a nice dog. Looks like a smiling fox.'

'With wonky ears,' Kat added with a grin as she took the route around the back of the book café, because Angelique wasn't allowed through the front, even when the place was closed. After settling her canine buddy in the office, she had just enough time to put up her hair and wash her hands before the trays of pastries and cakes arrived in a white van. Staff members Romain and Antoine hurried in, calling, '*Salut! Ça va?*'

'*Salut! Je vais bien,*' Kat called. Soon she was lost in a welter of white trays of fragrant baked goods, using a spatula to carefully nestle crisp, flaky pastries in neat rows punctuated by pink, green, yellow and brown macarons, neatly domed cannelés and circular tarts filled with scarlet strawberries or glistening brown chocolate. Behind her, Romain set up the coffee machine and Antoine emptied the dishwasher to begin the day with stacks of clean crockery. Kat completed her arrangement with *pain au raisins* and *pain au chocolat,* red and white napkins cupping each pastry, and then took the remainder of the order out to the kitchen chiller.

'Opening time!' she cried, as she returned, smoothing her apron. Another day at the book café began to the usual soundtrack of a hissing coffee machine and chattering customers, the air fragranced by good things to eat, the backdrop shelves and shelves of enticing books. The sun shone, brightening red shopfronts as Kat went out to the outside tables.

She drew in a deep lungful of warm summer air. Her job was the loveliest in the world.

*   *   *

Noah left the park office after a fifteen-minute discussion with an admin guy about whether Noah's boss Marcel, the lake area manager, had already been sent updated staffing numbers for the summer. Marcel said not. An impatient man in his late fifties, he found it easier to send Noah to the office to sort it out than to type an email. Noah didn't mind because Marcel was washing down the kayak slipway in Noah's stead. Used to a high-paced, logistics-based environment with emphasis on customer relations, Noah could have offered to type the email for Marcel. But why turn down a stroll across the park?

That he'd ended up being escorted by Solly's sister had only added to his enjoyment of the bright June morning. Kat seemed sunny and uncomplicated. Matters with his ex-wife Florine had become so extraordinarily complex that to talk to a woman whose conversation wasn't cloaked in secrets or evasions had almost tied his tongue.

Now he glanced across at the book café and saw Kat and a young guy in glasses popping open green parasols as early customers settled around the tables. Kat's dark, curly hair was gathered in springs on top of her head by a red bandana that matched her shirt. Earlier, it had been loose, a curly mass writhing around her head in the breeze. Her eyes, as dark as her hair, had questioned him, the bridge of her nose wrinkling at his minimal part in the conversation. She must have thought him Mr Dull from Dullsville. When had he got so awkward that he couldn't smile at a pretty girl and ask her about herself?

All his thoughts these days were fixed on another female: Clémence. Pretty, delicate, blonde Clémence . . . his eight-year-old daughter who his ex-wife Florine and new-husband Yohan had taken far across the country. Without Noah's permission.

His neck bunched up every time he thought of it. Fear and worry woke him at night to lie awake and listen to Solly mumbling in his sleep through the prefabricated walls.

What Florine and Yohan were doing was against the child custody agreement lodged with the notary. It was also against everything that was fair or just, but they'd done it anyway. Clémence was living here in Alsace, close to the border with Germany, five-hundred-and-fifty miles from Castillon-la-Bataille, their hometown. That twat Yohan was at the bottom of it all, Noah had no doubt. He wanted to be more important to Clémence than Noah was.

And Florine was letting it happen.

But now Clémence had been able to send Noah a photo that included the name of the place where they were staying, and it was only a few miles away. Come Noah's next day off, he was going to this place, Kirchhoffen, to try and identify the actual house – he had a photo of that, too – and then decide how best to approach the ticklish problem of how to re-establish contact with his daughter without recourse to the law if at all feasible. Clémence was what her teachers called 'highly emotional' and it was best to keep the river of life as calm as possible for her. An appearance in court would send her spinning into an emotional vortex.

Noah not only understood Clémence, he also understood his ex-wife. Florine's father Henri had been a controlling patriarch and the accepted norm of Florine's childhood had been that Henri directed her life, along with that of her mother Violette, rewarding compliance with approval and punishing rebellion with icy, elaborately enacted disappointment. Violette had died young, leaving Florine to be brought up by exacting Henri, who'd had an unpleasant habit of analysing Florine's faults aloud in company. In the early days, Noah had quietly asked Henri not to do that in front of him, but Henri had continued whenever Noah wasn't around.

It had been a couple of years after Noah and Florine's marriage that Henri had exhibited the first signs of dementia. In the end, he didn't recognise his daughter, let alone attempt to control her. She'd been noticeably adrift.

Within months of her father's death, Florine had found a replacement controlling male in Yohan Gagneau – and fallen in love with him. *Just like that*. Noah had been stunned.

With Yohan's encouragement, Florine dumped reasonable, reliable Noah and fell into step behind Yohan like a trained dog. After the initial shock, Noah accepted the end of his OK-ish marriage . . . so long as Clémence, then five, was eased gently into the new situation with bags of love and reassurance to stave off her anxiety. And that, going forward, Noah would see plenty of Clémence.

He sent Kat a smile as he realised she'd paused in clicking open a parasol to gaze at him, probably wondering why he was standing there in a daydream, then he turned and strode out of the shopping arcade, clutching the printout Marcel had requested.

He swung right at the end of the last shop, passed the formal garden and the park train station, then loped down the long grassy slope towards the lakes, still thinking about Florine, who must be a sort of chameleon, taking on the personality of the man in her life, seeking input on everything from clothes to career options and floundering when encouraged to develop her own attitudes and aims. He recalled how his '*What do you want?*' had always prompted her '*I want what you want*' reply.

26

It had become tedious, like being married to his own reflection.

He hadn't been unhappy. Clémence had filled his heart from the instant he knew she was on the way, but he'd become bored. Still, he'd been faithful and would have stuck the marriage out for his daughter.

Until Florine found the controlling influence she apparently yearned for. Bloody Yohan.

As he continued down the greensward towards the boating lake, his thoughts were interrupted by the approach of the park's cream-coloured, three-wheeled truck and trailer. The truck was old-fashioned, but it was equally at home on footpaths or grass, so it was perfect for the grounds staff. Right now, it was burbling and burping along with a load of fat black sacks in the trailer, telling Noah that the current task of Solly, who was at the wheel, was emptying the park bins. The truck headed directly for Noah.

He dropped into a walk and Solly slowed the ungainly vehicle, the air around it hot and musty. He lifted his voice over the harrumphing of the engine. 'Hey, Noah. Could you do me a favour?'

'Maybe,' Noah answered cautiously, hoping he wasn't going to have to get too near the whiffy rubbish. He liked the young Englishman he shared the holiday home with, but Solly reminded him of a spaniel: bouncing and scatty.

Solly grinned engagingly. 'You know that girl, Ola, one of the drivers of the park train? She says I can ride in the cab with her during my lunch hour but I'm supposed to be taking Angelique for a walk because Kat can't. I'll buy you a beer later if you take Angelique instead.' As if prompted by Solly's request, the little train started noisily in the station behind them. Each day, the smartly painted black locomotive tootled maroon and cream carriages around the three-kilometre track. Families smiled and waved as they rumbled across bridges, around the lakes, through a green tunnel of leafy trees, then past picnic tables and the rollercoaster. Back at the station – the roof of which was painted maroon and cream to match the carriages – the train disgorged one lot of happily chattering passengers and waited for the next, chuffing and tooting like a miniature steam train, though it was actually powered by diesel.

Earnestly, Solly stressed, 'Ola's hot and she's in charge of a *train*.'

'Only a small one,' Noah teased, but he wasn't surprised Solly would want to take Ola up on her offer. A little younger than Solly, she certainly was pretty, her long ponytail swishing and trendy glasses glinting. Four drivers covered the seven-day week but the other three were men with knobbly faces and grey hair. Noah kept Solly hanging for another few seconds then said, 'Yeah, OK.'

Solly punched the air. 'Awesome! Kat will probably give you a free coffee and a pastry.'

'Awesome,' Noah parroted back. 'Awesome' had been cool-speak when he'd left Scotland twenty-seven years ago and he'd have thought today's kids would have found something new. 'Now I need to get to work before Marcel docks my pay.'

The truck's engine grumbled louder as Solly prepared to go. He hesitated before pulling off. 'You OK?' he asked diffidently. 'Only, when I drove up you were frowning like a goblin.'

That surprised a laugh out of Noah, though he was faintly shocked his troubling thoughts had shown so plainly on his face. 'I'm fine. Text your sister that I get my lunch break at one today and I'll be along then.'

'Awesome,' Solly repeated happily, and bumbled off in his noisome vehicle.

Noah resumed his jog down the slope, making an effort to keep his forehead unfurrowed, even if his thoughts immediately flew back to his little daughter, who was apparently so close that she might one day turn up at the park.

He wished she would. He looked for her every day.

Chapter Three

Kat went about her morning's duties quickly and efficiently, switching between chatting to browsers at the bookshelves and ferrying frothy coffees to tables. Her smile remained in place even when Romain dropped a tray piled high with crocks that he scrambled to clear up, his freckly face red, but it masked her troubled thoughts.

Still no word from Jakey.

Images of accidents and incidents bloomed in her mind's eye. She checked online for news of train crashes between Strasbourg and Paris or Paris and Rennes. Nothing. The only text she received was from Solly. *Can't take Angelique but Noah can. He gets off at one.*

Kat bit her lip. She hardly knew Noah, but she wasn't sure she could condemn Angelique to being cooped up in the office all day if he was kind enough to offer to take her out.

She messaged back: *That's kind of him. Are you sure it's OK?*

Solly returned a laconic, *Yep.*

Lunchtime proved unexpectedly busy for early summer.

The park ran group booking schemes and today a number of fourteen and fifteen-year-old British kids on an educational trip were taking their rest day at the park. Livres et Café had apparently been nominated for lunch. Park-issued meal vouchers were as good as hard cash, as the book café would be reimbursed, but it would have been nice if the teachers in charge had given Kat notice that thirty-plus customers would turn up at once. She would have got Justine or Pierre in. As it was, she, Romain and Antoine, a serious young guy with straight-up hair and brown-rimmed glasses, were kept flying around tables and dashing in to sell books while a crowd of excited teenagers topped up their sugar levels with fizzy drinks and cakes. It was wonderful to see the place overflowing with happy eaters, but also exhausting.

It was at the height of the rush that Noah arrived, hands in the pockets of the dark green trousers of the park uniform and golden-brown hair glowing. He smiled when Kat's gaze landed on him. 'I've come to take Angelique.'

Kat paused to catch her breath. 'Is it one o'clock already? It's so good of you to take Angelique, Noah. I can't leave unless another member of management's here, for insurance reasons, and it's Danielle's day off.' When Reeny and Graham had been available, there had been four of them to share the member-of-management-present duty.

He shrugged. 'I don't mind.'

'Let me show you how to get out the back way.' She led him swiftly indoors, dumping the order she'd just scribbled down for Romain to fulfil, telling him she'd be back in a couple of minutes to run the tray out to the appropriate table. 'She stays in the office,' Kat explained as she led the way. As if attached by string to the opening door, Angelique bounced to her feet with a pleased woof, her tail a blur, ears flat to her head – or as flat as they got. Kat gave her a fuss. 'Noah's taking you out today. Be a good girl.' She got Angelique's harness and turned to Noah. 'She won't give you any trouble because she's a sweetheart, but you'll need to keep her on the lead with the park this busy.'

She cleared her throat and felt her face heat up. 'There are bags attached to her harness, for, erm, you know . . .'

Laughter entered his eyes. 'Don't worry. I know what responsible dog-walkers have to do.'

She laughed, relieved. 'Oh, good. Also, I should mention that occasionally she barks at people shouting, especially if they're angry. She was a rescue dog and gets anxious. You can get her attention by doing this.' She pursed her lips and made kissing noises and Angelique instantly pressed close, wagging her tail and looking expectant.

He snorted a laugh. 'Blowing kisses will get me funny looks.'

'But it works.' She grinned. 'And don't let her kid you she's allowed on the big slide with the mats, because she's not. Leave enough time to have lunch on the house when you come back.' She passed him the lead.

'Thanks,' he said easily. Solemnly he made kissing noises at Angelique, who instantly turned his way, tail swishing.

Kat showed him to the back door. 'It's not locked during opening hours. Thanks again.' She closed the door behind him, washed her hands and hurled herself back into the melee, where every table was still full of eating, drinking, chattering customers, indoors and out. Many of the kids from the school trip, having spent their meal vouchers, began paying for further cakes and drinks with their own euros. The three accompanying teachers ordered fresh coffee, evidently content to sit and soak up the sun along with their charges.

A sweating Kat was just beginning to think someone must have cast a spell over the café area so that every table would remain full forever when a female voice came from behind her, a voice as hard and cold as icicles. 'You are Katrina?'

Kat, who had been about to take an order on her little pad, swung around at the English words spoken in a French accent. She found a woman staring at her through thickly made up flinty eyes, long dark hair falling in waves from the top of her head. Another woman and two little girls in shorts and T-shirts sat at the same table. 'Kat*e*rina, yes,' Kat replied, wondering who on earth was addressing her so stiffly.

The woman shrugged away the correction and indicated the others around the table. 'This is my sister and my daughters, Manon and Margaux.' The girls were fairer than her and flicked uncertain glances at their mother, no doubt catching their names but perhaps not understanding the rest. As if this were a signal, the sister rose and held out her hands to the two girls, whispering in French that they would visit the climbing frames while *Maman* spoke to the lady.

As the three hurried off across the paving, Kat gazed in bewilderment at the woman, unsure what was going on. But then the woman began to speak – or hiss. '*You slut. You bitch. You man-stealer.*'

Kat was shocked into stumbling back a step, the hubbub from the schoolchildren receding in her ears. 'What?' she demanded faintly.

The dark-haired woman jumped up, crowding Kat so that she joggled the table behind her, causing a chorus of protests. 'You,' she ground out, 'have stolen a man who has a partner and children.'

'Me?' demanded Kat, blankly. Blood began to thunder in her ears. '*Me?*'

'*Don't pretend!*' The dark-haired woman's voice rang out, silencing the chatter and laughter from nearby tables. 'You should be ashamed. I would like to spit on you—'

Her words began to garble in Kat's ears, hostility hitting her like a physical blow, turning her skin clammy and her legs to water. She hadn't suffered such intimidation since crossing the school bully. 'Stop!' she protested as a hate-filled, sweary torrent of words continued to flood over her, including 'whore' in at least three languages. It was time to gather her wits. '*Stop!*' Kat snapped this time, injecting steel into her voice. 'I've no idea who you are but it's not acceptable to—'

The woman howled loud enough to hurt Kat's ears. 'Do not speak to me of "acceptable". You have dragged my boyfriend into your horrible, sordid affair. Did you see our daughters? And you dare to try to break their home? I am Emma!'

The woman's words made no sense, though she spoke in quick, practised English. Kat became aware of a sea of faces craning her way, even passers-by stopping to watch the loud quarrel unfold. Antoine hovered closer, concern and shock written all over his young face at the tirade. She licked her dry lips. 'You've got the wrong person, Emma, but we can talk in the office—'

'*Non!* No!' Emma planted her hands on her hips, her face contorted with contempt and the desire to wound. 'Everyone should know you are a slut. Do not expect me to let you hide away what you have done.'

Common sense returned to Kat in a wave, along with

34

the first stirrings of anger. If this Emma woman wouldn't talk in a civilised manner, then Kat could only remove the oxygen from her fire – and that meant remove herself. Face burning, she shouldered the woman aside and stalked around the end of the parade of buildings towards the back door of the book café, away from the sea of gawking faces and listening ears.

'Come back!' Emma shouted after her, and Kat heard the scraping of chairs and tables and a new flurry of protests.

Kat didn't pause. Intent on moving the scene away from the book café, her responsibility, she picked up the pace until she reached the back door, then dragged it open and pulled out a chair to prop it ajar – which you weren't supposed to do because it was a fire door – so she could maintain her role of 'manager on the premises', however sketchily.

As Emma panted up behind her, Kat warded her off with an upraised hand. 'Hold it there. Now,' she drew in a long, calming breath. 'Tell me what you're going on about because not one word you've said so far has made any sense to me.'

Emma's nostrils pinched as she sucked air between her teeth. 'You,' she said with elaborate calm, 'are having an affair with my partner, the father of our children. Jacques.' Then, as Kat opened her mouth to argue, she added, 'Jakey.'

The area behind the shops was filled with parked cars, bins and used packaging. It all seemed to take a giant loop around Kat, sending her dizzy. Her blood, which had been pounding angrily, turned to ice. 'Jakey?' she croaked.

Satisfaction stole over Emma's face. She folded her arms. 'Oh? So suddenly you know? Jakey. Jacques. My boyfriend. We make a family together and you try to destroy it. You sleep with him, yes?'

Kat's lips parted but no words emerged. Jakey. *Jakey*. She tried to get her bearings. 'You're speaking about Jakey Marsaud?'

Emma tittered. 'So he does not even give you his correct surname! Marsaud is the name of his mother before her marriage.'

'But – but Jakey said he was single. I asked him! I wouldn't have an affair with someone who's not single. You must be confused. It's a different Jakey.' Even to her own ears, her protests sounded weak. How many Frenchmen called Jacques were known as Jakey? And if Marsaud was also Jakey's mother's maiden name . . . Horror descended on Kat like a shower of rain.

With the air of triumph, Emma produced her phone, angled the screen so Kat could view it, and began scrolling through her photo library. Jakey smiling. Jakey looking hungover – Kat had seen that Jakey a few times. Jakey grinning into the camera. Jakey with his arms around the two little girls who'd arrived with Emma today. Jakey kissing Emma and even Jakey with a dog, a dog who wasn't, of course, Angelique. Somehow this last hurt most of all.

Kat stared at the images, sick with guilt. 'Well,' she began tremulously. 'As he comes from Rennes, if he lied to me—'

'We live in Nanterre!' Emma cried, as if Kat saying otherwise was a fresh insult. Her cheeks were plum-red with fury, her eyes glittering like coal. She raised her hands and Kat recoiled, thinking for a moment that Emma would attack her physically.

Then a dog barked furiously. *Angelique!*

Obviously startled by the volley, Emma halted and glanced over her shoulder.

Heart pounding, Kat craned to look past her and saw Angelique pulling so hard against her lead that she stood on her hind legs, the tall figure of Noah hurrying along behind, a dark frown wrinkling his brow. 'Whoa,' he said. 'Are you OK, Kat?'

Before Kat could speak, Emma rounded on him. 'She is having an affair with my partner,' she spat viciously. 'She breaks the home of my daughters.'

Noah looked astonished and Angelique growled and threw in a snarl.

Emma took a step aside, as if suddenly noticing that Angelique was baring teeth like a set of white knife blades.

Kat began to shake. She addressed Noah. 'She just turned up and started shrieking at me. I had no idea that Jakey was with someone else.' Her voice vibrated with painful mortification. 'He said he was single.'

'Pah!' said Emma rudely. 'And you believed?'

'Yes,' Kat snapped, stung. 'Why shouldn't I believe him?'

Spite sharpened Emma's features. 'I tell you about Jakey. He likes to amuse himself. You are not the first. What reason did he tell you for being near Strasbourg some weeks?'

Noah interrupted, his eyes filled with compassion as his gaze fell on Kat. 'You're not obliged to answer these questions. Whether or not this woman's claims are justified, she's no business hectoring you. Shall I call security? They'll remove her from the park.' Angelique growled again, as if in agreement.

Emma looked shocked, perhaps taking in his uniform with Parc Lemmel embroidered on his shirt. 'But she is—'

'—a victim, by the sounds of it,' said Noah coldly. Brushing past Emma, he passed Angelique's lead into Kat's hand then took out his phone as if prepared to summon park security there and then. Angelique, rather than jumping up and performing her usual welcome dance when reunited with Kat, kept the lead taut and her attention trained on Emma, low growls shaking her from nose to tail.

Kat licked her lips, steadying now that she had back-up. 'Don't call them yet, Noah. I think Emma and I need to know the truth about each other.' She gave Emma a level look. 'So far as I know, Jakey works for a sports management company in Rennes. He manages and coaches promising young karters in Strasbourg.'

'Pah,' said Emma again, though more conversationally now, as if Kat's story wasn't even worthy of a proper snort of disbelief.

Anger tightened Kat's chest. How dare this horrible woman treat her this way? 'That's what he *told* me,' she emphasised.

'What is the name of his employer? Who are these "promising karters"?' Emma injected so much disbelief into her tone that she might as well have said 'elves and pixies' instead of 'promising karters'.

Kat's face burned. 'I don't know. I'm not into motorsport. He said his work's sensitive because he works with young people. We didn't discuss the details of his job because he's signed non-disclosure agreements—'

Emma laughed aloud, rolling her eyes. 'You believe in fairytales, I think.'

'I'm beginning to think the same,' Kat allowed, her eyes burning as hotly as her face. She was horribly conscious of Noah listening silently, a frown curling his eyebrows. Angelique had ceased her growling but still stared fixedly at Emma, her side pressed comfortingly against Kat's knee. 'So how did you find out about me? I presume it was you

38

who rang last night, pretending to be a colleague?' Kat demanded.

If Emma's lip had curled any further it would have blocked a nostril. 'Yes. I tried to telephone him on the evening of Saturday to tell him his mother has broken her arm. His phone was silenced, perhaps. He was with you?'

Sickly, Kat nodded. She'd cooked dinner and then Jakey had enticed her to bed.

'So,' Emma nodded. 'I telephone his hotel, the one where he should be, and they have no booking. I think perhaps he has changed the hotel he uses, and so I pause. His mother is not too terribly injured. I text. But then I worry because there is no answer to my message. On Sunday I telephone his employer, although I am not supposed to do that except in an emergency. A colleague, he tells me they could not perform their work on Sunday afternoon because of a system failure.'

That must have been why Jakey had turned up at Livres et Café, Kat thought. He'd had an hour to fill before his train home. He hadn't gone out of his way to see her, as he'd pretended, he'd been passing and thought he might as well call in for sex. Disgust crawled over her skin like a thousand ants.

Emma charged on. 'I suspect, of course. He arrives home and I ask about my messages and he say, "Oh, my phone is silenced. I forget. We have been busy at work in an important meeting and my manager is angry if our phones ring." So, I tell him about his mother, and he hurries to see her. She lives nearby.' Her face darkened. 'He comes home; he is tired. When he falls asleep, I take his phone and ring every contact I do not recognise. You were listed as "Gaston". But, Gaston, when he answers the phone, he is a woman, and one who knows much too much about

Jakey.' She spread her hands dramatically. 'I wake Jakey to discuss.'

Kat could only imagine what the 'discussion' might have felt like to Jakey, woken in the middle of the night with his partner confronting him about his affair.

'He admits and apologises, of course,' Emma went on, as if this part of the sequence of the events was of only mild significance. 'He tells me your name and where you work. I put my daughters and sister on the train this morning and we come to show you what it is you have risked.'

Kat gulped. 'What *I've* risked? But if I had known he had a partner and children I wouldn't have gone near him. I thought he was my boyfriend,' she added pathetically.

Emma leaned in, as if she'd like to come nearer but didn't want to test the sharpness of Angelique's teeth. 'So. I tell you some truth. Jakey and me, we are together for many years. After we live in England, we come back to live in Nanterre and we begin our family. Jakey's job . . .' Her voice trembled. 'For part of each month, Jakey, he works near the *Parlement Européen*, in Strasbourg. It is a private company that provides logistical support to the many visitors. It takes him away from us for a few days every two weeks but it's a good job.'

Kat was beginning to experience a swimmy feeling of shock. 'Then why the hell would he tell me he worked with young karters?'

'Pah!' exploded Emma once more. 'It is a little fantasy, I think. He makes a pleasant imaginary life with a stupid, gullible girl, but gives her no way of contacting him. He enjoys motorsport and knows enough to fool you.' Her lips whitened and her eyes turned to stone. 'But I will tell you what Jakey really wants from you. Free accommodation and free food. I think you say "bed and board" in English, yes? When I discover you last night, that is what he said to me. He puts his accommodation allowance in his pocket while he sleeps with you and eats your food for nothing.' Her contempt was like black venom aimed at Kat. 'You live close to a tram line. You are in all ways . . . convenient.'

Kat gazed at Emma through a haze of tears. Everything the other woman said, every accusation she spat, rang too awfully true. Kat hadn't been in an exciting relationship, as she'd thought. Instead, she'd been made a fool of by an unscrupulous, fantasising man. But what she wasn't going to do was apologise to Emma, because Kat had acted in all innocence and been hurt, too.

Emma looked down her long nose. 'How can you think a good-looking man of thirty-five has no partner in his life? And that he needs to date from the internet? You think I'm stupid to believe this?'

'I don't care what you believe,' Kat flared, incipient tears drying in fury at Emma's persistent refusal to believe Kat had been duped and betrayed. 'I'll tell you what *I* think of *you*, shall I? I think you're a poisonous, scorned woman who can't keep her man. Instead of blaming him for being a lying cheat, you blame his victim. You say I'm not his first affair and yet you stay with him, letting yourself be made a fool of over and over again. And you say I'm gullible and stupid? Well, right back at you!'

Angelique let out a sharp bark and growled at Emma. A canine declaration of *I stand with Kat!*

Noah interrupted again then, speaking for the first time for several minutes. Tone low and even, he addressed Emma. 'I think it would be best if you go. If Kat says she had no idea her boyfriend wasn't single, then I believe her.'

41

'*Boyfriend?*' cried Emma, looking freshly incensed at the inference that Kat had the right to claim Jakey as such. 'It does not matter what you believe.' She rounded on Kat with a hiss. 'You! You will not have him. He will change his phone number. I wish to hurt you as you have hurt me.'

'I don't want him,' Kat retorted hotly. 'And you can't do a damned thing to me.'

With a final, 'Pah!', Emma whirled and flounced away, around the corner of the building and out of sight.

Instantly, the dog lead slackened in Kat's hand and Angelique turned with her usual doggy grin, gazing up as if to ask, 'Are you OK, boss?'

Shaking, Kat ruffled the pretty dog's silky ears. Then her knees turned to water, and she plumped down on the chair she'd used to prop open the door, shock washing over her. Angelique put both front paws on Kat's knees and tried to give her a consolatory lick on the nose. Kat's laugh quavered perilously close to a sob. 'That was hideous.'

Noah came closer. 'It looked it,' he admitted awkwardly. 'I hope I did the right thing by sticking around.' With a wry grin, he added, 'I wouldn't have wanted Angelique to get in trouble for biting her.'

Kat had to wipe a tear from the corner of her eye, though she managed a weak smile. 'I understand Emma's fury, but I honestly didn't know Jakey was attached to anyone.' Her stomach gave an uncomfortable roll. 'He never acted as if he had anything to hide. What a bastard.' She groaned. 'Everything Emma said makes sense. Kirchhoffen is on the Tram B route and if Jakey works near the European Parliament buildings he can get off at Homme de Fer and walk the last bit. Bloody hell.' She clutched a hand over her eyes, a hand that Angelique immediately licked.

Antoine hurried up to the back door from inside. 'Kat, you are OK?' He looked worried and unsure of himself. 'The woman, she has gone.'

Wearily, Kat dragged herself to her feet. 'I'm OK, Antoine.' She told him briefly what had transpired. Then reading his awkward expression and wondering whether he was feeling abashed he hadn't done anything to help when Emma kicked off, she gave him a shaky grin. 'If we have any customers left, you go and serve. I'll settle Angelique in the office.'

Antoine looked relieved and hurried back indoors. Noah hesitated. 'Do you want me to hang around in case she comes back?'

Kat gave him a grateful smile, though, along with feeling sick and shaky, she was beginning to feel embarrassed that he'd witnessed her being hailed as a slut and a home breaker. But she didn't really have time to indulge in mortification. They'd had a flood of customers all morning and she had yet to update orders and perform other admin tasks. 'I'll be OK,' she said. 'But thanks.'

After a final searching look, Noah left. Trembling, Kat took Angelique into the office, where she settled down to snooze, then opened the computer. From this machine or her laptop at home, she could submit orders to the bakery wholesalers, sandwich makers, catering supplies company and book wholesalers, schedule newsletters or events, or post on social media, and an hour's admin would provide a valuable interval in which to collect herself. It was only then that she took out her phone and selected the thread of texts between her and Jakey. Humiliated, she reread her stream of messages checking he was OK and asking him worriedly to call. She refused to torture herself further by going back over the earlier, excited texts about their time together.

Instead, she sent one final text. *You shit. You sneaky, two-faced, unfaithful bastard.*

In reply, he returned, *I am sorry. This number is to change.*

She stabbed viciously at the letters on the screen. *It won't affect me because I won't be using it!* Nothing could be surer.

Chapter Four

Aware that his boss, Marcel, was covering his lunch hour, Noah hurried back to work, already five minutes late as he jogged down the grassy slope towards the lake, weaving his way between strolling visitors. He skirted the queue of tourists waiting to have wristbands checked or tickets taken and let himself through the staff gate to the kayak landing slip.

Marcel frowned and glanced pointedly at his watch.

'*Pardon.*' Noah edged close enough to whisper to the older man over the chatter from the queue and the occasional quack of one of the ducks that shared the lake with the watercraft. 'A female friend was being harassed. I had to make sure everything was OK.'

As the father of four daughters, Marcel had highly developed protective instincts towards women. His seamed face relaxed. 'All is well?' He passed over the ticket pouch and the wristband scanner.

Noah took them with a nod. 'She's fine now.'

Marcel rumbled a farewell before setting off towards the park's oldest ride, a flat-bottomed boat that shot down an enormous chute into the water, merrily soaking everyone in the vicinity. Marcel liked to keep an eye on the elderly winding mechanism that was responsible for dragging the boat back to the top, ready for the next plunge.

Noah turned to the queue and began getting tourists into lifejackets and then into yellow or red kayaks, keeping up his usual friendly chat about how to use a paddle and asking if they'd read the illustrated water safety code displayed nearby, important even in a lake less than a metre deep. He reassured a young girl that the swans, ducks, coots and geese would swim out of her way if she got too close and agreed with the anxious father of two teenaged boys that it was a bad idea to rock a kayak. It was easy work and Noah enjoyed the slow pace of the lake and being out in the sunlight that dappled its surface.

Once the full complement of kayaks was waterborne and Noah had checked there were none due in, he felt for his phone. A swift glance told him Marcel was at the top of the water chute, his back to the lake. Against the 'no phones at your workstation' rules, Noah tapped out a text to Solly. *I'm on the kayaks. Can you make an excuse to come by?*

He'd hauled several dripping kayaks from the water and up the slope, filled them with a new batch of tourists and pushed them smoothly off again before he found another moment to check his phone. Solly's answer was waiting: *Am stuck shovelling bird shit at the aviary. What's up?*

Noah glanced up the slope. The aviary, a netted dome that visitors could walk through to admire the birds in flight, could be seen right at the top of the park. His fifteen-minute afternoon break wouldn't give him sufficient time to jog up there, find Solly, have a conversation and jog back. He replied, *End of day coffee at your sister's caff? But meet me first as have to mention something.* They arranged to meet at the formal garden. Noah put his phone away, wondering how much Kat would appreciate him telling her little brother about Emma the witch and Jakey the weasel . . . but she hadn't actually instructed him not to say anything. If the positions were reversed and it had happened to Bex, his sister in Scotland, Noah would want to know.

As he watched a young boy in a kayak carve a meandering line across the lake, he went back over the violence of Emma's rant at Kat. A lot of people would have crumbled at such an onslaught but Kat, however white and pinched, had firmed her chin and returned to work.

His gaze roved methodically over the water dotted with brightly coloured rowing boats, kayaks and paddle boards. It was part of his duties to keep a watch out for people getting into difficulties, simultaneously awarding him the opportunity to enjoy majestic white swans holding up their wings to dry or geese waddling out through the reeds to menace passing tourists.

He loved being around the lake, breathing the vegetable smell of natural water, seeing the feathered backsides of swans and geese as they fed on the lakebed, hearing the laughter of kids, the rumbling and tooting of the little train or the yells carried on the breeze from the rides. At home, he'd worked either from his apartment in what had once been an old house in Castillon-la-Bataille or at the Bordeaux head office of the river cruise company that employed him. Climbing the career ladder had made his role land-based, unfortunately, but at least his love of water had been satisfied by paddle boarding or kayaking on the Dordogne River that flowed only a few hundred

47

yards from his home. Automatically, his mind strayed to his water-loving daughter. On their weekends together he'd often taken her upriver to Creysse, enjoying her grin as she perfected shooting her kayak like an arrow across the surface of the water, or to Cap Ferret on the coast where she got thoroughly overexcited as their hired speedboat bounced on the ocean waves.

Clémence. If only he wasn't carrying around the great black cloud that was his worry over his little girl. His heart clenched at the knowledge she was nearby, but he hadn't yet been able to discover exactly where.

Quashing the anger that threatened to feed on itself like a hurricane and sweep him into hasty, unwise action, Noah tucked the image of Clémence further back in his mind as a two-person kayak came in and he hauled it high enough up the slipway that its occupants could step onto dry land. Without waiting to be called, two boys in their early teens detached themselves from the head of the queue. One gasped in a very English accent, '*Excusez-moi, monsieur, un kayak pour deux, s'il vous plaît.*' Noah brought himself to the present and smiled at the boys. He could easily have replied in English, but he approved of their wish to communicate in the language of the country they were visiting. '*Mais oui, certainement.*'

They chorused, '*Merci,*' and he soon had them snapped into lifejackets. For safety, he switched to English to give them the low-down on paddle usage and safety.

The boys laughed. One said accusingly, 'You're Scottish.'

He settled them on board with their paddles at the ready and assumed a heavy mock Scottish accent. 'You haird ma accent? Ah've lived in France since I was aboot yur age. I used to live in Sco'land when I was a wee 'un, though.' Then he pushed them off and listened to them

48

immediately try and give each other instruction. He grinned. Another thing he liked about this job was that he was involved in people having fun.

The only thing wrong with working at the park was the pay, even if France's minimum wage was one of the highest in Europe. After tax and a deduction for the staff accommodation, his current income was pocket money compared to his real job – and he was still paying rent in Castillon while he worked out what was going to happen with Clémence. Still, he reflected, watching the wavering oars of a man zig-zagging a rowing boat towards the jetty some fifty metres along from the kayak beach, there was a lot to enjoy about this summer. Having leapt at the undemanding job in a panic, it was a huge bonus that the big park was such a great place to work.

By the time he got the nod from Marcel to end the session at four o'clock – to allow time to haul the kayaks into their rack and lock it – his thoughts were straying back to Kat's unpleasant encounter with Emma. He swung by the kiosk at the side of the boat shed to account to Marcel for his haul of tickets and return the wristband scanner, then signed off. Striding up the grassy slope among people walking dogs or playing games, he came within sight of Solly hovering at the gate to the formal garden, blazing orange marigolds filling triangular beds on the other side of tightly cut hedges.

'Hey,' Solly greeted him, as Noah arrived. 'What's up?'

Noah took a second to recover his breath from climbing the long slope. 'Just want to give you a heads-up. Your sister had a problem earlier.' Noah recounted what he'd witnessed as Solly listened in wide-eyed silence. 'Of course, she may not want you to know, but I thought you'd at least want to swing by and check on her,' Noah concluded.

He wanted to check on her himself, but it was only right he offer the honour to Kat's brother.

Scowling, Solly turned decisively towards Le Centre. 'Let's go. She shuts at five today and it's nearly that now.' The younger man hunched his shoulders, looking troubled. 'To be honest, I don't know whether she'll mind you telling me because I don't know her that well. I could smash that shit Jakey's frigging face in, though,' he added.

'Tempting,' Noah agreed before asking tentatively, 'Why don't you know your sister well?'

Solly grimaced. 'We share a dad but not a mum. I was born when she was twelve. I lived with Dad – and my mum – full time but she only came at weekends. Once she went to uni I saw even less of her. And now she lives in France and I usually live in England.'

Solly was striding so fast as he turned into the arcade that Noah – usually no slouch – had to hurry to keep up. 'My background's similar,' he puffed. 'I share both parents with my sister Bex and brother Tim but when we moved out here they had just been accepted to uni in Scotland, and so they both stayed in the UK. I was kind of an only child . . . but with siblings.'

'Yeah, that describes it well,' agreed Solly.

Shop canopies were already being wound in ready for closing and further up the parade Noah could see the young guy Kat had earlier addressed as Antoine carrying in chairs while Kat stood gazing at her phone screen, a cleaning cloth clutched in one hand, her red bandana holding her curls back in the breeze.

Solly waved. 'Hey, Kat.'

She looked up and smiled, though there was a notice-able droop to her shoulders. Noah wondered how she'd behave towards him. He felt as if witnessing the vitriolic attack on her had moved them on from bare acquaintances but wasn't sure to where.

Solly ploughed in with an opening gambit that made it obvious he'd decided not to try and pretend he didn't know what had happened. 'Are you OK now?'

Kat flicked a glance at Noah, but she didn't call him on telling Solly what had happened.

'Sure,' she said. Then her lower lip quivered for an instant and she conceded, 'A bit shocked. It's crappy enough to learn you've inadvertently borrowed someone's partner, let alone to have the information screamed in your face.' She blinked hard and her refusal to give way to the tears that obviously threatened squeezed Noah's heart. She went on, 'I've just received a text from Jakey. He points out that I never asked whether he was *single*, only whether he was *married*. He seems to think that frees him from mentioning a *partner*, or their two kids.' She let out a long, wavering sigh. 'I feel so stupid.'

With a curse, Solly enfolded his sister into his arms. 'You're not stupid. He's a turd to try to hide behind a supposed difference between "single" and "not married". How about I come back to your place this evening? We'll have a couple of drinks and I'll get a taxi back later or sleep on your sofa. We could get a takeaway from the restaurant in the middle of Kirchhoffen.'

Noah's ears pricked up. 'You live in Kirchhoffen?' He was as certain as he could presently be that that was where Clémence was staying. An urge rose up to pick Kat's brain, but he hesitated to pester her when she'd had such a bad day.

But then Kat gave him the perfect opportunity for a conversation. 'That's right, and the village restaurant, *À la Table de l'Ill*, does Alsatian meals as well as French.

Why don't you join us, Noah? You were great not to turn tail and run from that hideous scene earlier.'

'Yeah, come.' Solly rubbed his stomach with a dreamy smile. 'Kat took me to that resto when I visited a couple of years ago and they do an awesome stew.'

Noah didn't hesitate. 'Thanks. Sounds great.'

Leaving Kat finishing up at the book café, Solly and Noah returned to their place to shower and change. After calling at a supermarket for wine, it was nearly seven by the time Noah drove them into the pretty village of Kirchhoffen and Solly, with a quick check of Google Maps, directed Noah to Rue du Printemps. They drew up outside an imposing house that exhibited the Germanic influences of the area in its steep gables and balcony. Black beams crisscrossed the white stucco that earned the building its name La Maison Blanche – 'The White House'.

Noah, carrying two of the wine bottles, followed Solly out of the car and around to a door at the side of the house, which Solly, carrying a further two bottles, used his elbow to open. 'It's us,' he called. Angelique cannoned into the tiny hall, a rust-coloured fur ball, tail whirring as she greeted them like long-lost friends.

A muffled voice called from another room, 'Be out in a minute.'

'Sound like Kat's in her bedroom.' Solly, obviously passingly familiar with his sister's home, led Noah into a square salon with high ceilings and tall windows. The polished wood shutters on the inside of the windows reminded him of his parents' guesthouse. They'd retired to a modern riverside house four years ago – more convenient, but a boring box in comparison.

The salon floor was varnished wood with a patterned rug in cream and brown in the centre. The two sofas were unalike, a dull red one toning with the gold of the other. An oak bureau contrasted with a side table painted muted green. Nothing matched but everything went together.

Just as Angelique jumped into exactly the spot on the sofa where Noah had been about to sit, Kat appeared. She'd changed into denim cut offs and a white sleeveless top that, Noah couldn't help noticing, clung more than the Livres et Café top in which he'd so far seen her. Her eyes looked pink-rimmed, and he felt heartsore for her. Perfectly nice people got trashed in romance every day, but it didn't seem as if Kat had deserved it.

Solly held up his bottles of red and indicated Noah's bottles of white. 'We brought wine.'

Kat managed a smile. 'In generous proportions, I see. Let's go into the kitchen for the glasses and takeaway menu.'

Following Kat and almost tripping over Angelique, who was doing that peculiarly canine thing of trying to guess where the humans were going and then lead the way, Noah paused at the kitchen doorway.

'What a great room.'

It was long, and big enough for a pine table as well as the cabinets. At the end, French doors stood open to a riot of a garden, early pink roses rambling over the branches of a tree and heavy-headed peonies leaning chummily on a small conifer. Daisies and clover spangled the grass white and pink. His apartment in Castillon-la-Bataille was convenient for the bars and cafés of Rue Victor Hugo but it was on the second floor and without so much as a balcony. He missed the garden and house he'd shared with Clémence and Florine.

'The garden comes with this flat. It's worth the extra rent, isn't it?' said Kat, following his gaze as she took down a takeaway menu from beneath a magnet on the fridge. Then she opened a bottle of red wine with assured movements of her corkscrew and they settled around the plain pine table. Having decided on a family pot of baeckeoffe, the stew Solly had enthused about, Kat phoned the order through. Evidently, she knew the person on the other end of the call because she grinned as she explained that no, she hadn't found the appetite of a pig; her brother and his friend were visiting.

Birdsong filtered in from the garden as Kat heaped cutlery and placemats in the centre of the table. Noah liked the lack of ceremony. Florine would have ensured everything matched and was carefully set out, with neatly folded napkins rather than the kitchen roll Kat plonked down beside the wine bottle. One thing Kat did prove picky about was paying for the meal, saying, when Noah reached for his wallet, 'My shout because you helped me out today and you and Solly brought the wine.'

The washing machine, which had been whirring in a corner, picked up speed and volume. Kat glanced at it. 'Sorry it's noisy but I couldn't wait to wash my bedclothes because of—' Her voice caught and Noah realised that she must have stripped her bed to rid it of any trace of Jakey.

Solly obviously caught the same inference as he leaned in and gave her a quick hug. 'He's a shit, Kat.'

'Yeah.' She sniffed. 'When that bloody woman ranted at me, I realised how gullible I'd been, falling for Jakey's lies.' Kat folded her arms. 'I've been checking out what Emma said and she's right that Tram B from Kirchhoffen would take him close to offices by the *Parlement Européen*. I *was* just a convenience.'

She heaved a great sigh, then straightened her spine.

54

'Well, I've wasted enough time on that tosser. Turns out that being treated like crap is an instant cure for infatuation. Let's not talk about him anymore.'

The doorbell rang and she strode off to pay for their meal, Angelique bouncing and woofing at her side. After a quick exchange with the delivery person, she returned with a large foil dish of the regional delicacy. She set down the container, removed the lid, plonked a ladle in it, pulled half a round loaf from a bread bin and they were ready to eat.

Angelique wandered out to sun herself in the garden, evidently too well trained to beg at the table.

As the humans ladled fragrant, steaming baeckeoffe onto their plates, Solly relayed to Kat his and Noah's conversation about being brought up as an 'only child but with siblings'. Kat looked interested. 'Me, too, I guess. I was an only child until I was twelve; then Baby Solomon here' – she pointed her fork at Solly – 'was born after Dad got together with Irina and I spent weekends with Dad and weekdays with my mum.' Her expression shifted, though her tone remained light. 'Mum married Geoffrey and he moved in.'

Solly dropped his spoon and looked dismayed. 'Crap, Kat. I've just realised where this is leading.'

Noah glanced between them. 'Is it something you'd rather not share?'

Kat shrugged. 'It wasn't my tragedy.' But her eyes were troubled. She tore off a piece of bread and dipped it in gravy. 'Geoffrey had two daughters, Amber and Jade. They had a similar routine as me – with their mum on weekdays and their dad at weekends. That meant when I was at *my* dad's, they took over my room to be with *their* dad. I was fifteen and seethed a bit then got used to it. Then, when I was seventeen, their mum was killed in a car crash.' She ate the piece of bread and paused to wash it down with a gulp of wine. 'Poor Amber and Jade were only eight and ten. They moved in with us full time, of course.' She gave a wintry smile. 'I'd love to tell you that I took those two kids under my wing and made them welcome but actually I withdrew, alienated by having to share my room full time. Mum, to her credit, realised what they were going through and showered them with love, whereas I cleared off to uni in Cardiff. There, I did house shares instead of uni halls so I could live there year-round and not go home for holidays.'

Noah detected an echo of past confusion and pain under Kat's matter-of-fact telling of her history. Families formed and reformed all the time, but it did seem that Kat had felt overlooked just as she reached the crucial years of adulthood. 'That sounds tough for you all.'

She wrinkled her forehead. 'Sure. Then Mum died about ten years ago.' Her eyes glinted with the suspicion of tears. 'I miss her. Geoffrey, Amber and Jade emigrated to Canada soon after. We exchange Christmas cards but that's about it.'

Noah topped up Kat's wine and decided this might be a good time to change the subject. 'How do you like living in Kirchhoffen? It seems a nice village.'

Her expression cleared. 'Love it. I've lived here for two years. I was in Muntsheim when I first arrived in Alsace. I worked part time at the book café, which was in the town centre, then.'

'Kat was a journo before she left the UK,' Solly put in. He was drinking and eating with relish. 'Then she bummed around Europe, writing travel articles.'

'And doing a spot of waitressing,' Kat added wryly. 'It was different to being a staff writer on a regional maga-

56

zine. There are opportunities for freelance writers . . . but not all of them are paid.' She circled back to Noah's question. 'I liked Muntsheim, too. Reeny and Graham, my bosses at the book café, they let me stay in their pool house until I got on my feet and could rent my own apartment. Then, a couple of years ago, I found this garden apartment in Kirchhoffen that meant I was able to have a dog. I really owe Reeny and Graham.'

Noah tried to gently steer the conversation. 'Do you know many people in the village? You seemed friendly with the people at . . . what's the restaurant called? *À la Table de l'Ill?*'

She nodded. 'I do have village friends, mainly from the book group I run with a lady called Mathilde. We meet at the *salon de thé* each month. And then dog owners always chat to other dog owners, of course.'

He tried to sound as if an idea had just come to him. 'Do you cover a lot of the village when you're exercising Angelique? Because I have some family friends who I think moved here but I don't have their address. My parents are visiting mates in New Zealand right now but Mum wanted me to find them.' His conscience gave a twinge that, like Jakey, he was misleading her with an artful choice of words. The 'family friends' could more properly be described as his daughter, his ex-wife and her new husband, but at least his yawning omissions wouldn't hurt Kat. He just wanted more information before he shared the full truth behind being in Alsace. He went on, 'I had contact details, but they were related to their jobs, which both changed. I have a picture of the house, though, and it's so distinctive, I wonder whether you know it?' On his phone, he scrolled to the picture Clémence had sent him of a wood-clad house

57

with triangular windows in the steep gables and circular windows studding the rest of the walls.

'Cool,' Solly commented, craning to inspect the contemporary design.

Kat's eyes crinkled and she had to struggle to swallow her mouthful before she could answer. 'Oh, *les maisons expérimentales!* They've been constructed from as many natural materials as possible and made energy-efficient, hence the "experimental" tag. They're on the edge of the village.' She sipped her wine. 'I hear a lot of disapproval of *les maisons expérimentales*, mainly from those living in *les maisons traditionnelles*, which probably leak heat in winter and fill the air with boiler fumes.'

Noah laughed along with her, though inwardly he was storing every word. 'Do you know the name of the street?'

She shrugged. 'No, now you mention it.' She'd almost cleared her plate and, while Solly took a second helping from the foil container, she consulted her phone, scrolling with her thumb while holding her wine with the other hand. 'Looks like it's so recent that it's not named on Google Maps yet.' She turned the phone so he could read the screen. 'It's here.' She pointed to a stub of road that, according to the map, led to a blank space.

'That's great, thank you.' His heart began tapping at the walls of his chest like a woodpecker. He searched out the same spot on his own phone map and dropped a pin, then finished his meal in silence.

Presently, Kat turned to Solly, asking sympathetically, 'Is it really over with you and teaching?' One of her eyebrows curled in concern.

Solly shrugged, misery creeping across his face. 'Getting dismissed when you're a newly qualified teacher doesn't send out the right message to future employers, does it?'

Noah had already heard about Solly's unfortunate escapade. He'd got so drunk on a stag weekend that he decided that, rather than risk being late for school on Monday, he'd wait overnight on the doorstep, singing bawdy songs while beating time with an empty champagne bottle. It was almost inevitable he would be seen by a passing parent . . . who videoed him and posted it on her social channels. The head, hit by a torrent of complaints from other parents, had had no choice but to act. Solly had paid a high price for his idiotic, immature episode.

Kat touched Solly's hand. 'Are you going to tell me the whole story? I've only heard bits.'

Noah hit on an idea that would allow Solly the privacy to dissect the disaster with his sister while Noah satisfied his burning desire to find the house in the photo. 'How about I take Angelique for a walk while you two talk? It's not dark yet and I'll have a quick look for that house. Mum'll be pleased if I can get an address.' So would his whole family. Everyone was worried about how Florine had moved Clémence away without a word to Noah.

Angelique ran indoors, ears twitching at the sound of her name and the word 'walk'. Kat glanced between the dog and Noah. 'She does normally have a run after dinner. Are you sure?'

Noah got up. 'Absolutely. We got on perfectly at lunchtime, didn't we, Angelique?'

Angelique gave him a goofy doggy grin and wagged her entire rear end, wiggling and waggling so much Kat could barely get her into her harness. Finally, she passed the lead to Noah and soon he and the prancing dog stepped out into the last of the light, leaving the others to their discussion.

Noah headed towards the centre of the village, following

his phone map while Angelique sniffed at gateposts and waved her tail at a couple of dogs across the street.

Kirchhoffen was a pretty village, largely made up of the traditional painted and timbered houses. He passed the restaurant *À la Table de l'Ill* and a building that housed a boulangerie, pâtisserie and *salon de thé* – bakers, pastry shop and tea shop – with space for tables and chairs outside. A sign bearing a yellow cartoon bus with feet instead of wheels told him Kirchhoffen was on *Ligne A* for the school bus and the familiar colours of yellow and dark blue indicated the post office. Silvery track and overhead cables showed where the tram passed through, and the signs near a white church with a pointed steeple indicated the way to a cycle track, a park, and the nearby communities of Ostwald and Lingolsheim. Kirchhoffen was the kind of place residents might refer to as 'le village' but close to the tram line was a 'hotel de ville' or town hall, so it obviously thought of itself as a town. The roads weren't busy enough to really disturb the evening tranquillity and Noah listened to birds singing goodbye to the day and nodded to another dog walker, who looked curiously at him as if recognising Angelique and knowing she wasn't with her usual human.

Once through the centre, the blue dot on his Google map told him he was drawing nearer to *les maisons expérimentales*. Excitement rose that he no longer had to wait for his day off to snoop around the village . . . yet his footsteps slowed.

He'd approached the situation cautiously so far and didn't want to spoil things now by letting the wrong person catch sight of him. Clémence was highly intelligent but also highly emotional. Once upset, her anxiety levels sent her into storms of tears during which she seemed barely able to control herself. She liked things that made sense, like maths and science, timetables and calendars. She was knocked off-balance by unpredictability – like being uprooted from her life and transplanted to Alsace without warning and without seeming to know if the move was temporary or permanent. Unable to reassure her, because it was exactly the sort of question he wanted an answer to himself, fresh anger at Florine and Yohan hit him. Her worried texts were never far from his mind. *I was scared when you didn't answer . . . we have a nice house in a nice place but not near my friends . . . I want to see you . . . I ask Maman when I'll see you and she just says she's not sure yet . . . Yohan says we're very lucky to be able to go travelling like this.* 'Travelling' was what they'd told the school, apparently, with no information as to whether that meant a week away or a year's backpacking. Angelique paused to look back, ears cocked enquiringly, as if sensing his mood. He made the kissing noise Kat had recommended and she frisked back to be reassured with a pat before resuming her inspection of gateposts.

Noah forced himself to stop fulminating over why the hell Florine had let Clémence be left in limbo and concentrated on following the phone map until he reached the point where the road ended on the screen. In real life, however, the road continued as Kat had described. Fresh asphalt swept down to a row of wood-clad houses exactly like the one on the photo, patterned with triangular and round windows.

Dizzying relief flooded through Noah. Had he really found his daughter?

He paused to check the photo again, fixing in his memory the exact features. Two triangles in two gables; one triangle in one gable, five circular windows along the ground floor. Spiky plants and a four-car drive. He persuaded Angelique out of snuffling down a hole and then took to the wooded area opposite the row of houses, counting on the long shadows to disguise him.

House one had too many triangles. House two not enough. House three – his heart leapt – the right number of triangles . . . but too many circles.

And finally! It was the last house, right down to the four-car drive, which contained two new-model Renaults. The mailbox at the end of the drive displayed the number '8'.

His heart pumped so loudly in his ears that he could no longer hear vehicles passing on the road he'd left behind or the breeze soughing through the trees above. He gazed at the house, his feet rooted to the earth and last year's leaves. A light came on upstairs in one of the triangles and he wondered, chest aching, whether it might be Clémence's room. She'd love having a triangular window. She'd probably measured its angles.

Not wanting to draw undue attention by lingering, he continued past the house and further into the trees, where a narrow footpath showed up in the gathering dusk. A few hundred yards took him to the bank of a stream, and he paused there to calm his thumping heart. Then he turned around and made his way slowly back the way he'd come, past number 8 and its neighbours. At the end he saw a temporary-looking sign he'd missed on the way down. 'Rue du Kirchfeld'. He had an address.

A mixture of joy, relief, satisfaction and disbelief swept up, almost choking him.

At last! Clémence.

Chapter Five

The twilight had turned dark purple and a chill stole into the kitchen. Kat rose to close the French doors. 'Noah's been a long time, Solly. I thought he'd just take Angelique for twenty minutes or so, but he's been an hour.'

'Noah's a bit of an enigma.' Solly stumbled over the last word, upending the second bottle of red wine and splashing the last of it into his glass. He snorted a laugh. 'Did you b'lieve that story about family friends he's searching out for his mum?'

She took down a couple of white mugs and a jar of Ricoré de Nestlé instant coffee. She and Solly both took coffee black and unsweetened, and it looked as if he'd be needing his. 'I don't know. Why would he make it up?' She boiled the kettle, spooned coffee, added hot water and then deposited both steaming coffee mugs on the table. She cleared away the wine glasses and empty bottle. It felt a bit mean not to ask Solly if he wanted to open another bottle, like saying he'd already had too much, but, well . . . he'd certainly had enough.

Solly pulled one of the mugs closer to him, apparently

unsurprised it had replaced his wineglass. 'Dunno. But at the van, he's always preoccupied' – he struggled to get that word out neatly, too – 'and kinda secretive. Checks his phone constantly. I reckon he's seeing someone who's married or something and she – or he – is giving him the runaround. They probably live in that house he showed you and he's gone to spy on them. Man with an agenda, I reckon.' He picked up the coffee and sloshed some over his hand. 'Ouch.'

Absently, Kat ripped off a piece of kitchen roll and passed it to him. She'd only just met Noah, but Solly's comments made her stomach feel heavy. Couldn't you trust any man? Now Solly was smirking over Noah's story, it did seem thin. She sighed. 'At least I didn't *know* Jakey was committed elsewhere. If you're right, he's aware the person he's having a thing with isn't free.' Disappointment in Noah settled over her. Wasn't he ashamed? He'd seemed so kind and decent.

At that moment, the doorbell rang, and Angelique's bark sounded from outside, notifying them she was home. Kat stepped into the tiny hallway and let them in. 'Have a nice walk?' she asked, concentrating her attention on Angelique, who was jumping up as if checking Kat had missed her enough. 'You didn't need to take her for so long. Twenty minutes would have done.'

'Have I put your schedule out?' Noah sounded unsure as Angelique finally stood still long enough to have her harness removed.

Kat could hardly say, 'You've made me suspect you might not be as nice as I thought,' so, instead of answering, said, 'You're in time for coffee.'

'Thanks, that would be great.' Noah strolled into the kitchen and resumed his seat at the table.

Feeling unreasonably annoyed that he requested both milk and sugar, which was much more faff than drinking it black, Kat reboiled the kettle.

Solly, cheerfully tipsy, demanded loudly, 'Find who you were looking for?' Then, more soberly, 'Noah? You all right, mate?'

Kat swung round to see that Noah was suddenly looking completely overcome, his face a dull red and eyes glassy . . . almost as if he might cry. For a long moment, she and Solly could only stare at such naked emotion.

Her heart softened. Whoever Noah was yearning for was clearly making him heartsick. 'Here's your coffee,' she said softly, putting it before him. Then, to take the spotlight off Noah, 'It was lovely of you to come home with me tonight, guys, but after coffee I think I'm going to kick you out, OK? I need a bit of me-time.'

Solly turned his head towards her, but his eyes stayed on Noah, making him look even drunker. 'Yeah, right,' he said slowly. 'That's solid.' Finally, his eyes flicked to Kat, widening as if to say, *Do you see how upset he is?*

Almost imperceptibly, she nodded.

The other man's silent desperation seemed to do more than the coffee to sober Solly up. While Noah struggled with whatever had etched the anguish on his face, Solly talked quite sensibly to Kat about Ola, the girl who drove the train, and who'd said she'd take Solly to see Strasbourg as soon as they could make their days off coincide. It gave Noah a chance to hide his face in his coffee mug and pull himself together.

When he finally put the mug down, he managed a smile that didn't reach his eyes. 'Ready, Solly? Thanks again for dinner, Kat.'

Mechanically she replied, 'Thanks for bringing Solly and the wine.'

In half a minute, the two men had left, Solly's feet still not quite with him as he followed Noah out.

Silence fell. Angelique had put herself to bed curled round like a fox-coloured doughnut. Irrationally, though she'd wanted to be alone, Kat now wished she hadn't been so quick to suggest it was time for Solly and Noah to go. Solly was tipsy and Noah might not have the right setting on his moral compass but they'd distracted her from thoughts of Jakey.

'Jakey won't be coming around anymore,' she said aloud, to test how it felt to hear this truth spoken. More humiliating than painful, she decided. She was too angry to feel the way betrayal ought to make her feel. 'He used me as a convenience,' she told Angelique, who twitched an ear but kept her eyes resolutely shut. 'I've been a proper mug.'

Angelique began to snore.

Kat breathed a laugh then cleared up before going into the salon to ground herself with the everyday task of checking her emails. There was one from her dad, which she read smiling at his pride in birdying a hole at golf today. Then he approached the subject of Solly.

Is your brother behaving himself? Irina's still in shock at him being dismissed, even though it was weeks ago. She doesn't know what to say to people. I just say teaching didn't work out and he's got a summer job in France.

Kat paused to wonder whether Howard ever had to sanitise the way he spoke of her. She'd given up a good job to travel, after all . . . But maybe he never thought to tell his friends about her. She read on.

Solly seems confident and affable but underneath he's unsure and anxious. He was gutted to lose his job. I find it interesting that he went to you.

The email concluded with hopes that all was well in Kat's life. With a wry smile, she closed the email, intending to reply in a few days. For a moment she let herself imagine typing: *Dad, I think Solly only came to me because I could get him a summer job in the sun, which beats the hell out of living where his mum can drop in whenever she feels like berating him. Oh, and by the way, hoping all's well in my life isn't the same thing as* asking *me whether* it is. *Nice that you're emailing me weekly instead of monthly . . . now you want an eye kept on Solly.*

She wouldn't say any of those things, of course. Her relationship with her dad wasn't bad, just distant. Irina had made sure Solly was Howard's major focus since the hour of his birth and Kat had long since come to terms with the fact that the child who lived with you all week forged a better relationship than the child who turned up only at weekends. She could have told Howard about her anger and humiliation over what Jakey had done but it was a long time since she'd run to Daddy with her troubles. Since her teen years, he'd seemed to be proud of calling her Miss Independent and she'd never felt able to respond, 'Aren't I Miss Got-no-choice?'

She took a moment to wonder how her relationship with her mum would have developed as 'the younger girls', as Joanne used to call Amber and Jade, had reached adulthood. Secretly, she'd waited for that moment, thinking that as Joanne became needed less as a stepmother, Kat could resume her proper place in her mother's life. She blinked back a tear that her mum's untimely passing had prevented it. Sometimes she thought everything would have been different if she'd still had her mum here.

At least she wasn't weighed down by parental expectation. She switched to the Livres et Café email account, finding four invoices to be paid, an updated price list from the patisserie wholesaler, a reminder that the insurance was due . . . but zero book orders or newsletter sign-ups. It just about summed up her day – all negatives and no positives.

She switched to Twitter to schedule posts for Livres et Café for the coming week and found herself staring at the page in disbelief. Livres et Café had attracted a 'pile on' of one-star reviews!

All appearing to come from different accounts, Livres et Café had been tagged into every post so Kat would see the crappy reviews. *Slow service . . . poor range of books . . . rude staff . . . stale pastries.* 'They bloody are not!' she snorted, then stopped, tilted back her head and closed her eyes. A vision swam into her mind of Emma's screaming face, rage flashing from her dark eyes as she threatened to hurt Kat. It wasn't a big stride from there to imagining her sitting on the train home to Nanterre, smirking as she arranged these one-star reviews, urging her friends to join in. The timing was too much of a coincidence for it not to be her work.

Presently, Kat dragged herself up and went to the bathroom to clean her teeth, then threw off her clothes and flopped onto the bed to read away her troubles with a wonderful novel about love and travel, two of her favourite subjects.

But it was hard not to find her thoughts straying dismally to cheating scumbags and one-star reviews.

When morning came, Kat, having tossed and turned for most of the night, woke with the heavy, dragging feeling of doom that comes with the knowledge of bad happenings. She hauled herself from her bed and opened the shutters with barely a glance at the world outside. Glumly, she got ready for work and applied her make-up.

Angelique yawned, flopped off her bed, stretched, shook, and was ready to face the day, prancing to the French doors with a polite woof to indicate she'd appreciate a moment in the garden. 'Dogs have it easy,' Kat told Angelique grumpily as she let her out.

When Kat was ready to leave a few minutes later, she returned to the door. The bright morning light was making Angelique's fur glow like new copper coins while she watched blue butterflies dance over white roses. Kat made a kissing noise. Angelique frisked indoors and soon they were settled in the hatchback that had an Angelique-sized space at the rear.

They drove past young children walking to the village school and older ones boarding the yellow school bus to Muntsheim. The colourful houses created a honey, blue, red, amber and cream patchwork at the edges of Kat's vision as she navigated around a bike. She usually drove through the village with a smile but today her forehead ached under the weight of a frown.

It took fifteen minutes to reach Parc Lemmel in the morning rush hour but as she hadn't felt like breakfast, she still had plenty of time for a walk. Angelique led the way toward the section of the park where the grass grew long and shaggy, her tail curled like a russet ostrich feather as she meandered along the dog walk, sniffing lacy white cow parsley where it lolled over the path like drunken brides. Traffic rumbled in the distance and the wind rippled the growing grass as they followed a path that swung gently downhill. With an unpleasant jolt, Kat realised she hadn't told Reeny and Graham about Emma's banshee act yesterday. As she was looking after their business, they had every right to expect her to report such upsets, but her mind had spun all afternoon and it hadn't occurred to her.

As it was a business matter and he was keeping as many worries as possible from Reeny, she selected Graham's number from her contact list. There would be no cheery FaceTime with Reeny on this morning's walk because Kat didn't feel equal to plastering on a grin and assuming the necessary positivity. And now was not the time for her to lean on Reeny, no matter how much she'd grown used to it.

'Hello, early bird,' came Graham's raspy voice when the call connected. 'Everything OK?'

Kat elected to keep her voice neutral and her words factual. 'Unfortunately, I had a situation at work yesterday.' She strolled on beside the hawthorns, following a path that was ankle-deep mud in wet weather but was now hard-packed earth, and the story sounded worse and worse in her own ears as she'd told it.

Graham heard her out. 'Well,' he said heavily when Kat had finally wound down. 'That's unfortunate.' Then, after a pause, 'So you think these bad reviews are coming from the woman?'

'It's too big a coincidence for both things to happen on one day.' Kat's heart had slithered down into her comfy flat shoes at the worry in Graham's voice. She was supposed to be keeping problems off his shoulders, not causing them, and no amount of blue sky and early summer birdsong compensated for that unpalatable fact.

'OK,' Graham said when they'd exhausted the discussion about one-star reviews without conjuring up a way to counteract them. 'Once something's out on the internet, it's out. We can't change history.'

'No,' Kat answered despondently. 'How's Reeny this morning?'

Worry sharpened Graham's response. 'Not great. The chemo nauseates her and makes her feel weak. Nothing to be done but plod on and hope for the best.'

'Give her my love,' Kat murmured, choked that she'd brought added worry to her friends.

They ended the call as Kat left the wild area and stepped onto the mown-grass slope. Much of the park lay spread before her, the rollercoaster and go-karts, one of the smaller play areas, the lake with the rowing boat landing stage and the slope where the kayaks slid into the water. Several figures moved around the water's edge and she wondered whether any of them was Noah. She made her way to Livres et Café and settled Angelique in the office with a breakfast of crunchy dog food and a bowl of water. Justine and Antoine arrived in time to deal with the food delivery, transferring pastries and filled rolls to the display cabinet and setting out the tables and chairs on the pavings while Kat unlocked the stock room and restocked the books. Then she opened the book café's doors and soon it was buzzing with customers chattering in a mixture of languages as they consumed late breakfasts or early elevenses.

Antoine hurried indoors with a long order from a group of young mums and pre-school children who were fuelling themselves with snacks before heading over to the free play area to let the kids burn the sugar off on the climbing frames. Kat weighed in to help, frothing coffee and selecting pastries. She carried out the first laden tray and Antoine the second. Like magic, children who'd been scampering around returned to their seats to scoff *pain au chocolat* and peach juice, chirruping like baby birds.

Kat was just turning away when she was brought up short by the surprising sight of Reeny and Graham stepping out of the book café and glancing around. Her heart misstepped. They must have parked at the back and walked through, Reeny's hand tucked in Graham's arm. Her face was so thin it hurt Kat to look at it, and her complexion was like tallow wax.

Shoving aside her disquiet at what this unexpected visit might mean only a couple of hours after the awkward phone conversation with Graham, Kat swept over. 'How wonderful to see you're well enough to be out,' she told Reeny, giving the older woman the gentlest of hugs. Somehow she looked more shrunken in real life than she did on FaceTime and Kat was shocked. Where was the robust, laughing Reeny of old?

'I'm fine,' Reeny answered unconvincingly, her silver hair thin and lifeless above her eyes. 'Hello, darling. You look wonderful.'

Kat bestowed a quick hug on Graham, too, the solidness of his frame only exaggerating Reeny's frailty. 'Sit down. What can I get you?'

Graham gave Reeny his hand while she lowered herself into a seat, but he wore a frown. His grey hair needed cutting and his beard trimming. His shorts looked clean but as if he'd put them on unironed. '*Café au lait* and a slice of Parisian flan for me. What do you fancy, Reeny?'

Reeny adjusted herself carefully in the chair, as if scared her skin would split if she made an unwary movement. Her arms were like sticks. 'Just a hot chocolate, please, dear.' She smiled at Kat and the old Reeny's twinkling eyes peeped from the mask that illness had made of her face.

Graham shook his head. 'Bring Reeny a tarte framboise,

as well, Kat.' Then, to pre-empt the protest Reeny was obviously about to voice, 'The doctor says you have to try and eat, darling. Just have a mouthful or two and I'll have the rest if you don't want it.' His forehead was furrowed with worry.

Kat tried to smooth any anxiety from her own face because it wouldn't help Reeny if everyone around her looked horrified. 'Coming right up,' she sang brightly, and hurried inside to prepare the tray, casting surreptitious glances around the premises as she did so to check all was in order because Reeny and Graham were her employers as well as her friends. Happily, everything looked great. Justine served at the book counter and Antoine took money at the café till. Tables were full, customers were smiling. Kat could sail back outside with an easy conscience.

'Reeny, I've brought you a knife,' she said, as she was deftly unloading the contents of the tray. 'Then you can cut your tart up. It's easier to fancy something if it's in small pieces.'

Graham nodded approvingly. 'Good idea, Kat.'

Kat smiled and whirled away to clear a nearby table and continue with her duties.

Twenty minutes later, Graham came inside to where she was neatening the bestselling books display. Reeny had stayed at the outside table and Kat could see her listening to the lady who ran the soap and natural remedies shop opposite, smiling and nodding but saying little. 'A word with you?' Graham rumbled.

'Of course.' Kat left her task and followed Graham to the office, where they were nearly flattened by Angelique's greeting. Kat flushed as she clicked her fingers to send her pooch back to bed. Graham was perfectly aware she brought Angelique to work but somehow, on top of the problem she'd had to report to him, the dog's presence felt unprofessional.

Taking the big black leather chair behind the desk so Kat had to take the smaller one facing him, Graham sighed. 'Tell me the whole story again so I can take it in.'

Awkwardly, Kat did so, prickling uncomfortably under the weight of Graham's unwavering gaze. 'I honestly didn't know he was committed elsewhere,' she concluded miserably. 'I'm not the kind to trespass.'

He flipped his eyebrows up and down as he did when he was uncertain. 'I'm sure that's true. But it's tricky when a staff member brings their troubles to work with them.'

The back of Kat's neck turned hot with embarrassment. 'I'm sure it is,' she said. 'But if the staff member has been unwittingly drawn into a situation . . .' She licked her lips, worried that there wasn't much sign of support from her boss. Perhaps he was wondering whether leaving her in charge was the right thing to do. Half of her was sorry, if so, because he had enough woes, with Reeny being ill in France and his mum ill in the UK. But half of her was affronted. She'd taken on a lot of additional responsibility with little financial recompense. She didn't deserve to be made to feel like a naughty kid. She added, 'I'm not sure things would have gone differently if you'd been here.'

'Maybe not,' conceded Graham, rocking back in the chair and folding his hands.

She sat up straighter. 'Only "maybe"? I was taken completely by surprise when this Emma woman began haranguing me. I dashed around the back of the building, hoping she'd follow me – which she did – to remove her from other customers. I don't know what else I could have done.'

74

Graham looked at Kat while he stroked his beard with finger and thumb. Then he shrugged. 'I'm just saying that I thought I'd left the book café in safe hands.'

Horror rose up to choke Kat. What she saw as Graham's unfairness stung her more than Emma's attack and her voice came out a strangled gasp. 'Do you want to find someone else to look after your business?' Angelique jumped up and trotted anxiously over to Kat, tail at half-mast. For once, Kat didn't reach out to reassure her.

Without answering, Graham snatched up an empty takeaway coffee cup Kat had left on the desk, screwed it up and hurled it across the room.

Angelique pounced on it and brought it back, depositing it on Graham's lap for him to throw again.

Kat wanted to laugh at Angelique's expectant expression but Graham's face twisted in scowl. 'Bloody dog.'

Angelique's tail went down at his gruff tone.

'She hasn't done anything wrong either,' said Kat icily.

Graham gave a great groan and put a hand across his eyes. Then, in a quite different tone – dreary and flat – muttered, 'I'm sorry, Kat. Please don't resign. I can't cope. Reeny's got to have more treatment and Mum's anxious about whatever's wrong with her. The kids are trying to help but none of them live nearby. I should go back to the UK for Mum, but I've got to stay here for Reeny.'

Slowly, Kat's anger drained away. Alarm and sorrow flooded in to replace it. She sat back, recognising that Graham was at his wits' end. 'That sounds awful.'

'It is.' He raked his fingers through his hair. 'When men joke about having to choose between their wife and their mum, they don't mean like this, when they're both in danger and all you can do is let one of them down.'

Hearing a quaver in his voice, Kat slipped out and got

a bottle of chilled pamplemousse from the drinks chiller and poured it into a glass. Back in the office, with Angelique still glancing between the humans like a linesman waiting for the umpire to make a call, Kat poured the drink and pressed it into Graham's big hand.

'Thanks,' he said in a muffled voice. When he'd polished off half the drink, he lifted his gaze to her, his grey eyes red-rimmed. 'Had any bright ideas about these one-star reviews?'

Kat shrugged tiredly, the results of her disturbed night welling up to engulf her like a grey fog. 'I suppose we could encourage happy customers to leave good reviews in mitigation.' She managed a smile. 'You saw how busy we were when you turned up, so the one-stars don't seem to have made any difference so far. Most of our custom's passing trade and wouldn't necessarily read reviews.'

Graham brightened at her logic. Coaxingly he suggested, 'Be a darling and just ring this bloke and see if he'll call his girlfriend off, will you? Might work.'

'I could try, I suppose,' Kat agreed reluctantly. But when she did, a robotic voice told her the number was not in service. She sighed as she passed the information to Graham, who sighed, too.

They talked the situation over for a few more minutes without any brighter ideas dawning. Then Graham realised Reeny would be tired and needing to go home. Before he left, he gave Kat a hug. 'Don't mind me,' he said gruffly. 'And for goodness' sake don't go off in a huff. Right now, we need you like never before.'

Chapter Six

The next day, Wednesday, was Kat's day off. It would have been great to sleep late but by six a.m. she was awake and staring at the rim of light showing around the shutters. Her mind circled. Had she missed signs that Jakey had been using her to live his double life? Had she been gullible and naive? She presumed he still worked in Strasbourg for part of each month, and, thanks to Emma, she knew roughly where. Would lying in wait for him and kneeing him in the nuts get her in too much trouble? Maybe not if the *gendarme* and the *procureur* were female . . .

Her mind jumped tracks onto yesterday's uneasy meeting with Graham. From there it was only a quick mental hop to worrying how Reeny's poor depleted body would cope with yet more chemo. She already looked as if the breeze off the lake would blow her away like a dandelion seed.

Kat threw off her bedcovers. Lying here indulging in catastrophic thinking would help no one.

She had two days off. She should book in at a

pet-friendly Airbnb somewhere. Take her camera and collect material for a travel piece. With taking on additional responsibility at Livres et Café and spending so much time with Jakey, she hadn't written a feature for weeks. Maybe she could head down the shores of the Rhine – Le Rhin in French and Alsatian, Rhein in German, Rijn in Dutch – hunting for content to sell to one of the river cruise operators for their website or newsletter. She began to write copy in her head. *The mighty Rhine begins in Switzerland and flows through Germany, forming the border with France for a while, before rolling on past the Netherlands. The tributary River Ill flows into Strasbourg and beyond and the Rhône joins both of these rivers in the water network of the Rhine basin.*

She jumped out of bed. Angelique, who'd been sleeping on the rug, lifted her head blearily, one ear bent forward and the other back.

'I'm going travelling. You coming?' Kat asked.

Angelique dropped her foxy head again and looked unsure.

After a quick shower, Kat dressed in a favourite outfit of embroidered denim dungaree shorts and her cropped white T-shirt, both soft and comfy.

Angelique gave up her attempt at a lazy morning, rolled to her paws and shook. Kat let her out into the garden then returned to the bedroom to throw things in an overnight bag, buoyed at the idea of a couple of days away. Back in the kitchen, she filled another bag with bowls and food for Angelique then took down the dog lead and jingled it. 'Angelique! Better go for a walk if you're going to spend a while in the car.'

Angelique bounded in, tongue lolling and eyes gleaming, and they set off on their favourite path around the village, passing the stream where Angelique could stare suspiciously at the coypu. Trees linked their leafy arms above them to form a canopy that allowed glimpses of the blue sky dotted with puffs of white. A trickle of people passed on their way to school or work. In no hurry herself, Kat stepped aside with just an occasional, '*Bonjour.*'

When the path ended, Kat and Angelique were again among coloured houses nestling between hedges. Passing the *salon de thé*, Angelique looked up and barked her pleased 'Woof!' of welcome. Kat glanced over at the outside tables, expecting to see one of Mathilde's family, as they ran the tea shop. Instead, it was Noah Toleman she spotted, hunched over a coffee cup and gazing unseeingly down the street. She hesitated. Noah in Kirchhoffen at just after eight a.m.? It fitted uncomfortably well with Solly's theory of him trying to effect some romantic rendezvous.

On the other hand, he'd been visibly distressed after searching for that house on Monday evening. Perhaps someone didn't want to be found? Perhaps it was unrequited love rather than the affair Solly had suggested, which would explain that tortured expression. Perhaps Kat had been a bit judgy . . .?

Whatever the situation, Noah would probably like Kat to leave him alone with his thoughts, she decided. Unfortunately, Angelique had other ideas. She barked again, more insistently.

The heads of almost everyone seated at the tables swivelled towards the sound, including Noah's. As he smiled rather than looking shifty or worried, she waited for a car to pass, shortened Angelique's lead and crossed the road to greet him. '*Bonjour.*'

'*Bonjour*,' he replied as he fussed over Angelique. He

gestured to the vacant chair across the table. '*Café, peut-être? Ou petit déjeuner?*'

Kat's stomach rumbled as she caught the mouth-watering aromas of coffee and croissants. 'Well, it is my day off. Thanks.' After checking with Noah, she went inside to order for them both and was served by one of Mathilde's warm and chatty daughters. Mathilde's three daughters – and any number of their teenage kids – were the workforce of the *salon de thé*. Now in her eighties, Mathilde only visited socially and – as her family grumbled good-naturedly – to boss them about.

Once the order was given and Kat had enquired after the family, she returned to where Noah still waited. Angelique had taken up station beneath the table, an excellent spot from where to clear up croissant crumbs.

'Odd to find you here in Kirchhoffen,' Kat said to Noah, as she sat.

He shrugged. 'It's my day off, too.' And before she could probe further, he went on, with the half-smile she was getting to know, 'How are you feeling about things, now?'

'Glad to have a couple of days to lick my wounds.' Thinking of Jakey's perfidy gave her emotional indigestion, complete with a burning in her chest. 'Still hard to believe I was so stupid.'

Noah paused while a young man served them a plate of croissants and jam and steaming coffee mugs before repeating, 'Stupid? He lied to you – great big, hairy lies made all the more plausible because you wouldn't expect anyone to be so audacious. I don't think you should blame yourself.'

Warmth blossomed inside her at his support. 'Thanks.' She broke off a corner of hot, flaky croissant to chew while she wrestled with the fiddly opening of the jam tub.

'You were looking very thoughtful before Angelique and I disturbed you.'

His smile vanished like the sun slipping behind a cloud. 'Just trying to decide how to handle a situation.'

Remembering that tortured expression again, she made her voice gentle. 'If you were hoping to meet someone, I can change tables.'

His hair blew into his eyes, and he brushed it back. 'Not expecting. Hoping against hope, maybe.'

She studied him, thinking he had a cheek to condemn Jakey if he himself was having an affair. He seemed like such a straightforward guy, too. 'Are you divorced?' she asked, saying what was on her mind without thinking it through.

His head tilted in the same way Angelique's did when she was curious about something. 'Yes. I'm thoroughly single.' A smile hovered around his lips.

Kat flushed, realising that he'd probably construed the question as interest on her part. 'Solly asked if I knew,' she mumbled unconvincingly.

His smile broadened, eyes crinkling at the corners. 'I'm surprised your brother's got time to be interested in my love life. He's getting all excited about his day off, tomorrow. I don't know if you were expecting to spend the time with him, but he's asked that girl Ola to show him around Strasbourg.'

She grinned. 'He mentioned it. I guess he hasn't bothered telling her that he's visited Strasbourg several times.' Her first croissant finished, she began to spread jam on a second.

He watched her movements. 'He's visited you in France before? I thought perhaps not when he explained that you don't know each other very well.'

Shock shimmered through Kat although she lent half an ear as he went on to chat about how his brother and sister, Tim and Bex, had been expected to join Noah and his family after uni but had remained in the UK. *She and Solly didn't know each other very well?* It was unpleasant to have it put so baldly, though it must have been what her dad was hinting at when he said he found it 'interesting' that Solly had come to France. She ate mechanically, turning the idea over.

While she'd been feeling she'd been nudged out of the nest at both her dad's house and her mum's, had her little brother been wondering where she'd gone? The idea made her heart feel as if it didn't fit properly in her chest. She was familiar with feeling unnecessary to the lives of others and the realisation that she may have made Solly feel unwanted in hers swamped her with guilt.

Now was the time to make it up to him and hopefully grow closer.

Noah had paused and she realised he'd asked whether she had plans for her day off. She told him about the feature she had planned. 'I'll drive south, further into the Rhine basin, and see what material I can find.'

Noah looked interested, his hair catching the sun and looking more gold than brown. 'I work for a river cruise company. We're small and not represented on the Rhine but I have contacts. Let me send a couple of emails to press officers to ask whether they work with freelancers or only with agencies.'

She stared at him, distracted from the subject of her brother for an instant. 'You work for a cruise company? Because you do a good impression of someone who works at the park.'

His face fell and he took a breath as if to speak . . . but no words came.

*   *   *

Damn. That had just slipped out. All Noah's instincts had told him to fly under people's radars in Alsace while he focused on his mission – yet, somehow, he'd fallen into friendship first with Solly and now with Solly's sister. He reminded himself that he didn't owe Kat explanations. 'I meant I *used to* work for one,' would let him off the hook. But Kat had just been lied to by Jakey and Noah recoiled from the thought of being bracketed with that rat.

As the silence drew out, Kat propped her elbows on the table and cupped her chin with her hands. Her dark curls were piled up to form a pom-pom behind her head that jiggled in the breeze. She narrowed her eyes. 'I've been a bit self-centred. I haven't asked you much about yourself.'

Noah could only shrug. 'I told you about my family and coming to live here when I was young. Not much more to say.' But he knew she was asking why he'd tripped himself up about his job and then failed to come up with an explanation.

Her next words, accompanied by a meaningful little quirk of the eyebrows, confirmed it. 'Well . . . I'm wondering why you're hanging around a village several miles from where you're living. It's none of my business, of course. I'm just hoping no one will get hurt by whatever you're here for.'

Noah met her unafraid gaze. Everything he'd learned about Kat so far was that she was honest and straight-forward. Her colleagues liked her. Her bosses trusted her. She'd got her little brother a job. She was nice to dogs.

She was someone he could tell.

Someone he could tell . . .

Confiding in her would be like knocking the weight off a pressure cooker lid so the steam could pour out. The tight, frightened feeling in his heart and head might ease. He heard himself say, 'If anyone's getting hurt, it's me.' He saw her blink, as if that wasn't what she'd expected. 'But my real worry is Clémence being hurt and confused. Clémence is my daughter,' he added, realising Kat didn't know this.

Kat's lips parted and formed a silent, 'Oh . . .'

Now he'd started, he found he couldn't stop. 'When a marriage ends, adults take the decisions, and the kids just have to roll with it.'

'True,' Kat agreed, gently.

He remembered that it was exactly what had happened to her and flashed an apologetic smile. 'Clémence is emotional. A bit different. Likes things with precise answers. She's scared and anxious about so many things and suffers emotional episodes.' Feeling he wasn't doing his darling girl justice, he added, 'She's also clever and sweet and funny and I miss her *so* much.' Then his heart jumped into his throat and, to his horror, his eyes began to burn. He pressed them shut with his thumb and forefinger, feeling as emotional as a teenage boy being dumped.

'I'll get you another drink,' Kat's voice said softly. He heard her get up and leave, Angelique whining from beneath the table because she wasn't taken along. Kat's voice floated out to him, speaking in French, ordering more coffee and requesting a dish of water for the dog.

By swallowing hard, he'd just about regained his composure when she returned with Angelique's water, which the dog lapped noisily. Kat smiled at Noah, her dark eyes soft. 'They're bringing more coffee.'

He nodded his thanks. They waited for several minutes, the two of them in a bubble of silence but surrounded by the chatter from surrounding tables, the clatter of crockery and scrape of forks. The traffic on the road running past had thinned. School runs and journeys to work must be over. Eventually, the young guy appeared to serve them more coffee – café crème for Noah and espresso for Kat.

'*Merci*,' Noah mumbled. When he'd added sugar and taken several steadying sips he spoke again. 'I would have jogged along in our marriage for our daughter's sake, but Florine, my ex-wife, met Yohan. He's controlling,' Noah added bitterly. 'That was the attraction. Florine's dad Henri was the same. Her mum died young, leaving Florine completely under her father's influence. Henri died and she was a bit . . . undocked, I suppose. According to her, I should have been "stronger with her" and "more of a bastard" – I mean, really? – and my encouraging her to be her own person was "unhelpful".' His throat felt raw, flayed by voicing painful facts. 'I was only upset for Clémence. I'm the first to admit our marriage had become lukewarm.'

Beneath the table, Kat's knee brushed his as if in sympathy. 'How old is Clémence?'

'Eight, now. Five when we split up.' He took another draught of the coffee. It was a little hot for comfort but it eased his throat. 'The split began OK. We share responsibility for Clé, as is the norm in France, so we reached amicable agreement to that effect and lodged the paperwork with the notary. We continued to make joint decisions about Clémence, and I saw plenty of her when we all lived in Castillon-la-Bataille. She likes paddle boards and kayaks, like me.' He cleared his throat. Kat was watching him, lips half parted, the tiniest crease of concentration between her eyes.

'After a year, when the divorce came through, Florine married Yohan. He began to try and influence things.

85

Having tucked Florine safely under his thumb, it seemed his next target was to rank above me in Clémence's affections. Earlier this year, Florine asked if I'd be prepared to allow Yohan to adopt Clémence. He, apparently, thought this was only fair.'

Kat made an inarticulate noise of protest.

'Yeah, I know,' he said wearily, slumping in his chair, shoving back his hair as the breeze blew it in his eyes. 'I told her not till hell froze over. I was already unhappy with his approach to being a step-father. Clémence is bilingual but he doesn't like her speaking English – probably because his is of schoolboy standard – and pulls stupid passive-aggressive stunts like acting sympathetic if she "has" to see me.' He felt his fingers clench around the handle of his cup. 'It was confusing Clémence and making her anxious. Yohan declined the opportunity to discuss this with me, so I told Florine that Yohan's frigging presumptuous behaviour was unacceptable.' He took a long, slow, steadying breath. 'And a few months later, in March this year, they disappeared. The first I heard of it was when the school called me to discuss the way that Clémence had abruptly been taken out of school "to travel", with no information about if and when Clémence would return. While the teacher was going on about the school calendar being set by the Ministry of Education and not by parents, my head was spinning. Then, I got a text from Florine saying they were taking Clémence on holiday "for a while" – again, no end date. She didn't answer my calls and when I went to their house it was empty. Clémence didn't answer my calls either. I'd never had Yohan's number. I realised that because I'd refused him the right to adopt Clémence, he'd simply taken things into his own hands. It was terrifying.'

'What the hell?' demanded Kat. Her indignant scowl contrasted with the pretty embroidery along the denim straps of her dungarees. 'People can't just act like that.'

'Not in law,' he allowed. 'But, in fact? They can. They keep their plans quiet; they pack up and leave. My brain nearly exploded. I was incandescent. But I was also scared to death. Suspecting that my number had been blocked, I used a friend's phone to text Clémence. Sure enough, she came straight back demanding to know why I hadn't been answering her when she tried to contact me. She was . . . upset,' he added inadequately, remembering the way he'd clutched the phone in impotent fury as he read her sad, confused messages. He gave himself a moment to regroup by sipping his coffee.

Kat sipped, too. Her eyes were just the colour of the espresso in her cup. 'And they've moved her here?' The cup rattled on its saucer as she put it down because her attention was on him rather than on what she was doing.

His laugh was strained. 'Yes, but it took me a couple of weeks to figure it out. I told her not to unblock my number on her phone in case Yohan checked it, then I bought a burner. I got her to write its number down somewhere rather than store it in her phone and delete our messages once our conversations were over. That shit Yohan,' he added contemptuously. 'Fancy exercising his pathetic power plays over a little girl. When she asked him the name of the village they're living in, he told her not to worry about that and wasn't she a lucky girl to spend a summer in such a wonderful place? He has this treacly cooing voice when he's making his outrageous attempts to control people. As an eight-year-old, it might be hard to shove back against such unreasonable coercion, but what on earth's Florine's thinking . . .? I assume he's blocked my number on her phone, as well as Clémence's. People think controlling behaviour is about loud voices, outright aggression, accusations and physical violence. But it doesn't have to be. It can be about emotional manipulation, isolation, using teasing or guilt as weapons.'

'Maybe Florine's infatuated,' she put in quietly. 'It seems to make you gullible.'

He shrugged in disgust. 'Brainwashed, more like. Clémence eventually found the opportunity to take photos of things in the village and one was a war memorial for the fallen of Kirchhoffen. That's how I knew where she was. I've taken a leave of absence from work and moved here while I figure out my next move. I'm still paying rent on my apartment in Castillon-la-Bataille so the job at the park with accommodation was a heaven-sent way of making ends meet.' He gazed down the street, barely noticing window boxes frothing with pink and white blooms.

Kat sat back and let out a long breath, shaking her head. 'It's almost unbelievable. I presume the house you were searching for is theirs?'

He nodded. 'Clémence sent me the picture.' The sun was gaining in strength, and he adjusted his position so the light didn't blind him.

She frowned thoughtfully. 'You couldn't just go to the door and demand to see your daughter?'

'I could,' he agreed. 'But what if that prompts Yohan to move them again? We're close to the border with Germany here and he speaks good German. What if they moved across the Rhine in the same stealthy way that they moved clear across France? What if he made that permanent? It could take ages to get Clé back. I'd win in the end, but how long would it take? Would I have the necessary financial resources? And most importantly of all, what would it do emotionally to my daughter?' His head had begun to ache, not just with the sun but with the stress, the fear that dogged him every day, every moment.

'Then go to court,' she protested fiercely. 'Go to the police. You have rights. Your ex and her new bloke can't just flit hundreds of miles and hope you'll let it happen. It's against the law and morally wrong.'

Gently, he pointed out, 'But that's exactly what they've done. It's *fait accompli.*' From beneath the table, Angelique sighed, moving around and settling across one of Noah's feet. He went on. 'You're right, I can go to the law. Florine's in breach of our agreement. But the case would be sent to the family court. Before that, social services would need to make an assessment. They'd question Clémence and she'd be called to court to speak there, too.' He gave a quick, decisive shake of his head. 'I'm not criticising the French system but I'm not putting my little girl through that if I can find another way. Clémence is already confused and upset. In many ways, she gets on fine with Yohan because he presents everything in the guise of doing the right thing and knowing what's best for an eight-year-old. He buys her and her mother gifts and takes them to nice places and I don't think she's old enough to know about gilded cages.' Decisively, he shook his head. 'I need time to assess the situation and decide how to go about things the best way.'

'Wow.' Kat shook her head. 'You're more patient than I am. I'd be rampaging about and banging on their front door.'

The snap in her eyes made him grin, despite the heavy weight in his guts. 'That might come. But my priority is to see Clémence somehow. I texted her and asked her to find an excuse to come here this morning if she could, but she's a touch young to be given free rein, even around a safe little village like this one. She hasn't answered and I feel rubbish about encouraging her to deceive her mother and stepfather. Also high on my to-do list is a conversation with Florine. I'm shocked and disappointed that she's allowed herself to be sucked in by a manipulative tosser but mainly I'm frightened that I might do the wrong thing for Clémence.'

'Wow,' Kat said again, her eyes big and soft with sympathy. 'It's really shitty.'

'Another reason I took the job in Parc Lemmel,' he said. 'If I had all day every day to brood on exactly how shitty it is, I think I'd go completely mad.'

Chapter Seven

Their coffee cups were empty. People visited the boulangerie and patisserie or passed by with wheeled shopping baskets on their way back from the mini market. Kat watched Noah check the time and sigh. She wondered how long he'd sit there just hoping his daughter would arrive.

Her blood boiled for him. How dare this Yohan arse try and take Noah's daughter away? 'I suppose you could fight fire with fire,' she suggested. Then, when he raised one querying eyebrow, she clarified, 'I mean turn up and take Clémence back to Castillon-la-Bataille.'

He gaped. 'Like, break into a private house?'

She wrinkled her nose. 'I meant more if Clémence was ever able to get out to meet you.'

He pushed his coffee cup away with a moody gesture. 'I could. It would make me as bad as them though, and poor Clémence would be more upset than ever. She loves Florine, and Florine loves her. It's just Yohan. He's the adult version of a spoilt kid who covets someone else's toy and can't bear even to share it, so he steals it instead.'

Angelique came out from under the table, laid her face

in Kat's lap and blew out a hot sigh. 'Angelique's not finding this much in the way of entertainment,' Kat began. Then she halted, the word 'entertainment' echoing in her mind. She narrowed her focus onto Noah. 'I can see why you're cautious about turning up at Florine's front door unannounced, but someone else could. Like me. I could put on my good neighbour's hat and ask if they'd like to join the village book group. I could deliver flyers to all that row of houses, so it won't look suspicious if they happen to be in the front garden and see me coming.'

Noah's attention fixed on her with laser intensity. 'For what purpose, exactly?'

Kat shrugged. 'If someone answered the door, I could probably confirm it's the correct house, at least.'

For the first time that morning, a tiny gleam of positivity flickered in Noah's eyes. 'Really? That could help because it doesn't look as if Clémence is going to turn up here. If you're sure you don't mind being involved in my domestic crisis—'

Kat was already on her feet, glad to do something to return the support Noah had given her in the face of Emma's wrath – was that only two days ago? 'Let's go to my place to pick up the flyers and you can hang out there while I pop along with them.' Angelique frisked to her paws the moment Kat moved, feathery tail beating.

'Take Angelique with you,' Noah suggested. 'Clémence likes dogs.'

It took only ten minutes to put their plan into action. Noah – plainly on pins – parked himself in front of Kat's TV while Kat and Angelique set out with pretty, lemon-coloured paper flyers at the ready. It took only a few minutes for them to reach Rue du Kirchfeld and its row of contemporary homes. Although the triangular and circular windows gave the high-end development an air of modernity, she preferred La Maison Blanche and its traditional peers, herself.

She made her way from house to house, tucking flyers through the handles of front doors rather than the slots in green mailboxes that were common at the end of drives in France, to create the impression she was going properly door-to-door. Nerves tingled up her spine. She was not naturally a sneaky person but what had happened to Noah was so out of order that she was prepared to see what she could discover. And, who knew? Florine and Yohan might actually want to join.

Then she was there, 8 Rue du Kirchfeld. She strode confidently up the drive past two Renault cars on one side and landscaped garden on the other. She rapped the knocker and took a polite pace back.

A tall, willowy woman answered the door. Her blonde hair was short and chic. She wore what looked to Kat like a designer shirt and jeans, both black. In full make-up, including peach-coloured lipstick, she could have been a model for Sézane or Germanier. '*Bonjour*,' she said, polite but cool. Behind her, a double-height hall allowed Kat a glimpse of a dog-leg wooden staircase with glass balustrades.

'*Bonjour*.' Remembering her French manners, Kat extended her hand, saying – also in French – 'I'm Katerina Jenson, one of your neighbours in Kirchhoffen. I've come to welcome you to the village and invite you to join the book group—'

A man appeared behind the woman. His dark hair was brushed straight back, his dark eyes gleaming from behind black-framed glasses. He frowned. '*Bonjour. Vous sont Anglais?*'

Kat allowed herself a giggle, as if amused at such an unusual opening gambit as demanding to know if she was English. '*Oui!* But I've lived in France for several years. I manage a bookshop in Parc Lemmel. It's always such a pleasure to meet neighbours that I'm here to invite every household in Rue du Kirchfeld to the Kirchhoffen book club, which meets once a month at the *salon de thé*.' Was it her British accent that had brought him to the door? Or did he vet all callers, even if his wife was dealing with them?

The man seemed to relax and shook Kat's hand, though as he took the lemon-coloured flyer he said, sniffily, 'I doubt a village book group would share my taste in literature. I don't see my social life as being in Kirchhoffen,' he added condescendingly.

Kat nodded understandingly, though she wondered what his taste in literature was. Homer in the original, perhaps? 'But as well as the *salon de thé*, we have a nice restaurant in the village.'

His nostrils flared, as if needing to rid himself of a smell. 'Not for us, I don't think.' So, only high-end restaurants in Strasbourg were good enough for him, then? Kat turned back to the woman. 'I'm sorry. I didn't catch your name.' She repeated her own.

The woman glanced at the man before murmuring, 'Florine Gagneau.' *Bingo!* Kat smiled, exultation spurting in her chest, then turned an enquiring smile on the man. 'Yohan Gagneau,' he said tersely.

Then down the wooden staircase behind him trod a small, slight figure. The blonde hair hanging down her back was wavy, like Noah's. Her eyes were blue – also like Noah's. She looked as wary as a baby deer, but her gaze was fixed on Angelique, who'd been standing on the path beside Kat's leg as if waiting politely to be included in the introductions and wondering if they were to be invited in rather than left standing in the sunshine.

'*Bonjour!*' Kat cried to the little girl, beaming because this surely was Clémence and she'd be able to tell Noah she'd caught a glimpse of her. 'Would you like to meet my dog? Her name's Angelique.'

The child stepped forward with a shy smile, but Yohan put out a hand. 'With respect,' he said to Kat, 'we don't know your dog and we're very careful with our little girl.' He turned his smile on the child. 'Clémence, we must be careful. I couldn't bear it if anything happened to you.' His voice was soft, caressing. Kat remembered what Noah had said about Yohan's 'cooing' way of manipulating people.

Angelique sat with a wide doggy grin, as if to demonstrate how unthreatening she was but Yohan's restraining hand remained on Clémence's shoulder, though the girl wore a longing look as she gazed at Angelique. 'Of course,' Kat murmured. She turned back to Florine. 'We have events for children at the book café where I work, right in the middle of Parc Lemmel. Its address is on the flyer, too. Have you visited the park yet, on the edge of Muntsheim? It's a wonderful place, with everything from wild walks to rollercoasters.' She thrust a flyer at Florine, though Yohan already had one.

Florine held it loosely, as if unsure what she should do with it.

Kat smiled widely at everyone. 'Do you like the village? I love these new houses and I've been curious about what they're like inside. Have you moved far?'

'We're just on holiday,' Clémence began in a high, sweet voice.

Yohan smiled. 'Thank you for calling but we must go now.' In a very few moments, Kat was left facing a closed door.

She turned and hurried home, clutching the rest of her flyers, Angelique trotting at her side. At La Maison Blanche she fell in through the door and Noah shot into the hall from the salon, his hair rumpled as if he'd spent the entire time she'd been away thrusting his fingers through it. 'It's them,' Kat gasped.

Noah took a stunned step back, as if he hadn't quite been able to let himself hope. His Adam's apple moved compulsively and he absently stroked Angelique's head, as she'd reared up on her hind legs to allow him to greet her. 'Yes?' he croaked.

Quickly, Kat unclipped Angelique's harness and ushered Noah back to the sofa, dropping down beside him to recount every detail of what had been said and what she'd seen as nearly as she could remember. 'Clémence seemed fine, apart from Yohan not letting her pet Angelique,' she concluded, realising that at some time in her babble of words she'd seized one of his hands in both of hers and he'd let it lie there, warm, their fingers curled together.

'That's his way,' he whispered. 'Controlling every little thing.' Then he dropped his gaze and made a strangled gasp that could have been thanks.

Kat squeezed his hand before she released it. 'You sit there. I'll fetch a glass of cold water.'

By the time she'd hurried to the kitchen to pour two glasses and add ice, he'd recovered himself enough to say a proper, 'Thank you for doing that.' And he sank most of the water in one draught. His colour, which had swept from white to red and back again, returned to his normal healthy hue. 'Weren't you going away somewhere today?' he asked suddenly.

'Oh. Yes.' Kat had become so wrapped up in her sleuthing that she'd completely forgotten her plan to take her mind off Jakey with a couple of days of research. She pulled out her phone to check the time. 'Wow. It's nearly eleven-thirty.' She considered. Getting out of the apartment seemed less urgent than when she'd awoken in a glum mood. She'd almost made up her mind to say that she'd go next week when her phone rang in her hand. She read the screen and said, 'Sorry but I should take this. It's Danielle at Livres et Café. *Allô*, Danielle?'

Danielle sounded harassed and cross. 'You didn't cancel all the pastries on today's order, did you?'

'Of course not!' Kat had been slouching but now she sat up straight. 'Don't tell me they weren't delivered.'

'Cakes, yes; pastries, no,' Danielle confirmed gloomily. 'I've spent ages arguing with the bakery and they insist the change to the order came from the Livres et Café's account with them.'

'Shit,' cursed Kat, her throat tightening. 'Leave it with me. I'll phone them.' She ended the call, then scrolled through her contacts and stabbed at the screen muttering under her breath, 'What on earth?' In a few moments she was explaining to a confused sales department that despite their perfectly valid-looking amendment through their own system, she had not cancelled half of their daily order. No, she hadn't. No, she truly hadn't. 'I can't explain it. What can you deliver to us today?' She groaned when she was told 'nothing' but refused to be brushed off. 'What can you let me have if I come and fetch it? OK, that's better than nothing. I'll be there in fifteen minutes.'

She was on her feet and ready to head for the door before she remembered Noah and turned back.

Unexpectedly, he was already on her heels. 'I'll come with you. It will be quicker to load and unload with two,' he said.

'Thank you,' she said fervently.

She made sure Angelique had water and food before they tore out of the door. All the way to the bakery wholesaler on the industrial park just inside Muntsheim, which she always passed on her way to work, she was conscious of Noah's vehicle behind hers, his slate-grey SUV with both roof rack and bike rack proclaiming his sportiness. Presently, she swept to a halt in front of a roller shutter and Noah got out and followed as she ran in through a personnel door beside it. Unfortunately, she discovered that she wasn't getting a single croissant until she had explained herself all over again to the sales manager.

Mme Philippe was a small, middle-aged woman with a perfect bottle-black bob and a habit of folding her arms and staring while she considered what had just been said to her. And she considered slowly. 'The cancellation came from the Livre et Café account,' she observed.

Kat shrugged. 'But I didn't make it. I'll check with the owners, but I doubt it was them.'

Mme Philippe's black brows met above her nose. 'Then someone else must have access to your computer. Or you have been hacked,' she pronounced.

Hacked. Kat's stomach dropped. What, more trouble?

'In future,' Mme Philippe added, 'you must back up your orders with emails to protect us both, you understand. Sudden cancellations cause us work-flow problems.'

Kat bit the inside of her cheek. 'If someone has hacked our computer, they've hacked our email.'

Once again, Mme Philippe considered slowly. 'Then you must text me or my assistant.' It was not until Kat had the phone numbers safely in her contact list that Mme Philippe instructed her staff to throw up the roller shutter and reveal the trays of pastries already packed up and ready to go.

At least Noah, Kat discovered, had spent the wait putting down his rear seats to form a flat surface to receive the trays. 'Thank you,' Kat said gratefully as white-smocked bakery staff wheeled out a trolley full of sturdy plastic trays.

Ten minutes later Kat was pulling up behind Livres et Café and watching Noah park alongside. They unloaded in record time, Noah ferrying trays to and from his car and Kat wielding the tongs to fill up the chilled cabinet. It wasn't quite one o'clock so there was still plenty of trade. Danielle, Justine and Antoine reached past her to fulfil orders or use the till, reminding her why this operation was usually conducted before they opened. The area in front of the cabinet was thronged with people who didn't want to await table service. Most of the tables were full. The bookshop side was busy, too, with a queue for Justine to ring up purchases. Laughter and happy chatter filled the air, at odds with Kat's mood.

'Hey,' said a chirpy voice. 'Thought it was your day off.'

Kat didn't have to look up from arranging palmiers on a rectangular plate to recognise Solly's voice. 'Hey,' she answered briefly. 'Small issue.'

Solly ordered a sandwich from Antoine along with a millefeiulle, which was a triumph of pastry layers, cream and icing, and a cup of coffee. 'Takeaway, *s'il vous plait*,' he added, obviously considering 'takeaway' an international enough word to get by on, or not knowing *emporter*. He raised an eyebrow when Noah arrived with the final tray and paused with the two white paper bags in his hands. 'Is everything OK?'

With a meaningful glance at her customers and staff, Kat said, 'Tell you later.'

Solly still hovered. 'I'll wait.'

Something turned over in Kat's heart at the staunch jut to his chin as if to say: *if there's something the matter, I want to know. I'm your brother.* She couldn't help smiling. 'I'll be ten or fifteen minutes.'

Solly nodded. 'I'll take a table outside.'

Noah said, 'I'll dump the last empty tray in my car and hang out with Solly.'

'Thanks,' she said gratefully. 'Antoine, give Noah coffee and a snack on the house, please.' Then she escaped to the office to call Graham to share the possibility that their computer had been hacked.

Kat plumped down at the desk with butterflies doing the salsa in her stomach as she dialled.

Graham answered, puffing for breath. 'Kat! Just going to call you. Shit has hit the fan. We're at the hospital. Reeny began a chest infection that's gone to pneumonia. They're taking her to the high dependency unit now. She looks like a ghost.' This was followed by what sounded suspiciously like a sob that he turned into a cough. 'Mum's been taken into hospital in Surrey as well because of chest pains. I'm sorry, darling, but I'm at my wits' end and whatever it is I'm just going to have to leave it with you to do your best. In fact, I'm going to have to dump everything on you. I've got to be with my Reeny. My eldest's with Mum but she's had to leave work and drive over to be there. What if one of them dies and I'm with the other one?' His voice cracked. Then, with a bitter attempt at humour, 'If I still have my sanity when things calm down, remind me to pay you a bonus.'

Kat could hardly keep up with all the information he was hurling at her, putting in, 'Oh no . . . I'm sorry . . . yes, of course . . . give my love . . . poor her . . . yes, OK. Oh, no!' Then fast, before Graham disappeared completely, 'I need to talk to the web designer. There's a hitch somewhere.'

'Yes, yes,' Graham said distractedly. 'You know Ulrica's email address. I give you full authority over everything in my absence. Look, Kat, I'm going to tell you where to find the access information for the internet banking and the secure key thingy. Luckily, I didn't go with any of that voice recognition nonsense. Just keep the account in credit – that's all I ask.' A few hurried details, then he was gone while Kat was simultaneously scribbling notes and trying to send her love to Reeny.

For several seconds, Kat stared at her phone screen. Holy crap. Her heart tumbled with anxiety for Reeny.

And Graham had left Kat steering the whole ship. She had to worry about the bank account. What if she couldn't stay in credit? What if she'd stocked too many niche titles or the park suffered some disaster and there were no customers to put money in the till? Just because every table had been full for weeks didn't mean . . .

Then she shook herself. 'This is no time for a wobble,' she said aloud. 'The summer holidays are less than four weeks away. The bank account will get fatter and fatter all summer so long as you carry on doing everything you've been doing. Just let Graham concentrate on helping Reeny.'

Still feeling shellshocked, she remembered Solly and

Noah and went to find them, stepping outside and shielding her eyes against the sun. At a small, round table, the two men waited, Solly just finishing his lunch. 'Drama upon drama,' she said gloomily, before recounting Graham's gabbled phone call. She lowered her voice. 'I have to check with the web developer to see if someone's messing with the computer. I'd better tell Danielle all about it, too. So much for a day off.' She rubbed the spot above the bridge of her nose where an ache was beginning.

Solly's thick, dark eyebrows flipped up, his – currently unused – credentials as an IT teacher coming to the fore. 'You've changed your passwords, I hope?'

Kat's stomach felt as if she'd just gone over the top of the biggest loop on the rollercoaster. 'Oh hell, I'll do it right away.'

He tutted. 'And don't use any whole words or easy-to-guess crap. It should be random letters, symbols and numbers.'

She pulled a face. 'What, like the "strong" passwords my phone tries to persuade me to accept? But we need something the customers can type in easily for the free WiFi. Every café has free WiFi.'

Solly's eyes almost rolled from his head. 'You're not telling me your business computer is on the café's free WiFi?' He picked up a WiFi card from the menu holder. '"Livresetcafe22?" That's your password? It's like *inviting* a Man in the Middle cyber-attack.'

Kat had only heard vaguely about 'MITM' attacks but knew they were rife in cybercrime. Her cheeks felt as if they were on fire. 'Graham set it up, not me. But yes. There's just one WiFi.'

Solly shook his head and climbed to his feet. 'I've got to get back to work or my manager Liliana will probably sack me. I suggest you change every password you can think of, then I'll come back tonight and sort out your network so you can keep your gormless password for the punters, but the business is physically separated and properly password protected. Sheesh.' He shook his head. 'I was going to invite you to the van for pizza anyway because I've got something to show you. Let's do that when I finish work, then we can come over here and see what's what.'

'Thank you. I do like pizza,' Kat answered meekly, not pointing out that big sisters weren't supposed to be told off by little brothers. Solly obviously knew a lot more than her about IT.

So Solly returned to work, Noah disappeared to enjoy the rest of his day off and Kat gloomily sentenced herself to a stint in the office to change the passwords of their website and email until Solly could work his magic on the network. This morning's plans to drive away and happily lose herself on the banks of the Rhine seemed a distant memory.

After changing the passwords, she spent an hour on the phone with Ulrica, the web designer, straining Kat's technical ability and sinking her heart to her boots. Tentatively, she recounted the story, including Solly's fears about the network being accessed.

Ulrica said, 'Hmm,' in a foreboding tone. 'Your brother could be right about the nature of the attack. In which case, the hacker can eavesdrop on anything going through the network connection. Your computer could be infected with malware to intercept connection with selected sites, such as the wholesaler you had a problem with. The attacker can also modify your transmissions.'

'And this won't be put right by Solly increasing our security?' Kat asked, already knowing the answer.

'*Non*. The malware is in the machine. He's just making you more secure for the future.'

'But if I only log in from my own computer at home from now on . . .?' Kat tried optimistically.

Ulrica had sounded sombre. 'If she's gained the ability to log into the site, the threat actor has probably infected the site, too, concealing malware code in an image or a movie. Leave me to look, hmm? If the attacker is this Emma, or a hacker employed by her, she will probably be content with attacking Livres et Café and not install code on the sites of your suppliers. That would be a much greater offence.'

She made a sound like somebody blowing out their cheeks. 'So . . . motivation. If there's no blackmail or attempt to make financial profit then it's all about mischief.' The waterfall-like sound of fingers flying over a keyboard came to Kat down the phone before Ulrica added, 'Yes. The newsletter has been disabled, and the online shop.'

Kat groaned and left Ulrica to travel into the bowels of the admin area while she examined what Ulrica called the customer-facing website. There she found testimonial quotes mangled into outlandish complaints about Livres et Café . . . recognising the same phrases as the one-star reviews that had begun appearing on Monday evening after Emma's visit.

In the three days since Sunday, when Jakey 'went dark', as the military thrillers would term a sudden lack of communication, Kat felt as if she'd suffered enough stress for a month. Doggedly working through her tasks, she spent another hour changing passwords for every account they held with a supplier – making them all different and random and compiling a handwritten list rather than make a digital record that might also be accessed.

At four, Kat drove home to fetch Angelique, taking the opportunity to swallow some painkillers and then relax as well as she could under a lukewarm shower. She had little appetite for dragging her headache back to Muntsheim, but she must get Solly's help with the network . . . and the thought of being with Solly and Noah was more attractive than being alone. She couldn't think of a single other occasion when she'd sought comfort from her brother but, despite their long absences from each other's lives, she was becoming aware of their connection strengthening.

She'd felt the same tug on the day her twelve-year-old self had inspected the crumpled, red-faced newborn Solomon Howard Jenson, who'd squirmed in her arms. She remembered the incredible softness of his skin, the bagginess of his white sleep suit and the way his tiny fingers had clutched the air until he found her finger to cling to. Her heart had burned with love. She'd wanted to hold him forever, but his mum Irina had said, 'Howard, take the baby back from Kat. You can't be too careful.'

Kat had flushed to think that anyone would assume she would be careless with her tiny, precious brother. But Irina had been at pains to say 'half-brother' at every mention – making it plain that what was important about Baby Solomon was that he was Irina's son – and had continued to boss and fuss whenever Kat got too near. Hurt, Kat had maintained a distance, but as soon as Solly was old enough to crawl he'd set off after her. When Irina had tried to interest him in something else, he'd howled for Kat to build bricks for him or play clapping games, to grasp his damp hands as he learned to walk. It had even been Kat who'd taught him to ride a two-wheeled bike just before she'd left for uni.

The bond had been buried under the years of Kat once again being encouraged to keep her distance, but now Solly had grown up. He was old enough to shave, to work abroad, to be sacked in disgrace from his first real job. And he'd come after her again.

Heart swelling at these thoughts, Kat dressed in fresh clothes and she and Angelique travelled the few miles back to Muntsheim.

She parked behind Livres et Café and, as there were so few people likely to be about between the service area and the staff lodges, let Angelique run ahead without her lead. The soft, summer evening relaxed her, and butterflies danced above the cow parsley. It would be light until about nine-thirty, but the blue of the sky had hazed over and everywhere was so still Kat could hear bee-buzz and birdsong as plainly as the swishing of her sandalled feet through the grass.

At the two-tone green caravan, she found Angelique already greeting Solly beside a scooter. Black, with a rusty exhaust, it looked well used but had rakish lines. 'What's that?' Kat asked as she came up with them.

Solly gave the handlebars a stroke. 'It's an MKB Booster,' he said. 'This is what I wanted to show you. I can't afford to run a car here, so I bought a scooter. Two hundred euros. What do you think?'

Kat walked a careful circle around the little black runaround, noting a slit in the saddle cover and scratches on the mudguard. The tyres had plenty of tread though and all the lights looked complete. 'It looks fun,' she pronounced, because it was obvious from Solly's eager expression that she wasn't meant to pick fault. 'Great for the price.'

Looking suitably gratified, Solly gave his new steed a

last pat and then led the way indoors. 'The pizzas are in the oven. Noah's keeping an eye on them.'

Kat followed her brother up the metal steps and in through the lightweight door that sprung back on you if you didn't hold it open. Angelique bustled ahead with a bark of welcome.

From inside, Noah's voice said, '*Bonsoir*, Angelique.'

When Kat had taken the three strides necessary to clear the galley kitchen – surprisingly hungry now she could smell the pizza – she saw him uncoiling himself from a corner of the U-shaped sofa, laying the time-travel paperback she'd sold him face-down on the cushion. Kat wasn't one of those purists who couldn't bear to see spines cracked, books folded back, or corners dog-eared. In fact, it always made her smile to see someone enjoy the hell out of a book. In shorts and bare feet, his T-shirt hanging loose and his hair looking darker than usual from the shower, he greeted her with a smile. 'I can vanish if you and Solly want to talk.'

It seemed as if her headache lifted a little. 'Nothing secret. I hope the pizzas won't be too long. I've just realised I missed lunch.'

His eyebrow quirked. 'You haven't eaten since those two croissants this morning?'

Kat flushed, aware of Solly turning to regard them with interest. 'We met by happenstance this morning,' she said, without giving details because it would bring out things that were very much Noah's business.

They ate the pizza with their fingers and washed it down with Meteor beer. Kat decided a drop of alcohol would relax her while she recounted everything Ulrica had told her this afternoon.

Solly paid close attention to the details Kat spilled.

'I suppose if it all comes from spite it might stop sooner or later,' he said dubiously. 'Guess you have to leave it to Ulrica to find what code she can and eradicate it, but it can be like playing Whack-a-Mole. The hacker could just come back from another angle. Are you looking to prosecute, by the way?'

'I hadn't thought of it. I just want the problem to go away,' Kat sighed.

Afterwards, Noah volunteered to take Angelique out so Kat and Solly could retire to the office of Livres et Café. Kat sighed, her headache threatening to make a comeback at the very sight of the big laptop computer. She spent the next two hours watching Solly's fingers pirouetting over the scratchpad like mini ice-skaters while he sighed and tutted about crappy passwords and system vulnerabilities.

Twice Kat protested, 'Graham chose the password, not me,' then she fell silent and let any further scolding wash over her. If Solly needed to grumble while he worked, fine. He was here, helping. She tried to think of something to do for him but, apart from rewinding time and abandoning Jakey in favour of Solly during his first week in France, came up blank. So, she did the only thing she could think of. She slid her arms around him and said, 'It's great to have you around, little brother.'

'So I can fix your network?' he asked with a snort. But a smile blazed across his face, and he took his hands away from the keyboard to hug her tightly in return.

When the changes had been made and the password for the secure area written down, they returned to the van and joined Noah for coffee. Noah told Solly about his weird domestic situation, which made Solly almost spit out his coffee. Solly explained he was getting over his teaching-related disappointment and thinking of trying for an IT support job in the UK in the autumn. Kat vowed not to think about Jakey or Emma anymore.

She sent a quick text to Reeny to say she was thinking of her, then settled down to relax with her brother and Noah. Maybe the worst was behind them.

Chapter Eight

'I can't believe it's nearly the end of June already,' Kat said to Danielle, a couple of weeks later. They were clearing a corner, ready for a Wednesday afternoon children's event at Livres et Café while the bustle of customers went on around them. The local primary schools closed early on Wednesdays, leaving time for extra-curricular activities. 'I'm glad to see the back of June with its heartaches and headaches. At least Reeny's out of hospital for now, and I can FaceTime her tonight. Ulrica seems to have plugged the gaps in the website security and Livres et Café is busy as hell, so the one-star reviews haven't hurt us.'

Danielle twinkled as they carried an indoor table outdoors to make space for the anticipated influx of children. '*Oui*. And Justine, Antoine, Romain and Pierre have finished university for this year, so we have a full staff roster even without Reeny and Graham.'

Kat liked the way Danielle pronounced 'Reeny' – like 'René'. She sighed as they deposited the table on the sun-baked pavings and returned for the chairs. 'I wonder if we'll ever see Reeny back here. Graham told me she's presently too frail even for another round of chemo. I texted him to see what he thought about me visiting Reeny now she's home, but he said' – she assumed a deep, Graham-like voice and a South London accent – '"Sorry, darling, we can't have you bringing in germs. Even the common cold could put her back in hospital." So, it's just FaceTime again.'

Danielle shook her head sorrowfully. 'I suppose restricting visitors is the correct thing to do. But poor Reeny.'

They returned inside to put out floor cushions for the children's event, the last before the school holidays, which would begin in a little over a week. A local author, Helene Sagan, was the guest of honour and the children attending would receive a copy of her previous book, *L'incroyable Elodie,* with a voucher for half-off the brand-new sequel, *Elodie et Rose.* The character of Elodie was a ten-year-old girl who was full of courage and saw it as her task to instil courage in others. Kat had read *Elodie et Rose* and thought Elodie would do a lot better to let her responsible adult handle dognappers rather than tearing off on her own to rescue her dog, Rose, but who was she to say? Kids loved adventures and Kat would probably have rushed off to rescue Angelique, if she was in Elodie's place.

The author arrived in a colourful clash of harlequin pants, purple canvas sneakers embroidered with daisies and a T-shirt bearing a picture of the cover of *Elodie et Rose.* In her bag were *Elodie* bookmarks, notebooks and pencils to give away, swag guaranteed to please young children. Fifty-ish, Helene had a mop of wiry brown hair and a twinkly smile.

Danielle, who usually took the lead with the running of events, made Helene welcome and provided her with coffee. Kat joined in the chorus of, '*Bienvenue!* Welcome!' but her role had been the behind-the-scenes organisation, liaising with the publisher doing the promo. Before Ulrica had had a chance to increase security, the website had been changed by their hacker to read that Jacqueline Wilson was the visiting author. Luckily, Kat had noticed immediately so no one had turned up expecting the superstar Jacqueline.

Helene was already seated on a floor cushion, greeting children as they arrived with their parents and handing out bookmarks when a tall woman with short blonde hair entered, a little girl beside her, who handed in her ticket with a quiet, '*Bonjour.*'

'Oh!' Kat managed not to utter an overexcited, 'Oh, you *came*, Clémence!' saying, merely, '*Bonjour!* You've come to meet Helene Sagan? How lovely.' She turned to Florine with a smile. 'The children are to sit with Helene and talk about her books and listen to Chapter One of *L'incroyable Elodie*. The adults usually take seats at the tables.'

Florine smiled and nodded. 'Of course.' She looked tired, with tiny creases beside her eyes. She settled Clémence, who chose to sit shyly at the back of the group, bought an espresso and retired to a table in the corner, alone.

Kat's brain was whirring as she took the last ticket and then nodded to Danielle to announce that three o'clock had arrived and they should begin. She must text Noah! This was perfect. Retiring a couple of steps towards the office, she took out her phone and, after a moment's thought, typed in: *Can you come to the café right now? Important!!!* She purposefully elected not to give him a reason, deciding that it would better all-round if his meeting with his daughter appeared accidental. Then she

112

retired behind the chilled cabinet to serve cake and pastries while Helene Sangan began telling the children how she'd created Elodie to be exactly the brave girl Helene herself had wished to be as a child.

After ten minutes, Noah arrived, his hair tumbled by the breezy day. He crossed to the counter where Kat still stood but before he could say a word a shrill voice cut across poor Helene Sagan's carefully rehearsed reading. '*Papa!*' The shout was so loud that Kat heard Angelique bark in reaction from the office. Clémence leapt up to bump and scramble through the other children, crying, 'Papa!' again.

Noah spun on the spot, his gaze zeroing in on the little body hurtling his way. 'Clémence,' he breathed, eyes wide in disbelief, crouching to gather her up against him, staggering against the display cabinet with the force of Clémence's joy.

It was everything Kat could have wished for, she thought with satisfaction, watching Florine jump up, too, but only to stand rooted to the spot, lips parted in alarm. Noah wearing the uniform of Parc Lemmel robbed the situation of any whiff of set-up, as did his obvious shock and Clémence's joyous tears as she clung to him. Kat's own eyes burned. She felt sorry for the visiting author as every single member of her audience was now watching Noah and Clémence instead of listening to Elodie's adventures, but she was sure Helene would grab their attention back with the free pencils and notebooks as soon as the emotional scene was over.

Noah rose, Clémence still clinging to him and sniffing, and his gaze caught on Florine over their daughter's head. Noah strode across to her corner and murmured something. She nodded, and the three of them went outside.

Kat, feeling queerly churned up as the little family left her and everyone else behind without a backward glance, turned her attention to smiling brightly and getting the event going again.

Noah's heart was thumping as if trying to break out from behind his ribs. After more than three months, he could scarcely believe his darling daughter's hand was clasped in his. A crowded place wasn't where he wanted to talk to Clémence and Florine, so he murmured, 'Let's go somewhere quieter.' Though he was bursting with gratitude for Kat, he'd come back and thank her later.

Florine nodded and followed him out of the arcade and down the grassy slope to an area where no one was picnicking or playing ball, selecting a nice patch of sun-warmed grass. She was wearing her hair shorter now, but it suited her high cheekbones. He thought she was thinner than last time they'd met, in March. Always willowy, her severe jeans and short-sleeved shirt made her almost androgynous, reminding him of David Bowie on the covers of his mum's albums. The Florine he'd been married to had liked feminine, filmy dresses . . . or had she just been trying to reflect Noah's own tastes back at him?

'So,' he said, setting Clémence among the daisies but keeping one arm looped around her thin shoulders. 'This is where I work, at the moment.' He waved an encompassing arm at the lake. 'I look after the kayaks for Parc Lemmel and live on-site in staff accommodation.'

Clémence shook her fringe out of her eyes. 'We're here on holiday.' But her voice sounded thready and unsure and her smile wavered. 'But last night Yohan said that in September I'm going to school here . . .' She trailed off, sending her mother a questioning look.

114

Noah fired a questioning look at Florine, too, his eyebrows flying up in the age-old indication of, 'You . . . *what?*'

Pale pink flushed Florine's cheeks. 'We *came* for a holiday.' She took a breath before adding, 'But I think we might be here a while.'

Clémence frowned down at the daisy she'd picked and was now twirling between finger and thumb. 'I won't see my friends in Castillon, ever?'

Noah's heart squeezed so hard it hurt. 'I'm sure that whatever happens, visits can be arranged,' he said, comfortingly. 'Have you made friends here yet?'

Without looking up from the daisy, Clémence shook her head, her hair dancing around her downcast face.

Wordlessly, he stroked her shoulder, wondering how best to proceed. He needed to talk to Florine without Clémence overhearing, but without scaring Florine off. He couldn't let today's giant stride be lost.

'Tell me what you've done while you've been here, then, Clé,' he suggested gently.

Clémence brightened, glancing up with a flash of blue eyes so much like his own. 'We've been on a boat on the river in Strasbourg. All the bridges have pretty flowers and the roof is glass so you can look up at the buildings. We've eaten at restaurants. And we've walked and been to the cinema and we've been bowling. And we've biked around a lake and eaten ice-cream.'

'You, Maman and Yohan?' he prompted.

Clémence nodded. Luckily, she'd never seemed scared of Yohan, because if Noah ever thought Yohan had given her cause to be frightened, he wouldn't have been able to control himself. It was, however, still tricky to deal with her stepfather, with his manipulating ways, heading people off like a sheepdog until they took the paths he chose.

He noticed Florine check the time and was prompted to do the same. They'd been talking for more than half an hour and it was close to four o'clock. He didn't want her to declare it time she went home to prepare the evening meal. Inspiration struck. 'Would you like a short turn on one of the small kayaks, Clémence? The lake's less than a metre deep and children of eight years and up are allowed to go alone if they wear a life vest.'

Florine's eyes widened uncertainly but Clémence jumped to her feet. '*Mais, oui!* I haven't been on the water at all since we left Castillon.'

Aware that now it was he who was being manipulative by not involving Florine in this decision, Noah scrambled up, taking his daughter's hand, small and trusting, in his. A rush of love swept over him as he led her away, leaving his ex to follow, chatting about the park and how great it was to work with boats all day, watching people have fun. Clémence listened happily. She didn't ask how or why he'd turned up in a new job in Alsace and he was glad. That was a conversation for the grown-ups.

'Is your kayak here, Papa?' She gave a little skip of anticipation.

'No, just those belonging to the park,' he answered. 'You don't think I'd let tourists crash into each other in my kayak, do you?' He was rewarded by her giggle.

When Noah had left his workstation with barely a word of explanation, Marcel had stepped into his role. Now, Marcel's iron-grey eyebrows crawled up his forehead like caterpillars as he caught sight of his absentee employee calmly stepping through the gate onto the kayak slipway.

Noah clapped him on the shoulder, gambling on Marcel's family-mindedness. 'Marcel, I'd like you to meet my daughter, Clémence. Isn't she beautiful?'

116

The creases in Marcel's leathery skin changed direction to form a smile. '*Tu es la fille de Noah?*' You're Noah's daughter?

'*Oui,*' Clémence murmured shyly.

After introducing Florine as 'Clémence's mother', Noah explained, 'I've promised Clémence a paddle in a kayak.' Soon, he and Marcel were holding the jolly red kayak broadside so Clémence could slide on board bum-first and settle her feet on the pegs. Confidently, she pushed off with her paddle, and they watched her glide towards the centre of the lake.

Noah turned to Marcel, who was regarding him with curiosity. 'She's been kayaking either with me or in her own kayak since she was five years old.' He lowered his voice. 'I'm sorry I've deserted my post, but I have something very important to sort out.'

Marcel frowned, but after a moment he nodded shortly and moved down the slipway to help a mother and daughter out of a two-person kayak.

Noah edged Florine to a spot where they could lean on the fence like any other proud parents watching their offspring, ready to wave whenever Clémence looked over. Voices drifted to them on the breeze and a pair of ducks set up a great flapping and quacking to shatter the glittering surface of the lake. As if encouraging them on, a goose honked from the shore. Noah fixed his ex-wife with his gaze. 'You owe me quite an explanation. The first I knew of you moving Clé away was when the school called me in a snit about it. I received one text and eventually worked out that my number had been blocked on Clémence's phone. And maybe on yours? Is that why you didn't answer any of my increasingly frantic calls? Didn't you think I'd be panic-stricken at my daughter just

117

vanishing? Or even worry that I might send the gendarmes after you? You need to be transparent with me now, Florine, because I have taken legal advice,' he said, which was a bald-faced lie. 'The only reason I haven't acted yet is because I don't want our little girl to have to go through the process with the social workers and the family court if I can avoid it. But *only* if I can avoid it,' he added meaningfully. In his pockets, though, his hands were clenched. He was so aware of the border with Germany only six or seven kilometres from where they stood.

Florine's gaze dropped to her fashionable leisure shoes like a child knowing she'd done wrong. 'I'm sorry. I never intended things to happen quite as they did,' she murmured.

Though Noah was churned up inside, he dug deep and managed not to let his rage show. 'Then tell me how everything played out.'

She lifted her gaze to Clémence gliding across the sun-dappled lake against a backdrop of trees, her orange life vest clashing merrily with the red kayak. 'Yohan,' she began in a scratchy voice. She hesitated, shaking back the wing of hair that fell across her forehead. 'Yohan presented me with a fait accompli,' she confessed in a low, strained voice, unwittingly repeating the phrase Noah himself had used when explaining the situation to Kat. 'Though he called it a surprise, an opportunity to experience another region of our magnificent country. He'd already rented the house we're staying in and he . . .' Again, a hesitation, as if she were only just now marshalling her thoughts on the subject. 'He . . . thought I'd already agreed to do it, I suppose. He said he'd like to spend a summer in this region and I said it would be nice. I didn't realise he took that as the go-ahead.' A thread of defensiveness underlaid her words, as if she expected Noah to pour scorn on the explanation.

Then she smiled and lifted an arm to wave. Noah saw Clémence grinning at them and he broke into exactly the same proud parent smile as he, too, waved. Their daughter was all that connected he and Florine, now. Once, he'd been attracted to her pretty smile and her interest in everything he did. It had felt like togetherness. They'd been looking for an apartment to share when they'd been surprised by her pregnancy. Marriage plans had been the obvious response and the search for an apartment had become a search for a house with a garden for the child to play in.

At first life had seemed happy. Florine was a caring mother, enchanted by the little pixie who'd made them a family.

After a couple of years Noah accepted that their marriage had moved from 'happy' to 'OK' and knew that if Clémence had never come along, their relationship would've run its course much earlier.

When, three years ago, Florine fell under the spell of Yohan's domineering personality it had been a shock but Noah had simply focused his attention on their daughter, making certain she was nurtured and eased through the big change in her life. He hadn't deserved to be traumatised by that daughter being spirited away from him.

Tightly, he prompted, 'So, what happened next?'

She sent him an apprehensive look. It was a look he remembered, an expression she'd worn when waiting for her father to react to something she'd done or said. 'We packed up and came.'

'Why did you give the school no notice?'

Her growing apprehension was visible in her eyes.

119

'Yohan said it was best, in case they made a fuss about her being taken out of school in term time. It was a way of getting around the rules.'

Noah thought that the school would have been perfectly correct to have raised such a 'fuss' but he let that slide. 'I'm her father, not Yohan. Why wasn't I consulted?' His hands had clenched in his pockets again. Deliberately, he looked away from Florine and watched Clémence practising the long, slow, even paddle strokes he'd taught her. Deliberately, he reminded his ex-wife, 'You're in breach of our parental agreement.'

Florine's breathing caught. 'I texted you.'

'Once!' he bit out.

Her voice wavered. 'You didn't answer so I thought . . .'

'Bullshit,' he said wearily. 'Yohan somehow persuaded you that it would be good for family unity or something to distance yourself, while he quietly blocked my number on yours and Clémence's phones. Having taken over my wife, he wanted to be more important to my daughter than I am. A pathetic power trip.' He still managed – somehow – not to snap and snarl but he was determined Florine should know how unacceptable the whole situation was.

They watched Clémence propelling the kayak faster and faster, less adept kayakers pausing to watch the way she turned around the tip of her paddle and arrowed back the way she'd come.

He felt oppressed by the sheer selfishness of Yohan's actions. The other man literally considered only himself and saw his wife and stepdaughter as possessions. There must be an appropriate label for him such as 'narcissist'. Or 'douchebag'. Yohan and that Jakey character who'd

120

used Kat so shamefully made a fine pair, trampling over others without even a glance at a moral compass.

'How did you find us?' Florine asked quietly. It was typical of her that she didn't defend herself with anger or defiance and that only apprehension lurked in her pale blue eyes.

Noah thought suddenly of Kat and her steady, dark-brown gaze, of the way she'd helped him, first by leaving the information about today's event with Florine and then by contacting him when Florine and Clémence showed up. Big-hearted Kat had shown him nothing but warmth and friendship since he'd come to Alsace, and he'd begun to realise recently how often he visited her café and how much he looked forward to doing so.

He shook Kat out of his head and focused on his ex-wife. Communication with Clémence had been unexpectedly re-established and he intended to seize the moment. 'When Clémence disappeared, my first instinct was to go to the police,' he said, watching her pale. 'But I suspected someone had tampered with her phone and I texted her from a friend's. She was terribly upset at not hearing from me – and so am I,' he added, not seeing why he should sugar coat the facts. 'Obviously, Clémence has been yanked away from the life she's always known because I refused to allow Yohan to adopt my daughter. But a new school at the opposite end of the country? What the hell?'

She hunched a defensive shoulder. 'Yohan has been head-hunted for a directorship in Strasbourg. He's renting out our old house and arranged for a company to pack up the rest of our things and store them. He says we can buy a house when the rental period's up, if we want.'

Noah actually forgot to keep an eye on his precious daughter as he stared at his ex-wife in horror, his worst

121

suspicions realised. 'He's moved you and Clé hundreds of miles away from Castillon *permanently*? By stealth? By manipulation? Who the fuck does he think he is? You don't seriously think this fab new job and all his plans have just happened, Florine? He must have been scheming for months!'

She didn't reply but her eyes grew enormous. Probably, Noah thought, he'd never sworn at her before.

He thrust his fingers through his hair and tried to calm down. 'What's the name of the new organisation he'll be working for?'

A frown puckered her forehead. 'Why do you want to know?'

'Because,' he said through gritted teeth, 'I want to know if the company's French. If it's a German company, indicating that he's heading towards getting you both across the border, then I'm going straight to the authorities.'

'Oh. It's a French firm,' she said eagerly, sounding relieved to be able to say so. She mentioned a company that developed stock control systems for warehousing and distribution. Noah checked on his phone and breathed more easily to discover they had no German offices listed but were represented in east and south France alone.

Clémence paddled closer to them wearing a half-smile, glancing from one of them to the other. Noah realised she was getting tired of kayaking alone and looked for a way to head her off from joining them just yet. 'Just ten minutes more, Clé, OK?' He made sure to sound regretful.

As he'd hoped, she reacted by not wanting to lose any of that time. 'OK.' With an expert swish of her paddle, she headed back into the centre of the lake, swerving around a yellow kayak and a white rowing boat.

Noah looked back at Florine. She was pale again, almost

pasty, beneath her make-up. 'Are you happy with the situation?' he asked. 'Happy with a husband who's disregarded any wish you might have and acted so unacceptably? Happy that Clémence's real father is being treated so shabbily? Happy Clémence has been separated from her friends? And, OK, my parents are travelling for a few months now, but they'll return. You've separated her from them, too, the grandparents she's known all her life.'

She shrugged apologetically, but her gaze dropped.

He battled to stifle his anger and think clearly. Maybe Florine thought she had no alternatives? If that was the case, perhaps he could offer her one. He dropped his voice, making it ooze with sympathy. 'If you want to return to Castillon-la-Bataille I can take you and Clémence. Find you somewhere to live. Any time. Just say the word.'

But she was already shaking her head. 'I do . . . love Yohan.'

He couldn't really see how anyone could love a manipulative shit who tricked you and your daughter into giving up your whole lives so he could start a great new job conveniently far away from said daughter's dad, but he, at least, wouldn't attempt to dictate to Florine. He tried something subtler. 'So, you didn't get a chance to say goodbye to your friends? And neither did Clémence?'

She shook her head.

'You didn't help choose your new home?'

Again, a headshake. He sighed. He wanted to shake her. But that, of course, was not how you handled a difficult situation. 'Put my new number in your phone and don't let him block it. Make it possible for me to spend time with Clémence. Don't let him move you again without my knowledge,' he said flatly, abandoning all efforts to coax.

She looked at him uncertainly so, as Clémence was paddling into the slipway now, the late afternoon sun burnishing her pale blonde hair into white gold, breaking his heart with her angelic beauty, he made his stance abundantly clear. 'That's what it will take for me to hold off involving the authorities. And just suppose – hypothetically – that Yohan *does* think you're conveniently close to Germany here, how would he feel if he tried to take Clé across and got stopped at the border? Got a criminal record? I've made it impossible for Clémence to leave the country without my consent.' He hadn't, but it was beginning to seem an increasingly good idea to find out if it was a possibility. 'You might put up with Yohan's shit, but I'm not going to,' he concluded, his reasonable voice roughening around the edges.

She cleared her throat. 'I-I don't think it would be a good idea for you to try to confront Yohan.' It sounded as if the mere notion made her feel faint.

Noah deliberated. It would give him a lot of pleasure to have a stand-up, drag-down row with Yohan Gagneau. However, he contented himself with saying, 'I'll hold fire on that for now because arguments upset Clémence. She's all I care about. But he's not taking my daughter away from me. Understand that.' To reinforce his intention to play hardball if he had to, he added, 'How would you feel if I ever took her to the UK without telling you?' He made it a question rather than a threat, but he saw her flinch as his words hit home.

Florine couldn't get any paler. She whispered, 'You wouldn't?'

As a tough guy seemed to be all she understood, he replied, 'Wouldn't I?' He saw her eyes widen with horror so reined back. 'You know that's not my style . . . unless

I get desperate – and I've been pretty close to desperation already.' The qualification was cold comfort and he meant it to be. He pushed himself away from the fence as Clémence turned the kayak into the shallows, ready to be pulled in.

Uncertainly, Florine said, 'but you don't know where we live.'

He tossed back over his shoulder, 'It's 8 Rue du Kirchfeld.' Then he went to help his little girl onto dry land, fresh joy flooding through him that she was here, in his life, as she should be.

Chapter Nine

At Livres et Café, Kat helped Danielle restore the café furniture to its usual places with smiling efficiency, even if most of her mind was on Noah and the way he'd caught his daughter to him, joy and anguish warring on his face.

Author Helene Sagan had already finished her event, drunk a cup of coffee and left. The children had scattered back to their parents, gleefully clutching their notebooks and freebies. Kat had enjoyed redeeming vouchers for Helene's new work and, along the way, selling a few paperbacks to parents. The event had gone well.

She was repositioning the last table when she saw Noah and his family entering, Noah resting an affectionate hand on Clémence's shoulder. Kat had to blink away a prickle of tears at the love in their eyes when they glanced at each other. Florine walked a step behind, expression carefully blank.

'I kept a goodie bag for you,' Kat said to Clémence. From the shelf beneath the till she pulled out a white paper bag with *Livres et Café* printed in flamboyant, grass-green script and passed it to Clémence, whose blue eyes sparkled as she peeped inside.

Noah looked surprised but pleased. 'That was thoughtful of you, Kat.' He spoke in English although Kat had addressed Clémence in French.

Clémence, followed his lead, proving that she was, as Noah had claimed, bilingual. 'Thank you very much. Helene Sagan's one of my favourite authors.' Her accent held a hint of Scottish – unsurprising considering her father – but her English was effortless.

'You're so welcome,' Kat replied.

Noah and Florine each duly admired her gift and then Noah said, 'We thought we'd stop in for a drink.'

'Of course,' Kat answered breezily. 'Give me your order and I'll bring it over.'

'Peach iced tea, please,' said Clémence promptly. Her gaze slid sidelong to the nearby cake counter. She tilted her head and looked from one parent to another. At Noah's nod she chose a slice of chocolate tart. Noah asked for a latte and for Florine an espresso, then they went back outside to an empty table.

Kat crossed to the café counter to fulfil the order, where Danielle was fulfilling an order of her own. She lifted an eyebrow. 'Is he taken after all?'

'After all what?' Kat demanded with a shrug. 'That's his ex, if that's what you mean.' She turned to the espresso machine.

'And his child?' Danielle asked, in the same soft, teasing voice.

'*Oui*,' Kat responded briefly, pouring first the espresso then adding the steamed milk to Noah's to make his a latte.

Danielle wasn't to be deterred with brusque replies. 'I have been watching how you look at Noah.'

'How I . . .?' Kat tried to frown Danielle down.

Danielle merely grinned. 'And he looks at you in the same way. An ex is an ex. In the past.'

'Obviously.' Kat selected the largest piece of chocolate tart for Clémence and, grabbing a bottle of peach tea from the drinks chiller, hurried outside. What did Danielle mean? How did Kat look at Noah? He was a very nice man, of course – a very nice-*looking* man, too.

Blimey, had she been making eyes at him?

To offset any such impression, she made sure to smile at Florine as well as Noah and Clémence. 'There are weekly events here, during the school summer holidays, if you're interested. We'd always be happy to see you.'

Florine smiled, a smile that began slowly, as if she were uncertain. 'Thank you. Perhaps Clémence would like that.'

Clémence nodded emphatically. 'And to see Papa.'

Ah. Kat tried to assess Noah's reaction, but he was smiling, so presumably whatever had taken place in the past hour had gone reasonably well. She turned back to Florine. 'And don't forget the book club in the village.' She disregarded the fact that Yohan had already refused on behalf of all three of them. 'Quite a few children come, too, especially in the summer. I'm keen to keep kids reading and away from screen activities, of course. I have to look after my future audience, after all.'

Florine looked interested. 'So Clémence might meet children from Kirchhoffen?'

'Definitely. And you – and your husband, if he comes – can meet people, too. The next meeting is on Friday evening. We meet inside the *salon de thé* at seven-thirty. Just come along if you want.' With a last smile, Kat swept off to cash out the book counter till while Danielle and

Pierre served any last stragglers and wiped down the café tables.

She couldn't help keeping one eye on Noah and co as she signed in to the till and instructed it to report the day's takings. Subtracting the one-hundred-euro cash float in her mind she saw they'd had a good day, thanks to the author visit. She requested the non-cash transactions and was about to carry the till drawer into the office to make sure everything balanced when she spotted Noah entering the book café once again. Through the glass shop front she spotted Clémence and Florine walking away.

Kat smiled at Noah, her fingers pausing on the catches of the till drawer. 'All OK?'

'It was so fantastic to see her.' For an instant his eyes shone with emotion. 'I came in to ask you out to dinner this evening, to say thank you for texting and getting me up here. Running into them here got over the huge obstacle of whether to call at their house and risk having the door slammed in my face.'

Kat would have accepted, but she remembered Danielle's hint that Kat had been making eyes at Noah. Had he noticed, too? Perhaps that was part of what had made him feel obliged to offer? Her face flamed. 'You don't need to thank me,' she said. 'I know how much Clémence means to you, and I was glad to help.'

For an instant he looked unsure, vulnerable. Then he took a step nearer, dropping his voice. 'OK. I won't thank you if you don't want me to, but will you come out to dinner with me anyway?' His smile was slow.

Conscious of Danielle clearing the unsold cakes and pastries nearby, Kat felt as if her face was literally on fire now. 'Oh! In that case, that would be lovely.' They made

129

arrangements for him to pick her up at home later and he left.

Kat finally managed to get the till drawer out of its housing. As she turned towards the office, she saw Danielle's broad grin and demanded, 'I suppose you think you're clever?'

Danielle laughed as if, yes, that's exactly what she thought.

'Good to see you back at home,' Kat said to the on-screen Reeny she'd summoned up via FaceTime. Kat's phone was propped against a roll of kitchen paper at the table. 'We had an author event today – Helene Sagan. Went very well.'

Reeny ignored the doings at the book café and brought her face closer to the screen as if to inspect Kat. A cool evening breeze was swirling in through the French doors and Kat had pulled on a denim jacket over her white summer dress. Reeny's voice was reedy. 'Pretty dress.'

Kat laughed self-consciously, glancing down at the golden sunflowers printed on the fabric. 'I'm going out. I've never got the hang of French chic and I'm out of touch with British fashion so I've created my own look. I call it: "I wear whatever I feel good in."'

The eyes of the older woman crinkled. 'Who?' she asked economically. Talking tired her since her last hospital stay and Kat was getting used to her popping in verbal landmarks from which Kat could create the rest of the conversation.

'Oh' – Kat waved an airy hand – 'a friend of Solly's.' Then, with Reeny's encouragement, she told her a little about Noah's predicament and how nice he'd been to take Angelique out when neither Kat nor Solly could. How he'd offered to take her out as a thank you and when she'd dismissed the idea said he'd like to take her out anyway.

'A date,' Reeny decided. 'And your brother?' Her silver hair was brushed to one side instead of lying in its normal fringe. She probably didn't feel up to submitting to the ministrations of a hairdresser but it made her look uncharacteristically ungroomed.

A warmth crept over Kat's skin. 'We're getting to know each other. It's awesome but it's also strange.' She hesitated, searching for the right phrases. Reeny knew all about Kat's distance from her dad and Solly and the gap in her life where her mother Joanne should be. Kat regretted both, but at least she had Reeny. 'Solly's becoming *real* to me again, like he was when he was a kid.'

A thin hand came into shot as Reeny wiped the corner of one eye. 'Lovely. You need family.'

Kat had to swallow a lump in her throat at Reeny's evident emotion. She managed to hold back her own tears in deference to her mascara. 'Thanks for listening, Reeny.'

Reeny blotted her eye with the back of her hand. 'Some families are made from blood and some from love,' she said wisely.

'I think I'd better end the call before we both end up in floods,' Kat said, half laughing. 'Try and get better soon, so we can have you back at Livres et Café. I miss you every day.' The call ended with a couple of blown kisses and Kat, checking the time, called Angelique in from the garden in preparation for Noah's arrival.

He was punctual. When she heard tyres on the gravel and spotted the dark grey bulk of his car through her salon windows, she strolled out and hopped into the passenger seat of his car before he had a chance to leave the driver's seat.

131

'This is the first time I've worn a proper shirt since I came to Alsace,' he said, sounding rueful. 'In fact, it's the only one I brought with me.'

His words reminded Kat of the circumstances surrounding his stay in Alsace. She wondered how much longer he'd be around now he'd established contact with Clémence. 'Don't worry,' she said, perusing the plain cotton. 'You look great. You've gained a suntan from being outdoors all day and the white shows it off beautifully.'

He coloured but a smile danced in his eyes. 'I sound clueless, all but demanding a compliment. I should have told you how lovely you look. I have taken women out since my divorce, but I expect it doesn't seem like it.'

She laughed, charmed by his lack of pretension. Maybe she didn't have to worry about French chic – even if he had been married to the elegant Florine. 'Shall we leave it that we both look amazing? Where are we going?'

He started the car, checked over his shoulder and reversed into the road. 'Le Jardin Thiery, by the river on the edge of Eckbolsheim. It has good reviews.' He flashed her a grin as they set off past the neighbouring houses. 'Google Maps says Eckbolsheim's about twenty minutes by car – far enough away to seem as if I've made an effort but not so far that you fear being abducted.'

She imagined him searching for the right venue online. 'You've really given the evening some thought,' she said, copying his jokey tone.

He glanced across at her, then returned his gaze to the road. More seriously, he answered, 'I have, actually. I wasn't sure if it was too soon after Jakey for you to be dating. Thanking you for your help today seemed like a great opportunity, until you left me stranded by declaring that you didn't need thanking.' He headed the big car onto the road leading from the village and blew out his cheeks with comical gusto. 'I had to either say, "Oh, right" and trudge off looking like an idiot, or go for it.' He sent her another sidelong look.

'Oh, sorry,' she said. 'I just didn't want you to feel obliged.'

'Obliged to take you out?' He shook his head mock-sorrowfully. 'Yeah, that would be a giant burden.'

'Oh,' she said again, her face heating up along with her insides, then she cringed at how breathless she sounded. 'Now *I* sound like an idiot. Shall I tell you a story about Angelique stealing biscuits out of a lady's bag outside a shop, instead?'

The tale of Angelique's crime saw them along roads lined with droopy willow and upright birch between the usual many coloured timbered buildings with balconies, steep roofs and dormers. The road joined the towns like a necklace of beautiful beads, yellow sunflowers or purple lavender glowing from fields in between. Kat admired knobbly squashes ripening atop walls and wondered why she and Noah were both exhibiting first-date jitters. They'd been acquainted for over three weeks. He'd seen her screamed at, crying, enraged, anxious, in her work gear or scruffy home-clothes . . . yet he felt awkward about having nothing better to wear than a standard white shirt. The thought he might want to impress her sent butterflies flitting inside her. She hadn't mentioned that she'd tried on six dresses before settling on the one she wore.

As the miles passed, they slowly managed to relax into their normal conversation. Arriving outside the restaurant, they found it was a beautiful stone building that had been a water mill a couple of centuries earlier. 'You certainly like anything to do with water, don't you?' Kat asked, alighting from the car and gazing at the River Bruche, which shone almost luminously in the evening light as it made white water over boulder-strewn ledges.

He took her hand to steer her towards the restaurant entrance below a great wooden porch. 'The river did actually influence my choice of restaurant, particularly as they've done something quite special with it.'

Kat cried, 'Oh!' in delight when she discovered what he meant. Their table stood in a room with a glass floor over rushing water that was illuminated by soft golden light.

Noah looked pleased. 'Isn't it awesome? It's the race that used to power the mill. I hoped you'd like it.'

'It's gorgeous. Look at the way the candle lamps are reflected in the glass, too.' It was all beautiful, she thought, as they were shown to their table: the stone walls, the white linen tablecloths and gleaming glass and silverware. Even the simple bunch of lavender and grape vine leaves in the centre of the table was well chosen. A murmur of conversation rose from diners at other tables, but she thought she could detect the burbling of the water, though it was locked behind what she knew must be incredibly thick glass.

It was refreshing to go on a date with someone she'd got to know and trust over a few weeks. Online dating, while fun, felt slightly transactional in comparison. *Find each other's profile photo attractive. Message. Talk on the phone.* By the time you reached *Meet in real life* you'd already agreed where and when and probably how you were dividing the expenses.

As if reading her mind, once they were settled in their wooden chairs and had been furnished with menus, Noah asked, 'How are you feeling about Jakey, now?'

She sniffed. 'Any good feelings I had for him are long gone. And with all the website problems that cropped up the moment Emma found out . . . I wish I hadn't bothered.'

He gave an understanding nod. 'Are you sure Emma's behind the hacking problems?'

'I don't have proof,' she allowed, sitting back so a waiter could place a glass of water before her. 'I'm just hoping no one else hates me enough to do it.'

His eyes narrowed as he sipped from his water glass. 'And you're sure that the malice was aimed at you and not the book café's owners? Or even just the business itself? People do all kinds of stuff to eliminate a competitor.'

She gazed down at her menu, marbled cream with curly brown writing. 'Ulrica, our web designer, thinks the motivation was to make trouble, which I think must have come from a thirst for revenge. Anyway, thankfully, Ulrica seems to have solved the problems.' She glanced up to give him a rueful smile. 'We attracted a heap of one-star reviews but it's not like this place, where people might study its website and the reviews before making a booking. Our business comes from park visitors. I feel guilty that I prompted the whole thing when my bosses have so much other bad stuff to contend with.'

'The hacker's to blame, not you,' Noah observed.

She agreed – if only sort of – and they ordered, moving on to talk about poor Reeny's illness and Graham having his wife sick in one country while his mother was ill in another. Kat sighed. 'I keep FaceTiming Reeny, but only for five or ten minutes at a time. She's incredibly weak.' Remembering how papery and thin Reeny had appeared when she visited the café, her once-lustrous hair flat and lifeless, Kat turned the conversation to happier things. 'So, tell me how it felt to see your daughter today.'

Noah's face lit up as if someone had placed three extra candle lamps on their table. 'Amazing. Fantastic. Wonderful. I can't put it into words. And though you don't seem to want my thanks, I am incredibly grateful that you sent that text.' His eyes glowed at her across the table. 'I literally couldn't believe my ears when I heard her shout, "Papa". I had to grovel to Marcel for taking half the afternoon off,' he added sheepishly. 'But I came clean about the situation and he was understanding. He got too emotional to speak, in fact, and kept clapping me on the shoulder.'

Her heart gave a squeeze at the image. 'I only know Marcel by sight. He's such a quiet, unsmiling man that I can't imagine him getting choked up.'

'He has four daughters of his own.' Noah put down his fork. He'd ordered mussels and now-empty shells edged his plate as if waiting for someone to notice their pearly insides and make them into a necklace. 'I keep savouring how it felt to hug Clémence again,' he said huskily. 'The relief.' He took another drink while Kat quietly finished her chicken in Riesling with golden herb-sautéed potatoes, then recounted how he'd got Clémence out on the lake so he could speak privately to his ex-wife, who'd broken the unwelcome news that the supposed 'holiday' Yohan had sprung on Florine and Clémence had been a front for him taking a new job.

Kat dropped her fork with such a clatter that people on nearby tables paused to look at her. 'You're not serious?' she gasped.

He gave a snort. 'All too serious, I'm afraid. The jerk.' He paused, then went on more moderately. 'Today was a godsend. I don't have to storm the ramparts of their home or ask Clé to sneak out to meet me. I watched Florine put my new number into her contacts – she's put it under "Livres et Café" actually, in case Yohan snoops her phone.' His mouth twisted. 'I'm encouraging her to sneak behind her husband's back, which is wrong, but, exasperatingly, it seems the only way she feels comfortable. She's incapable of calling him out on his behaviour.'

He paused while a young woman with spiky hair cleared their empty plates. 'I think she's genuinely perturbed to realise how far Yohan's hubris has made him go.'

Kat felt a dimming of her pleasure in the evening. She took several bolstering sips of wine, a delicate rosé that probably hadn't been the correct choice to go with chicken, but she liked it. 'Maybe she'll see the light? Return to the Dordogne? Then you'll be able to go back, too, and pick up your life. You'll see Clémence at weekends again.' A picture of her own dad flashed into her mind. She'd seen him each weekend but still the failure of his marriage to her mum had created a distance between them, vigorously cultivated by her stepmother Irina.

Her mother had said, 'In my experience, men don't leave unless they have someone new to go to,' and it had been true of Howard. He'd moved into Irina's home and Solly had arrived. Kat had only ever been a visitor from then on. Why hadn't Howard fought for his relationship with her as Noah seemed willing to fight for his with Clémence? Unexpected tears clogged her throat.

She sipped her wine again so she could ask, huskily, 'What would you have done if Yohan had told you about his new job and asked your permission to move Clémence to Alsace?'

His eyebrows flew up into his hair. He'd shaved tonight so was minus the golden stubble he often wore. 'I don't know.' Trouble clouded his eyes. 'Then he would have

137

deserved my consideration, I suppose. Florine insists she's in love with Yohan, even though she's had time to see through him in the couple of years they've been married.'

The waiter arrived with dessert menus and Kat ordered a fresh glass of wine. Noah, as he was driving, hadn't drunk alcohol at all. Kat took the menu, thinking hard. 'Showing consideration for Yohan would have been magnanimous of you, after everything he's put you through.'

Noah barked a laugh, one containing precious little humour. 'It would have been facing cold, hard facts. My daughter lives with him and I must do whatever keeps her world calm and happy. The point is moot, anyway, as he was obviously unable to lower himself to ask my permission.'

She studied him, this man whose feelings had been treated with contempt. 'Most men would just get the law on him. He's a shit.'

He turned his water glass in circles on the tablecloth. 'I think if I work things out without the law, the result will be better. The acrimony will be easier to smooth over. Clémence is only eight. We have another decade before she can be an independent person and the lives of the adults won't affect her so much. My goal is that we three adults find a solution that we can all live with.' He leaned forward and took Kat's hand, the one not occupied by her glass. 'Yohan's already taken the new job and left the old. I have to accept that it could be impossible for me to manoeuvre him, and therefore Florine, and therefore Clémence, back to the Dordogne.'

She liked the feeling of his fingers closed around hers – warm, and with the cat's-tongue roughness that came from outdoor work. 'So, you've accepted that he's won,' she said slowly.

He shook his head, his eyes seeming to reflect every single candle lamp in the restaurant. 'I still have my daughter's love. He can't really win, so long as I have that.'

Kat put down her glass to clutch her heart. 'Did every single person in this restaurant just say, "Awwww?" You're amazing.'

He laughed, his blue eyes reflecting the candlelight. 'I'm not amazing. I'm just a parent. That's how we think.'

Kat had to work to hang onto her smile. 'Not all of them.'

His smile faded. 'I'm sounding mature and measured now but I was anything but when Florine told me about Yohan's wonderful new job. I had to fight not to bellow with rage. But since then, I've had a couple of hours to think hard. My options are limited because Clémence is well looked after by Florine and they love each other. It's unfortunate that Florine loves Yohan, too, that's all. I have to live with the consequences of that. Anyway,' he went on in the voice of one who was ready for a change of subject, 'do you know your brother's out with Ola who drives the park train?'

'Again? I didn't know, but I'm not shocked. He talks about her a lot.' Kat picked up the dessert menu, though she was full already.

Noah grinned. 'They're at a club in Strasbourg and I'll probably be woken up at four when Solly crashes his way into the van. Mostly, the van's great for two blokes – but the walls are thin. Also, we need to get another mirror. This evening, I was trying to shave while he was peering over my shoulder to put styling clay in his hair.'

Kat envisaged the scene. Was 'the van' a bit of a comedown for Noah? 'Tell me about your place at Castillon-la-Bataille.'

He shrugged. 'It's a nice apartment in an old, three-storey house in the main street, Rue Victor Hugo. I have the second storey. The kitchen and bathrooms are modern but it's a bit like your place, I suppose, in that some of it's more traditional – a big black fireplace and ornate plasterwork.'

Though she was aware he'd already steered attention away from his situation once, something made her want to peep into his future. 'What do you think will happen at the end of your summer at the park?'

A bleak expression stole into his blue eyes. 'Big question. My leave of absence from my employer in Bordeaux will be up. Park Lemmel will wind down for winter around October time. Yohan taking a permanent job in Strasbourg has made my choices pretty stark – I either resign myself to a long-distance relationship with my daughter; I go to the authorities to try and force some kind of solution, which might result in her unhappiness; or I move my life to Alsace.'

At his last words, her heart leapt like the water rushing beneath their feet, but she didn't let herself think why. 'Clémence's unhappiness . . . through facing the social workers and the courts, you mean?'

He grimaced. 'That's the most likely scenario but there are others. There might be some chance of me winning the right to take her back to Castillon, but then I'd be doing to Florine what she's done to me. If there's any chance it would split Florine and Yohan up, Clémence would be affected by another divorce. As much as I dislike her stepfather, I don't want that for my daughter.'

They fell silent. The room had filled, each arriving group pausing to exclaim over the glass floor and the rushing mill race, and the noise level increased along with the

140

consumption of wine. Kat studied Noah's frown. It furrowed the skin above his thick, fair brows and her heart ached for him. 'You've obviously got a lot to worry about.'

His gaze flew up to meet hers. 'Oh, shit, I've gone on and on about my problems, haven't I?' he demanded remorsefully. 'I meant to ask you about your journalism and what you were writing at the moment.'

'I've only contributed a few fillers about France to magazines since the summer began. And I kept asking,' she pointed out, discomfited at the way he'd taken her words.

He took her hand again. 'After Jakey, probably the last thing you want is to start something up with a bloke who's up to his neck in family drama. If you want to end the evening early, I'll understand. But don't miss dessert just to get away from me.' He tapped the menu, his expression open and honest, maybe a shade rueful. But there was no gathering storm of anger on his face, as she had seen so often on Jakey's when things didn't go his way.

Heart beginning to scud with feelings she couldn't quite identify, Kat leant forward so only he'd hear her words. 'Tell me more about the starting something.'

His shoulders relaxed, his eyes gleamed and the whole atmosphere between them changed. He mirrored her position, bringing their faces as close as was possible over the table. 'I'm hoping tonight won't be our only date. I've come to like you over the past few weeks and' – he smiled – 'I'm attracted to you. I think about you a lot.'

'I think about you, too,' she said, flushing, admitting the truth to herself as much as to him. 'I've eaten all I need to. We could return to Kirchhoffen and give Angelique her last walk. Then I'll switch on my posh coffee machine.'

Her words seemed to smooth the last lines of apprehension from his face. 'That sounds fantastic.'

They paid the bill and drove home, the headlights of Noah's car cutting through the darkness between golden halos cast by streetlights. Kat, watching a couple stroll hand-in-hand to a painted house that looked luminous blue in the night, felt unexpectedly content. The corner Noah had been backed into by Yohan was tight but that didn't mean the summer couldn't be special. For Solly, it meant a spell working abroad. For Kat, it meant steering the book café through its busiest time and bringing it safely through for Reeny and Graham. For Noah, it was a period to process what had happened to his daughter and how it would affect his own life.

And for Noah and Kat . . .?

Who knew? A summer romance? People had them all the time, a happy oasis with no lasting expectation.

Once finally back at Kat's apartment, Angelique met them like a furry cannonball, tail lashing, ears back, panting with joy at humans re-entering her life. Laughing, Kat crouched to pet her to avoid her jumping up and marking her dress. 'Fancy a walk, Angelique? We have a guest with us tonight.'

At the word 'walk', Angelique shot across to where her lead hung on a hook on the kitchen wall and waited expectantly. Kat laughed. 'I think it's safe to assume she's happy to have you along.'

'It would have destroyed me if she'd voted me off the walk.' Noah took Kat's hand as they stepped out of the apartment once more and gestured to encompass the summer evening. 'We have moonlight and starlight. And perfume from . . . this flowery thing.'

'Honeysuckle,' she supplied helpfully, as they passed a vine almost smothering a neighbouring fence, its distinctive scent heavy on the air. Above them, the moon was a crescent, as if smiling at the stars.

'Honeysuckle,' he repeated, as if he'd known that all along. His hand tightened around hers. 'Are you working tomorrow? I could take Angelique for a lunchtime walk for you.'

She smiled at him, wondering whether his offer sprang from thoughtfulness or an excuse to see her. She was happy either way. 'Danielle will be at Livres et Café tomorrow, so we might be able to go together.'

Discussing how best to make their lunch hours coincide, they passed the *salon de thé* and its neighbouring patisserie and boulangerie in their night-time cloaks of darkness, calling '*Bonsoir*' to a man walking a portly terrier. Angelique, spotting that Kat and Noah were walking hand-in-hand and that her mistress was paying attention to Noah instead of at her, shouldered her way in to walk between them.

Noah said drily, 'She's reminding me she's Kat's dog.'

When they passed the entrance to Rue du Kirchfeld, Kat noticed Noah glancing down the dark slope. Quietly she said, 'I'm so glad you've made contact with her again.'

He gave her hand a squeeze. 'All thanks to you.'

Angelique abandoned her role as Kat's chaperone in favour of following up interesting scents under a garden hedge. Somewhere an owl hooted, and insects swooped as they sauntered through the night-time village. Noah said, 'Do you mind me asking about your experience of being a stepchild? I'd be grateful for the insight.'

She understood his anxiety for his little girl. 'I think most people blend families more successfully than either

143

of my parents did. I felt as if it suited my stepmum down to the ground if Dad was more focused on his second family than his first, so my relationship with her is not warm. Mum's husband, Geoffrey, is a nice enough guy. My stepsisters losing their mum was a horrible tragedy and I can see why he gave them so much love, but it did stop me getting to know him really well.'

She concentrated on casting her mind back as a car swished past, its headlights criss-crossing the cones of light from streetlamps, music drifting from its open windows. The evening felt quieter in its wake. 'He didn't bother with me much after Mum died,' she admitted. 'Even so, I got on better with Geoffrey than with Solly's mum, Irina. I suppose it was the different situations. Amber and Jade are my *step*sisters but Solly's my *half*-brother. We share a dad, but Irina dismissed that. She had no other children; Solly was of primary importance to her, so she wanted him to be top of Dad's priority list, too. Maybe I was hostile towards her? I didn't think so at the time, but I blamed her inside, so maybe that came through.'

His footsteps had slowed as he listened. 'I'm sorry to hear that.'

She shrugged. 'It's in the past. But, in light of the situation between you and Yohan, if you're asking whether either of my stepparents expected to be more important to me than my natural parents, the answer's a resounding no. They were delighted to take the back seat.' She gave a short laugh. 'And now I'm sounding whiney.'

'Expressing your true feelings isn't whiney,' he observed as they crossed a quiet road, completing their loop around the village and arriving back at La Maison Blanche. They had to unlink their hands to negotiate the narrow path down the side of the house but before Kat could get her key in the lock, Noah slid his arms around her from behind, his breath making her neck tingle. 'Do you think your canine chaperone would let me kiss you?' he murmured.

Heart stepping up its pace, she turned in his arms, so their faces were close. 'Yes. And more to the point, *I'll* let you kiss me.'

The light from the streetlights made his hair a halo as he dipped his head towards hers. 'I've been wanting to for weeks.' Then his mouth found her lips, first brushing soft, fleeting kisses, then breaking off to trail down her neck and along her collar bone, which instantly turned into the most erogenous zones she owned, shortening her breath and swooshing heat down to interesting places. He returned to savour her mouth properly, taking his time over a sweet, caressing exploration of her mouth. One of them – or both – was trembling as he gently cupped the back of her head and deepened the kiss until her head spun.

But then a whining Angelique jumped up and tried to get her damp muzzle between them, scrabbling with her paws.

Kat broke away, laughing as she rubbed the furrows Angelique's claws had made in her forearm. 'Let's go inside for that coffee I promised you.' She didn't add that then she could check the dog had food and water and then shut her in the kitchen for the night. Or, at least, whatever portion of it was to involve Noah.

But, as she let them all indoors and unclipped Angelique's harness, her phone rang from her bag, which she'd discarded on the table. She dragged it out and inspected the screen. 'My boss Graham is calling,' she said, with a hint of alarm. 'I hope Reeny's no worse. I'd better answer.'

'Of course,' Noah's mouth said politely, though his expression was more: *Oh, bollocks.*

Into the phone, Kat said, 'Hi, Graham. Is everything OK?'

'No,' he said flatly. 'Everything's shit. Mum's got to have some heart device implanted tomorrow.' He made a swallowing noise. 'Reeny said you talked earlier so you won't be surprised to know she's in no fit state to be left at home alone. St Clare's Hospice has offered her a three-day respite so I can fly home to the UK and see Mum.' He cleared his throat, plainly having trouble forcing the words out. 'The hospital wouldn't be doing this procedure on Mum unless they thought there was a reasonable chance of success but I'm an only child and I'd hate to think I'd missed my chance—' This time, his voice broke completely.

Kat visualised his lined, woebegone face and she had to swallow, too. 'Oh, Graham. I'm sure Reeny understands and, hopefully, your mum will be better for the procedure.'

'Yes,' he agreed, still sounding strained. 'I know I'm already putting on you enormously but if you could swing by the hospice to see Reeny and take her a book or something, I know she'd love to see you properly. You won't be able to hug her because of the germs but the hospice thinks a visitor at the foot of her bed would make a difference to her. I'm flying tomorrow morning and will be back late Saturday. I've booked a Travelodge near the hospital so I can see Mum as much as possible while I'm there and stay in touch with Reeny by phone. Our girls are doing the same, of course.' He swallowed audibly.

Despite Graham's obvious anxiety, Kat's heart leapt at the thought of seeing Reeny in person again. At the same time, she felt for Reeny and Graham's daughters who were helping with their grandmother as much as possible while watching their mum go through things from a distance. 'Of course, I'll visit,' Kat said. 'I can call in daily. St Clare's isn't far off my route home from Muntsheim and I know not to stay too long.'

'That would be so appreciated, Kat, I just can't tell you,' Graham answered hoarsely.

At some time during the call Noah had drifted off to the salon to give her privacy. Now she heard his phone ring over Graham's words and his voice float back, muffled and indistinct. Then he reappeared at the kitchen door, saying into his phone. 'Can you hold on a moment, Mum?' He paused and glanced at Kat.

Kat said into her own phone, 'Can you hold on a moment, Graham?'

Noah gave a wry smile. 'Mum wants to know all about my meeting with Clémence. I left messages for her and she's only just picked them up. See you tomorrow?'

Resignedly, she smiled. 'Yes, see you.' Then she settled down to give Graham assurances that he could go off to see his mum with a clear mind because everything was going beautifully at the book café.

Chapter Ten

The next morning, Kat took a delivery from the book wholesaler. Surprised by the number of boxes, she slit them open as soon as she got them on the stockroom floor – and found every box filled with the same English language book: *The Girl Who Stole a Man*. Her initial reaction was exasperation that it was 'girl' in the title instead of 'woman' but that was swiftly subsumed by dismay that she had nearly four hundred copies of a book she hadn't ordered by an author she didn't know.

The wholesaler was going to be well hacked off because they must have had to be exported from the UK and now Kat was going to return the entire consignment.

Shutting the stockroom door with something close to a slam, she stalked into the office, accepting Angelique's welcome with one hand while she logged onto the appropriate wholesaler account with the other and checked her order history. Damn. The order was there so it wasn't a mislabelling of the boxes. She groaned. If this was Emma's work again it meant Ulrica hadn't been successful in stopping the cyber-attack after all. She picked up the phone and a few moments later was speaking to a disgruntled sales manager.

'But you must have seen the confirmatory email,' the sales manager protested.

'There hasn't been one.' Kat knew there hadn't been, but she scrolled through to make sure as she talked, just to make certain. She hesitated, unsure whether to confess that Livres et Café's system had been hacked before and the wholesaler was an unfortunate victim. 'I'm going to have to return them.' The bookselling world still used the 'sale or return' system and though never had she been gladder of it, her conscience was afire.

The sales manager attempted to get Kat to keep just one box but when she refused ended the call with an angry, '*Pfft*', which Kat translated as 'Up yours'.

Her next call was to Ulrica. Soon Kat was describing the latest situation and listening to Ulrica trying to stifle a sigh before she said, 'I'll find it. She's very clever this one. She hides code like little wormholes she can squeeze through to cause mischief.'

Kat groaned. 'I thought she'd gone away.'

Ulrica snorted. 'I expect that's all part of the fun. She likes you to relax so she can wind you up all over again.'

'Evidently.' Kat ended the call, assumed her customer-facing smile and went out to sell books and pastries.

She looked forward to Noah arriving at one, having promised herself a proper break today. It was a perennial problem that customer numbers were highest just when café staff needed their own lunch. The schoolchildren poured in at twelve; adults could stay any time until three. Kat was quite used to taking a break if, and when, she could get it. But today . . . well, Noah.

In bed last night, she'd laid awake reliving his kisses.

The man kissed like a dream – heated, intense, yet caressing. Their interlude had been over too quickly, thanks to the combined efforts of Angelique, Graham and Noah's mum, but his lips on her skin had raised every hair on her body in a delicious, sensuous wave, making her forget that it was just a summer romance. Honeysuckle on summer evenings would always make her think of him, she suspected. In fact, she thought of him all the time she was working, when all she could smell was coffee, sugar and the suntan lotion of tourists.

And just when she was looking up, expecting every person who entered to be him, the person who did arrive with a dramatic cry of, 'Kat!' wasn't Noah at all. It was a middle-aged Englishwoman with a dark, blow-dried bonnet of wavy hair, gasping as if she'd just received an unwelcome shock. She snatched out a chair almost from under the hand of another patron and collapsed into it. 'Kat, I need espresso.'

Kat gaped, her mind refusing to believe the evidence of her eyes. Then, 'Irina?' she said uncertainly. What on earth was her stepmother doing here? They only ever met when Kat travelled to the UK and the last time had been for a pre-Christmas visit more than two years ago. Howard passed on any Irina-news in emails or phone conversations, but, otherwise, dutiful birthday cards were the main points of contact between the two women. 'Is Dad OK?'

'Yes, yes,' Irina answered impatiently. 'Howard has business with a customer on an industrial estate near Strasbourg Airport. They supply bangles and belts and all that stuff his company sells. We decided to make a long weekend of it and see Solly. And you, of course,' she added.

This obvious afterthought made Kat's stomach cramp. Solly was in France, so his parents had come to see him.

Not unreasonable. Kat wasn't sure why she hadn't anticipated it happening. But her dad not even sparing the time to tell Kat . . .? Who'd have thought she'd be hurt by having her family status made so obvious, even after all this time?

Irina's face had screwed up like an irritated baby's. 'Make that espresso a double-shot.' She craned to see into the chilled cabinet without leaving her seat. 'And give me one of those strawberry tart thingies.'

As Kat already held an order on a tray in her hands – and was nettled at Irina turning up out of the blue and making demands – she summoned a smile. 'In a moment.' Then she swept outside to pass out croissants, madeleines and iced tea to the waiting customers.

When she returned, she placed an espresso and tarte framboise on the table before Irina along with a napkin-wrapped cake fork and, after a quick glance to make sure Danielle and Pierre could cope with the flow of customers, took the vacant chair at the table. She hid her indignation at Irina's autocratic manner while she dug for information. 'Does Solly know you're here?' At that moment, she saw Noah arrive, halting just inside the door when he saw she had company. Kat smiled and held up an apologetic finger to signify, 'One minute.' He nodded and leant against the glass shopfront to wait.

Irina forked up a mouthful of tart with all the urgency of a smoker taking the first drag of a long-awaited cigarette. 'Yes, Solomon does know,' she said tersely, when she'd swallowed. But the sugar seemed to steady her and she paused to take a sip of espresso, then sat back with an unhappy sigh. 'As Howard's working today, I took the tram to Muntsheim and came to the park.' Her voice wavered. 'I thought I'd be a sur-surprise because Solomon had said it was his day off. So, I found his staff quarters – do you know it's a *caravan*? – and the door was open and I went in and . . .' Her face bloomed tomato-red. 'He was with some girl . . . in the bedroom.' Her voice dropped to a mortified whisper. 'He's going through such a rebellious patch. First throwing his teacher training away and now this.'

Relieved Irina's agitation arose from nothing worse, Kat couldn't quite hide her smile. 'But he's twenty-five and adults do have sex lives. I'm sorry you're disappointed in him but, well, he got drunk and lost his job. Now he's met a girl. It's all part of joining the adults.' She smiled in an attempt to take any sting out of her words.

But Irina threw down her cake fork and fixed Kat with a mean-eyed glare. 'I wouldn't have come in here if it hadn't been the first café I saw. I'd have warned Solomon off coming to this park if he'd asked me. I shouldn't think you're a good influence on Solomon at all.'

Kat's blood chilled. She got to her feet, newly aware of Noah quietly waiting and conscious of her time with him wasting away while she listened to Irina's disagreeable complaints. 'Maybe I shouldn't have smiled,' she said evenly, 'but you don't know me well enough to hold an opinion on what kind of person I am. Now you'll have to excuse me as a friend's waiting.'

Irina had the grace to look abashed but muttered an ill-natured, 'How was I to know that?'

Kat headed towards Noah but was almost bowled over by a crowd of schoolchildren surging in through the door. Even Noah was shuffled aside by the sudden influx. His eyes smiled at Kat over their heads. 'Kinda busy?' he asked.

She looked at the crowd around the counter and saw that every table was full. She groaned. 'I'm not going to be able to get away after all.' She just wasn't the kind of manager to abandon her staff to the rush while she sneaked off to skip through the daisies with Noah.

Noah nodded understandingly, though his face fell. 'I'll take Angelique for half-an-hour, shall I? We might grab a coffee together when I come back.'

Kat gave him a grateful smile. 'Fantastic.'

But when he did return, coming in the back way and popping Angelique into the office, they were still run off their feet and Kat felt even more annoyed with Irina for preventing her from escaping with Noah before the mob of schoolchildren arrived. She just had time to whisk together a coffee and sandwich for him to take away.

'Text you later,' he said softly, as her hands brushed his. They exchanged a long look and Kat, at least, imagined the kisses they could've had. Then they returned to their respective jobs.

The afternoon was crazily busy at Livres et Café, not helped by two chatty British women who seemed to want to monopolise Kat's attention every time she passed their table.

The first woman had a round face with dark eyes that almost disappeared into her laughter lines when she smiled. 'You're so busy, dear! Is it often like this?'

'Pretty much,' Kat sang gaily, clattering crocks together at top speed and thinking that if the woman was in a child's picture book her face would look like a currant bun.

The second woman had a bob brushed straight back from her long face, a little like a friendly pony. 'It must be a goldmine.'

Kat knew it was and that her wobble when Graham

put the finances in her hands had been unjustified, but Reeny and Graham's business was just that – their business. She gave a vague smile and, having loaded her tray with a teetering tower of plates, hurried back to the kitchen.

Next, the friendly women appeared inside to browse the bookshelves. 'What a good idea to sell several languages with the tourist footfall, here,' Currant Bun murmured to Friendly Pony. She tried to involve Kat in the conversation, though Kat was busy selling a Harry Potter in Italian to a couple with a small son. 'Do you sell all these languages year-round?'

Kat and the Italian couple had been trying to understand each other's French. Distractedly, she said, 'Some, but I increase French language stock in winter, as the locals use the park more.'

It was four o'clock and the sides of Kat's stomach were almost sticking together with hunger before she finally escaped the chatty tourists and got a chance to take a brioche and a cup of coffee into the office. Angelique positioned herself with her muzzle on Kat's lap, a mixture of affection and being in a good spot to hoover up crumbs. Between bites, Kat hastily emailed two students on the list for summer jobs to see if they were still available.

Then Solly burst in. 'Danielle said you were in the office,' he explained. With his oversized sneakers and big T-shirt, he looked as if he ought to have a skateboard beneath his arm. 'My bloody mother turned up without warning.'

Though Irina's visit had been anything but a pleasure for her, Kat still giggled, knowing Solly's venting came from exasperation rather than rancour. He loved his mother, however much her blunt and possessive ways drove him crazy. 'I've seen her. She caught you, erm . . .?'

Solly widened exasperated eyes. 'Holy shit, she *told* you? It was Ola's day off, too, and I invited her for coffee. Things . . . progressed and I didn't think to shut the freaking door because I didn't suspect my freaking *mother*, who was supposed to be in *England*, was about to barge in. The staff lodges are more or less deserted during the day.'

'I think she was disappointed in you,' Kat reported gravely, though she knew her eyes must be full of laughter.

'She was disappointed?' he snapped. 'How disappointed do you think I was? Ola got dressed, jumped on her scooter and rode away in a strop. Mum wasn't tactful.'

'Not her strong suit,' Kat said diplomatically. 'But Dad's in France, too.'

'Yeah. I had lunch with Mum and she told me.' Solly flopped down into the other chair.

Kat absorbed the fact that Irina and Solly had evidently lunched somewhere else.

Solly's attention was obviously not on how Kat felt about that because he added discontentedly, 'I've got to go out to dinner with them tonight so I can't even see Ola to smooth things over. They want to come to the park tomorrow, too. I'm still off but will you be working?'

After taking out her phone to check for texts or emails or anything else that might look like an invitation from her father – there were none – Kat slid it away again. 'My busy time. But tell Dad hello from me. I've got to get back to work now.'

'Oh-kay.' Solly hesitated. Then came around the desk and gave Kat a sudden hug. It felt like sibling shorthand for *I just realised you should have received your own invitations. This is awkward. You're obviously hurt and you are, like, you know, my sister.*

Glad of the silent support and enjoying this evidence

of their strengthening relationship, Kat hugged him back. 'I'm sure Ola was just embarrassed. Promise her you'll lock the door next time.'

He laughed and gave Kat an extra squeeze. 'You can bet on that.' Then he headed off.

Although they were only officially open until five o'clock until the end of June, trade was enough that Danielle agreed with Kat to stay open till five-thirty. It was the first of July tomorrow, after all, and there were plenty of takers for cold drinks or coffee in the late afternoon sunshine, even if the businesses around them were rolling in their canopy blinds and locking their doors.

Kat was taking an order when her neck prickled and she turned and saw Noah taking an empty seat. His hair was ruffled, his dark green polo shirt open at the neck and he looked tanned and outdoorsy. Ignoring the rule that she'd imposed on Irina about customers being served in the order they arrived, she made a beeline for him. 'Hey. Coffee?'

'Hey.' He gave her a long smile. 'If you're still serving, though I actually just came to see you. Are you looking for someone to help you walk your dog this evening?'

She flushed with pleasure. 'Absolutely. Come over and I'll cook dinner first.'

'Sounds perfect.' His smile made his eyes crinkle and, after making his coffee last until closing, he helped carry tables and chairs indoors. Danielle cast significant glances between Kat and Noah, but Kat couldn't bring herself to be embarrassed. She was feeling pretty confident she could look forward to more of those kisses this evening. It made any lingering sadness about her dad's silence about dinner fade away.

There was nothing new there, anyway.

* * *

Noah parked outside La Maison Blanche and picked up the silly gift he'd bought for Kat – a ceramic plant pot in the shape of an orange dog, its oversized tail and bent ears bearing a passing resemblance to Angelique's. In it was a potted plant with tiny, rust-coloured flowers. He'd greet Kat with a sweet kiss – nothing too heavy – and present her with the dog to start the evening with a smile. After being taken for such a mug by Jakey, she deserved to be wooed gently.

He exited his car, and, glancing up, realised he was the subject of curiosity. An old couple leant out from a balcony up in the eaves of the house and two men stared from the middle-floor window. Noah nodded pleasantly. The old couple waved and smiled. The two men withdrew. Maybe they were offended by a dog-shaped flowerpot.

He strode down the side of the building to Kat's door. She must have heard him arrive because suddenly Angelique was bounding down the passageway while Kat's gorgeous smile beamed from the doorway. Her dark, springy hair was down, brushing shoulders that were bare but for the straps of her misty green sundress. 'I hope you like chicken,' she said, stepping back to let him in.

He had to step around Angelique to follow Kat. 'I like anything. It smells delicious.' He squeezed himself into the tiny hall and presented her with the ceramic dog.

As he'd intended, Kat's dark eyes danced. 'A mini Angelique! And kalanchoes. How pretty. Thank you.'

'Is that what the flowers are?' He didn't manage the greeting kiss as Angelique got up on her hind legs to sniff the planter and, not wanting a repeat of wet nose and dog breath intruding into their kisses, Noah simply followed Kat into the kitchen.

She positioned her gift carefully on a sunlit windowsill

and turned to Noah with promise in her eyes. Angelique chose that moment to run to the French doors and utter a gruff woof and Kat turned away again. 'Just let me let Angelique out. Isn't it a perfect summer evening?'

Thinking that this last remark signalled her intention that they should go outside, Noah followed. But then Kat closed the door behind Angelique and turned around and somehow he ended up catching her in his arms. 'Whoops!' she said. Then she smiled and slid her hands onto his shoulders, stretching up so her mouth could meet his. At the feeling of her in his arms, something taut inside him loosened – the thing that had been winding tighter and tighter as he abandoned his old life and careered across the country to find his daughter, tortured by a mind full of worst-case scenarios. Kat had provided the last couple of stepping stones he'd needed to see his daughter again and having her in his arms felt right.

She kept the kiss slow and thoughtful, as if she were attuning herself to him, learning something fundamental. What *he* learnt was that he wanted her like crazy. Electricity zinged through him. The gentle wooing thing tried to slip his mind, especially when his hands stroked up her back and encountered bare flesh where her dress ended. It made him ache to explore further but he wasn't disrespectful enough to think that the moment a woman kissed him he could make free with her body. Kat Jenson had become important to him in the few weeks he'd known her, and he could stand right here and kiss her all night and be satisfied. OK, he amended, aware of the growing throbbing in his groin, maybe not exactly *satisfied* . . .

From a place on the nearby wooden counter, Kat's phone began to ring.

Gently she ended the kiss and, after a moment gazing

up at him with her dark, bottomless eyes, said, 'Sorry. That's my dad's ringtone.' She didn't pull away but just reached out and picked up the phone.

As she was still encircled by his arms, Noah couldn't avoid hearing a male voice say, 'Darling! I understand Irina's given away the surprise that we're in Alsace for a long weekend. We're having dinner in Lingolsheim. Come over and join us.'

Noah's heart sank but he began to slacken his hold on Kat's waist, assuming she'd want to take the invitation up. Lingolsheim was only a ten-minute drive from Kirchhoffen and if her parents were over from the UK . . . He hadn't been aware of that, maybe because his path hadn't crossed with Solly's after work.

Kat, however, didn't budget a centimetre. 'It's nice to hear from you, Dad. Irina did tell me you're in Alsace but I'm afraid your invitation's a little late. I have someone with me.'

Her dad hesitated infinitesimally before saying in the same jolly voice, 'We are going to see you while here?'

'That would be great, but it depends on your plans, I suppose. I can be free either of the next couple of evenings.' Kat sounded polite rather than warm. Then she corrected herself, 'Oh, sorry, not tomorrow evening, Friday. It's my book club.'

'You can't skip that?' Her dad sounded surprised.

'I run it,' she said quietly. 'How about Saturday evening?'

The line became muffled while her dad presumably consulted with another party. Kat stared absently into thin air, a hint of wistful resignation in her expression. Then her dad's voice returned. 'We're visiting Parc Lemmel tomorrow. Why don't we discuss it then?'

'If we can all be free at the same time, that would be

lovely,' said Kat. She ended the call with courteous fare-wells and carefully lodged her phone back on the counter.

'Are you all right?' he asked tentatively, trying to read her suddenly shuttered expression. 'I couldn't tell how well that conversation went.' He lifted his fingers to her hair, stroking a few curls so they stretched and then sprang back into place. 'If you'd like to see your dad tonight, we can meet up another time. My feelings won't be hurt.'

She gave a rueful smile. 'Well, mine are, which is why you just heard me being deliberately standoffish with my dad.' The smile wobbled. 'He and Irina are only just now inviting me, whereas I know they invited Solly much earlier today. Taken in isolation, it's nothing – just one of those things that happens – but the bigger picture is that that's exactly how things work out all the time, leaving me feeling about a quarter as important to them as Solly is.' She firmed up her smile with a visible effort. 'If he'd called this afternoon and asked me out to dinner then, I would have been thrilled. When you suggested we meet up I'd have just asked if we could make it another night. But the sequence of events is all too obvious: Irina planned to see Solly for dinner and when she told my dad he thought he'd better invite me, too. Or maybe Dad just assumed Irina would have invited me and didn't bother to check, hence the phone call when they're already at the restaurant. Or maybe it even took Solly to draw their attention to the fact that I should have been there, too.' She blinked. 'Irina could easily have mentioned it. It was her I was with at Livres et Café when you were waiting at lunchtime.'

Shock shimmered through him. That unsmiling woman Kat had been talking to so stiffly was her stepmother? The *froideur* between them had been palpable. No wonder

160

sadness lurked in Kat's eyes if she had to go through that chilly relationship to access her father and, till Solly came to work at the park, her brother. Why wasn't her dad more proactive in their relationship? 'Do whatever makes you happy,' he said. He wanted her to be happy. He could think of lots of ways of making her that way, most of which would have the benefit of making him happy as well.

As if reading his thoughts, she edged closer, her breasts brushing against him. Through his T-shirt, his skin tingled. She slid a hand up and behind his neck to ease him down until his mouth was once again on hers.

Excitement hit him like a train. He felt hyper aware of her body beneath her pretty summer dress, the scent of her warm skin and tumbled hair.

She broke off to kiss along his jawline and down his neck. 'How about we turn dinner down low and take a glass of wine into the salon?'

'Fantastic.' He sounded as breathless as a teenager getting his first snog.

She poured out two glasses of red and passed one to him. She opened the French doors ready for when Angelique had finished soaking up the last rays of the sun slanting between long shadows, but closed the kitchen door behind them so the dog could get no further. Kat turned to kiss Noah again and he turned dizzy with a wave of sensation and emotion.

Still kissing, instead of heading into the salon they somehow drifted off-course until they ended up in the doorway of the only room Noah hadn't so far visited – Kat's bedroom. The shutters were half closed against the evening sun that flitted over a green-painted wardrobe standing beside an old-fashioned polished wood dresser with a speckled mirror. Kat didn't seem unhappy with their situation. His heartbeat filled his head. 'You're a gorgeous woman,' he murmured, nuzzling her hair. He was getting the idea that the gentle wooing strategy wasn't working out but clung onto his wits long enough to whisper, 'You're not feeling rushed?'

Breathlessly, she laughed. 'No. Are you?'

He laughed back, giving in to his desire to crush her hard against him, letting her press against his arousal so there were no doubts about what he was thinking. 'I'm on fire for you.'

'Me, too,' she whispered.

He eased down her shoulder straps and followed their progress with his mouth. She moaned in the back of her throat. They staggered towards the bed and Kat spared a hand to give the shutters a neat shove that closed off the view of anyone passing the front of the house. The bed caught Noah behind his knees and he sat, drawing Kat with him, so that she stood between his legs. It was a tall bed and his face ended up level with where her dress met the top of her breasts.

She looked glorious, her straps down around the tops of her arms and the weight of the dress fabric threatening to uncover her.

He reached behind her and found the zip fastener, trying to slide it down but succeeding only in getting it caught, swearing under his breath, which made her laugh, until finally he could ease her dress down. 'You are so beautiful,' he murmured. Her breasts were cupped by a rose-coloured bra, her pale skin gleaming luminously in the half-light. He flipped the catch and got rid of the filmy fabric, trying to get his mouth to her, losing his grip on any last attempt at slow, gentle foreplay when she pulled his T-shirt up and

162

over his head in a sensuous movement that turned his skin into a shower of sparks. She pressed him back and they fell together onto the bed. He was aware of her kicking the quilt aside so they could tangle together on the cool cotton sheet, of them getting rid of his shorts and boxers in a combined endeavour, of her panties disappearing, and soon he was losing himself in her heated, silken flesh.

Kat made love in the energetic, pragmatic, open-hearted way she seemed to do everything.

When she slid down his body to take him in her mouth he almost lost his mind, certainly lost the power of speech and – almost – lost control. He dragged her up so he could pay court to her flesh with his mouth. She was a delight, open in her responses, clutching his hair, gasping, stroking, until, finally, he searched out the place his shorts had fallen, located a condom in his wallet and rolled it on. Then slowly, slowly, savouring every moment, he slid inside her tight, heated body. She made a tiny, 'Grr,' in her throat, the sexiest sound he'd ever heard, and wrapped her legs around him.

From that point, nothing was slow. She clung, she thrust, she bit and kissed while he pounded into her in a wave of the fiercest passion he'd ever experienced, consuming his head, heart and soul. It was joy. It was satisfaction. It was completion.

Later, when she lay across his body, snuggling her face into the crook of his neck, he murmured, 'I had made up my mind to woo you slowly.'

Her body shook with laughter. 'I'm happy with the way things went.'

He tugged her closer. 'Me, too. Ecstatic, in fact.'

*　　*　　*

163

Later, they ate in the garden, the herby chicken and potatoes dry but edible, moths dancing in the light that streamed through patio doors. The table had a wrought-iron base that had once been part of an old-fashioned sewing machine, Kat explained. 'I rescued it from a charity shop.' It fit beautifully with the half-wild garden that pulsed with the rhythm of the night. The moonlight picked out leaves on tumbling shrubs and the breeze carried the scent of their flowers.

Noah liked that Kat didn't care that her garden wasn't tidy, her furniture wasn't new and didn't match, that she made napkins from kitchen roll and had slipped her dress back on without underwear. She looked relaxed and happy, except for when she told him about visiting Reeny, one of her employers, at the hospice on the way home.

Then, her eyes misted over. 'She's so frail,' she told him. 'Like a doll made of wax and paper.'

'I'm sorry,' he whispered, slipping his arms around her and holding her against his heart.

She sniffed. 'She used to be so lively and chatty. Today she listened and smiled but she hardly said a word. She was brighter than that on FaceTime a day or two ago.'

When their plates were empty and they'd picked out scraps for Angelique, Kat regarded him, a dreamy smile in her eyes. 'Will you stay tonight?'

Though he'd thought himself sated, heat pooled low inside him. 'I'd love to. But what if Solly asks where I was?'

She shrugged. 'Tell him. Did he tell you about his mum walking in on him and Ola this morning?'

Noah was intrigued. 'No – I haven't caught up with him today. What happened?'

She recounted Irina's disappointment in her son and

Solly's exasperation with his mum, making Noah laugh. All the turmoil and anxiety that had brought him to Alsace, even the gnarly problems he had yet to solve concerning Clémence, seemed to have taken a step back.

Being with Kat soothed him.

Chapter Eleven

Kat began Friday with a broad smile and the kind of delicious tenderness that came from a night of joyous sex. It made a memorable way to greet July.

She and Noah had said a sensuous farewell that left no time for breakfast and driven separately to the park. Noah had needed to change into his uniform before starting work at nine, and she imagined him yawning as he cleaned down his workstation with a pressure washer ready for the attractions to open at ten.

Kat munched a cereal bar as she and Angelique roamed Parc Lemmel for their morning exercise, chilling in anticipation of this being the first day they'd remain open until eight in the evening, kicking the dew off the lush grass and watching various members of park staff dragging covers from rides. Her favourite was the gaily painted horses of the carousel, saddles red, manes streaming, nostrils wide and legs frozen in a perpetual gallop as they circled endlessly on the end of golden barley-twist poles.

She gave Angelique time to investigate the bases of trees and to scratch at a molehill that had erupted in the middle of a patch of pretty purple wildflowers. Then it was time to turn towards Livres et Café ready for delivery of the day's bakery order.

It coincided with the arrival of a text from her father.

We'll eat lunch at your café today. Hoping that that way, at least, you'll be able to join us and we'll be sure to get a table. x

Irritated by that 'at least', which seemed to suggest she was being difficult to pin down, she left Antoine to begin filling the chilled cabinet while she replied.

Dad, I don't really get a proper lunch hour! But happy to reserve you a table if you advise inside or outside. x

No such advice arrived so she left Antoine to his work, the light from the cabinet glinting from his glasses, and turned to tidying and restocking the bookshelves, forming a pretty display of the signed books left over from Helene Sagan's author visit and putting aside a few she'd take to book club tonight in case any of the parents there wanted to buy them for their children. Justine was putting out the tables, which tended to signal 'open' to early tourists, and a couple came in to browse the books. Kat saw no reason to turf them out just because they were ten minutes ahead of opening time.

She greeted them with, '*Bonjour,*' as they were in France, though she was pretty certain from the man's England football shirt that they were Brits. She added in English, 'Anything I can help you with?'

The man was already headed for the biographies, but the woman looked relieved to hear her native tongue. 'I like a love story.'

'Me, too.' Kat showed her where she could find the popular books with pretty covers. Then, seeing Justine,

Antoine and Romain had everything in hand, Kat slipped into the office. She was waiting for Ulrica to email that she'd finished implementing the 'multi-factor authentication' that would make it harder for Emma to make changes on the website because no one would be able to log in without a code sent to Kat's phone – or Graham's or Reeny's, if they ever came back on the scene. Until MFA was in operation, Kat was checking through the website and their supplier order histories daily to catch unauthenticated changes.

Kat opened the email inbox. It was full to the top with complaints that a newsletter had been sent out earlier this morning advertising sex toys.

'*Bitch*,' she hissed through gritted teeth, and hastily composed an apology to the mailing list, explaining that the organisation was currently the victim of cyber-attacks and offering a 5% discount on book purchases via the website in an effort to make amends.

She was changing the email password yet again, even if it was a futile gesture until the multi-factor authentication was in place, when Justine opened the office door and said in formal English, 'Your father is here to visit you.' She sounded intrigued.

Kat hid her surprise at a glimpse of her dad behind her young assistant, his smile lifting his florid cheeks. 'Thanks, Justine. Come in, Dad!' She rose to greet Howard Jenson as Justine opened the door wider and ushered the visitor in.

Howard's thinning silver hair was brushed back so his ears protruded between his hair and his fulsome sideburns. He was holiday-smart in open-necked shirt and tan trousers. 'Darling!' He spread his arms and Kat stepped into his hug. She did love her dad, but hugs were so rare that it was hard not to feel awkward. Nevertheless, she said, 'Lovely to see you,' and kissed his shiny cheek.

Neither of them prolonged the embrace. Kat asked Justine to bring coffee and then resumed her seat behind the desk, leaving the other chair for her father. 'I thought you were coming at lunchtime.' She checked the time on her open laptop. It wasn't yet eleven.

His smile became fixed. 'As you're too busy to join us for lunch, I thought that by coming earlier I might gain a little of your precious time.' There was no mistaking the pointed nature of his words.

Slowly, Kat shut the laptop and pushed it aside, so that there was no physical obstruction between her gaze and her father's. 'Where were you yesterday, Dad, during working hours?'

From the way his gaze flickered, her question hit home. 'At work,' he admitted with a rueful smile.

'Just as I am,' she said softly. 'And I had plans last night and I have plans tonight. I'm thrilled to see you but—'

'—I can't just crash into your life and expect you to be free?' he finished for her.

She gave a little shrug that she felt answered in the affirmative. She'd lived in France long enough to be fluent in the language of shrugs. Justine arrived with the coffee then, black for Kat and white for her father.

'So,' Howard said cautiously, when they were alone again, 'do you have a few minutes for me now? Irina's gone off to find Solly.'

She tried to relax the atmosphere with a joke. 'I hope that this time she knocks first.'

Howard's eyes gleamed in amusement. 'Quite.' He raised his eyebrows. 'As you've brought that subject up, I hear you and Irina didn't see eye-to-eye on that subject.'

Kat nodded, taking the first sip of coffee. It stung her lips because it was so hot. 'I didn't appreciate her suggestion that I'm a bad influence on my brother.' She put her coffee down and before her father could express the surprise she could read in his eyes, rushed on, 'Dad, I'm really happy to see you. It's lovely to have Solly around and we're getting to know each other all over again. I'd really like to join you in a family meal. How about tomorrow?'

Howard rubbed his jaw. 'We've been invited out with colleagues.'

She managed a smile. It was exactly the kind of thing she'd suspected had lain behind the muffled conversation last night when he'd covered the phone to confer, no doubt with Irina. They'd probably been invited somewhere swanky, somewhere Irina would not want to miss. 'And I expect you need to travel home on Sunday,' she said.

Then, smile fading, what had been festering inside her found a voice. 'If you – or Irina – had invited me for dinner yesterday evening earlier in the day, as you did Solly, then I would have loved to have joined you. But to ring from the restaurant when the meal was in progress . . .' She shook her head, aware that she might be putting still more distance between her and her dad but powerless to prevent the words of pain and disappointment from tumbling out. 'Have you any idea how uncaring that felt? How obvious you make it that Solly's your focus? Every arrangement you've made for your long weekend has been about Solly. You're literally only seeing me because I'm in his vicinity.' A slow, hot tear leaked from the corner of her eye, and she dashed it away with an inelegant sniff. 'Anyway. I'll have to get back to work. It's my assistant manager's day off and I can't leave three part-time staff to cope alone.'

But Howard didn't move. He stared at her, coffee cup neglected, eyes haunted. 'It's not like that,' he protested.

She'd half risen but now she dropped back into her seat. 'It is. From the moment you left Mum and me, you moved your new family to the top of your list.'

'Katerina!' he protested. 'It *wasn't* like that.' Feebly, he added, 'At least, I didn't realise you thought it was. You seemed so independent.'

She swilled down the rest of her coffee to dislodge the lump in her throat. 'Independent like those birds you see tipped out of the nest on wildlife programmes.'

Slowly, his face crumpled, and his eyes grew moist. 'I was . . .' He drew in a wavering breath. 'I was worried about you, you know. I-I got Irina pregnant when I was still married to your mother. It made it hard to meet the eyes of my twelve-year-old daughter.' He swallowed convulsively. 'I'm sorry. I hadn't realised how all the changes felt to you. I just thought you'd become a bit withdrawn. You know . . . girls . . . puberty.' He waved a helpless hand.

Kat's heart had taken on a heavy, sickening thud. Angelique got off her bed and whined uneasily, butting Kat's hand as if to say, *I'm here. You'll feel better if you stroke my ears.* Automatically, Kat did exactly that, feeling the soft silkiness slide through her fingers. Her throat was tight with unshed tears. 'It was. Apparent, I mean. And I wasn't withdrawn, I was left out. Irina didn't want me around and she directed all your attention to your new baby. She was possessive, stopping me interacting with you and Solly whenever she could. Recently, I've learned that Solly feels he doesn't know me very well. Isn't that sad? My own brother? But at least we've got the chance to get to know each other now and I'm enjoying it. I hope he is, too.'

She rose and went around the desk to where Howard sat in stunned silence. 'Sorry, Dad. Did I get too much off my chest all at once? It just kind of came out.' Tentatively, she laid a hand on her father's shoulder, soft and warm through his smart summer shirt. Her voice was husky. 'I thought I'd got used to all this a long time ago but Solly being around has brought it all back. And the way things have gone down the past couple of days with Irina trying to blame me for Solly having sex with another consenting adult and you acting all injured because I'm not free to see you at a moment's notice brought it bubbling to the surface.' She breathed in slowly and tried to manufacture a smile. 'I really do have to go back to work. I genuinely can't abandon my plans tonight to see you because it would mean leaving an old lady to run the book club on her own and missing a visit to a dear friend who's in a hospice while her husband rushes back to the UK to see his sick mum.' She patted the shoulder again. 'You stay and finish your coffee. Please don't let Angelique out when you leave because she'll come galloping into the food area.' She dropped a perfunctory kiss on his scalp where it showed through his hair and then left the room, swallowing down a lake of tears so she could run a book café for tourists.

She would have given a great deal to sit down somewhere quiet with a good book and a big slice of cake herself.

Kat signed in at reception in the serene atmosphere of the hospice and followed a light, bright corridor to Reeny's room, silently thanking Danielle for closing up this evening to leave Kat free. Even though she'd visited the woman who was both employer and friend only the evening before, she still had to pause anew to absorb Reeny's waxen pallor. She lay in bed, eyes closed, her head looking shrunken on the pillow. Part of Kat knew that the chemo would make Reeny worse before getting better but sometimes it was hard to believe the improvement would ever come.

She hovered. Should she leave Reeny to her rest? But then Reeny's eyes blinked open and her familiar smile dawned. 'Come in, Kat,' she croaked. 'Don't look so worried. I'm only in bed because I've got a boil on my bum.'

Half reassured by the feeble joke, Kat progressed close enough to take the visitor's chair at the foot of the bed, keen not to transmit some tiny germ that she wouldn't even know she had but which could weaken Reeny or hold up her treatment. She didn't bother with, 'How are you?' knowing a blatantly false, 'Fine, thank you,' would be the invariable response. Instead, she said, 'Angelique's sulking in the car because she's not allowed in, but she says she'll share her biscuits with you when you're well.'

Reeny's eyes crinkled at the corners, making her skin look like baking parchment. 'I look forward to that.' She asked about Kat and everyone at the book café then said, 'Graham FaceTimed a few minutes ago. His mum's doing well. Now, if her heart stops, the implant will kick it off again. Isn't that amazing? They've also put a couple of stents in to ease the angina so once she's rested, she'll be good as new.'

Kat marvelled at Reeny's capacity to care about others and take pleasure in their successful treatment when hers wasn't going well. 'Modern medicine's awesome, isn't it?'

'It is. I'm glad for Graham's sake, as well as Mum-in-law's. He's under so much strain.'

As Reeny had apparently tired herself by stringing together several sentences, Kat took most of the conversational burden from there, chatting about her dad and Irina's visit, glad to have something to talk about other than Livres et Café. Kat didn't want to give this warm, wonderful woman even one more worry by highlighting further cyber-attacks, not sure whether Graham had ever told Reeny that they'd begun. She'd sorted out the newsletter issue and Ulrica was on the case with further website security.

Crossing her fingers that Solly wouldn't mind, she related the story of Irina walking in on Solly and Ola, which made Reeny laugh until she coughed. 'Awkward,' she said on a gasp, wiping her streaming eyes on the sheet. Kat giggled too, wishing she had Reeny for a stepmum rather than the difficult Irina.

Soon she kissed Reeny and left her to rest while she raced home to eat, shower and grab what she needed for book club. Then she strode off to the *salon de thé*. The redoubtable Mathilde, whose family owned the business, was there before her, and had set some of her grandchildren to putting out seats.

'*Bonsoir, cherie*,' Mathilde called in the throaty voice that could switch between a purr or a growl. She treated Kat to a brisk air kiss beside each cheek. 'You look worn out. I will find a grandchild to serve you coffee.' With three of Mathilde's daughters running the place, there were so many grandchildren helping out that even she didn't seem to bother with their names.

She bustled out in her purple dress and broken-down sandals, leaving Kat calling, '*Merci*,' after her. She didn't mind being told she looked worn out. She *was* worn out. She'd spent half the night having sex and all day working hard and having difficult conversations of one kind or another.

Other book club members began to wander in. Gaston,

174

who had known Mathilde at school and was her favourite person to argue with; Anaïs, who taught at the village school; single mum Yasmine, who brought her two daughters; single dad Rayan, who brought his two sons, and Kat suspected, attended mainly because he fancied Yasmine. Others followed, clutching copies of the book under discussion, notepads and, in most cases, a drink that they'd bought on the way in.

Mathilde returned with a grandchild – male – bearing black coffee for Kat. 'To wake you up,' Mathilde declared.

By the time everyone had arrived, there were fourteen chairs occupied in the circle, four by children who would go first in talking about the graphic novel they'd been reading. Kat, having slurped down half her coffee and managed a few words with each person, was about to ask Yasmine's eldest daughter, Flavie, whether she'd enjoyed the book, when two more figures stepped tentatively through the doorway.

Kat was startled to recognise Florine and Clémence.

Florine's blonde crop was neat and chic. Clémence's longer blonde waves were caught in a clasp and then rippled down her back. Her eyes were wide, like Angelique's had been when Kat first brought her home from the shelter and she'd seemed to expect attack from any quarter.

'*Bienvenue!*' Kat called easily, thinking mother and daughter looked poised to turn and leave. 'This is Florine and Clémence, everyone. They haven't lived in Kirchhoffen long.'

Mathilde beamed. 'How lucky that we have two empty chairs. Please join us.' Others chorused their welcome to the newcomers and gestured them to the empty seats.

The idea of texting Noah again flitted across Kat's mind, but she dismissed it. Noah had made initial contact and it was down to him and Florine now. She smiled. 'I won't bamboozle you by introducing everybody at once, Florine and Clémence. We'll carry on and let you get a feel for things.'

'But they have no drinks,' Mathilde objected. 'I will fetch a grandchild.' This time the grandchild proved to be female and provided iced tea while Kat showed Clémence which book the younger members had been reading.

Although she looked on pins, Clémence listened to the other kids talk about the story while Kat prompted them, encouraging them to think about what they'd read. The children's time was soon up and they moved over to the table in the corner where Kat had provided bookmarks to colour in from the stash of marketing materials she collected. She was pleased to see Clémence, though looking shy and hanging back, follow the others.

After that, Kat could chill. She began the discussion of the contemporary romance they'd read last month, most of which centred on whether men really thought as the female author had depicted. Gaston, Rayan and another man whose name Kat had forgotten made comments that ranged from acerbic to thoughtful and soon the discussion became lively.

Kat's mind began to stray.

Were Solly, Irina and Howard out together again this evening? Had Howard taken Solly aside for a manly chat to demand, *What on earth's eating your sister?*

Her mind jumped back into the present situation when Mathilde demanded loudly, 'Why do readers like romantic fiction?'

Gaston answered, with an air of pronouncing an incontrovertible truth, 'It's a chance to fall in love . . . but without endangering their marriages.' Everyone laughed and no one came up with a better definition. The discussion moved back to the specific book read and after an hour the formal part of the meeting broke up. Both the grandchildren serving that evening came in to take last orders for further beverages and snacks as the *salon de thé* only stayed open this late for the book club or similar events. The children plumped down onto beanbags to eat their snacks, including a shyly smiling Clémence.

Over coffee, it was Gaston's turn to choose the next book and she was interested to see if he'd choose another romance as he'd certainly seemed to enjoy this one. Tomorrow she'd send a group email notifying all members of the choice. Some would buy the ebook or borrow from the library. A few would take advantage of the book club discount and buy via Livres et Café. She was just popping a reminder in her phone to include the discount voucher for July in the book club email when she realised Florine was hovering in front of her.

'Hi,' Kat said, with a tiny jump. She switched to French. 'Can I help you with something? It's nice to see you here.'

Florine took the chair beside Kat, which had been vacated by one of the children. 'Clémence would like to attend your next children's event at Livres et Café. Is it Wednesday?' She crossed one long, designer-jeans-clad leg over the other.

'School ends on Thursday so we're making it Friday the 8th instead. The details are on the website and Clémence can sign up there. I've never turned anyone away, but it helps to give me an idea of how many will come.' Then, cautious about the website since the cyber-attacks began, she checked the events page on her phone to make sure it wasn't suddenly saying that the reading would be given by an elephant or something. As it all looked fine, she turned the screen so Florine could see it, gratified when she got her own phone out and signed her daughter up there and then.

'It's good for Clémence to meet other children,' Florine said. With a smile of thanks, she uncrossed her legs and made as if to rise.

'You know,' Kat said, words tumbling out before she could examine them, 'the children of park staff can have a free wristband each month, giving them unlimited rides.'

For several seconds, Florine regarded her gravely, quite obviously having no trouble in putting two and two together. 'You know Noah quite well?'

Remembering just how well she'd got to know every inch of him last night, Kat's cheeks flooded with heat. 'He shares accommodation with my brother. I know how much he loves his daughter,' she mumbled, wondering why she felt so guilty when Florine was currently married to another man, but some people were possessive of their ex, even when they'd moved on themselves.

Florine, however, just answered, 'Thank you, I'll contact him.'

Relief that Florine didn't seem put out flooded through Kat. But it was closely followed by the realisation that she'd possibly just thrown Florine and Noah together. She shook herself at such a stupid thought. They'd had constant contact over their daughter when they all lived in Castillon-la-Bataille so why should anything be different now?

Once Florine had moved away, Kat chatted to Rayan and Yasmine about a TV dramatisation of a book that the book club had read last year. Then Kat's attention was caught by Mathilde clucking about, '*La pauvre petite.*' Kat realised with dismay that Florine and Mathilde were clustered around little Clémence, who had tears pouring down her cheeks.

Deciding that her status as book club organiser made it perfectly OK for her to involve herself, Kat hurried to join the group. 'Is something the matter?' She smiled down at the blonde child who was wiping tears with her sleeves and looking self-conscious.

Florine had her arms around her daughter. 'One of the other children told her about her dog running away. She feels things very deeply.' To Clémence, she murmured consolingly, 'I expect the dog will find his way home.'

Flavie, whose dog it was, declared reassuringly, 'He's probably having an adventure. He left home twice before but he came back the next day.'

'Really?' Clémence sniffed, looking happier, and the tears began to dry up.

Kat, hovering to make quite certain everything was well, got a glimpse of why Noah was so dead set on Clémence being spared the enquiries of social workers or the family court. If Clémence tapped into the sorrow of others so easily that she'd be so upset over a scamp of a dog she didn't even know, she must find it hard to cope with trauma of her own.

A picture drifted into her mind of Clémence sobbing when she was reunited with Noah at Livres et Café. Most children would have reacted the same in that moment of mixed shock and joy but, still, it made her eyes prick with tears even now.

Yohan was a monster to separate Clémence from her father so callously. Kat had only met him briefly, but she felt as if his negative influence infiltrated everyone around him, creating shadows of uncertainty and unhappiness in good hearts.

Chapter Twelve

Noah and Solly lunched at Livres et Café on Saturday, securing a table inside as the sun had been baking them both all morning while they performed their duties at the park. The opportunity for air-conditioned comfort was to be relished.

Kat greeted them cheerily, racing past with a tray full of cold drinks and pastries to deliver to an outside table. She'd twisted her hair up in some complicated fashion today with a clasp that looked like a big purple butterfly securing it to the back of her head, though occasional curls escaped to float about her face. With her eyes bright with purpose and lips curving into her ready smile, just the sight of her made Noah's heart beat faster.

One of the assistants, Antoine, came to the table to take their order. Solly ordered one of the crusty ham and cheese rolls he liked and a chocolate cake. He certainly loved his sugar. Noah chose a sandwich and the largest cup of coffee available. He needed caffeine after helping tourists in and out of kayaks all morning. As those on the 'rescue' paddle boards had been seconded elsewhere today, Noah had had to jump into a kayak and swish off into the lake twice to give people a tow back or recapture a lost paddle. Hapless tourists tended to think such mishaps hilarious, but it was a pain in the arse to Noah, even if it entertained the queue of visitors waiting for empty vessels.

Solly's phone rang and with an explanatory, 'It's Ola,' he took the call, his end of the discussion comprising: 'I don't know yet. I've got to talk to my sister. Yes, I'm waiting to talk to her now, but she's busy working. Yes, I'll text you and let you know.'

While Solly carried on negotiating with Ola, Noah watched Kat carrying and hurrying or stretching up for a book on a high shelf. It was no wonder her body underneath those clothes was so firm. She smiled at the elderly gent she'd retrieved the book for and he looked as if he'd been hit by a truck.

Noah knew how he felt. When was he going to be able to spend time with her again? A phone conversation late last night had only fed his appetite for her, even if much of the conversation had been taken up with the news of Florine and Clémence attending the book club and Kat having told Florine about free wristbands for children of the staff, something he should have remembered to say himself. Kat was a star to have thought to bring the subject up and he hoped Florine would follow up that lead and bring Clémence to Parc Lemmel while Yohan was busy at work.

He'd decided to offer to take Angelique for a run when he'd eaten, though it was small reparation for what Kat had done for him.

He'd deliberately ordered his lunch first today, so Kat didn't feel constrained to feed him on the house in return, which was how things had worked out on previous occasions. Solly didn't seem to have a problem with it, but

Kat managed Livres et Café and Noah didn't want her to get in trouble for handing out freebies. Worse, she might be putting the lunch costs in the till herself so her employers wouldn't suffer, which, in Noah's view, would be worse.

Solly had just put his phone away and said, 'Ola never seems to think, "I don't know yet" is a reasonable answer,' just as Kat dashed by, swerved behind the counter and asked something of Antoine, who smiled and nodded, then, making up a tray in a blur of motion, she arrived with their order plus a huge coffee and a sandwich for herself.

She plumped down in a vacant chair. 'If I don't get something to eat, I'm going to collapse. How are you both doing?' Rosy-cheeked and eyes sparkling, she didn't look at the passing-out stage, but she took a bite of sandwich and munched at top speed like a rabbit.

Solly got in first, a faint note of indignation in his voice. 'I'm waiting for you to make your mind up about tonight, so I know what to tell Ola about what I'm doing.'

Kat swallowed, eyebrows quirking. 'What about tonight?'

With a sigh of overdone patience, Solly answered. 'Dad's texted you to say they're changing their arrangements so we can all have dinner together, if you're still free. But if you're not, they'll stick to their original plans and so will I. So, what's your situation?'

Solly's scowl and the face Kat pulled in return struck Noah as much more sibling-like than a month ago, when they'd been like friendly strangers. He grinned at their nearly matching expressions of frustration.

'I haven't seen a text,' Kat retorted with impatience and indignation of her own. 'Some of us are too busy to check our phones at work.' She took another swift bite of sandwich to munch on while she fished out her phone. 'Oh.

Right. Yes, it's here.' She stared at the screen then back at her brother with a lightning change of direction. 'I'm free, but would you rather I said I'm busy, so you don't have to go, Solly?'

Solly frowned at her. 'No. I'd rather you went so we can all be together.' Then, as Kat's cheeks coloured and her eyes took on a gleam of pleasure, he added, 'I'll tell him from both of us.' Solly began texting rapidly. He plonked down his phone and tackled his lunch once more. 'I told them you'd probably be there, too, mate,' he mumbled around a mouthful.

Noah started. 'Me, do you mean? I wasn't invited.'

At the same time, Kat exclaimed in a scandalised tone, 'Solly!'

Solly regarded them both with an air of injury. 'You're together, aren't you?' he demanded, waggling his finger between the two of them to indicate togetherness.

Kat's flush darkened to one of annoyance. 'I apologise for my idiot brother, Noah. I'll text my dad. For fuck's sake, Solly, people are usually seeing each other for longer than a couple of days before they meet bloody parents. Are you taking Ola?'

Solly looked aghast. 'No! We're not serious.'

'You've been seeing each other longer than we have,' Kat fumed, snatching up her phone.

Noah laughed. Solly's heedless action had caught him by surprise, but he said, 'Happy to be your plus one, Kat, but I'll understand if you want alone time with your folks. You know I'm curious about stepfamilies, with everything that's happening with Clé. Maybe the more I understand, the better I'll deal with it.' Really, he wanted to support Kat and he didn't think that meeting the parents was the last step before buying rings and booking a wedding.

She halted with her finger poised over her phone screen, dark brows forming little arches of surprise. 'Really?' She wrinkled her nose in thought. 'Maybe it will make things easier if you're along. Thank you. Where's the meal to be, Solly?'

He grinned. '*À la Table de L'Ill*. Dad would like to see your apartment, too.' Then he laughed at Kat's stunned expression. 'What? You told Dad off about not being involved enough in your life, didn't you? Well, he's involving himself.'

Kat muttered, 'I didn't think it would mean having to tidy my apartment.' She began to pile crockery back onto the tray. 'You're not worried about being caught in the village by Yohan, Noah?'

'Not overly,' he said tersely, irritated at the way Yohan had everyone tippy-toeing around him. 'Especially as you told me he doesn't see his social life as being in Kirchhoffen.' He slipped his hand onto her knee, her skin bare and warm beneath his hand. 'It'll be fine. I'll bring Solly over in my car and park at yours and we'll walk down to the restaurant together. OK?'

He felt some of the tension leave her. She smiled. 'Sounds great. I don't have to visit Reeny tonight because Graham's got an earlier flight so he can see her before bedtime.'

They went their separate ways, Solly to see if he could grab a word with Ola to tell her he wouldn't be available until late this evening, Kat to hurl herself back into the busy whirl of Livres et Café and Noah to get Angelique and enjoy a peaceful stroll beneath the dappled shade of the trees before returning to the tourists splashing merrily on the lake.

Solly, despite Noah's offer to drive him, had decided to go directly to the restaurant on his old banger of a scooter so he'd be free to meet Ola later. Kat and Noah strolled down into the village, the sinking sun setting light to the pink and yellow roses hanging over garden walls. The booking was for nine, which worked well for Kat as she had been on duty until eight this evening.

Noah had news to share. 'Florine messaged me. I picked it up on my afternoon break. She says she's signed Clémence up to your event on Friday and asked if I want to see her. It's not my scheduled day off but one of the lake team's happy to swap days so I'm going to take advantage of the staff wristband scheme and spend the whole day with Clémence.'

He sounded so excited that Kat halted in the middle of the pavement to fling her arms around him in a glad, hard hug. 'That's fantastic! You must be over the moon.'

He hugged her even harder, treating her forehead to a smacking kiss. 'I am. And I have you to thank for planting the seed with Florine.' As his arms slackened, a sigh escaped him. 'Pity that Florine doesn't feel she can be open with Yohan, but my primary goal has to be to spend time with my daughter. Clé called me when I'd finished work. She's so excited, already planning what to wear and what to put in her backpack, asking which rides she's allowed to go on. She got so excited that she cried.' He paused to swallow before going on huskily, 'It broke my heart to have to remind her to delete the call history at the end of the conversation. I'm fighting the urge to confront Yohan but Florine came on the line after Clémence to say he'd just drawn up outside so we had to end the call.' He groaned. 'I hate the sneakiness but it's important to make Florine comfortable with me seeing Clémence. The future will have to look after itself for now.'

Kat took Noah's arm consolingly, having learned enough

185

about him to know how badly subterfuge would sit with his open and honest personality. 'It's astonishing how one person feels comfortable grabbing all the power in a relationship. I'm not saying Irina's as bad as Yohan, but she's always tried to keep Dad and Solly away from me just as Yohan's tried to keep Clémence away from you.'

'Florine's played her role,' he said quietly. 'She seems incapable of calling Yohan on arranging a "holiday" that was obviously always a permanent move, keeping Clémence out of school from March to July. Her old school hasn't been in touch with me again, so I assume Florine's now told them they've moved out of the area.'

They arrived at the spot where the road broadened and the blue-painted restaurant stood, bedecked with white petunias and red geraniums. Solly lounged at an outside table, enjoying the cool evening air with a long glass of lemonade before him.

'Hey,' Kat called as they approached the wooden table, surprised by a flutter of butterflies in her stomach now the family meal was upon her. Used to limited contact with her dad or stepmum, she found herself glad of Noah's presence. The dad who once used to fetch her home from a friend's house where she'd been doing homework, or who'd sneaked extra biscuits into the shopping trolley when her mum Joanne wasn't looking, had ceased to exist when he'd left the family home – and everyone had seemed to expect that she'd simply accept the change.

Now, twenty-five years later, when he'd acknowledged that he'd fallen down in his post-divorce fatherly role and seemed to be making an effort, she wasn't sure how to go on. Would Howard have told Irina of Kat's complaints about the way they'd treated her? Almost certainly, she decided, taking a seat opposite her brother. Would that have put up Irina's back? Again, almost certainly. And put her dad in a difficult situation? Yeah . . .

'Hey.' Solly grinned, looking comfortably chilled, giving her a hug and clapping Noah on the shoulder.

Irina thought the world of Solly, but Kat resolved she wouldn't let her set brother and sister against one another. Somewhere in the past few weeks she'd started thinking of Solly as properly her brother. No 'half', no distance, no excuses, no division. 'Have you started a tab?' she asked.

Solly nodded, looking about himself for a server. 'What do you want? I'll try out my French.'

The manager, Cindy, came over with her order tablet, and Kat and Noah hid their grins when Solly got *vert* and *verre* mixed up so that he ordered 'a green of white wine' instead of 'a glass' but he managed Noah's orange juice OK. Cindy nodded and smiled and whisked off again. She spoke better English than Solly did French, but Kat wasn't going to rain on Solly's attempts to speak the language of his hosts by telling him so.

The drinks had just been delivered when a familiar voice cut through the gentle chatter of those at other tables. 'I'm not sitting out here with all the bugs that come off the river. I'll get eaten alive.'

Solly looked up, clearly unsurprised at his mum's opening gambit taking the form of a grumble. 'Hi, Mum, hi, Dad.'

Kat smiled and greeted them, too, wondering why Irina couldn't say her hellos first and then ask if people *minded* moving indoors as she was the kind insects liked to feast on? It was on the tip of her tongue to suggest Irina clear off inside while the rest of them stayed out here where it was cool, but she opted for displaying her own good manners instead and introducing Noah.

Howard smiled and shook Noah's hand. 'Evening. Nice to meet you.'

Irina just did the handshake.

Solly rose. 'Suppose we'd better go inside, then.'

Kat baulked. 'Shall we ask whether they have a table inside for us, first?' Almost every outside table was occupied and she didn't want to give it up and end up with nothing. Catching Cindy's eye as she sped past, they had a brief conversation, then Kat translated for those who hadn't followed the French. 'Cindy says there's just one table left, if we'd like to follow her in, we can have it.'

Irina strode past everyone else with a toss of her head, though her blow-dried helmet of hair was too fiercely lacquered to move. 'I hate restaurants that won't take bookings but then don't have tables available.'

Cindy turned back with a smile. 'We are a little rustic here, madame.'

Irina had the grace to look abashed at having her English so readily understood.

After that, everyone seemed on their best behaviour for a time. Kat made an effort to include Irina when she told Howard about her apartment and invited everyone back for coffee so that they could see it, adding, 'I have a coffee machine so I'm not condemning you to instant,' before Irina could ask, knowing her stepmother to be a coffee snob.

'Lovely, darling,' Howard said heartily.

Irina tried to migrate to a one-to-one conversation with Solly by asking who he was texting all the time. Solly grinned. 'You've already met her – kinda, anyway,' alluding to Irina walking in on him and Ola.

Irina flushed, clearly not comfortable with that subject.

Noah, who'd been largely silent till now, diverted Solly's

188

mum's attention. 'What do you think of France, Irina? Have you visited often?'

Luckily, as quite a few people at nearby tables probably spoke English, Irina did like France. She waxed lyrical about Alsace, the pretty, differently coloured houses and the network of rivers and canals that created the region's many moods. Kat relaxed and listened, grateful that Noah had hit on something to bring out Irina's positive side.

After they'd each perused the menus brought in neat black folders and given their orders to a young female server, Kat translating a couple of times when laborious holiday French wasn't understood, Solly put away his phone and joined the conversation. 'How about you, Dad? You enjoying *la belle* France?'

'Absolutely.' Howard rubbed his chin and glanced at Irina.

Kat thought she caught Irina return a small nod. She was still pondering this when her father cleared his throat and spoke again.

'Actually, we want to talk to you both about that.' Howard smoothed his wings of silver hair back behind his ears. 'Things haven't been going well for us in the economic downturn. I've been given notice of redundancy from the accessories wholesaler I work for and Irina's been put on a zero hours contract.'

Irina pulled a face. 'And some weeks, that actually means zero hours. I don't know how they expect people to live. They're trialling automated phone systems in the call centre where I work so it's only a matter of time before I'm entirely replaced by robots.'

'I'm sorry to hear it,' Kat said sincerely. She loved her own job and could only imagine how hollow she'd feel if she lost it. Noah, too, murmured sympathetically. Solly didn't speak, so Kat decided he must already be in possession of these facts.

Howard cleared his throat. 'We still have a mortgage and payments on the car and so on, like everyone.'

Kat nodded sympathetically. People who started a second household, as Howard had, would naturally still have mortgages when they were fast approaching sixty. He might not yet be in a financial position to exist on a pension . . . supposing he had one. They lived in the Cotswolds, where property prices were lively, and Irina was a full eight years younger than him so they might easily have a mortgage that would carry them past Howard's sixty-fifth birthday.

Howard's colour, always high, rose higher. He propped his elbows on the table and clasped his hands. 'But we've been thrown a bit of a lifeline.'

'A potential lifeline,' Irina corrected, holding up crossed fingers.

Howard nodded. 'We're in talks with someone who wants to take a partner into their small manufacturing business. They operate in the area I'm in now – handbags, belts, costume jewellery – and they want a partner to take on the role of sales director. It seems like a good opportunity. Employers aren't keen on taking on people of my age and this way we'd have things more in our own hands.' He smiled suddenly, twinkling at his wife. 'We're about ready to sign on the dotted line, aren't we, Irina?'

Irina smiled, looking quite excited. 'Very nearly.'

'That's great,' said Kat. 'I hope it goes brilliantly for you.'

'Mega,' Solly added approvingly.

Howard's grin broadened and he made fidgety little movements with his shoulders as if trying to conjure up words. 'We're glad you feel like that,' he brought out in the end. 'Because we'd really like it to be a family firm. We'd buy in and employ you and Solly. Later, we'd pass it on to you.'

'Or you'd buy us out,' Irina amended.

Kat couldn't have been more shocked if he'd stripped off all his clothes and done the limbo. She made the first objection that entered her head. 'But I live here.'

'The company's here,' Howard pronounced jubilantly. 'My partner would be a guy my current company's dealt with for years, Phillipe Mercier. His premises are out near Strasbourg Airport and he wants to build up the export side. That's who I've been seeing this week. We didn't say anything before we came because we wanted to tie up loose ends and be sure of getting our business visas. Once the agreement is signed, we hope to be able to move here in about a month.'

'A month? Like . . . early August?' Kat blinked, trying to absorb this completely unexpected turn of events, wondering what it would mean for her. Her heart rate picked up. Would living close to her dad bring them closer? Then her stomach sank. Or would Irina succeed – again – in pushing them apart, and distance Solly from Kat, too?

At Kat's silence, Howard went on. 'We can apply for our residency permits once we're over here.'

'*Carte de Sejour*,' Irina added, as if Kat might not know that, even though she was a Brit living in France herself. Then, to Noah, 'Do you have that?'

He nodded, shifting so that his leg rested against Kat's, as if to remind her he was beside her while this bewildering conversation took place. 'I've lived here since I was eleven, so I applied as soon as I was eighteen.'

'Hang on,' said Kat, feeling as if everyone was going too

fast. 'You want Solly and me to work for you? But I have a job, one I love, and I wouldn't abandon my employers at the moment anyway. They're depending on me.'

'What if we're depending on you?' Irina put in. 'Your family. That's how a family concern works.'

Kat gazed at her, with her blow-dried hair and righteously pursed lips, fighting the temptation to snap that Reeny and Graham had been more like family to her than Irina had ever been. She had to fight to summon a smile to take the sting out of her next words. 'You can't really depend on someone without asking them first if they'd like to be involved.'

Howard rubbed his jaw. He wore a close-cropped beard now, which Kat thought made him look older than when he'd been clean-shaven. 'You'd be a real asset, Katerina. You speak French far better than us and you're integrated into the country. Family firms are tight-knit, and everybody pulls together.'

Kat felt her eyes narrow sceptically. Working for a 'family firm' probably meant that extra commitment was expected of you in the name of loyalty. She tried, and failed, to envisage arguing for pay rises with her dad or stepmother. 'But you're only buying half the company, aren't you? How can that be "family"?'

Irina leaned forward. 'Phillipe's already got his wife and children working in the company so it would even things up nicely. Howard and I will deal with the exports, especially into the UK and US. We thought that Solly could be trained up in the management and you could run the onsite shop, Kat. And help a bit with translation, like your father said,' she added, generously.

Kat couldn't hold in a shout of incredulous laughter. Irina – and, so far as she could see, Howard – were *still* prioritising Solly. It was astonishing in these circumstances, but there it was. *Solly could be trained up in the management and you could run the onsite shop.* She'd been quite clear with her dad how slighted she felt and yet not a thing had changed. She tilted her head enquiringly. 'Why shouldn't I be part of the management? I'm already a manager and I speak French so I'm by far the best applicant.'

'That's true,' Solly observed. 'I don't mind running the shop.' He smiled at Kat engagingly. 'If you teach me how.'

She laughed again, but more genuinely this time, grinning at her brother's sweet smile. 'Would you be interested in joining Dad and Irina? Staying in France?'

Slowly, he nodded, his round, boyish face becoming serious. 'It's worth giving serious consideration. I like it here. You're here already. I'd probably like being part of a family – or two-family – concern and' – he grinned wickedly – 'my lack of references from my last job wouldn't be a problem.'

She gave his arm a tiny shake. 'Don't do it for that reason. I'm sure one indiscretion doesn't need to destroy you for all other employment. But it would be great to have you around if you were to stay.'

'I could try it for a year or so,' Solly pondered. 'Why not? I'd have to improve my French.'

'We're doing the same,' Howard put in eagerly.

Kat nodded. 'Yes, it's not one of those countries where you can get by with English full time, even if you are exporting to English-speaking countries.' She turned back to Howard and Irina. 'I'm sorry I can't join you in the business, but I'm happy to help you find somewhere to live and deal with the letting agent, or other bureaucracy, so far as I'm able.'

'Thank you, darling.' Howard reached over the table and gave her hand a squeeze.

'Yes, thank you,' echoed Irina, but frostily. 'If that's the best you can do.'

Noah had sat silently through this exchange, probably feeling that family business had nothing to do with him, but now, as Kat took a breath to flash back a hot retort at her stepmother's ungracious rider, he smiled disarmingly at Irina. 'Aren't you lucky to have such a savvy, kind stepdaughter to smooth your path, especially with such a compact timeline for the move here? When my parents moved to France to set up a business they made all kinds of mistakes, got ripped off and fell afoul of local bylaws because they knew absolutely no one at all. I'll bet they would have been immensely grateful to have such an incredibly generous offer, especially considering how hard Kat's already working.'

A pause. Then Irina inclined her head graciously. 'Thank you, Noah.'

In an instant, Kat switched from red fury to wanting to once again roar with laughter. How on earth had Irina translated Noah's thinly veiled reprimand as a compliment? As if Irina had actively chosen to have Kat in her life?

Luckily, the meals arrived just then. In the flurry of uniting each person with the correct meal, the conversation became more general. Kat tried to explain a little of the process of gaining the *Carte de Sejour*, but Irina was quick to reply that they knew all that.

An hour later, when dessert had been eaten, Solly checked the time. 'Anyone mind if I bail out? Some of the others from the park are having a barbecue at the vans.'

Irina looked disappointed. 'You've just eaten,' she pointed out.

Solly grinned his irrepressible grin. 'But I haven't drunk yet, Mum.' He jumped up and hugged each of his parents, giving his mum a smacking kiss on the cheek that spoke of the love between them, regardless of how overbearing she could be. With a quick, 'See you, Kat; see you, Noah,' he hurried out of the restaurant to spread his social wings in a different direction.

Immediately, Irina checked the expensive-looking watch on her wrist. 'Katerina, would you mind if we took a rain check on seeing your apartment? If we leave soon, we can have coffee with Phillipe and his wife and tie up whatever else we can before we leave for the UK tomorrow.'

Howard looked surprised but Kat wasn't. Golden boy Solly had left the building and Irina's desire to be at the gathering had left with him. Kat wasn't sure she could blame her stepmother this time because she was feeling the strain herself. 'Not at all,' she answered sweetly and truthfully. It would leave her alone with Noah, after all.

As Solly had skipped, obviously expecting that someone would deal with the pesky matter of the bill, Kat made to pay his share, but Irina seemed to take that as a slight and insisted they 'would pay for Solomon'. By the time she'd painstakingly done the maths and informed Kat that tips weren't necessary in France, Kat wished she'd just paid the whole thing, her cheeks burning as Cindy patiently wielded the contactless payment machine while Irina told each person what they owed.

Once they were back outside, Howard kissed Kat goodbye but Irina just jumped into their rental car and started the engine. Howard murmured, 'I'll be in touch,' and joined his wife in the car.

'Phew,' Kat said, catching hold of Noah's hand when they'd waved the car off and were alone. They headed for Rue du Printemps through the soft evening air. 'Tense, or what? What did you discover about step-relationships?'

Noah shrugged. 'That I hope Clé can have a better one with Yohan than you do with Irina. Yours looks painful and I wouldn't wish that on her.'

Kat sighed. 'Was I prickly? Irina brings out the worst in me. But honestly, I bet she backs out of Dad's scheme if Solly doesn't get onboard.'

'If that was you being prickly then you're an incredibly sunny and tolerant person,' he said frankly, making her laugh and lean her head against his arm for an instant, feeling comforted by his undemanding presence.

'Katerina,' he said thoughtfully, swinging her hand as they turned into the leafy street where she lived and drew within sight of La Maison Blanche and its lofty balcony.

She laughed again. 'What?'

'I didn't know it was your name. I suppose I thought you were a Katherine.'

'Reeny's a Katherine,' she said helpfully.

'Katerina's a beautiful name.' He slowed his footsteps, pulling her close in against his side so she caught the smell of his aftershave. 'Can I take you to bed, Katerina?'

A warm, tingling wave of desire started at the soles of her feet and swept up to the top of her head. 'If you call me "Katerina" in that sexy Edinburgh growl you can do pretty much anything you want.'

He slid his arm around her and brought his mouth close to her ear and murmured, 'Deal.'

Chapter Thirteen

Never had six days passed so slowly as those leading up Clémence's visit to Parc Lemmel.

Noah had more than half expected Florine to text a postponement, probably based on Yohan working from home that day or taking Friday off. The thought had made Noah grind his teeth but the reality of finding himself waiting alone at the hedge beside the formal garden was much worse. It was well past the appointed time, ten o'clock in the morning on 8 July and his stomach was screwed up in disappointment.

Florine had agreed to bring Clémence to the park. They were to have wristbands to go on the attractions and take in the children's reading event at Livres et Café this afternoon. So why had he been stood up?

He fidgeted with his phone, dying to message or call either his daughter or his ex-wife but wary of causing a problem for them. It wasn't Noah who had to live with Yohan Gagneau, after all.

Twenty past ten.

Twenty-five past.

The sun beat on the top of his head and he wished he'd bought a bottle of water.

Then a movement from his left caught his attention and he turned to see a slight, blonde figure racing towards him, face almost split in two by her huge smile, her mother walking more sedately in her wake. 'Papa!' Clémence shouted when she was close enough. 'Papa, I'm here.'

Heart soaring as if someone had filled it with helium, Noah jogged towards his daughter, swooping her up as he had when she'd been a toddler, swinging her around and making her giggle. 'Hello, little one!'

She laughed in delight as he set her back on her feet. 'Can we go in the kayaks? What about the rollercoaster? Maman says I can have a wristband and go on anything I like.'

'Maman's exactly right.' He smiled over Clémence's head as Florine joined them on the grass. 'I'm going to have a wristband, too, so that I can join you. And maybe Maman would like one?' He hadn't pressed Florine on how they'd tackle today. If seeing Clémence meant having Florine along then that was fine with him. They hadn't done that when it was his turn to have Clémence when they all lived in Castillon-la-Bataille but he wasn't about to spook Florine with demands he be left with alone with his daughter. Not at this sensitive stage.

Florine smiled. 'I think I'll watch, thank you. I'm afraid we were delayed by roadworks between Kirchhoffen and Muntsheim.'

Noah managed not to say, 'Oh? They weren't there at seven.' Roadworks could sprout up like morning mushrooms and why invite questions on his early morning exit from Kirchhoffen? He wasn't remotely worried over Florine's feelings about him sleeping with Kat, but he didn't want to say anything that might make Kat uncomfortable. Also, he wasn't sure it was a good idea to make Florine aware that he was frequently in the same village as Yohan. She might easily grow flustered and nervous, which might cause her to keep her distance, making everything trickier with Clémence. He smiled, didn't ask why one of them couldn't have sent a text to warn him they'd been held up, and said easily, 'Never mind. You're here now. Let's head for the ticket office.'

He took Clémence's little hand in his to queue at the kiosk for the wristbands he'd reserved, explaining how they clipped on and that they'd be scanned at each activity. Clémence was possessed of lively curiosity about the way things worked.

The next two hours passed in a flash. They glided yellow kayaks over khaki water while Florine sat on shore and read, and when the half hour was up, they took the lakeside path beneath sweeping green willows to the rollercoaster to ride the clattering, flying, giant silver caterpillar with whoops of joy, howling as they were flung around within their restraining harnesses. After striding up the long grassy slope – which Clémence accomplished with an impatience that made her pant – they climbed astride gaily painted horses to whizz around on the carousel. Clémence was half afraid of the next ride, the flying chairs, where centrifugal force threw her seat on chains out high above the watching tourists.

Back on solid ground, Noah noted her white face and gave her a comforting hug. 'You weren't so keen on that ride, were you? Let's try the big slide.' Clémence did indeed prefer sitting on a red mat and swooping down the turquoise slide over a series of humps to land in a laughing heap at the bottom, and then she proved herself a ruthless bumper in the bumper cars.

Finally, the little girl declared, 'I'm hungry.'

'Let's find Maman,' he replied.

They returned to the bench where Florine waited. All morning she'd sat on benches with her e-reader or wandered over to look at the gardens through her designer sunglasses. Noah was grateful that she hadn't inserted herself too much into the brief time he had to spend with Clémence, this small person, this part of him who'd possessed his heart since the day she was born. Her first thin cry had stirred in him a protective love he hadn't known existed. From that instant, it had been his mission to do whatever was best for Clémence. He'd paced the floor with her nestled into his shoulder when she was a sleepless infant, offered unstinting hugs and reassurance when she became a nervous toddler and continued that reassurance when she'd grown into the bright but sensitive child she was now.

Florine loved Clémence equally deeply, though, and Noah felt a pang of guilt that she'd waited so patiently while he had fun with their daughter. When Clémence had hurled herself at her mother and babbled out an account of every ride they'd been on, he murmured, 'Maybe Maman would like to choose where we eat lunch?'

Florine stroked their daughter's hair. 'Let Clémence choose. It's her day.'

Clémence danced on the toes of her turquoise and pink trainers. 'The café with the books.'

'Don't you want to look at the others?' Noah had never tried Park Lemmel's other eating places because they didn't have Kat in them, but he added, 'There are two more and sometimes there's a burger van, too.'

Clémence gave an emphatic headshake. 'I like the pastries and the peach tea. And the books. Can I have a book today, please?'

'Maybe. Let's see what happens at the story event this afternoon.' He felt her hand slide into his again and smiled down into her trusting blue eyes, heart melting. Every tiny thing about her, from the cute wisps of hair that grew in a rosette at the front, to the way one small foot turned in a smidgeon when she walked, was indelibly imprinted in his mind's eye, yet he couldn't stop looking at her. He paused so Florine could take station at the other side of Clémence, and they listened to their daughter chatter about the rollercoaster as they went.

'We can go on the rides again later,' Noah told Clémence. 'Your wristband lasts all day.' He caught a tiny movement as Florine checked her watch. 'If there's time,' he added, being punctiliously fair, even if he felt Florine should have made sure this day was free after depriving him of Clémence since March, whether or not it had been her or self-centred Yohan who had planned it.

When Clémence turned enquiring eyes in her mother's direction, Florine smiled. 'I think we should leave at four so that we have plenty of time.' She didn't say for what and Noah didn't feel he could express disappointment that the curfew was so early, not within earshot of Clémence.

But as they reached the entrance to the arcade and Clémence caught sight of Livres et Café, she let go of their hands and ran, calling back over her shoulder, 'I'll find a table.' Her blonde ponytail streamed out behind her, bright in the sun.

The moment she was out of earshot, Noah turned to Florine, speaking in French because it was easiest for her.

'Thank you for bringing her. It's been unbearable to be apart.'

Colour flooded her cheeks. 'I am sorry about what happened.' She sounded regretful but also worried.

He kept his voice low and easy because he'd made his feelings clear last time they'd met and now he wanted the atmosphere between them to be as good as it could be in their circumstances. 'I understand how it came about.' He changed the subject. 'If you want to go off and have a few hours to yourself this afternoon, it'll be fine. I have the whole day free.'

She looked uneasy as they made their way over the pavings, approaching the table where Clémence was already seated, beaming at them from under the shade of a green parasol. 'Yohan doesn't work late on Fridays.'

'Ah.' He took a few more steps, wondering whether now was the time to broach the question of the future. Should he let Florine have more opportunity to absorb the reality – that he wasn't here to rock her family boat, but neither was he about to go away? 'Florine,' he began.

At the exact same moment, she said, 'Noah—'

They laughed. 'You first,' he said.

She halted, turning to face him. 'I know we'll have to talk about where we go from here,' she said haltingly. 'But I need time to think.'

His nod was slow, but his brain worked quickly. Perhaps leaving Florine to reach her own conclusions was the best way? Knowing that she didn't think well for herself, his instinct was to demand, *But what are you thinking? Because I'm thinking that Yohan has acted like a knob and it's time I told him his actions in moving my daughter hundreds of miles away are unacceptable. I'll deal with him. Leave him to me.* But Noah bulldozing Florine was

202

no more correct than Yohan doing so. He adopted his usual reasonable tone. 'OK. I don't have to rush any decisions. We have a little time.' He put slight emphasis on 'a little' so she didn't think that he was going to spend the rest of Clémence's childhood snatching moments with her in this stupidly clandestine way instead of resuming his shared custody role.

However, it was all too apparent that his choices had narrowed. Florine loved Yohan, so despite the high-handed, selfish way he'd presented her with a *fait accompli* once they'd arrived in Alsace, she'd continue with her marriage. Yohan had begun a fabulous new job in Strasbourg and she'd already registered Clémence at the village school. It wouldn't be good for Clémence if Noah embarked on a battle to take her back to the Dordogne . . . and it wasn't a battle that he'd necessarily win, no matter that Florine had acted against the notarised custody agreement. The family court might take a dim view of Noah carrying Clémence so far from her mum and having to settle her into new childcare arrangements, even if they were based around her old school. He wasn't sure he was keen on that scenario himself. Wasn't it him who didn't want Clémence desperately upset?

All this meant that, sooner or later, Noah would be making his permanent home in Alsace and Yohan would be informed of that and warned of the consequences of trying the vanishing act again. For *now*, he was prepared to let Florine decide whether she should be the one to explain the facts to Yohan.

But only for now.

He'd reached this conclusion a few nights ago, lying awake listening to Kat breathing gently beside him, her skin warm against his. Moving to Alsace permanently would be an upheaval. He'd have to resign his job in Bordeaux and try and get a new role with one of the river cruise companies on the Rhine, give up his apartment in the Dordogne and find one in Alsace. His parents were accepting of his decision but were dismayed that they'd no longer be living within a couple of miles of their son and granddaughter upon returning home from New Zealand, as his mother had been quick to tell him in their last phone conversation.

Apart from living near Clémence, uppermost in Noah's mind was the blossoming thing with Kat, the strong, independent, hot, sexy woman who occupied his mind whether or not he was with her. Maybe if he stayed, he could have Kat long term. He'd move on to a new relationship just as Florine had done and everyone would prioritise Clémence's well-being – with the possible exception of Yohan, who would prioritise himself.

Though his brain was whirring with these possibilities, he gave Florine a casual smile. 'I think Clé's hungry.'

Her face cleared, as if she was relieved he hadn't pursued the difficult conversation they needed to have. 'We'd better buy her those pastries and peach tea.'

As they approached the waiting Clémence, he saw Kat emerge from inside the book café, balancing a full tray despite her usual warp-speed. She checked, changed direction and swerved towards Clémence's table. Clémence smiled shyly and pointed. Kat looked up, and Noah could tell the exact moment she caught sight of them. He couldn't read what lay behind her smile but just the sight of her made him feel grounded and calm. She said something to Clémence as Noah and Florine arrived.

Clémence wiggled in her seat, beaming, greeting her parents with an excited, 'Kat says that the dog came home safely.'

Florine said, 'Oh, good,' and offered Kat a friendly greeting as she took a seat.

Noah glanced at Kat in surprise. 'Angelique ran away?'

Kat laughed and shook her head. 'When Clémence and Florine came to book club last Friday, another little girl, Flavie, told Clémence that her dog had run away.' She turned her gaze to Clémence. 'You were sad, weren't you? But he's arrived home, hungry but happy.'

A small frown creased Clémence's forehead. 'But where has he been?' She lifted her hands as if asking for a satisfactory explanation to be placed into them.

Kat obviously understood Clémence's need for satisfactory answers. 'Flavie's maman thinks he found a doggy girlfriend.'

'Oh,' Clémence nodded, apparently convinced, while Noah grinned at this carefully censored explanation of a dog taking off after a bitch in heat. But Clé hadn't yet finished asking questions. She turned her wide, blue-eyed gaze on Noah. 'But who is Angelique?'

'Kat's dog,' he said, switching to English to see if Clémence got the joke.

After a second, Clémence did. Her ponytail swung as she switched her gaze between Kat and Noah, eyes crinkling. She switched to English too, making Noah proud that she'd kept it up so well despite not having been in his company for the past few months. 'Your name is Kat and you have a dog? That's funny. Why is your name Kat? Is a cat not your favourite animal?'

'My full name's Katerina.' Kat turned to the back of her order pad and printed K-a-t-e-r-i-n-a and then, underneath, K-a-t. 'And my dog's called Angelique. She comes to work with me, but she has to stay in the office. Your daddy has taken her for a walk for me a few times.'

Clémence swung on Noah, eyes wide and enquiring. 'Have you?'

He nodded. 'Kat's brother and I share staff accommodation, here at the park. One day, he'd offered to walk Angelique and couldn't make it, so he asked me to do it for him.'

Clémence's eyes grew round with longing. 'Can I take Angelique for a walk, too? Today?'

'If it's OK with Kat,' Noah said doubtfully. He recognised Clémence was beginning to get fidgety, an incipient sign of what he privately thought might be hyperactivity, but he'd expected her to want full value out of having unlimited access to the rides. 'But we have our wristbands . . .'

Clémence waved the point away. 'I'd like to go on the little train later, but can we walk Angelique, please, Kat?'

Kat shrugged. 'Of course. You'll have to keep her on the lead, though, because the park's busy.' She took their order, waiting patiently while Clémence debated over her choice of sandwich and pastry, then whisked off to carry on her day's work. It was the young girl, Justine, who served them after that, though Noah occasionally caught a glimpse of Kat through the glass shopfront, busy with customers in the book department.

The moment Clémence had finished her lunch, she began to bounce in her seat. 'Can we take Angelique now?'

Noah exchanged glances with Florine, the kind of wordless parental exchange that said, *Kids, huh?* Aloud, he said, 'If you're sure you'd rather do that than the rides, we can. We should be back here by three for the story event, though.'

Florine chimed in. 'I think I'll stay here with another coffee and read.'

206

Noah raised his eyebrows. 'Are you sure?' It felt like a positive development, so he didn't push her on it any further. 'OK. We'll have to go through the café to the office and take the dog through the back door. I'll order your coffee at the same time, Florine.' He rose and Clémence grabbed his hand to tow him, as if she could make him go faster. Inside, he paid the bill at the counter and ordered an espresso to be served to his ex-wife when ready.

Turning away, he caught the eye of Kat, who was ringing up a book purchase. 'OK if we get Angelique now?'

She smiled while her customer fussed with a payment card. 'Sure. She'll be delighted.' She winked at Clémence. 'See you for the story event.' She returned to her work, looking completely at home amongst the clatter and chatter, her dark curls corkscrewing high behind her head, one hand propped on the curve of the hip he'd nibbled last night.

Noah would have liked to press a kiss on her mouth as he passed, but that wasn't exactly appropriate, so he just smiled a slow smile, and watched her blush.

Kat had done everything she could to be ready for the story event. She cast her eye around her domain. A woman at the bookshelves was reading a bestseller with a misty image on the cover that hinted at emotional content – Kat hoped she was going to buy it, sooner or later – and a man was crouched near a bottom shelf, cricking his neck as he tried to read spines. The café tables were still busy but not as full as the height of lunchtime. Justine, Danielle and Romain were serving. Through the glass, Kat could see Florine still sitting at a table, an e-reader in her hands, her coffee cup empty.

Acting on impulse, Kat went out to her, the heat of the sun causing a sudden beading of sweat around her hairline. 'Can I get you another cup of coffee?'

Florine looked up with a smile. Her hair had fallen forward as she read. '*Merci.*' Unexpectedly, she added hesitantly, 'Will you join me? I know so few people in Alsace.'

The expression in Florine's eyes was wistful. Kat checked the time. 'I haven't had a break so yes, I will.'

She scooted back inside, made the drinks and carried them out, taking the seat opposite Florine. 'I'm sorry you haven't made many friends yet. Kirchhoffen is a friendly village. I was recognised in the village shops within a few weeks of moving there.'

Florine raised her steaming cup. 'We have our shopping delivered. My husband likes the convenience.'

'I do that too, sometimes, but the boulangerie and patisserie provide bread and pastries that are nicer than from any supermarket.' Kat hid her impatience at the mention of Yohan's preferences. He didn't have to control every detail of what went on in his household, did he? She was beginning to feel sorry for this willowy woman. When Kat first heard Noah's story of Clémence being moved across the country without his knowledge, she'd thought badly of Florine.

But now . . .

Did she simply not know how to resist an overbearing man? Noah had told Kat that Florine had been brought up with a controlling father so perhaps she'd been trained to expect it. What else had Noah said? That Florine had been 'undocked' by her dad's death? Yohan might have recognised that in her and smoothly 'undocked' her from everything else she knew in her life, too. Kat had read a feature in a magazine about coercive control recently and it did seem that some people could home in on those it was possible to shape. The journalist had utilised case histories to illustrate the different types of control: Alexandre was a steamroller, ordering everything his way with complete disregard for others; Benoit was anxious that if he didn't keep control everything would go wrong; Cybelle was insecure, needing others to show their love by constantly putting her first. The feature had suggested various forms of self-help or counselling for those seeking to escape control but at no time had it suggested 'tell him he's a selfish bastard and refuse to kowtow,' which was how Kat would have treated Yohan.

How could Florine prefer Yohan to Noah?

That question started Kat thinking of the comfortable, familiar manner in which Florine, Noah and Clémence had lunched together, the way Noah had paid for all of them and ordered Florine more coffee on his way out to have some fun with their daughter.

She realised Florine was speaking again. 'We've been out in Strasbourg more than Kirchhoffen, admiring the cathedral and acting like tourists,' Florine said. 'I'm glad you let us know about the book club and the events at Livres et Café because I should like to get out locally while I can. After Clémence is settled at school I'm going to look for a new job.'

They chatted about the local amenities for a few minutes. 'Of course, there's a lovely park in Kirchhoffen too,' Kat said. 'Nothing like Parc Lemmel – just a village park. It has playthings for the children, circuit training equipment and trails in the wooded area. I take Angelique there sometimes.' Obeying another impulse to do something for this isolated woman, she rummaged in her pocket for her order pad and scribbled down her phone number. 'Here – if you fancy coming for a walk sometime, contact me and we'll arrange it.'

Looking surprised but pleased, Florine took the scrap of paper Kat ripped from her pad, murmuring her thanks. Kat wasn't sure whether she'd ever use it but that was up to her.

She was half surprised that Florine hadn't asked again whether Kat had something going on with Noah when the subject of Angelique's walks had come up earlier, but it was really up to Noah whether Florine knew they were seeing each other. He was the one with a stake in that. Just as Florine's upbringing had made her malleable, Kat's upbringing had made her good at fading into the background when required.

It was with almost a feeling of kinship that she said to Florine, 'I'll have to go in for the children's session now but do phone me sometime if you'd like to.'

There was no time for Florine's reply because Clémence burst out from inside Livres et Café, Noah following, his fair hair windblown. Clémence was giggling almost uncontrollably. 'Oh, Angelique was so naughty,' she spluttered. 'She pulled her lead out of my hand and ran right up the slide then jumped on someone's mat and slid down to the bottom!'

Noah was grinning broadly, blue eyes glinting. 'No one seemed cross. The parents of the child whose mat Angelique hitchhiked on asked me to let her do it again so they could video it.' He slid an affectionate hand onto Clémence's shoulder. 'I thought Clémence was going to fall over she laughed so hard. We've settled Angelique back in the office,' he added.

'Thank you. Angelique does love the big slide if she

gets a chance to go on it.' Kat laughed too, but as she hurried in for story time, she reflected on the way Noah's focus was on Clémence – as it should be. Florine, too, seemed a doting parent.

What a lucky little girl.

Chapter Fourteen

The next week was one of unending sunshine. Kat and Noah were able to both get Thursday off and hired a tandem paddle board at a water sports centre on the River Ill to spend the day getting wet and tanned. Angelique stood at the prow like a figurehead, turning to wave her tail at them every time they laughed or whooped as they splashed or wobbled.

On Friday, Livres et Café had once again hosted a successful children's activity where Danielle had led the creation of a group story with the aid of fridge magnets and coloured pens on a whiteboard. Amidst gales of laughter, the children created a story of a mouse who lived in Parc Lemmel and jumped on the rides when nobody was looking. Clémence, who'd come with Florine, told the story of Angelique's adventure on the big slide and the dog was promptly added as the mouse's friend.

Business was so good that Kat added two more part-time assistants to the roster, a student called Frederik and a sixty-something woman, Hilda, who wanted a retirement job. 'I'm not used to being with my husband all day,' she'd mock-grumbled to Kat, '"For better or for worse", yes – but not for lunch.'

Saturday, unfortunately, began badly when people began turning up with vouchers on their phones for free coffee.

Every single person on the mailing list had received one, it transpired, when Kat checked, and the free coffee event had mysteriously appeared on their website calendar. *Bloody Emma!*

Thinking fast, she decided the honour of Livres et Café was more important than admitting they'd been duped and argue with disappointed customers. She decided to treat it like a planned promo, hid the disposable cups and said, 'I'm afraid we're not a takeaway.' It meant everyone with a voucher had to sit down to drink their freebie and most bought snacks to go with the drink and even book sales went up.

Late in the afternoon of a long and tiring day, Kat telephoned Ulrica to confer and was baffled by talk of 'man in the middle' versus 'man in the browser' cyber-attacks and the hacker combining the two. Ulrica promised to install yet another kind of authentication.

Analysing the day's takings afterwards, Kat determined two things: there was no need to bother Graham with this latest blip as they'd been run off their feet all day; if Ulrica couldn't find a way to stop this hacker, then Kat must.

And that meant beginning with Jakey. 'Not a prospect to look forward to,' she told herself aloud, frowning as she swiftly entered the takings on the appropriate spread-sheet. As Angelique was the only other in the room, she obviously decided she was the one being addressed and stood on her hind legs beside the chair to snuffle Kat's neck, which at least made Kat laugh.

Cheering up, Kat read an email from her dad confirming that he and Irina had completed the formalities to leave their current jobs and had asked an estate agent to let their house in the Cotswolds. It would give them a fallback position if they later decided to return to the UK but Howard sounded determined to make the move work. She reread the email, examining her feelings now things were happening. Would having Howard and Irina close help them build bridges? Or would she discover life had been easier without them around?

She gnawed her lip as she fluctuated between the two possibilities.

No conclusions drawn, she closed down the computer, locked up, and she and Angelique strolled over to the staff vans to a barbecue, eating slightly charred burgers and drinking Meteor beer as darkness fell. Angelique heartily approved of the party as people threw her titbits to see her catch them in mid-air.

Noah curled his arm around Kat's waist as they chatted to various members of park staff, who were drawn from many nationalities. Solly adopted a similar pose with Ola, his round face wearing a beatific smile whenever his eyes met her artfully outlined ones behind fashionable statement specs.

Kat enjoyed teasing her brother about Ola, who teased her right back about Noah.

Solly's French was improving, and Kat began to imagine that if Howard and Irina completed their plans to move to Alsace, he'd be an asset to their enterprise. Howard's potential new partner, Phillipe, apparently wanted English-speakers to deal with English-speaking markets, but that wasn't going to work well if those English-speakers couldn't understand what their colleagues said to them in French.

214

As the evening wore on, Kat and Noah settled back on the grass to look at the stars, enjoying the cool of the evening and listening to the buzz of insects alongside the chatter and laughter of humans. Angelique, when discouraged from burrowing between them, snuggled up to Kat's left leg, sighed and went to sleep. Kat told Noah all about the day's 'free coffee' debacle. 'I'm going to have to try and track Jakey down,' she concluded gloomily.

Noah, playing with a lock of Kat's hair with one hand, scrolled around the internet on his phone with the other. 'Trying to find Jakey, Emma and their family on social media or anywhere else online isn't going to be easy without knowing the correct surname. I'm googling their first names with the place "Nanterre" but getting nothing. Maybe they keep their names off the internet.' He turned his head so he could press a kiss on her temple. 'Have you tried Jakey's phone lately?'

'No.' Kat hesitated. 'Of course I have wondered whether the "out of service" message I heard before was a trick and he hasn't changed his number after all. By now, he might be curious enough to answer a call or a text but if Emma monitors his phone, which I think is likely, she'll know I want to talk to him. If it's her behind the cyber-attacks, as I suspect, then it will alert her. No, I've come to the conclusion that I need to meet him in person.'

He propped himself on his elbow so that he could see into her face, his fair eyebrows curling in concern. 'Seriously? How are you going to do that?'

She sighed. 'The only thing I've come up with is to go into Strasbourg to hang around the area Emma said he works. That sounds lame, doesn't it?'

Slowly, he sank back down onto the grass. 'I'd say . . . optimistic.'

Before he could add any more, Kat's phone began to ring. She dragged it out with a sigh and checked the screen. 'Oh. My boss wants to FaceTime.' She sat up and brushed grass out of her hair, her stomach giving an uncomfortable lurch. Had Graham somehow learned of the 'free coffee' trick that had been played on Livres et Café and was calling to give her a bollocking? She fought to look unconcerned as she accepted the call. Then she halted. Next to Graham sat Reeny, pale, as usual, but smiling, almost disappearing into a big white dressing gown. 'Hello, you two,' Kat cried gladly.

'Hello, gal,' Graham said wearily. 'Just checking in. We know we've been leaving everything to you. We're sorry. But with Reeny and my mum both in trouble, it's hard to be interested in anything else.'

'Everything's fine, don't worry,' said Kat, wincing because she knew that, in normal times, they'd want to hear all about the fake coffee vouchers. 'How are things Reeny?' Guilt crept over her that she'd only sent a couple of texts to Reeny in the last few days and allowed herself to be lulled by the equally brief replies she'd received in return.

Graham's long sigh wobbled. It was Reeny who spoke, looking composed compared to Graham, whose thin hair was on end. 'I've been offered a bone marrow transplant.'

'Oh,' Kat breathed. She knew very little about transplants of any kind, but it always sounded like a last resort.

Graham took over. 'They reckon her own's been damaged by the chemo and . . . well, it's her best chance of having a normal life.' He took another wavering breath. 'It's pretty intense. She'll be in hospital three or four weeks then have to stay home and not mix with people.'

'But at the end of it I stand a good chance,' Reeny put in, gazing up at Graham, courageously trying to reassure him.

'Shit,' breathed Kat, her recent supper suddenly sitting uneasily in her stomach.

But Graham hadn't finished. 'Mum—' He paused to clear his throat. 'Mum's going along nicely, considering her age. The device is keeping her heart stable, but it's a hard time for her to be alone. She's being that brave . . .' He had to pause again, and Kat waited, eyes prickling at his distress as Reeny laid her head on his shoulder. What a woman she was. Finally, he managed, 'Our two daughters, they took turns to take a week's annual leave to stay with Mum but now that's up. They both have jobs and their own children. And they must reserve some leave to come here to see Reeny—'

Kat waited a minute, having to wipe her own eyes as Graham gave a little snuffle, obviously fighting tears. Softly, she did her best to reassure them. 'I promise the bank account is in the black. We're having a busy July. Danielle's brilliant, the summer staff are reliable. Just forget about Livres et Café, both of you. Honestly.'

'Thanks, gal,' Graham managed to croak. 'I have got a lot on my plate.'

Kat murmured her sympathy, fighting the wobble in her voice. 'All my love, Reeny. I hope everything goes brilliantly and you'll be on the mend in no time.' After urging Graham to look after himself, too, Kat ended the call. Such an emotional situation must be draining for Reeny.

Noah, who'd remained beside her, encircled her once again in his arms. 'Poor them,' was all he said.

Kat sighed. 'Absolutely.' She used her forearm to wipe her eyes, prompting Angelique to jump up and snuffle anxiously, tail at half-mast. She gave the dog's silky head a reassuring pat. 'This makes me even more determined to get hold of Jakey and make him sort this out. I'm pretty sure all this trouble's coming from Emma. She's a bitch. No offence, Angelique,' she added.

A couple of days later – a Monday – Noah and Kat both had days off. Noah had arranged to spend the afternoon with Clémence, who'd telephoned to request that he bring Angelique.

Noah laughed. 'She's not my dog, sweetie, so how about I invite Kat, too?' As he was having morning coffee in Kat's garden clad only in shorts as he spoke, it seemed only good manners. They'd spent the night together, shutting a disgruntled Angelique in the kitchen as she knew no boundaries when it came to other people's love lives. Kat's bedroom had been a place of naked flesh, exploring hands and gentle caresses, which Noah infinitely preferred to a cold nose, sharp claws and dog breath.

Kat raised an uncertain eyebrow, but Clémence piped, 'But, yes! Maman says two o'clock.'

'Fantastic,' said Noah, and when the call had ended pulled Kat onto his lap to kiss away any doubts she might have. Accordingly, just before two, Kat showed Noah the way to Kirchhoffen Park along the shady tracks through the woodlands. The sun filtered through the branches and the coypu dashed for the safety of the stream as they approached.

They found Florine and Clemence waiting by the climbing frames. After a genial greeting, Florine kissed Clémence goodbye. She looked quite comfortable with the situation and smiled at Kat, but still Kat hovered, feeling anxious and gooseberry-ish, though Noah and Florine had been divorced before this long French summer had begun.

As Florine turned for home, Noah swooped on Clémence

and tossed her in the air. 'We'll have an English-speaking day, today, shall we? Two-and-a-half people here are British, after all.'

Clémence giggled at the idea she could be split in half and clung onto her father's hand after he deposited her back on her feet. She chattered about being invited to Flavie's house to play later in the week. Falling into step beside the pair, Kat noted how relaxed Noah was, grinning at Clémence and swinging her hand.

Over the past weeks he'd revealed himself to Kat as a laid-back guy with a sly sense of humour and a keen way of reading people. He had an inner strength, though. He *seemed* content to let time pass, for now. He *said* he was giving Florine a chance to handle her own life. But he'd told Kat that if matters weren't clearer later in the summer, he'd approach Yohan and tell him everything Noah felt his daughter's stepfather needed to know – and Kat believed him.

Now Clémence turned to Kat. 'Can I play with Angelique? Throw sticks?'

'She'd love to play with you,' Kat said with a smile. 'But I don't throw sticks for her in case she gets one caught in her throat. I have a Frisbee in my bag. Can you throw that?'

'Yes, yes!' Clémence cried, though she proved seconds later that she was best at throwing it behind herself.

'Like this.' Noah took the green plastic disc, curled his arm back and straightened it with a flick. The Frisbee shot through the air and Angelique gave a joyful bark before setting off in hot pursuit, capturing her prey in mid-air with a gymnastic leap.

'*Oui, oui!*' Clémence squealed in excitement. Then, obviously remembering this was an English day, cried, 'Yes, yes. I'll throw it now.'

* * *

And throw it she did, for the next half hour, until both she and Angelique were panting.

'They both need to calm down,' Noah murmured to Kat, though his eyes were brimming with laughter. 'Let's go to the tearoom for drinks and ice-cream.'

Kat was getting overheated just standing out in the sun, so she readily agreed. 'If we take the path back through the woods it'll be shady and Angelique can drink from the stream.'

The next hour passed pleasantly lazily, Angelique snoozing beneath the table at the *salon de thé* as the humans tucked into cold drinks and ice-cream. Kat made sure to take the backseat in the conversation, joining in but never trying to monopolise Noah's attention. Then came the time to take Clémence back to meet Florine in the park.

'I don't know why I couldn't have dropped her at her home, really,' Noah murmured to Kat.

But Clémence demonstrated the acuteness of her hearing by saying, 'Oh, because of the . . .' She frowned. 'I don't know the English. *La surveillance par télévision en circuit fermé.*'

'It's almost the same in English – closed circuit television, or CCTV,' Noah instructed her gently. But Kat saw from his profile that his smile had vanished.

A few minutes later, Clémence caught sight of her mother turning in through the park gates and ran to her across the grass, Angelique gambolling gamely at her heels.

Florine laughed, throwing her arms wide to receive a daughter who was considerably hotter and more dishevelled than when she'd last seen her, listening with all the admiration and fascination an eight-year-old could desire as the little girl recounted the events of her afternoon.

Kat hung back while Noah, Clémence and Florine said their goodbyes.

As they strolled home, Noah was quiet. Kat led the way into the apartment, which was beautifully cool because she'd closed the shutters against the afternoon sun before leaving.

In the kitchen, Angelique lapped noisily from her water bowl and then collapsed onto her 'Kat's Dog' bed with a sigh.

Noah said, 'Mind if I have a beer?'

'Of course not. I'll have one, too.' Kat took two cold bottles of Meteor from the fridge.

Noah took his and leaned his bum against the kitchen units as he frowned into the distance.

Kat opened the French doors to welcome any passing breeze and sipped her beer. 'You OK?' He obviously wasn't but she felt as if he needed encouraging into conversation.

A black frown married his brow. 'I hate knowing Clémence is beginning to see it as normal that I shouldn't go near her home,' he growled. 'At eight years old she knows Yohan will check the CCTV and see who's come and gone in his absence. That's how twats like him work. They "normalise"' – he made air quotes – 'the abnormal. People begin to accept it.' He slapped the table suddenly, making Kat jump. 'It's bullshit! Fucking bullshit, that's what it is.'

Wordlessly, she gave his forearm a sympathetic stroke, feeling the hair on the back of his wrist, soft yet coarse beneath her fingertips.

He gave her a crooked smile. 'You must be sick of my shit.'

'Makes a change from my shit, of which I have plenty,' she answered calmly.

Noah, though he smiled, remained distracted as they moved into the salon to watch a movie. It wasn't until Kat received a text in the middle of the evening and exclaimed, 'It's from Florine,' that he seemed to come out of his deliberations.

'Really?' His eyebrows arched.

She tapped at the screen. 'I suppose I forgot to tell you, but I gave her my number and said she and Clémence could come for a walk with Angelique and me some time. She seems so isolated that I felt sorry for her. Now she's asking if that's possible as Clémence wants to play with Angelique again.'

'Right,' he said slowly.

Kat studied him, trying to gauge how she should approach the next thing on her mind. 'I take it you haven't told her we're . . . seeing each other?'

He expression softened. 'I haven't because I hadn't asked you if it was OK. Also, saying, "Hey, by the way, I'm having a thing with Kat," just out of the blue would feel weird. I'd rather find the right moment.'

She leant her head against his shoulder, enjoying the size and warmth of his body as she searched her heart. 'And if I say, "Hey, by the way, I'm having a thing with your ex-husband," now she's made an overture of friendship, it might make her uncomfortable. What I definitely don't want is to muddy things for you when you're involved in this delicate situation with her and Yohan. It's so recently that Emma screamed at me about being "the other woman" that I'm feeling raw about it.'

His blue eyes clouded. 'You're not "the other woman" because I'm single.'

'I know.' She struggled to order her thoughts. 'I just feel as if one of us taking Florine aside and telling her right

222

now would make me feel that way. Would it be OK to leave it for a bit?' Neither of them knew what the future held. It might be embarrassing to make an announcement as if she and Noah were this whole big thing, when really Noah might disappear from Kat's life as abruptly as he had appeared.

He gathered her into his arms and nuzzled her neck. 'Only if that's what you really want. You're a good person, Kat, you know that?'

She flushed with pleasure, preparing to text a reply to Florine, but said mockingly, 'Yeah, that's why my last boyfriend's girlfriend is trying to make me lose my job.' She made it a joke, but she hadn't forgotten that she still had to do something about that.

As she'd suggested to Noah a few minutes ago, she had plenty of her own shit.

Noah wasn't off on Tuesday, as he needed to pay back the Friday he'd swapped with a colleague over a week ago, so Kat spent the morning outlining a feature to be called *Food, Wine and Nightlife in Alsace* for a train excursions website then went alone to meet Florine and Clémence in the Kirchhoffen park, a tennis ball in her bag for Clémence to throw for Angelique.

When Kat's gaze fell on Florine, she couldn't help wondering if Noah's ex indicated the kind of woman Noah really liked. Florine's shorts were black and tailored with an immaculate matching leather belt. Her sandals were also black leather and her nails glossy red, her smart haircut freshly trimmed. Kat's own shorts were sawn-off jeans with a smiley wearing sunglasses embroidered on the bum. Her nails were short and bare – hygienic when you worked with food. Her hair was long because long hair could go ages without cutting and she liked to wear it casual with elements of wild. Maybe Noah being with Kat was – like the rest of his summer in Alsace – designed to be a short-lived digression from his usual life.

She didn't let any of that show on her face, though. Clémence's laughter rang out as Angelique raced after the ball like a furry, rust-coloured arrow and Clémence raced in her wake.

Initially, conversation between the adults was stilted. Kat asked Florine about her new home and how she liked living in one of *les maisons expérimentales*. Florine told her about the solar-generated power, organic insulation and untreated larch cladding. 'My husband likes it,' she added, as if that was all that was important.

Having, so far, seen little to suggest Yohan was worried about anyone or anything other than himself, Kat suspected it was a compulsion to be on-trend, rather than concern for the planet, that had motivated him to choose an eco-friendly house.

'And you?' Florine asked politely, as they watched Angelique drop the ball at Clémence's feet, tail a blur as she waited for it to be thrown again. 'You must like Kirchhoffen to have left your own country to live here.'

Kat was always ready to wax lyrical about the pretty village and the travels that had led her there. Their conversation became more natural until Florine saw Clémence was pink in the face with exertion and visibly overexcited. To cool down and calm down, they walked through the wood to the *salon de thé*, just as they had with Noah. As they settled at a small table, Kat queried, 'What other plans do you and Clémence have for this lovely summer?'

Mother and daughter sighed in unison, then glanced at each other and laughed. 'It's a quiet summer for us,' Florine said apologetically. 'My husband's taken up with his new job and sometimes even works at the weekend.'

'We left all of our friends behind,' Clémence put in wistfully. Then she glanced at her mum and flushed, as if aware of speaking out of turn. A small frown appeared on Florine's brow, but she stroked her daughter's hair without verbalising whatever thought had put it there.

Kat was in no doubt that Florine loved Clémence but couldn't help suspecting that Florine had noticed Clémence censoring what she said. Wouldn't that make Florine question whether Yohan was the cause and reflect on the damage an overly controlling person could do? Kat said nothing, however, but smiled warmly at the little girl, so pink in the heat yet letting Angelique lean against her bare legs and make her hotter.

Clémence seemed at ease with Kat. 'We rode the little train in the park, Papa and me. We rode twice. The track, it's six hundred and ten millimetres wide and three kilometres long. It's over ninety years old. The locomotive is black and the carriages are red and cream. Dark red. I can't quite remember the English word for dark red.' Her blonde eyebrows knitted together at the bridge of her nose.

'Burgundy or maroon,' Kat supplied, struck by how much detail Clémence had absorbed. 'Probably burgundy is used most. It's funny that the English word is a place in France, but I expect it was named after the colour of Burgundy wine.' An idea occurred to her. 'My brother Solly's friend is one of the drivers of the little train. Her name's Ola. It might be possible for me to arrange for you to ride in the front of the train one day, when she's driving. Would you like that?'

Clémence's eyes almost popped from her head. '*Mais*

oui! But, yes, please, so much.' She sounded breathless with awe.

Kat turned her gaze on Florine, who was smiling at Clémence's excitement. 'Would it be OK if I find out if it's possible? Ola already knows Noah because Solly and Ola are seeing each other. In fact, she knows Noah better than she knows me.'

'But of course. Thank you very much,' Florine responded. Then, to a beaming Clémence, 'You must be patient. Kat will find out but if it's not possible then you must not be upset.'

Clémence nodded, gazing down into her cold drink, already looking woeful at the idea that the treat might not come off. But then she perked up and asked whether she could take Angelique up and down the pavement on her lead. 'If you stay where I can see you,' Florine told her after looking to Kat to check it was OK with her.

When she'd stepped off the decking onto the dusty pavement, Angelique's tail waving gently at the promise of a fresh expedition, Kat turned ruefully to Florine. 'Sorry. I should have asked Ola first and then you, about the train. I don't have children, so I'm not quite used to the best way to deal with them. I hope I haven't set Clémence up for disappointment.'

Florine waved the apology away. 'You're trying to do something nice. I understand. Clémence loves things like the little train and we read its history together on the park website.' Her hair blew forward in the breeze and she stroked it back into place. 'I admire the way you see a possibility and seize it. You are independent, seeing opportunities rather than obstacles. You wander around Europe on your own and settle in a new country. To arrange a treat for a child, it is easy for you.'

226

Kat was surprised by this perspective on herself. 'I suppose I do try and make things happen, but some people would consider that impetuous. As for independent . . . that was expected of me from a young age.'

Francine looked wistful. 'For me it was the opposite.' She changed the subject. 'When's the next book club?'

'Not until 1 August, another couple of weeks away.' When Kat saw Florine's face fall, she added, 'Although we're going to have a social evening for the book club, next week. Will you come?'

Francine dropped her gaze. 'I think so. If it's a convenient evening.'

'I'll send an email when I've checked the date with Mathilde,' Kat answered easily. Inwardly, she translated *If it's a convenient evening* to *I'll have to clear it with Yohan first* but just in case childcare was the issue, she added, 'Children will be invited. Flavie almost always comes to book club and I think perhaps her little sister will be in Clémence's class when they start school.'

Florine looked more interested. 'I think that's true. I took Clémence to play at Flavie's home one afternoon. Thank you for introducing them.'

Kat waved her thanks away, not letting on that the idea for the social event hadn't entered her head until just now, when she'd decided Florine needed a helping hand to get out more, especially if the book club seemed somewhere she felt able to go without Yohan.

Almost as if the thought had conjured him, Kat caught sight of a dark man with black-framed glasses walking towards them up the road, his eyes firmly fastened on Florine. 'Erm . . . is this your husband now?' she queried.

Florine turned to look. 'Why, yes. He must have arrived home early and found us via the phone app.' She gave

Yohan a little wave and called, 'Clémence? Time to go.' She smiled at Kat. 'Enjoy the rest of your day.'

Clémence returned and handed Angelique's lead back. 'Goodbye, Kat. Thank you for lending me your dog.'

Yohan had paused when he saw Florine and Clémence preparing to leave. He gave Kat what might have been a nod of recognition so she nodded back, then watched elegant Florine join him, wafting down the street hand-in-hand with her blonde and beautiful daughter – who just happened to be Noah's daughter, too. Though she disliked Yohan for all the trouble he'd caused, she acknowledged to herself that his wife and stepdaughter seemed happy enough to see him.

Kat was left to take herself off through a couple of village streets to Mathilde's house, which was small, bright and hard to ignore, much like Mathilde herself.

'Come in, come in,' Mathilde cried, beaming when she answered her door and saw Kat.

Kat followed her into an old-fashioned kitchen, where Mathilde took juice from the fridge and poured two glasses for them to carry outside to a swing seat in the shade, providing a dish of water for Angelique. The juice was passionfruit, Kat's favourite. She sipped it contentedly then asked, 'Do you think your daughters might make the back room available one evening next week so that the book club can relax over drinks and snacks?'

Mathilde creased her face into an enormous smile. '*Oui!* The very thing. I will arrange a discount on cake, leave it to me.'

Despite her eager adoption of Kat's idea, Mathilde then needed to discuss it thoroughly and it was an hour before Kat left for home. Instead of continuing to work on the feature she'd left earlier, she emailed the book club members with a colourful invitation to the *salon de thé* for coffee, cake and chat.

It wasn't until she pressed 'send' that Kat wondered at her urge to help Florine. Life would surely be easier if Kat kept her distance from Noah's ex-wife, rather than befriending her and feeling increasing sympathy for her situation.

Chapter Fifteen

Perhaps it was watching other people enjoy themselves on the water all day, but when Noah decided to take Kat on a really nice date, he chose an evening cruise around the waterways of Strasbourg.

A little research told him that a new glass-topped boat had recently come into service. *La Dame du Fleuve* – the Lady of the River – was smaller and prettier than the normal broad, functional tourist barges, and had tables to allow on-board dining rather than seating passengers in rows.

He arranged the treat for the next Monday evening. They'd fallen into the routine of both trying to secure Mondays and Tuesdays as their off-duty days. Now, at the height of summer, the park was open until eight p.m. and sometimes nine, when sunset glittered off the lake. If Noah worked into the evening he didn't begin until eleven a.m. or noon, but Kat frequently worked the entire day. She deserved a treat and Noah hoped Graham would also reward her when he was less overwhelmed by the illnesses threatening his loved ones. Noah knew the fear must be paralysing, but the fact that Kat's employers would still have a business at the end of their tribulations was down to her. She tackled the responsibility and long hours cheerfully, frequently only having time to walk the dog before falling into bed at the end of the day.

That it was Noah she fell into bed with several days each week was a joy, though.

Making love, then sinking into sleep with her in his arms brought him an enormous sense of well-being and . . . well, rightness. Was that even a word? He just knew that her skin against his felt right, sleeping and waking with her felt right, and her strength and sunny nature was right up his street.

Although he'd arrived in Alsace in a state of high anxiety and anger as he searched for Clémence, with a couple of flyers and a timely text, Kat had stabilised his situation. As it looked as if Alsace was going to be where his daughter lived, it was an almost unbelievable piece of serendipity that Alsace was where he now wanted – needed – to be. With Kat.

After a lazy day of sunshine, of picnicking on Kat's lawn on crusty bread, Munster cheese and tomatoes sprinkled with oil and basil before walking Angelique through the shadiest parts of the wood, they spent the rest of the afternoon in the cool atmosphere of her shuttered bedroom – only some of it sleeping. As the beginnings of a purple dusk stole over the sky, they took the tram into Strasbourg and sauntered down to the landing jetty on the softly gliding river spanned by black, wrought-iron bridges edged with a tumbling profusion of flowers.

Kat wore a dress of vibrant red poppies on a muted green background. Her sandals were poppy-red, too, displaying the delicate arch of her foot and her slender ankles. 'I haven't been into Strasbourg for weeks,' she exclaimed as they joined the embarkation queue, her dark eyes glittering more brightly than any of the stars emerging above the River Ill. She gave his arm a squeeze, pressing her soft curves against him. 'Don't the timbered houses and pointy churches look awesome, all illuminated? This is going to be a lovely date.' She kissed him then, just a peck on the lips, but it sent his temperature soaring.

Then, sobering, she added, 'I have to come in again tomorrow to try and hunt down Jakey.'

Noah hated the way the joy faded from her eyes. 'You want company for that expedition?' The queue began to move and they stepped onto the sloping wooden ramp that led down to the landing stage. A pleasantly cool breeze caressed their skin.

She wrinkled her nose at the vegetable smell of river water. 'I think it's something I have to do alone. If Jakey catches sight of you he'll think I've brought a minder and run away. If I see him at all, which seems, as you said before, optimistic,' she added.

He frowned. It was their turn to board. With a smile of thanks Kat accepted the helping hand of a crew member, a guy in navy shorts and a white shirt. Noah grasped both handrails and swung himself aboard behind her. A smiling girl in the same shorts and shirt showed them to a small square table at a port-side window that reflected the gleaming glassware and cutlery.

When they were settled, Kat leaned over the table to continue the conversation. 'Also, Jakey doesn't like to lose so he's quite capable of sulking if he gets any hint we're together. Then my chances of a conversation will be down the toilet. If you fancy taking Angelique for the day, though, I'm sure she'd love you forever.'

Her words hit him like a blow in his stomach. *Love you forever* . . . He imagined her saying those words to him one day, just before that delectable, smiling mouth came down on his. Words spilled from him before he could consider their wisdom. 'I'm more interested in how her owner feels about me.'

Kat's eyes widened.

Other passengers brushed past on their way to their own tables, and a female host distributing menus paused at their table to welcome them aboard and ask whether either of them were vegetarian or vegan. Would they be taking wine? Should she bring water? Or perhaps they'd like a sparkling wine aperitif while they perused the menu? The boat would be leaving the quay in a very few minutes. Their captain this evening was Jean-Marie, experienced both on river and canals. The cruise would take approximately two-and-a-half hours, carrying them through the quaint Petite France District, the statelier German Quarter and past the European Parliament Building.

Though he smiled in response, Noah cursed the interruption and his stupidity for plunging into an important conversation amongst the bustle of departure. His nerves zinged while they chose a sparkling wine aperitif and accepted menus but when the helpful woman finally moved on to the next table, he reached over the table to stroke Kat's arm. Ruefully, he said, 'I planned this evening with the idea of instigating a romantic conversation. Now I'm thinking it might have gone better in the privacy of your garden, even with Angelique panting hot breath all over us.'

Her eyes were still big and round, her lips half parted. The soft thrum of idling engines rose and the boat rocked as they were pushed off from the quay. The crew led the

233

passengers in applause to mark the beginning of a special evening. Some of the city's oldest timbered buildings towered over their glass roof just before they slid beneath the first black-painted bridge, its iron wrought in a dozen lacy patterns.

Kat made to speak but a young guy bustled up to place a flickering faux candle on their table. Her eyes began to dance and she giggled. 'Perhaps we should select from the menu to pre-empt the next crew member who dashes up to interrupt us.'

He relaxed. Trust Kat to remove the tension from the situation with a well-timed giggle. 'It won't take long. There are only two starters and desserts and three main courses. The galley on a boat this size can't be too ambitious.' He chose pâté, fish and *fromage blanc tart*; Kat went for *salade Alsacienne*, chicken and *torche aux marrons*, a dessert of chestnut cream and meringue. He ordered a bottle of rosé. A young guy took their order, screeching to a halt at their table seconds later like Road Runner to inform them that, regrettably, that particular rosé was not available this evening. Would they care to choose again? Noah said tersely, 'As there's only one other rosé, we'll have that.'

Kat sniggered, rubbing her bare knee against his beneath the table. 'I thought you were going to bite him when he came back.'

His heart swelled and he took her hand. 'I don't think I've known another woman like you. Do you *ever* complain about anything?'

The laughter in her eyes faded but she spoke lightly enough. 'Complaining doesn't change much. However, you might recall that when we first met, I was hissing like a dud firework at the situation Jakey had put me in.'

234

He didn't want to let Jakey intrude into this evening any more than he already had, so when their sparkling wine arrived, he took the opportunity to clink glasses. Around them, the chatter rose as people pointed out landmarks, and then the PA chimed in, droning a commentary about the canals and covered bridges of Petite France, first in French and then in English. Seizing his chance as the PA clicked off again, Noah leaned towards Kat and finally said what was on his mind. 'How would you feel if I stayed in Alsace?'

He was rewarded by a blaze of pleasure in her eyes, but she replied guardedly. 'If Clémence is settled here, then I could see why you'd want to do that.'

He ignored a couple from one of the tables down the centre of the boat standing up and craning too close to their table, intent on viewing something on the shore. 'But leaving Clémence aside, despite her being the reason I'm here. I wish . . .' He stumbled, face reddening, aware he'd been about to say, 'I wish to know your feelings' like some posh git from a bygone age. He paused for breath. 'On our first date, nearly a month ago, I didn't know what we were starting. I liked the region but still felt as if my life was back in the Dordogne, where I've lived for twenty-odd years. I was still grappling with the idea of somehow reversing the stupid situation Florine's got herself into.' His voice became husky. 'I'd no idea how fast that would change; that I'd want to stay near you and try for something lasting. I've tried to imagine going back to my rented apartment in the Dordogne without you, and . . .' He gave a little shake of his head. 'Even though my old life is there . . .' He ran his knuckle down the incredible softness of her cheek. 'You're here,' he ended simply.

Her dark hair curled around her face and down onto

shoulders bared by her summer dress and when her eyes softened, she almost stopped his heart with her beauty. 'Really?' she whispered. She cleared her throat. 'I thought . . .' She looked unsure.

'What?' He squeezed her hands as if he could encourage her response.

She licked her lips. Then her eyes dropped. 'It's just that I look at Florine and I can't believe how different we are. She's so chic with her stylish clothes and hair, so willowy she could make it on the catwalk. I'm kinda . . . messy.'

He laughed. 'You're not messy,' he contradicted firmly. 'You're spontaneous, glorious, warm, colourful and very much yourself.' He hesitated when Kat didn't smile or look relieved. Was she really troubled as to whether he was genuinely attracted to her?

Hoping that no helpful crew member would pick that moment to begin rearranging cutlery or flapping out napkins ready for the first course, he brought his head so close to hers that even in the candlelight he could pick out the exact point where her large pupil met her slightly less dark iris. 'Florine and I are over,' he said firmly, aware he'd said it before but feeling that Kat needed to hear it until she believed it. 'But when we were together, she wore pretty dresses and her hair was a softer style. If she was with a mountaineer, she'd wear snow suits; if she married a garden gnome, she'd buy a pointy hat and carry a fishing rod. She tries to be whatever the man she's with wants her to be.' He ducked forward far enough to press a kiss on the corner of Kat's mouth. 'Florine's not important to me. I think about you all the time. I'm happy when I'm with you. And in bed . . . you already know you drive me crazy.'

She did manage a smile at that, but it wasn't the fulsome, excited beam he'd hoped for.

The first course arrived and Kat picked up her fork but didn't begin her multi-coloured salad.

Noah ignored his own plate, feeling it far more important to convince Kat of his sincerity. 'I care about you. I want to be near you. I know I'd never have come to the region if not for Clémence,' he added fairly. 'But now I'm here, Clé's here and I've met you, I'm happier than I've been for years.'

Her smile grew at that. 'So am I. I care about you, too.' Then the light in her eyes dimmed. 'What about your parents? They're used to you and Clémence living in the same area as them.'

He felt a tug at his heart. 'They were disappointed when I told them on the phone that I'm not bringing Clémence back to Castillon,' he agreed. 'But they travel a lot since they retired and families relocate all the time, as they did themselves. Their other children and grandchildren live in the UK. At least Clémence and me will stay in France.'

'Oh,' she said, looking almost shy. 'Well. You've taken me by surprise.'

He caressed her bare calf with his. 'Good surprise? Or bad?'

She caressed his calf back. 'Good.' She sucked in a deep breath and then let it out on a rush of words. 'But I'm scared that if we start making plans it'll jinx it. Yohan will find out you're here and move Clémence somewhere else. Then you'll have to leave.'

A beautifully illuminated Strasbourg was sliding slowly past them almost unnoticed. Other passengers craned between mouthfuls, pointing out particularly beautiful buildings to each other or leaping up to take photos. The PA had been piping up periodically about the *Ponts Couverts* or covered bridges, cobblestone streets and narrow alleys, the sixteenth-century Tanners' House and seventeenth-century bridge and dam. Noah had been half aware of it all going on but was too focused on the woman in front of him to care.

He snatched up her hand, almost dipping his forearm in his sauce vierge. 'If that's worrying you then I've obviously let things drift for too long,' he murmured. 'I'll go and see him. I'll explain the law and what I'm going to do if he tries the same trick again. I'll tell him that I'm a fixture in the area and we'll be setting up a proper schedule of visitation for Clémence. I'll look for a permanent job – maybe with one of the Rhine cruise companies – and give notice on my old job. I am here to stay, Kat.'

Her eyes turned suspiciously moist at she gazed at him, looking gorgeous in the candlelight with the lights of the city behind her. 'Really?'

'Really,' he confirmed.

She let out a long, wavering sigh. 'Maybe everything will be OK. You'll sort out Yohan, I'll sort out Jakey.'

He took that as a result, putting down her initial reticence to her being taken by surprise. She'd always struck him as so fearless, but she genuinely seemed worried that they could 'jinx' their happiness by embracing it too readily. But if she cared for him, as she said, then all he had to do was show her that happiness was theirs for the taking.

They settled down to enjoying the tasty food and beautiful evening, tentatively talking about a shared future.

Chapter Sixteen

The idea of tracking down Jakey by hanging around the area where he worked evoked the words 'needle' and 'haystack' in Kat's mind. If she hadn't needed to contact her one-time infatuation, he would be firmly consigned to memories labelled, 'Who?' or 'What on earth was I thinking?' or 'How facile, in comparison to what I'm feeling now.'

All she really wanted to think about was yesterday evening's cruise around the waterways of Strasbourg, when Noah had told her he cared about her. The way he'd set about the conversation had been so typical of him. Straight-talking, kind, unafraid and yet sexy and hot.

Wow. She was still reeling, hardly daring to hope. Loads of people her age would have been married twice and had kids by now but somehow it hadn't happened for Kat. She'd been filled with happy disbelief when they'd agreed they were 'together', and that Noah wanted to remain in Alsace. He'd been so certain, so positive that Yohan wouldn't manage to upset any plans they made that she'd accepted the idea that her fears were groundless . . . at least on the outside. Inside, she couldn't help recalling the way Florine and Clémence had jumped up to join Yohan the instant he appeared outside the *salon de thé* and felt a thread of worry that it wouldn't be as easy as Noah thought.

At least her doubts weren't about her feelings for Noah. Last night, when they'd returned to her place, had been incredible, the lovemaking gentle and tender one moment then fast and joyous the next. Noah had finally left her this morning only when he grudgingly accepted that she really wasn't going to let him accompany her to Strasbourg on the Jakey hunt. He'd sighed and said, 'Suppose I'd better go and get my damned laundry done, then,' before driving off. Kat had had her own chores to do, too, hence only just setting out, a couple of hours behind him.

Her heart did the salsa and she gave Angelique a big hug. 'Lucky you to spend the day with Noah while I go on what's probably a wild goose chase after Jakey – if geese chase snakes, that is.' Angelique wriggled free, wanting only to get into the car and embark on whatever the journey brought.

Kat laughed and opened the hatchback for Angelique to bound into. Soon her little Citroën was bowling out of the village towards Muntsheim. Glorious early sunshine brightened the dusty green of crops growing in the fields and the yellows of wildflowers in the verges. She sang along to her favourite playlist and Angelique contributed the occasional 'woof' as if she were the percussion.

Inside the park, Kat slowed to the required sedate pace and drove to the staff accommodation, where they'd agreed she'd leave her car. Her heart gave a hop. 'Don't be ridiculous,' she scolded herself under her breath. 'Noah only left you a couple of hours ago.' But her heart continued to hop at the idea of seeing him again, adding in a skip and a jump for good measure.

She took the dusty track towards the green park home that stood amongst the others and drew to a halt on the patch of grass behind Noah's big grey vehicle and Solly's jaunty old scooter. Most units were shut up as it was nearly ten and many staff members who weren't on their rest days would be in the park, ready for the public to descend. Noah and Solly's door stood open, though, and Noah, clad in a pair of shorts, stepped through it to greet her, blonde hair damp from the shower, golden hair spangling his chest.

Kat jumped out and drew in her breath. 'Trying to tempt me, huh?'

His smile was hot and slow as he waggled a suggestive eyebrow. 'Your brother's in his room but we could be quiet.'

'Maybe later,' she grinned, approaching the back of the car to release Angelique, who bounded out and up the four steps to fawn at Noah's feet.

'Hey, Ange,' he murmured, giving her a fuss that sent her into doggy paroxysms of delight. 'If we're lucky, Florine might bring Clémence over to walk with us this afternoon.'

Kat pulled out Angelique's bed, bowls and food and shut the hatchback. 'That sounds great. Tell them both hello from me.'

Noah jumped down the steps, Angelique frisking around and barking as if sure his action signalled some great new game, which, naturally, would include her.

But Noah's attention was all on Kat. He drew her into his arms, blue eyes intent. 'My plan is to try and grab a few words with Florine today. Tell her that I'm going to sort things out with Yohan.'

Kat's stomach felt funny. 'Will it frighten her, do you think?' The underlying lost child she'd detected in Florine had loomed large in Kat's imagination.

His brows drew down. 'I hope not. I'm satisfied that Yohan's controlling, not abusive, or I would have got Clémence out of there long before this.' He paused, then kissed her. 'Sorry. That came out a bit sharp, didn't it? Maybe I'm tenser than I'd realised.'

She kissed him back, feeling his stubble brush her lips. 'I understand. It's tricky.'

'Yeah,' he agreed. He contemplated her, drawing in a breath as if ready to speak but trying to gather his thoughts. Finally, he said, 'How do you feel about me not telling Florine about us until I've got Yohan sorted? I think they ought to be two separate conversations.'

She snuggled into his body. 'I don't mind.' She gave a small laugh. 'To be honest, I still feel a bit guilty. She's a nice woman and you have a child together . . .' She tailed off.

Noah pulled back sharply to frown at her. 'I don't want you to feel guilty or like a secret I'm ashamed of. Maybe I should tell her today after all. I don't see why it should make any difference to her, anyway.'

Doubtfully, she pulled back. 'You don't have to.'

But evidently Noah had made up his mind and turned his attention to kissing her instead. Eventually, she had to come up for air. 'I need to catch the tram.'

'Sure I can't come along?' He nuzzled her neck.

'I'm sure it wouldn't go well with you there. He'd pout, despite the way things ended between us and the family he conveniently forgot.' She tilted her head, relishing the tingles that spread through her body.

A few kisses later she left, heading across the park on

foot towards the main road that would take her to the nearest tram stop. She was just approaching the dully gleaming rails sunk into the asphalt when she heard her name called. When she turned, she saw Solly loping up behind her.

'Hey,' he said insouciantly. 'What are you up to? I'm getting the tram into the city.'

She regarded him narrowly. 'Did Noah send you?' She could imagine Noah, refused permission to ride shotgun himself, slipping Solly into the role, knowing Jakey could hardly object to the presence of a brother.

His eyes grew wide, though a smile lurked. 'Noah? Why would he do that? I want to buy new T-shirts and boxers and stuff. He can buy his own. Are you shopping, too? You can show me some cool places. Are there any markets?'

'Most of the markets are on Wednesdays, not Tuesdays,' she answered slowly. 'Or maybe you should wait for the market in Muntsheim on Saturday.'

'Have you ever tried to get a Saturday or Sunday off from Parc Lemmel?' he demanded reasonably.

He had her there. Whether Noah had interceded or not, she could hardly forbid her brother to get on the same tram as her and it wasn't long before they were whooshing out of town, through villages and past gardens, rocking gently with the motion as they whizzed closer to the suburbs and the scenery became gradually more built up. Solly was in high good humour and didn't ask again what she was doing but recounted an exasperating phone conversation with his mum, Irina, instead.

'Honestly,' he complained. 'She calls me up, I'm knackered after working till eight and trying to chill with a beer, and she starts asking me all kinds of things about living in France. I keep saying, "You should ask Kat. I've hardly

243

been here two months yet." So, she asks me something different and my answer's the same.'

Kat snorted. 'She won't ask me. Not when asking is an excuse to call you.' Then, remembering she was talking about his mum and that no matter how annoying Kat found Irina, Solly loved her, added, 'She worries about you.'

It was Solly's turn to snort. 'Most of the time her "worries" are just excuses to talk to me, even though I've told her it's fine just to call me to chat.'

Obviously, Solly had more insight into his mother than Kat had realised. Curiously, she asked, 'From Dad's emails, he and your mum are well along the road to coming to live in Alsace. Will it work for you? You've pretty much said you'll join their new company, haven't you?'

Solly nodded, meeting her level gaze. 'I'm not settled into anything permanent here, like you are. I think it could be good for me and help me grow up.'

But, only ten minutes later when they alighted beneath the glass circle at the *L'Homme de Fer* terminus, and she tried an experimental, 'OK, guess I'll see you later,' she found he'd rediscovered his childhood.

He grinned irrepressibly. 'Dad said you're my big sis, so I've got to stay with you.'

She planted exasperated fists on her hip. 'Noah did send you, didn't he?'

Solly sobered, taking his hands out of his pockets and laying them gently on her shoulders, disregarding the crush of people jostling past. 'No, he didn't. He told me about your mission today and I decided to come after you. This Jakey's shown himself to be an untrustworthy prick, so I don't think you stalking him alone is a good idea. If you find him, I'll hang back a bit while you talk, if you want, but I'm not abandoning you then worrying all day.'

Unexpectedly, Kat felt tears gather hotly at the backs of her eyes. She would probably have taken a similar stance if it had been Danielle or Reeny going off to confront a man alone, but she was unprepared for how it made her feel to know that Solly wanted to look out for *her*. Also, more of Solly's company would be great. Since he'd come to Parc Lemmel, they'd become closer, but between them getting different days off, Solly seeing Ola and Kat seeing Noah, she hadn't spent an entire day with him. In fact, they probably hadn't spent an entire day together since his sixth birthday, when he'd chosen Alton Towers as his birthday treat. Even then, he'd mainly held the hand of either Irina or Howard and Kat had only come into the picture when Solly had wanted a companion on a ride that Irina or Howard had felt beneath their dignity. The twelve years between the siblings hadn't been enough to make Kat mind sitting in oversized teacups or undersized cars while Solly squealed and whooped.

Now Solly was an adult, a bit of a scamp but a good guy, and he'd given up his day off to make sure she was OK. The thought warmed her from her toes up. She abandoned her arguments. 'I think we should start at the European Parliament buildings. If we take the E line tram it'll save us a twenty-minute walk.'

After that short tram journey, they alighted in sight of the *Parlement Européen*, with its distinct glass tower. Glancing around as they disembarked, Kat felt like an idiot as she surveyed not just an ant-like population filling every pavement but traffic-filled streets in all directions, many edged by trees. And, behind the parliament building itself . . . a great expanse of flowing water. 'Crap,' she groaned. 'I assumed that wherever he works would be near this tram stop but the River Ill and the Marne-Rhine Canal intersect here. He could be based the other side of the water and still be near the parliament buildings. They're vast.' She'd been able to see them from the boat last night but hadn't exactly been paying attention. Now she saw that it might take the rest of her life to happen on a company that might prove to be Jakey's employers. 'Needle in a haystack' had been understating the magnitude of the search.

'I don't think well when I'm hungry,' Solly announced, rubbing his stomach. 'We passed a café back there. Let's get something to eat.'

One more look at the teeming traffic and flood of pedestrians and Kat's shoulders slumped. 'Might as well.'

They retraced their steps as far as Solly's café. He wolfed four pastries and Kat nibbled a *pain au chocolat* and sipped coffee while Solly consulted his phone, googling all kinds of combinations of words, in both French and English, that he hoped might provide a starting point for their search.

Kat was just beginning to appreciate the mixture of creativity and logic in Solly that had produced a first in computer science, when he sat back, looking disgusted. 'This is rubbish. Tell me more about this moron. I only met him for a few seconds.'

Kat sighed. 'He was a lying git so nothing I remember can be relied upon.' Hoping for some little fact that might inspire them, she began to recite the routine she and Jakey had fallen into – but then halted in horror, her hand clapped to her head.

'What?' demanded Solly.

Kat groaned. 'This is Tuesday. What was I thinking?' At Solly's mystified expression she tried to explain. 'His imaginary "work" was supposedly based around a kart track but his real-life job must involve a rotation or shift pattern placing him in Strasbourg from Wednesdays to Sundays, every other week, because he spent Monday and Tuesday with me – which he must have persuaded Emma were working days.'

'The lying shit,' Solly put in helpfully. 'So, even if he still works in this area, it wouldn't be today?'

'Exactly.' She gulped the rest of her coffee in morose silence, barely noticing the rich liquid in its smooth porcelain cup. Solly returned to messing around on his phone.

'What,' he said slowly, 'if he really was at a kart track part of the time? Not all that bollocks about managing young karters, but going karting himself? It would explain how he had enough basic knowledge to come up with the fantasy about sports management. There are only three kart tracks around Strasbourg. It wouldn't hurt to check them out.'

'I suppose . . .' Kat took her brother's phone and frowned over the list of kart tracks he'd pulled up, along with their locations. The third one sent a jolt through her as if a door had flown open in her mind. 'Fegersheim! It's on the correct side of the city.' She met Solly's dark-eyed gaze, so much like her own. 'There are direct bus links between Muntsheim, Kirchhoffen and Fegersheim. That would explain how he turned up at the park that last day. His plans didn't work out for some reason and he needed to pick up the tram line to Strasbourg's mainline station so he thought he might as well call in on me to . . .' She broke off, deciding not to say, 'get some sex' to her brother.

Solly looked puzzled. 'He travelled to Strasbourg by train, not car?'

'Driving's slow and stressful and parking's an expensive nightmare. It would take longer to drive, too, from Rennes.

247

Or Nanterre, if Emma's to be believed,' Kat corrected herself, remembering that Rennes seemed to be part of the whole Jakey fantasy.

Appetite returning with a rush, she ordered more pastries – she'd eat healthily tomorrow – and pored over the kart track website, searching out likely pages for patrons to be mentioned, which seemed confined to the intra-club league tables. No sign of a Jakey or a Jacques. Kat sighed in disappointment. 'Seems as if entrants assume a username or use their surname, so that's no help.' She did check for 'Marsaud' in case Jakey was using his mother's maiden name for karting as well as for duping innocent women into giving him a side-order of sex, but there was no such entry.

Solly, meanwhile, had been studying how the circuit operated. 'Each session lasts eight minutes, starting on the hour, leaving time between for safety stuff and changeover. It's eighteen euros a session, or three for forty-seven euros.'

She craned her neck to view his screen. 'To use three sessions, you'd have to be there half the day?'

He shrugged. 'That's what it looks like. There's a bar and games room so I should think you could while away any downtime happily enough.'

Kat stared through the window at the cylindrical tower of the European Parliament, which always looked half finished to her, rising above buildings and treetops. 'Every other week, he arrived on a Monday morning and stayed at my place until the following Sunday evening. During that period, he was supposedly "at the circuit" during the day Wednesday to Sunday managing young, up and coming karters.'

Solly, who seemed to have at least some grasp of motor sport, objected. 'This track looks like a club. I don't think there would be any championship rounds held there.'

'I think we've established that he built a fantasy world,' Kat said drily, neither knowing nor caring how championships worked. 'But say his real-life work pattern was Wednesday to Saturday, one week in Nanterre and one week in Strasbourg – or one week with his family and one with me, in effect. Changeover day would be Sunday, so that was probably his day off. He'd spend it having fun at the kart track while Emma looked after the kids, then go home pretending he'd just finished work.'

Leaving Solly writing this on a napkin to check he followed it, she browsed the karting website noting phrases that had littered Jakey's conversation. *Latest generation karts . . . bioethanol . . . safe and eco-responsible driving . . . timed practice.* Could this karting place be the link to finding him again?

She drained her coffee cup. 'It may be clutching at straws but it's all I've got. I'm going to check out this kart track place.'

Solly put away his phone. 'Lead on.'

They travelled back to Muntsheim on the tram, using the forty-minute journey to conjure up – and usually discard – various fibs they might tell about why they were looking for Jakey but didn't know his surname. Solly wanted them to be undercover detectives; Kat suggested they pretend he'd won a big cash prize. Both seemed far-fetched and unlikely to stand up to scrutiny. At last, they agreed on a story: Kat had been commissioned by Jakey to make something for Emma's birthday but had lost all her contacts when drunken friends had thought it a hilarious prank to delete them. 'I'll act like a vague, artistic type,' Kat declared, and tied a bandana in a knot above one ear to make her hair spring out in what she thought might be a bohemian manner.

They hurried from the tram stop, cutting a diagonal line across the park to pick up Kat's car. The van was closed up and silent, so Noah was obviously out. Kat wondered whether he'd been able to arrange to see Clémence. Was she paddling about happily in a kayak so Noah and Florine could talk over how they were going to manage Yohan? She pulled herself up. They each had things to sort out. He had to deal with Florine and Yohan and she had to deal with Jakey, and that's what she should focus on.

With Solly navigating via his phone map, they drove for a quarter of an hour to an area south of Strasbourg. Fegersheim itself Kat knew to be a pretty town with the same colourful timbered buildings as the rest of the area, but the kart track proved to be in the extensive commercial zone near a soccer park. Heart thumping uncomfortably, she parked, and they entered a large, industrial-looking building, brightly lit and smelling of machinery.

Pretending her French was poor, Kat blagged her way past the front desk by saying her brother thought he might want some sessions for his birthday and they just wanted a look around. She pretended to be impatient with Solly and said she didn't think they'd be long.

The guy behind the desk was the right age to be a student on a summer job. He didn't look confident to argue with Kat and, with a queue of people waiting for his attention, said, 'Go to the bar. There's a viewing area.'

Kat was fine with that. It would no doubt be impossible to get near the actual track without paying for sessions and learning to kart, which did not appeal. They followed signs to the bar along an echoey grey corridor, then took a flight of metal stairs to a huge room with one glass wall overlooking the circuit. The track itself was more attractive than Kat had anticipated, like a small, smooth road that had been gently squeezed around and in on itself so that corners came thick and fast between the barriers. Blue and pink uplighters created columns of light, prettifying the concrete block walls. As they watched, white-helmeted figures appeared, clambering aboard small, metallic green vehicles arranged two-by-two which formed, Solly told her, 'the grid'.

'They look like the bumper cars at the park,' she commented, seriously wondering why people would bother.

Karters clutched steering wheels with gloved hands. Staff members in blue shorts and tops walked between the karts, checking safety harnesses. Then most stepped off the track, just one remaining to release each karter in turn to buzz off towards the first corner. 'They're quieter than the bumper cars,' Kat admitted. 'I always thought motor sport was about screaming engines. These things just whoosh.'

'Electric karts,' Solly explained. 'It does seem weird that the tyre noise is the loudest sound.' He remained at the glass along with a dozen other people, watching the session get underway. Some spectators looked as if they might be the parents of karting kids on a school holiday treat but others clustered together earnestly, driving imaginary steering wheels to illustrate their conversation.

Kat turned to survey the room. At the back, a long bar offered refreshments. A fifty-something guy served, assisted by a young woman, while a young man cleared the many occupied tables. 'Got room for another coffee?' Kat asked her brother as she began to move in the direction of the bar.

He glanced around with a grin. 'I've room for a beer.'

It did sound attractive, and they sold Meteor *sans alcool*, she saw, which would do for her, both for driving and keeping her wits about her. She ordered, then hopped up on a stool. The fifty-something guy brought her drinks. As she paid, she took a bold line. 'Have you seen Jakey here today?'

'Jakey?' He looked blank as he tore the receipt off the card reader and passed it to her.

She kept to the same expectant tone. 'Everyone here knows Jakey, don't they? He comes here so much.' Leaning closer over the matte black counter that contrasted with the stainless-steel coffee machine and gleaming glass bottles, she gave a rueful smile. 'I've got to find him because I'm in a mess over his Emma's birthday present. He commissioned me to make a piece of jewellery for her.' She gave him the drunken friends story, adding a tearful catch to her voice. 'Some joke! They're costing me my business.'

Solly arrived beside her and picked up his beer. Playing the role they'd selected for him, he growled, in English, 'If you had any business sense, you'd have your contacts backed up and then I could have restored everything for you.' He shook his head and addressed the man. 'My sister's crazy.'

The man just gazed at him, not giving away whether he'd understood the English or not, though Solly pointing to Kat when he said 'sister' and his head when he said 'crazy' probably provided some clues.

Kat glared at Solly then dragged out her phone to show the barman a photo. 'This is Jakey. Everyone knows him here, don't they? Is he here today?'

The man glanced at the photo but shrugged. 'People keep their business private.'

Damn.

'Told you no one would help,' Solly said with faux triumph.

Kat made her lip wobble. 'But I'm going to lose out on so much money – the materials and all those hours.'

The man spoke with the tiniest hint of sympathy. 'But he must have your details? He will contact you, perhaps.'

Kat sniffed. 'That's what I'd been hoping, but . . .' She lifted supplicating hands. 'He hasn't yet. It's Emma's birthday on 2 August. We're running out of time.'

The man shrugged in what might have been apology then moved off to serve someone further down the bar. The female server hurried past with her hands full of coffee mugs. Kat turned to Solly mournfully. 'That didn't go well.'

Then the younger guy, the one who'd been industriously wiping a nearby table, spoke up. 'Jakey only comes on Sundays. I'm often in the same sessions.' He smiled modestly as they spun on their stools to regard him. 'We like to compete to win the record of the month. We're both in the Experts league.'

Kat's skin prickled. *Yes!* This younger guy apparently had a lot less discretion than his boss. 'Oh, thank you, thank you,' she babbled, trying hastily to organise her thoughts to capitalise on this unexpected lead.

Solly was ahead of her. 'Wow,' he said admiringly. '*Qui est . . . qui est le victoire . . .*' He turned to Kat, saying in English, 'I can't think of the phrase. Ask him which of them is winning this month.'

The guy smirked. '*C'est moi.*' He took out his phone and pulled up the league tables Kat had searched through earlier and switched to English for Solly. 'Here's my name at the top with a lap time of 30.866 seconds. My racer name is "Lucsi" because my name is Jean-Luc Simon. And Jakey, he is "LeBarbier", with 30.962. I beat him by a tenth.' He beamed, obviously expecting them to appreciate the achievement.

'Wow,' Solly breathed, looking positively starstruck. 'And what does "LeBarbier" mean?'

'"The Barber",' Kat stuck in, then worried that she should have let the two young guys talk while she listened.

But Jean-Luc plainly wanted to be the one to enlighten this overimpressed young Englishman. 'Jakey is Jacques Barbier,' he told Solly. Then, to Kat, 'Yes, it means "the barber", in English, but Barbier is also Jakey's name, of course.'

'Of course,' she agreed, because clearly someone executing a commission for him would already have known that. Her heart began to chug like a train. 'But I haven't been able to find him online. I suppose it's because his work is sensitive.'

He nodded. 'I believe so.'

'And Emma's, too,' she said, blindly feeling her way but desperate to find out everything she could. She laughed. 'She intimidates me with her knowledge of computers and mothering two daughters, as well. She's *so* clever.'

Solly snorted. 'You can hardly work a phone, dear sister, so you're probably impressed by anyone who can design a website.'

'But, no,' Jean-Luc protested, jumping earnestly to Kat's defence. 'She is right. Emma is a computer security expert. Her job is to test the computer security of organisations and tell them what they need to fix.' He lowered his voice. 'Government contracts. She has very high qualifications from university.'

Solly rocked back on his heels, assuming an expression of awe. 'She sounds like what we call an ethical hacker, or a "white hat hacker". I'm an IT teacher, so I know a bit about it.'

'Really?' Kat breathed, drawing out the word but thinking that there was nothing ethical about what Emma had done. She would rather call it criminal. 'Then she must need a very white hat to hold down a job like that. Whiter-than-white, in fact.'

'Just what I was thinking,' said Solly grimly, his eyes triumphant as they met Kat's.

'Thank you very much for helping me find Jakey, Jean-Luc.' Kat gave him her most grateful smile. Almost holding her breath, she took out her phone and poised an expectant finger over the screen. 'I'm to send the gift to his mother, Mme Marsaud, as she lives so close to him and Emma,' she said, dredging up information Emma had let slip in her rant. 'Obviously, he doesn't want it sending to their own home in case Emma opens it and the surprise is spoilt. If you can just give me his number, I can get his mother's address.'

Jean-Luc hesitated only momentarily. Then he smiled good-naturedly. 'I would not want to upset Emma.'

'Not for the world,' said Kat as she tapped the number into her contact list, thinking she'd like to do the opposite. She glanced at the number, which was, indeed, not the one she used to have for Jakey, stowed her phone and finished her beer with a satisfied slurp. 'This will be such an immense thing to Jakey, Jean-Luc.' No lie there. 'Thank you.'

'Yeah, thanks, mate,' Solly said, clapping Jean-Luc on his shoulder and then lowering his voice. 'That old guy's looking over here. Probably better get back to work.'

Jean-Luc hastily began polishing tables again. '*Merci.*' The two young men grinned at each other conspiratorially.

Kat couldn't get out of the building and into the car quickly enough, dialling as she went. 'I don't want Jean-Luc to decide he'd better warn Jakey he's just given his number out.' She clamped the phone to her ear as she slipped into the driver's seat, turning the ignition in order to get the benefit of the air con.

The single ringtone of France sounded in her ear. *Brurr . . . brurr . . . brurr.*

Then the line opened but it was a woman's voice that answered. '*Allo? Oui?*'

For half an instant Kat froze. Solly's eyes had grown round, as he obviously caught that the speaker wasn't Jake.

'*Allo? Oui?*' came again, but with impatience . . . and maybe suspicion?

Quickly, Kat went to speaker phone so Solly could hear everything. 'Hello, Emma,' she said silkily. 'This is Katerina Jenson.'

A silence that Kat liked to think was stunned. Then, 'You?' Emma hissed. 'You whore—'

'I'm glad you've answered Jakey's phone,' Kat interrupted ruthlessly. 'I was going to tell Jakey to call you off from your criminal cyber-attacks directed at my place of work but now I can tell you personally. Stop it, unless you want your "ethical" reputation besmirched so thoroughly that you'll never be given sensitive or government work again. Stop it, *arrête ça,*' she repeated, just to make sure Emma understood. 'Or I'll not only report you to the authorities, I'll pass the information to my fellow journalists who write for technology magazines and blogs. The story will blow up. Go viral. A few one-star reviews will be nothing compared to the nightmare you'll suffer.'

Emma vented a long list of swearwords in English and French, of which 'bitch' was the least offensive.

The worry and fear Kat had experienced since that very first bad review, all the scam emails and altered orders turned her anger molten. 'That's me,' Kat acknowledged gleefully. 'Your future is in my hands, so you'd better hope that we don't get so much as a dodgy email from now on, or your future will cease to exist. In fact . . . you'd better just hope I don't go for revenge. Just think of it. Any day, I can bring your life crashing down. Any . . . day . . . I . . . want,' she added for emphasis, and ended the call, cheating Emma of even that small satisfaction.

'Wow,' Solly whispered, eyes filled with respect. 'I wouldn't have suspected you had that kind of vindictiveness in you.'

'Me neither,' she confessed. 'It feels surprisingly good.'

As if someone had filled her with champagne, Kat drove home singing at the top of her voice, Solly punctuating her warbling with jubilant cries of, 'My sister is a badass,' and, 'Kat, one; Emma, nil!' He wanted to high five Kat, but it was tricky unless she wanted to let go of the steering wheel and end up in a hedge.

'That's the Jakey hurdle cleared,' she sang instead.

She wondered how Noah had got on with Florine.

Chapter Seventeen

Over a cold drink on the grass outside the van, Noah listened to Kat's jubilant account of her and Solly's sleuthing and Emma's fury at being outmanoeuvred. 'I wondered where you were when I came back and your car wasn't here,' he said. From a shady spot behind him, Angelique yawned and panted. She'd already performed her greeting dance for Kat and Solly and obviously felt entitled to chill. Solly had a date with Ola and the faint hissing of the shower that was audible through the van's open door informed Noah that date-night preparations were in progress.

Kat's dark eyes sparkled with excitement. 'It was awesome,' she kept saying, seeming hardly able to sit still. 'Visiting the kart track seemed such a slim hope but it worked beautifully. It's such a *relief* that the cyber-attacks should be over. I can see why people talk about "getting the monkey off your back" because it really does feel as if something awful's been clinging to me and now it's gone.'

They were perched on faded fold-up chairs that some

previous occupant had abandoned beneath the caravan and Noah's wobbled dangerously as he reached for Kat's hand. 'Your plans went much better than mine,' he admitted ruefully. 'I didn't manage to talk to Florine because she just left Clémence with me and hurried off into town.'

'It must have been nice to have Clémence to yourself, though.' Kat's smile held a world of understanding, though he thought the light in her eyes dimmed.

'I hope you don't think I'm reneging on my plan to tell Florine.' He was uncomfortably aware that events had conspired to make him skulk secretively about this summer. It wasn't characteristic and it wasn't comfortable, even though Kat seemed to understand Clémence's importance in his life and that he hadn't hidden his and Kat's relationship on purpose. She shouldn't be made to suffer doubts for even a moment, though. Her dad and stepmum might overlook her but he absolutely wasn't going to do the same. It wasn't the time to say so when her brother might burst onto the scene at any moment though, so he just added, 'Clé was Mademoiselle Chatty. She's had a play date with two girls she met via your book club, and she's seeing them again this evening at the book club social.'

Kat's eyes widened in sudden horror. 'The book club social! I'd forgotten all about it. Mathilde said she'd get the room booked and once I sent the invitations out, I left it to her.' Scrabbling about for her phone, she checked the time. 'It's starts in an hour. Holy shit, I'm useless. I can't leave poor old Mathilde to set out all those chairs.' She leapt to her feet and Angelique bounced instantly from asleep to awake, presenting herself at her mistress's feet ready to be included in whatever was about to happen. Kat glanced at Noah as she found her car keys. 'You're welcome to come along.'

Noah rose. 'OK, I'm up for cake and your company. I told Clémence I didn't think I'd be going so it will be fun to surprise her. I'll grab Angelique's stuff for you.' The social event might even give him a moment to explain to Florine how things were in his love life and then his conscience would be clear, as well as the way to whatever the future brought. His heart put in an extra beat at the prospect of sharing his life with uncomplicated, loving Kat.

She opened her hatchback and clicked her fingers to Angelique to jump in. 'I need to drop Angelique at home and then whiz to the *salon de thé* to help Mathilde. Best if I meet you there.'

'Sure,' Noah replied easily, resuming his seat. A quick peck on the lips then Kat was reversing her car onto the dusty track that ran through the staff quarters. A few minutes later, Solly buzzed off on his scooter and Noah was left to finish his drink, listening to the peaceful evening sounds of birds singing, exchanging nods or waves with the occasional colleague coming off the six o'clock shift. He even managed a doze in the late sunshine before he stretched and yawned and got himself ready to follow Kat to Kirchhoffen.

Ten minutes later, he parked on the gravel outside La Maison Blanche. The old lady from the top balcony called, '*Bonsoir,*' and he returned her cheery greeting. He wondered whether there were many places available to rent in Kirchhoffen. He'd grown to like the village and living here might suit him. He'd be close to Kat and Clémence, without crowding anyone. He wasn't sure how Yohan would feel about it, but neither did he care.

He wandered down Rue du Printemps, hands in his

pockets. The sky had hazed over and the evening was close and humid. Maybe there would be a storm.

When he reached the *salon de thé* he jumped up the step to the decking where people were enjoying coffee and snacks, then entered the interior, blinking as his eyes adjusted to the hard, artificial light, and headed for the back room where Kat said the book club was held.

He found himself following in the footsteps of a dark-haired man who stepped into the room and halted, so Noah had to pause behind him. The man glanced about then said to an unseen someone, 'I know you weren't expecting me. I was driving past on my way home from work when I saw you come in here, so I thought I'd stop.'

'It's the book club coffee evening,' answered a woman's voice uncertainly. Florine's voice. As she spoke, she took a step into view.

Noah took an involuntary step back, belatedly recognising the dark-haired man as Yohan Gagneau. He hovered, deciding on his best course of action, excruciatingly aware that the three of them now formed a tableau in the doorway and that Yohan wasn't yet aware of him. Whenever he'd thought of renewing his acquaintance with his daughter's stepfather, he'd imagined having some say in when and where, some opportunity for forethought.

But his options narrowed when a high voice suddenly called joyously, 'Papa, you came!' And Clémence brushed unceremoniously past Yohan to throw herself at Noah.

'Hello, little one,' he murmured, scooping his daughter against him, closing his eyes for an instant at the love that rushed through him when her little arms fastened around his waist.

He opened them in time to see Yohan half turn, his jaw dropping before he turned to glare at Florine, whose hand had flown to her mouth. Clémence froze. She glanced behind her at her mother and stepfather and whimpered, 'Ohh . . . *non*.'

The dozen or so people who'd already gathered in the room fell silent, no doubt wondering what was going on. Over Clémence's head, Noah met first Kat's wide-eyed alarm and then Yohan's dark, hostile stare. He smiled faintly, stroking Clémence's hair.

Clémence's frantic glance flew between her stepfather and her father and she burst into tears, burying her face against Noah's T-shirt and sobbing, 'Papa, I'm sorry.'

'Shh,' he soothed, wrapping her in all the love he could manage to convey with his embrace. 'It's OK. Don't worry. It's OK. Nothing is your fault.' But Clémence had rushed headlong into one of her inconsolable torrents of emotion, clinging to him, shaking, her feet pedalling against the floor in her anguish that she'd given the game away. His heart ached for the little girl who'd found herself an unwilling accomplice to the hubris of her stepfather and the inadequacy of her mother. Noah should shoulder his share of the blame, too, because he could have pushed for an earlier resolution instead of letting Florine try and muster the courage to stand up to her husband and tell him he'd been wrong to manipulate her and Clémence.

Now his darling little girl was wracked by guilt for welcoming her own father in the presence of her controlling stepfather.

When she suffered this kind of loss of control, Clémence was capable of literally crying herself sick, so Noah continued to soothe her, holding her close, telling her everything would be fine. Yohan took a step as if to brush past them, but Noah deliberately filled the doorway, his feet planted firmly apart, meaning Yohan would have to physically shove him and the crying girl aside in order to leave. In the background, someone murmured, '*La pauvre petite.*' Yohan fell back and Florine slipped by to join Noah in stroking Clémence's thin back and murmuring comfortingly.

At last, when Clémence's sobs showed signs of subsiding, Noah murmured to Florine, 'Will you take her now?'

'*Oui,*' she whispered, and eased the quaking girl into her own arms, laying her cheek against her daughter's hair and rocking her. She didn't make eye contact with her husband, and Noah wondered whether it was because she couldn't. Or because, for once, she was prepared to show Yohan her priority was Clémence.

Noah extended his hand. 'Yohan.'

Yohan just stared.

A step forward took Noah perilously close to being in Yohan's face. 'I was going to call on you soon,' he murmured. 'But now we can talk outside.' Then, when Yohan's lip curled into a sneer as if he was ready to refuse, he added softly, 'Man to man,' throwing down the gauntlet, knowing Yohan's pride wouldn't let him back away from a public challenge.

Eyes cold, Yohan glanced towards his wife, but she was concentrating on wiping Clémence's red, emotional face with tissues.

Noah turned and led the way past the counter, outdoors into the evening. He paused on the decking to check Yohan was following and then they strode side by side to a black metal bench facing the street, petunias nodding in tubs on either side. Noah sat. Yohan hesitated, as if a seat in the street was beneath his dignity, then finally perched as far from Noah as he could. His jaw was so tense Noah thought his teeth must be in imminent danger of cracking.

With no mental rehearsal for this tense meeting, Noah just went with his gut. 'It's unacceptable to move my daughter hundreds of miles away from me without consultation and block me on her phone,' he said calmly. 'Clémence was terribly upset. I'm not sure why you didn't simply tell me about your job offer so we could discuss the options. Did you assume I'd refuse to allow Clé to move? Regardless of that, your actions would appear dubious to any court. I have my own opinions on why Florine didn't inform me but she, too, put herself on the wrong side of the law by doing so. Do you have anything to say?'

Yohan's nostrils pinched. He stared straight ahead, his hands on the knees of his smart trousers.

Noah half turned on the bench so he could watch him. 'Can't you look me in the eye?' he asked quietly.

Yohan's head swivelled so fast he should have pulled a muscle, loathing and fury in every line of his face and the supercilious quirk of his lips.

Noah was unmoved by this thunderous expression and half disappointed it wasn't accompanied by an outburst. Noah's own temper had been simmering since March and he wouldn't mind unleashing it. 'I've had to track down my little girl and move to Alsace. The only thing that has prevented me from going to the law was putting Clémence – a highly emotional child, I expect you'll agree – through the system.' He pointed over his shoulder in the direction of the *salon de thé*. 'I wanted to minimise the kind of meltdown we've just seen tonight.'

Yohan said nothing but his dark eyes fairly glowed with fury.

Noah felt his lip curl with contempt for this arse who liked to push around people softer or timider than himself, but wasn't big enough to apologise for outrageous behaviour. Deliberately, he moved up the bench, impinging on Yohan's space, and spoke in a voice like iron. 'I won't be giving up my relationship with my daughter. You will not move her again without asking me. If you do, I will invoke the law without hesitation, especially if you try and take her out of France. Do you understand?'

A long silence. Eventually, as if his jaw had rusted and he could only free it with an effort, Yohan gritted out, 'I understand.' He looked as if the words were making his tongue bleed.

Noah edged back, adopting a tone as understanding as he could make it. 'I get that you're Clémence's stepfather. But *I'm her father*. Get that straight in your head.'

Yohan returned to the blank stare. Then he lifted one eyebrow and snapped, '*Fini?*'

'*Oui. Fini.*' Noah remained seated while Yohan jumped up, strode over to a shining black Renault Alpine parked nearby, slammed his way into it and roared off. Noah stared after him in disgust. Yohan had showed no remorse and offered no apology for his blatant attempt to cut Noah out of his own daughter's life. He muttered, 'Yeah, go and stew, you arse. Just know I've got your number.'

He sat on in the close, clammy evening for several minutes, letting his heartbeat steady, watching the heat haze form itself into purple clouds pierced by apricot rays from the sunset.

Then his mind flew back to the situation he'd left indoors in order to confront Yohan and he forced himself to rise and return to the *salon de thé*, hoping Clémence had recovered from her paroxysm. After the episodes of fear, frustration or grief Clémence suffered, she often flew to the other end of the scale and became overly talkative and cheery. It was a brittle mood, however, and it didn't take much for her to rollercoaster down to a new low. Florine was good at calming her, but Noah needed to see for himself how she was doing.

He was barely aware of the closed boulangerie and neighbouring patisserie as he passed because an outside gathering had caught his attention – Kat sitting with Florine and Clémence. Clémence *was* in chat mode, bouncing on her toes beside the table as if that would catapult words out of her mouth all the faster.

'I'm glad your brother is friends with Papa so I can be friends with Angelique,' he heard her gabbling to Kat as he came up on the table. 'Papa likes to walk her, doesn't he? And so do I. And Maman. We're sort of sharing your dog. Papa says dogs need lots of walks and you're working long hours.' Noah realised that Clémence was innocently reinforcing the myth he and Kat were just friends, but now definitely wasn't the time to make a contrary announcement. Clémence's gaze flew to him and she squealed. 'Here's Papa!' She whirled her way around the table and flung herself on him, wrapping him in all the strength of her slender arms. He stooped to hug her, feeling her little heart scudding. She was still up on the emotional high wire.

He patted her back and made his voice gentle and matter of fact. 'Yes, here I am. I didn't go far. I try never to be too far away from you.' He glanced up. Florine's eyes were red-rimmed, her face pale and apprehensive. Kat had risen and was moving away, though she sent him a small smile.

He felt terrible for enacting his family dramas under her nose but still he asked, 'Have you had a pastry yet, Clé? Perhaps Kat would take you.' He'd have to risk the sugar acting against his daughter's need for calm because it seemed the imperative thing here was for him to have a couple of minutes alone with Florine.

Kat instantly put out her hand. 'I haven't had mine, either. Would you help me choose, Clémence? Then you can bring pastries out to Maman and Papa, too.'

Clémence's arms fell away from Noah and she whirled and raced back to Kat. 'Yes, please! Is there *pain au chocolat?*'

Noah tried to send Kat a grateful look, but she was gazing down at Clémence bouncing at her side. As the pair disappeared indoors, he turned his attention to the still figure of Florine and took the seat Kat had just vacated. 'OK?' he asked, then, judging from her pallor and enormous eyes that she was anything but, conveyed the bullet points of his conversation with Yohan.

Florine nodded.

He took a deep, steadying breath. Someone had to take charge of the situation and, as it had throughout his marriage, it fell to him. 'I think Clémence should stay with me tonight. She can have my bed and I'll sleep on the pull-out in the lounge. Solly won't mind. He might be staying at his girlfriend's anyway. I don't want Clé any more upset.' He didn't have to add, 'By you and Yohan having a row in front of her.'

Florine gave a tiny nod. She had the look of someone who was numb with shock, unable to react fully.

He lowered his voice. 'Forgive me for intruding, but I have to ask. I know Yohan's never been violent with you but are you scared to go home?'

First, she gave a stiff shrug. Then she moistened her lips and whispered, 'Yes.'

He made his voice gentle, reminding himself that this

woman had once been his wife and though she could have prevented a lot of the agony Noah had been caused this summer, in another way she couldn't . . . because she was too weak. 'Why?' He had a pretty good idea, but he needed to hear it from her.

She spoke, barely moving her bloodless lips. 'It will be a difficult conversation. Clémence made it obvious that I knew you were in Alsace.'

He nodded and sighed. 'Yes. That's why she got overly emotional – she realised. What a mess.' Noah felt cornered. Part of his attention was on the doorway in case Kat and Clémence returned. He was screamingly aware that against his intentions he was side-lining Kat, but he felt obliged to make a basic effort to ensure Florine would be OK.

His thoughts were interrupted by a bright jingling that made Florine open her small bag and check her phone. 'It's Yohan,' she said colourlessly. 'He wants to know when I'll be home.'

Noah's stomach turned over on his ex-wife's behalf. Her anxiety was coming over the table in waves. 'Are you going?' he asked carefully.

Silence. A tiny sigh. 'Yes,' she answered eventually.

Noah turned the situation over in his mind. He and Florine were divorced. He had no right to interfere, yet . . . 'He's the one who has acted badly, not you,' he offered. 'Remember that.'

She nodded. 'I'll come and fetch Clémence in the morning.'

'OK,' he said, aware that he'd want to discuss the Yohan situation again with both Clémence and Florine before he let his daughter return to that household, but unwilling to further rock Florine's already rocky boat. 'I'm due to be at work from noon until eight p.m. tomorrow but I'll give it a miss if Clémence needs me.'

As he spoke, Kat and Clémence returned to the deck, Kat bearing a laden tray.

Florine drew on a bright smile and hugged her daughter. 'Papa says you can stay with him tonight. Won't that be fun?'

Clémence's gaze flicked between her parents as she smiled uncertainly. 'Shall I come home first and get my things?'

Noah had no intention of allowing that. 'I have a new toothbrush for you and you can sleep in a clean T-shirt of mine. You'll be in the park, so we'll make it like camping. It'll be great.'

'OK,' Clémence beamed. Though sometimes wise beyond her years, she was enough of a little girl to accept anything presented as a treat.

Noah shifted his gaze to Kat, wanting to apologise with his eyes because he was abandoning her and their plans for the evening, but Kat kept her gaze on Clémence. 'Doesn't that sound lovely?' she asked the little girl in an overly cheerful voice. 'I have to go inside to help my friend Mathilde now. Good night, everyone.' And she disappeared into the *salon de thé* without a backward glance.

Clémence set about her *pain au chocolat* with reassuring gusto, but Noah knew Florine's enthusiasm for sweet pastry was as feigned as his own. He watched her give Clémence several big hugs before setting off in the direction of Rue du Kirchfeld with a noticeably dragging stride. Noah and Clémence agreed it was a shame that Maman hadn't drunk all her coffee or eaten the last of the *chouquettes* Clémence had chosen for her, then discussed whereabouts in the caravan Clémence would sleep. At her insistence, he texted Solly to check he didn't mind.

Solly replied, *Fine by me. Staying at Ola's anyway. Back early as on at 9 tomorrow.*

Kat didn't reappear.

Noah checked his phone in case she'd sent a message, but there was nothing. He felt as if she'd come back from the kart track this afternoon trailing sparkling balloons marked *joy, triumph, relief*, and he and his family drama had been responsible for bursting every single one. He debated texting her . . . what? An apology? A row of kisses? A request to meet tomorrow? He didn't know what would happen tomorrow.

Clémence demanded, 'Are you texting? Has Solly changed his mind about letting me stay?'

'Of course not,' he assured her, putting his phone away. Presently, he walked Clémence back to Rue du Printemps to climb into his car and drive to the staff accommodation on the edge of Parc Lemmel, somewhere he now felt unexpectedly at home.

Together they changed the sheets on his bed ready for Clémence to sleep there – lucky he'd done laundry earlier – and transferred his sheets to the pull-out bed in the lounge. Then Clémence decided she liked the pull-out bed best. 'I've never slept on one,' she pleaded after they'd removed the big seat cushions and she'd inspected the ladder-like contraption that uncoiled from the base and hooked into the opposite seat. 'It's clever,' she pronounced. Clémence loved anything that functioned. 'Can I sleep here?'

Noah smothered a sigh. 'We'd have to change the sheets back over.' Which is what they ended up doing. The evening felt increasingly muggy and Clémence was pink in the face.

'Let's choose one of my T-shirts for you to sleep in,' he suggested. 'Then we'll do something quiet till bedtime.'

'Chess on your tablet,' Clémence decided. So they sprawled on the pull-out bed, Clémence proving so forward-thinking in her selection of chess moves that Noah had to concentrate hard.

'One day,' he said when she'd beaten him twice in a row, 'my daughter will be an amazing mathematician or scientist.' She'd also learn more mastery over her emotions and cope with difficulties better than she did now. Till then, she was his little girl and he'd protect her from anyone.

Clémence giggled with delight, set up the pieces again and promptly got him in check in six moves.

But when Noah saw it was ten o'clock and declared it quite late enough for bedtime, Clémence refused to sleep alone so they both settled down in the pull-out – texting Solly to let him know so, as Clémence stated, 'He won't be scared if he comes home and sees us.'

It meant a long night for Noah and gave him no opportunity to call Kat. Clémence swam restlessly in and out of sleep, waking hourly, it seemed, to check he was still there. Outside, the wind began to sough through the trees and thunder to rumble. When rain drummed on the metal roof of the caravan, Clémence woke as thoroughly as if she'd slept for ten hours.

'Let's just close our eyes and listen,' Noah said, hoping she'd fall asleep again. But he knew from her breathing that she was too alert and full of nervous energy, especially when lightning flashed through the van's thin curtains.

It was the storm that the muggy evening had promised but Noah hadn't bargained for the emotional storm that

271

had come first. It was that, rather than the noise of thunder and rain, that kept him awake.

He'd never feared storms but he sure as hell wished he wasn't so far away from Kat, geographically and emotionally, during this one.

Chapter Eighteen

Early August in Alsace was hot and airless, even when you worked right at the top of the open expanse of Parc Lemmel where there was usually at least a little breeze.

In some ways, Kat's life had settled down after a turbulent June and July, she thought wistfully, watching lilac butterflies dance over a swathe of white wildflowers in the rustling grasses, meandering behind Angelique's wagging tail on their morning walk. No one had messed with the website, sent out bogus newsletters or fake orders since her pithy conversation with Emma. Graham was on a more even keel now Reeny had got through her pre-transplant checks, had her stem cells harvested, endured yet more chemo and was in hospital to have the treated cells returned. Under the intensive, debilitating treatment she was taking calls only from family, but Kat knew from Graham that Reeny was 'doing as well as could be expected', and his mum was also picking up nicely, back in the UK. Kat and Solly's dad Howard had been scrupulous in updating them equally with his and Irina's moving-to-France plans. They were due to arrive tomorrow,

Friday . . . which *might* disturb Kat's peace, she reflected. As they'd so quickly completed the legal side of Howard's new partnership and let out their house in England, she suspected her dad and stepmum must have been a long way through the process before Kat had heard anything about it. Still, she'd been generous in her responses to Howard's various *we're hoping you can help us with* . . . emails.

As she trailed Angelique through the wildest, quietest part of the park where the ditches had run summer-dry and the hedgerow was dusty, her current unease centred on how things would work out with Noah.

He'd been troubled at having to abandon their plans when the time had come for him to confront Yohan. In the intervening nine days he'd apologised more than once. She'd been as reassuring as she could, in the circumstances. 'I made myself scarce so you could deal with things, but I wasn't upset. I'd *expect* you to put Clémence first. I'd be disappointed in you if you didn't.' It was, after all, easy for her to put herself in Clémence's shoes.

'Single parents encounter issues,' he'd gone on, rubbing his jaw. 'There are times when Clémence will need me.'

'I know,' she'd murmured, pressing a kiss to his lips. 'I understand.' All too well.

He was looking for a permanent job in Alsace and applying to river cruise companies, particularly excited by a role that meant that one week out of three he'd board a long, flat riverboat as its cruise director. He'd survived two interviews for the post and was on a short-list of three people. The role began in October, which was perfect for leaving his job on the lake team at Parc Lemmel and the accommodation that went with it. He'd also found a small and pretty house with a lawned garden in

274

Muntsheim that would fall vacant soon. He'd be only a few miles from both her and Clémence. Everything was falling into place perfectly.

Kat sighed. Except . . . for the teeny tiny worries that Yohan would pull something again, worries she'd decided not to share with Noah. He'd only launch into renewed apologies about having to put his little girl first – which she already knew.

It was better to spend most after-work evenings together and then fall into her bed; to join him and Clémence sometimes when they borrowed Angelique to walk her; to enjoy Noah giving every indication that he was a man intending to remain in her life.

Angelique paused and looked back, one paw lifted. The morning sun burnished her coat to the colour of a new copper coin and she looked like a canine goddess against the gold of the summer-dry grass. Then her ears pricked up, she switched around and raced back towards Kat, bounding through the long grass. 'What's up?' Kat demanded, but Angelique brushed past, her tail a banner behind her. Turning, Kat saw Noah approaching from behind them and Angelique flying like an arrow to receive the fuss that she clearly felt would be hers.

Noah's hair, too, caught the sun, almost the same gold as the grass now he'd spent a couple of months working outside. His smile blazed almost as brightly. 'Morning, gorgeous,' he called as he reached her, slinging an arm around her waist and dropping a hot kiss on her lips. 'I thought I'd take a wander and see if I could see you. I've just had an email from HR about that job I want. The shortlist is down to two people and they've invited both of us to join an overnight cruise and meet the directors. It's a smaller boat than the one I'd be attached to on my river-based weeks, of course.' His eyes danced. 'Best of both worlds – two weeks on shore and one on-board.'

She accepted the kiss, her heart tripping over itself at the brush of his body. She'd missed him last night as he'd spent it in his own bed, both of them having to catch up with their sleep and seemingly incapable of getting a full night if they shared a bed . . . Well, they had very full nights together . . . just not full of sleep. 'Fantastic,' she agreed, beaming as much at the sight of him as at his great news. 'Congratulations on getting down to the final two. I'll keep everything crossed for you.' Hoping those teeny tiny worries she'd been stressing over didn't sound in her voice, she slipped both arms around his solid warmth and squeezed.

He paused to regard her quizzically. 'What's wrong?'

'Nothing,' she protested reassuringly. 'Well, I *was* thinking about Reeny. I understand why I've been asked not to try to contact her but that doesn't stop me being sad that I can't.'

Though he made sympathetic noises about Reeny, he was too empathetic not to look deeper. He drew her gently to a halt, pushing her hair back so he could cup her face and meet her gaze. 'Shall I tell you what I've been thinking?' He didn't pause for her answer. 'That *you're* thinking that if I get this job, it will be Jakey all over again. Popping into your life when work permits, sidelining you the rest of the time.' Clouds shaded his face. 'If that's how it's making you feel then I'll withdraw. I don't want you to think you're not important.'

Tears stung Kat's eyes that he'd give up something he obviously wanted just to make her happy. Her heart swelled in her chest. 'You absolutely should not withdraw. If you're around two-thirds of the time, then I'd be a very demanding girlfriend not to be happy with that.' She laughed and settled against him for a kiss that she hoped would reassure them both, trying to be relaxed by the heat of the sun and the drone of bees amongst the buttercups.

'You're the least demanding girlfriend ever,' he said frankly, when she let him up for air. 'I'm not going to wait any longer to tell Florine about us. I want Clémence to know, too, so we can take her out together and be natural.'

His eyes smiled, and he waited, clearly expecting Kat to be pleased. Instead, her stomach cramped, mind flying back twenty-five years to when her parents had sat her down and given her the, 'Mum and Dad don't love each other anymore, but we both still love you' talk. Kat had sat frozen in horror between them. The 'It won't make any difference to you and me, darling' from her dad had proved to be hugely optimistic, as he'd known he had another child on the way. Her mother's red eyes had been scant reassurance that they'd 'all soon get used to things'. And every time another person was introduced into the nightmare – Dad's new partner Irina, their child Solly who turned up five months later, Mum's new husband Geoffrey and his children Amber and Jade – Kat had felt more unhappily out in the cold.

But this was different, she reminded herself. Noah and Florine had split up three years ago.

She wiped away sweat that had formed on her top lip, trying to separate young Kat's feelings from those of Clémence now. Noah knew his own child, didn't he? Just because he hadn't introduced Clémence to any other woman he'd dated in his three post-Florine years didn't mean the revelation would go badly.

Though neither did it mean it would go well.

'Is it the right time?' she asked uncertainly. 'You said that the two times you've picked Clémence up since Yohan found out you're in the area, he stood at the door and glowered. You must tell Florine alone, but he shadows her whenever you're around. He even came to book club with her on Monday. And you can't text her news like that.'

'You're talking as if you and I are sneaking around and our relationship's going to break up my marriage,' he said, frowning. 'It's been over for years. I don't owe Florine any more than courtesy. Still, I'll treat her sensitively, even if the conversation does have to take place in front of Yohan. I'm not the horrible type.'

She freed her hand so she could pinch his bum, suddenly feeling slightly better about things. 'No, you're not. You're the lovely type.' She sighed. 'I hope she's OK with me about it when it finally comes out. I really feel as if she needs a friend in the area.' She checked the time and turned back to the path, where Angelique was sniffing at nettles. 'I only have twenty minutes before I need to be at the book café.'

'I'll walk with you.' He laced his fingers with hers and they threaded their way through a stand of trees, an area that was thick with mud in rainy weather but now, in the height of the French summer, had cracked like an overcooked cake.

They didn't mention Florine again, but she was so present in Kat's mind it felt almost as if she trailed along behind them, looking blonde and chic, but abandoned.

On Friday, Howard and Irina arrived to take up their rented accommodation in nearby Lingolsheim, a town quite like Muntsheim but a little west. Kat got a text from

Howard: *We're here!* She texted back good wishes for their new life and said: *Tell me if/when you need help.* She envisaged a little light unpacking and maybe sharing a bottle of wine.

Instead, on Saturday, the phone calls began.

Howard and Irina had decided to wait until they arrived in France to worry about household utilities and now weren't certain they were reading FAQs properly, or they could make neither head nor tail of online chat conversations. At first, Kat tried to field the calls on her mobile between selling books and serving iced teas, but every table belonging to Livres et Café was filled. Kat, Danielle and all assistants on the payroll were fully occupied in hurrying to get customers their snacks and drinks so she was forced to begin ignoring the calls.

Her dad swapped to the shop's landline. 'I know you're working but I can't understand this bloke properly,' he'd explode. The 'bloke' would turn out to be a recorded message in French.

'Didn't the letting agent sort all this out for you?' Kat demanded, holding the phone between shoulder and ear and trying to make a cappuccino.

'The agent read all the meters,' Howard allowed. 'But Irina's worrying we're doing something wrong using gas and electricity when we're not signed up to anyone.'

Kat smiled at a female tourist waiting for the cappuccino and added a complementary biscuit to the saucer to make up for being on the phone. 'Sorry,' she mouthed at the customer. She pointed at the phone and rolled her eyes. 'My dad.'

The woman spluttered into laughter and Kat suddenly realised she was the woman who looked like a friendly pony who'd visited once before. She thought back. That first visit was weeks ago so either they had long holidays, or they lived locally.

'Do you have electricity and gas in the house?' Kat queried, checking the order Romain had just brought to the counter.

'All working,' Howard agreed.

Kat frowned. 'If everything's working, Dad, why worry just yet? Wait till Monday when I have the day off and I'll come over and go through things with you. I get my gas, electricity and broadband all from one company because it makes everything nice and simple.'

'OK,' said Howard, as if he hadn't sounded frazzled and confused just seconds ago. 'This is a smashing little house.'

'I look forward to seeing it. Got to go, Dad. Customers.' Kat dropped the phone back in its cradle, filled Romain's order and found Friendly Pony and Currant Bun waiting at the books counter to buy two books and a pen. Kat breezed over to them. 'Hello, again.'

Currant Bun smiled approvingly. 'You do well to remember customers when you serve hordes of them, dear.'

Kat kept to herself the thought that most customers weren't as memorable for being nosy as these two. 'You were so friendly,' she said.

'Got good staff here, have you?' Friendly Pony asked, taking out her card to pay for their purchases. 'Very young, most of them.'

Kat nodded. 'They're fabulous,' she said, wrapping the books. 'Danielle and I manage, and the others are part time, very bright and reliable. Excuse me,' she added, when the shop phone rang again, glad to get away as the nasty thought occurred to her that Currant Bun and Friendly Pony might be picking her brains because they were thinking of setting up in competition. She answered the phone with a friendly, 'Livres et Café.'

'Do you know where Solly is?' asked Howard's voice.

'He's working, Dad.'

'But his phone's off.'

'Because he's working, Dad. Park employees aren't encouraged to take calls and his boss can be tricky.' Kat tried not to sound ratty, but honestly!

Howard hadn't finished. 'Irina wants to know if she'll incur roaming charges on her phone, now she's living in France.'

'If it's a UK phone and her provider levies roaming charges then, yes,' Kat replied patiently, though clutching her head and pulling a 'scream' face that made Pierre, passing by, choke with laughter. 'She should check with her provider.'

Sunday was easier because Howard's new business partner, Phillipe, invited Howard and Irina to his house for lunch so Kat was saved from having to point out to her father that it was August and the park and book café were packed with tourists from ten in the morning until eight at night.

On Monday, after a morning walk with Noah, who was also off work but getting the tram to Strasbourg to refresh his office-clothes wardrobe in preparation for his cruise-cum-final-interview, she drove to the address Howard had given her in Lingolsheim. It was, as he'd told her, a smashing house, though not what she'd have called little. Judging by the dormer windows, its top floor was the size of her entire apartment and its garden covered at least four times the area of hers, full of well-stocked borders and trim hedges.

To Kat's dismay, she discovered that Howard was attending his first day of work at the bags and belts factory and Irina was in the full expectation that Kat's function was to act as her unpaid secretary and interpreter. Unfortunately, she wouldn't accept Kat's recommendation on which utilities company to register with but instead made her go through laborious comparisons and online chat conversations. She was full of disagreeable comments such as 'I would have thought you'd have told me', or 'you could have checked for us', or 'if only you'd said that in the first place we'd have been done a sight faster'.

Kat was soon wishing that she'd never offered to help Howard and Irina settle in because it seemed to have set up the expectation of doing the absolute minimum themselves. She was incensed to discover that the letting agent had offered them a package whereby the rent would include all utilities, meaning this wasted day wouldn't have been necessary, but they'd turned it down.

'Why?' she asked Irina blankly.

Irina bridled. 'It might not have been the most economical way.'

'But it might have been,' Kat couldn't help pointing out.

Irina switched tracks, gazing out at where Angelique was presently having a pee on the lawn. 'Did you have to bring that dog?'

'Yes,' Kat replied.

The only nice thing about the day was that Howard arrived at lunchtime with his new business partner, Phillipe. 'I wanted him to meet you, Katerina.'

Kat felt unreasonably touched. Phillipe proved to be a smiling man with big glasses and not much hair. 'You're very kind to help your parents,' he said, taking her hand.

Kat felt like saying, 'One parent, one stepparent,' but wouldn't be so rude, even if Irina had rubbed her up the wrong way. She smiled instead and returned to trying to find a gardener, Irina having decided the garden was too big for her to manage. By the end of the afternoon Kat was thinking wistfully of the days when she hadn't had much to do with her father and Irina.

'You're off tomorrow as well, aren't you?' Irina demanded as Kat prepared to leave. 'There's all kinds of things I need from the shops.'

Wishing that she'd never mentioned that she'd managed two consecutive days off this week, Kat tried to sound sincere. 'Sorry,' she said. 'I have plans tomorrow. Google should tell you everything you need to know, or you can order online. The French have Amazon, just like the Brits. Or maybe Solly can take you? He gets a couple of days off each week and he's probably dying to spend time with you.'

Irina visibly brightened at this idea and Kat sent a silent apology to her brother as she skipped out of the door.

Maybe it was the oppressive heat, or Kat's prickly day with her stepmother, but her feelings of uneasiness were in full force on Monday evening. It was a similar feeling to being outdoors as clouds gathered on the horizon, grey, then purple, and all the birds stopped singing.

Still, Kat laughed her way through Noah putting on an impromptu fashion parade, assuming what he imagined to be a languid catwalk prowl, modelling new trousers and shirt, a jacket slung casually over one shoulder. Then she watched him undress again and allowed herself to be slowly and sensuously undressed, too, then stroked, loved, kissed and caressed. It was the tenderest unwrapping Kat had ever known until urgency took over, and then it was the hottest. The hardest. The least controlled. The most exciting and special.

* * *

283

Later, in a cool lavender dusk, they walked Angelique, fingers laced, talking about the job Noah was feeling increasingly desperate to secure and how it was a pain he had to work at the park tomorrow. 'Only way to get the time off for the cruise interview next week,' he said, as pragmatic and even-tempered as ever. 'I'm on till eight, unfortunately. Shall I come over after? Or do you have plans?'

'I told Irina I did,' Kat giggled. 'But apart from a catch-up on household stuff, that plan is to spend a lazy day reading in the shade.'

They paused in the entrance to the wooded side of the park in the grey and purple shadows left by the sinking sun. He pulled her into his arms and nuzzled her neck, his mouth hot and exciting. 'I can't get enough of you, Kat. You're my addiction.'

Kat turned her face up to meet his kisses but an unwelcome little voice in the back of her mind suddenly spoke up sharply, *You'd give me up if you had to. Everyone does.* She physically shook herself. Where on earth had that come from?

Noah drew back so he could look at her. 'You OK? You shivered.'

'Fine,' she laughed. 'Your stubble tickled my neck, that's all.'

But then – while Noah was in the shower – came a phone call.

Kat stared at the contact detail that flashed up on the screen – *Jakey Barbier*, the name she'd assigned to his new number. Damn. What the hell could he want? She answered with a discouraging, '*Oui?*'

A hesitation, then Jakey's voice: 'Kat, *c'est moi.* Jakey.'

'It's late,' she said warily. 'What are you calling for?'

Since the spirited exchange with Emma on Jakey's phone, she hadn't heard a peep out of either of them.

Jakey's voice was tight – with tears? 'Our relationship is at an end.'

Disquiet prickled down Kat's back. 'It's been at an end for a couple of months,' she observed, confused. 'I ended it. Why contact me now?'

He tutted his frustration. 'Not our relationship. My relationship – with Emma. She wouldn't believe me that I hadn't given you my new number. She says I can no longer live with her and the girls.' He sounded stunned.

Kat digested this in uneasy silence. 'But I only rang you to try and get you to call her cyber-attacks off. I had no idea she'd answer,' she said at last.

'She does not believe that.' He sounded tired, defeated. 'Now I cannot live with Manon and Margeaux.'

Kat had sympathy with Emma doubting Jakey. It was hard to trust someone who'd cheerfully lived a double life – and more than once, apparently. Miserably, she said, 'I don't see what I can do. I'd contact her for the sake of your poor children but Emma's not going to believe anything I say, is she?'

'No,' he admitted sadly. He hesitated, then said, with a tentatively hopeful air, 'Kat, are you—'

Noah returned to Kat's bedroom, towelling his hair, gloriously naked and after-shower damp. 'When we can next get a day off together, how about we—' Then he saw Kat with the phone and said, 'Oh, sorry. Didn't realise you were on a call.'

In Kat's ear, Jakey's voice turned stiff. 'You have a man there?'

Was that a hint of accusation in his voice? Kat bristled.

'I'm sorry to hear of your troubles but I don't see what I can do.'

'There is nothing,' he mumbled. 'I don't know why I called.'

Kat suspected that she knew – if Emma didn't want him then he'd wondered if there was any way back to Kat. Hearing Noah's voice had scotched the idea – as if Kat would have entertained it for a nanosecond anyway! Goodbyes were short and she put down her phone, troubled.

Noah, who'd hovered indecisively once he'd realised she was speaking to someone, came to the bed and stooped to kiss her. 'You OK?'

Heavily, she told him what Jakey had said. 'Those poor kids,' she ended.

He scooted onto the bed and hugged her. 'You know that the breakdown of Jakey and Emma's relationship is Jakey's fault, not yours, though?'

'Mm,' she said, but she was thinking back to her own childhood, the splitting up of the family and the hatred that had welled in her twelve-year-old heart for her father's new woman.

Though she lay in Noah's arms that night, listening to his heartbeat, the vision of Margeaux and Manon kept swimming into her mind, smiling and sweet as they'd been when she'd met them for those few minutes at the park.

Her head told her that she was as much a victim of Jakey's grand deceit as they were and that she hadn't *knowingly* begun something with a man who wasn't free, as Irina had.

But she was still cold with guilt.

Chapter Nineteen

The next day brought the most beautiful morning Noah thought he'd ever seen, already sunny and hot as he used the pressure washer on the slipway before hauling the kayaks out of the rack ready for the tourists. August in France was all about holidays, no matter what nationality you were.

Dog walkers roamed the lakeside path and Noah couldn't help checking in case one of them was Kat. He'd left her in bed a couple of hours ago while he returned to the van for a clean uniform. Solly hadn't been home – they were each spending so much time with the women in their lives the van often stood empty. Shame, because Noah wouldn't have minded a word about Kat. She'd been so quiet since that dick Jakey had called her last night, cropping up just when Noah and Kat's future was looking bright and Noah was back in close contact with Clémence.

He understood that the thought of Jakey's children being parted from their father was bound to affect Kat; a corner of every person's heart was reserved for the past. That very corner of his heart was bothered about the minimal communication he was having with Florine. They texted to arrange for him to see Clémence, but she ignored any friendly add-ons such as him asking how she was. When he'd told her he hoped to have a house sorted out in Muntsheim soon, she'd acknowledged but not commented. As Kat had observed, Yohan hovered in the background whenever Noah picked Clé up, making Florine subdued.

Alone with Clémence, he'd checked that Yohan was OK with her now he knew Noah was around and she'd skipped and shrugged, so that was one thing less to worry about. Clémence was an emotional weathervane. Tears and a pale face went with unhappiness; anxiety brought on meltdowns. Skipping equalled 'happy'. Asking whether Maman also seemed happy seemed likely to alert Clémence to possible trouble, so he resisted. He hoped that Florine's reticence was just the result of tension with Yohan and would blow over in time, and yet the words of a song his mum liked kept revolving in his head: something about fear and taboos being worse than a bodily bruise. Just because Yohan wasn't violent didn't mean he couldn't inflict pain.

Soon, Noah had to focus on scanning wristbands, checking lifejackets, floating kayaks and keeping a constant eye out for anyone in trouble so he could alert the two young members of staff employed in high season to hop on paddle boards and rescue anyone floundering too badly.

He took lunch late, returning to the van and grabbing a sandwich and then a combat nap to counteract the heat of the day. When he returned to his station, he was ready to start heaving kayaks around once more. He'd lost a few kilos since coming to the park and his body had never been tighter. Probably plentiful sex had played its part in that, too.

Smiling at that thought, he was shielding his eyes from the glare bouncing over the water while he ran his eyes over the boaters and kayakers when he heard a familiar voice yell, 'Papa, Papa! It's me!'

Eager pleasure swept through him. He swung his gaze to the throng of tourists on the other side of the fence and homed in on Clémence's grin as she bobbed energetically at the staff gate. Florine, as immaculately presented as always, waited quietly behind.

Noah's 'trouble' radar began to ping at her unsmiling expression, but he sauntered to the gate and reached over it with a big hug for his child. 'Hey, you! This is a nice surprise.' He turned to Florine. 'Everything OK?'

She smiled and her mouth said, 'Of course,' but her eyes communicated, 'Not really.'

Clémence bounced on her toes. 'Is Angelique at the book café today?'

He shook his head. 'I don't think so because I believe it's Kat's day off.'

'Aw.' Clémence's face fell.

Florine touched her daughter's shoulder. 'That's not what we came to ask Papa, is it?'

Clémence's smile blazed anew. 'Oh, no! Please may I have a treat? Maman thinks perhaps I can take a kayak out.'

Noah glanced at his ex-wife and understood she wanted to speak to him alone. Parental communication wasn't something you blocked after divorce. He opened the staff gate. 'What a great idea. You'll have to wait a few minutes, but let's see what I can do.'

It was fortunate that two kayaks came in together as it meant he could pop Clémence in one and a tourist in the other, avoiding too much grumbling about queue hopping. Then he called one of the support staff over. 'I'm taking my break now. I'll still be nearby but can you deal with the changeovers for fifteen minutes?'

'*Oui.*' The young guy nodded and took Noah's scanner and ticket pouch.

Noah ushered Florine to a patch of shade from where they could watch Clémence sending her yellow kayak spearing across the shimmering surface of the lake. He'd barely opened his mouth to ask, 'What's up?' when Florine's lip began to wobble.

Her words came out like a breath. 'Please, will you take us back to Castillon, as you offered? I can't stay here.'

The unexpectedness of the words sent Noah dizzy. What? Back to the Dordogne? *But Kat was here in Alsace.* He'd almost completed the formalities to rent a house and was eagerly anticipating his interview for a great job. He'd given notice on his old apartment in Rue Victor Hugo in Castillon-la-Bataille and resigned from his old employer. *And Kat was here.* He stifled the urge to point all these things out and snap at Florine that she didn't have him on a piece of elastic.

But he forced himself to pause for thought.

It wasn't a simple situation. Where Florine went, Clémence would also go, unless she left Clé with him – most unlikely – or he got the authorities involved, which he'd worked so hard not to do, and might not even work out in his favour.

He *had* offered to take Florine and Clémence back to Castillon. It had been weeks ago, in June, when everything had been different, but it had been his idea.

'You don't need me to help you. You're an adult,' would be a waste of breath. There must be a problem for Florine to ask this of him. And any problem that affected

Florine would almost certainly affect their daughter. Stomach churning, he had to physically check the sunlit water for Clémence's happy face to reassure himself that she wasn't under imminent threat.

He moistened his lips. 'Why do you want to go back to the Dordogne? A few weeks ago, you said you were settled in Alsace and in love with your husband. Is it because you didn't tell him I'm living locally and he gave you a hard time?'

Her gaze dropped guardedly. 'He was sad and disappointed. He withdraws into himself, you understand. It's difficult.'

Noah allowed himself to feel relief. It was tempered with anger that the moody shit she'd married could create atmospheres to suppress the moods of others, but the situation didn't sound irretrievable. His focus shifted. 'Clé says he's OK with her.'

She lifted her gaze, wide eyes luminous with distress. 'He's at great pains to be kind and generous . . . to her.'

'Oh, I get it,' Noah said with heavy irony. 'Leaving you in no doubt that you're out of favour but keeping Clémence oblivious of it.' He thought rapidly, Florine's obvious unhappiness forcing him to reassess the problem. 'If you're asking me to take you and Clé back to Castillon then am I to assume you're leaving your husband?'

A single tear welled up. She nodded, lip quivering.

He made his voice soft. 'You're sure the current coldness between you is permanent? It won't blow over?'

She scrabbled in her bag for a tissue and dabbed her eye – being careful of her mascara – and choked, 'He wants me to have another baby.'

Noah rocked back on his heels. He hadn't seen that one coming, but even before Florine began to elaborate, he could see *exactly* why Yohan would suggest it.

She blew her nose again. 'He's "bitterly disappointed" in me but I could convince him of my commitment to him by having his baby. He says things like, "You know it's what I've always wanted" when I don't think it's ever been discussed.'

It sounded eerily like the strategy Yohan had utilised to get Florine and Clémence to Alsace in the first place – pretending existence of a discussion that had never happened. He stared out over the willows leaning over the lake as if waiting for someone to wash their hair. Clémence was paddling towards them now with long, effective sweeps, outdistancing the amateurs splashing about around her. The sunlight made a halo of her blonde hair and she lifted her hand from the paddle to wave. He waved back with a big cheery smile, even as he said to Florine, 'I take it you don't want another child?'

Her breath wavered. 'Not for his reasons.'

He licked his lips, needing to be sure he was reading her situation but aware he was trampling into sensitive areas. 'And what are his reasons, in your view?' His own interpretation was that Yohan, having failed to take over Clémence, now saw a child of his own as a way of creating a bond with Florine that would take priority over the bond she currently had with Noah. Once again, he was seeing relationships as a competition. Maybe Florine not notifying him the moment Noah contacted her had shaken him and he was seeking to mark his territory as well as tie her in. A baby made a good loyalty scheme.

Her lips wobbled again and this time both eyes began to leak. 'Control,' she admitted, surprising Noah with her candour. 'He wants me to stay at home with both children as his new job earns plenty for us to live on. He says it would bring us closer . . . but I'm suffocating already!

He's constantly checking up on me and letting me know if he doesn't approve of my plans.' She wiped her eyes, uncaring now about the mascara making marker-pen-like smears around her eyes.

Florine finally admitting the truth sank Noah's heart like a rock. The worm had turned, and she was desperate to wriggle free of Yohan before he trapped her completely. Three months ago, Noah would have given her a huge, jubilant hug. How he would have loved to have had this conversation when he first arrived in Alsace! And how little he wanted it now. *Because Kat was here.* He felt sick, all too aware that he'd told Florine he'd help her get back to Castillon 'any time'.

He could help her move back and then return here, of course, but then he'd be back to square one – living five hundred miles away from his daughter. He wiped clammy sweat from his forehead, cold despite the beating sun. 'It's only a few weeks since you told me you loved Yohan.' He was repeating himself, but it gave him time to think.

'I did. In a way, I still do.' Her voice broke. 'I love the nice side of Yohan. His intensity, his conversation, his knowledge, the places he likes to go. But all that is flawed by his need to arrange my life to suit him. Insisting on a baby of his own rather than discussing it with me . . . that's the way things were done a hundred years ago. It's too much.'

Noah agreed, obviously, but then he'd always considered Yohan 'too much'. 'Have you talked to Clémence yet?' It was amazing how calm he could sound when his heart was bouncing sickeningly inside his chest.

She sniffed. 'In a roundabout way. I asked whether she liked her friends in Castillon better than Flavie and her sister, in Kirchhoffen. She answered that she had more

293

friends in Castillon. I asked whether she preferred her old school and she said how could she know when she hadn't started the one in Kirchhoffen.'

'That's our daughter,' he said mechanically. 'Literal and logical.'

Then suddenly he heard Clémence cry out. His gaze flew to her, dismayed at the sight of tears now streaking her freckled face as she ploughed into the slipway. The young guy watching the kayak station ran to help her, saying something in a surprised voice that Noah didn't catch. Clémence abandoned the kayak and shoved past him, racing up the slope to Noah and Florine. 'Maman, why are you crying?' All the familiar signs of anxiety were in the rapid flapping of her hands, the tears, the pitch of her voice.

Both parents automatically turned their attention to soothing her.

'I'm fine,' Florine smiled. 'I was talking to Papa about my father and it made me a little sad. It's natural to be sad about some things.'

Noah reached out and stroked Clémence's head, admiring Florine for fibbing so quickly and effectively. 'Sorry, little one. I was talking about Grandpère, too. I should have known it would upset Maman.'

'Oh.' Clémence's breathing and crying slowed at this eminently reasonable explanation. 'I don't remember him very well.'

'He loved you very much,' said Noah, while Florine took out a fresh tissue to wipe the emotional little girl's eyes. To Florine he said, 'I don't start work until noon tomorrow. Why don't you bring Clémence back then? I could get her a wristband.' Parent-code for: *She will go on rides, making time for us to talk again.*

Florine looked relieved. 'That sounds wonderful, doesn't it, Clémence?'

Tears all but forgotten, Clémence bounced excitedly. 'Yes, yes!'

A few minutes later, Noah returned to work in a shocked daze, apologising to his co-worker for extending his break by five minutes, and began assisting tourists in and out of kayaks, more like a robot than his usual sunny self.

What the fuck was he going to do? Only half an hour ago he'd felt on the cusp of so much – new love, new job, new life. And now it was all under threat.

His stomach dropped at the prospect of the conversation he'd have to have with Kat. Once again, the picture of her when he'd left her earlier came into his mind – sleepy, sexy, sensual and warm. A woman who had captivated his heart.

He couldn't bring himself to spend the evening wearing a mask of contentment, deliberately keeping her in the dark about something so important. She deserved better. And he knew exactly what he was going to say.

Angelique jumped up to look out of the salon window and gave a single woof and tentative tail-wag, the alert that a car had pulled onto the gravel outside.

Kat's heart lifted when she made out the big, grey bulk of Noah's vehicle behind the headlights necessary at dusk. The evening being warm and sultry, she'd put up her hair and dressed in shorts and a strappy top while she waited for him to arrive.

She and Angelique went to the door. 'I have cold beer in the fridge,' Kat greeted him cheerfully. Then she took in his set lips and the bleak light in his eyes and halted, heart clunking. 'Are you OK?'

The corners of Noah's mouth lifted but no smile reached his eyes. 'Yes . . . well, no.' He stepped indoors. Angelique cavorted expectantly, but when he barely seemed to notice her, she dropped to all four paws, glancing uncertainly at Kat as if wondering if she understood the problem.

Noah closed the door and stepped in close to Kat. His warm arms wrapped around her and he tucked her against his body, laying his cheek against her hair.

Kat slid her arms around his lean torso, but her heart kicked into a gallop. She'd seen Noah sad, happy, worried, resentful, relaxed, horny, hungry and angry but she'd never before seen him quite this desolate. 'What?' she whispered. Had something happened to Clémence? Or one of his parents? But no, surely; he'd be on his way to them, if so.

Finally, after several more seconds of holding her in that frighteningly rigid embrace, he croaked, 'Gotta talk.' Slowly, his arms dropped to his sides.

'OK.' Kat hovered uncertainly, keenly aware of the empty space between them. 'I'll . . .' Unable to decide how to react to this bleak Noah, she fell back on automatic hospitality. 'I'll grab those beers.' She hurried to the fridge to pull two out, shut an indignant-looking Angelique in the kitchen and then led Noah to the salon sofa.

They each opened their bottle and took a bracing swig. Kat put hers down and took his hand, heavy with a feeling of impending doom. 'I've never seen anybody look more miserable than you do right now. Tell me the worst.' *Tell me the worst*. The words echoed in her ears, trite and meaningless. It was what you said to someone owning up to a mistake or presenting a big bill – not how you extended understanding to the man you cared about when he was struggling to speak and could barely meet your eyes.

Noah stared at their joined hands for several moments before lifting his gaze. When his voice emerged, it was dull and shocked. 'Florine and Clémence turned up at the park. While Clé was kayaking, Florine asked me to take them both back to Castillon.'

The two sentences were so blunt, so unexpected, Kat couldn't immediately make sense of them. 'I don't really get . . . I mean, why would she ask you that?'

Noah took her other hand, too, as if nerving himself to deliver bad news. His lips moved stiffly. 'The first time I caught up with her, in June, I did offer to take her and Clémence back to Castillon. I barely knew you,' he added quickly, as if Kat had offered a protest. 'Yohan had blown up my life by moving Clé and her mother over here and at that time I was hoping Florine was unhappy enough to accept my offer and return to her old life in Castillon so that I could return to mine. But she insisted she loved Yohan. He'd been high-handed but she was willing to look past it. Now,' he went on bitterly, 'she says Yohan's insisting they have a child together. He's indicated that she owes him a baby as proof of loyalty – and it's finally made her recognise his behaviour as controlling.'

Kat sat very still, lightheaded with shock. 'Oh,' she said huskily. 'She wants to return to Castillon permanently? Not just to see her old friends or collect things she left behind.' Although their hands were still linked, his skin warm against hers, she felt as if he was about to float away.

He nodded, his Adam's apple bobbing as he swallowed.

'Which means,' she whispered, gazing into his face, seeing his freshly shaven jaw and tumbled hair, 'that you're going back to live in Castillon, too. Because of Clémence.' A feeling of foreboding, of dread, began to clench like a fist in her chest.

He didn't answer directly. 'But we have to remember that Florine still doesn't know about you and me. I was about to explain but Clémence saw Florine was tearful and got upset so I couldn't say any more right then. Instead, I've booked a staff wristband for Clémence tomorrow and Florine will bring her to the park as soon as it opens so we can talk while Clé's on the rides. I'm not on shift till twelve. I'll explain that we're together, that I'm in the process of renting a house and getting a job. We'll find some other solution.'

'Like what?' Kat didn't mean to sound quite so sceptical, but the words flew from her mouth as hard and sharp as pebbles.

A guarded expression stole into his eyes. 'I don't know yet.'

'There is no "other solution".' Kat's hands were sweating. She withdrew them from his and grabbed her beer, taking a big slug to loosen the feeling of a drawstring closing around her throat. She wiped her lips, her mind flying along what seemed to open up as the only logical path. The *only* way Florine was capable of acting. The *only* way Noah could react. 'If Florine's leaving Yohan, then she's going to want to get right away from his controlling ways. Returning to the Dordogne is perfect because he's committed to a job here. Having you around is perfect. You're reliable and kind. She's not an independent person—' *like me* clogged her throat and she had to drink again to force the words back. 'She's probably not faced it yet but sooner or later she'll realise Yohan was a big error, and so, therefore, was letting you go. If marrying a controlling husband was a reaction to losing a controlling father – well, now she's got that out of her system. How comfy life would be for her if you, her and Clémence were all one family again.'

'*Kat.*' Noah sucked a breath in sharply, a giant frown on his brow.

She threw up a hand to silence him. 'Don't try and tell me it won't be like that. You were going to stick the marriage out before Florine met Yohan, so you won't be *un*happy. You'll have your old life and friends and your parents around when they're not travelling.' She swallowed hard. 'Think how happy Clémence would be with her *maman* and *papa* together again. And how it will feel to have your daughter living with you full time.'

Noah's eyes were shocked. 'That's not how it's going to go—'

'It *is!*' She wrenched away from him and jumped up, knocking the beer bottle spinning off the table, the dregs splashing on the floorboards in a fizz of foam. 'Florine will hint at or suggest it. You'll look into Clémence's dear little face, the person you love most in all the world, and you won't be able to find it in your heart to resist.' The words were pouring out of her because this wasn't something she had to think about. She had, as the saying went, *all the feels* – all the bloody, shitty experience of being the child tossed around by adult choices. 'It will be exactly like that and I refuse to be an obstacle to Clémence's happiness.'

He leapt up, too, snatching her hands, raising one to his lips. His eyes flashed. 'Kat, that scenario has come entirely from your imagination. It doesn't exist! I came here to ask you to consider moving to Castillon, too. We can be together there.' His eyes were burning into hers and his voice dropped to a near whisper. 'I love you, Kat. I didn't expect to be saying this to you quite yet, but Florine's bombshell has made me look inside myself. This sick, hollow feeling inside me can only come from the prospect of losing someone I love. That person is you.'

For an instant Kat lost herself in his words, the declaration of love she'd vaguely thought might not be far away . . . but she'd never dreamt it would be delivered like this. *This hurt!* She sucked in a long, slow, excoriating breath and did the hardest thing she'd ever had to do. 'But my life's here,' she said resolutely. 'I couldn't abandon Livres et Café when Reeny's in intensive care and Graham's terrified of losing her. My dad's depending on my French language ability to help him find his feet in Alsace. Solly's likely to take the job with Dad, too, and expects me to be around. And I'd only be in the way in Castillon.'

She swallowed her pain at the expression of bleak disbelief in Noah's blue eyes. 'I think you should go and try your marriage again, for Clémence's sake,' she finished. It was hard to draw breath. She physically hurt, as if a hand had reached inside her and was cruelly squeezing anything within reach. Her stomach ached, her neck and shoulders too; her chest felt as if it was slowly filling with cement.

His grip tightened around her fingers, gaze narrowing in on her, his brain almost visibly working as it processed her words. It took several seconds before he came up with a new angle of persuasion. 'I know you were hurt by your parents splitting up,' he said. 'But even if I entered into the pretence you're suggesting, it won't change that. You can't heal yourself by making a sacrifice for Clémence; you weren't the reason things ended with Florine any more than it was your fault Jakey and Emma split up. The fact is that sometimes people have kids . . . and yet, later, the relationship fails. Me getting back together with Florine wouldn't make us happy.'

300

She stared up at him, stricken that he wasn't getting the point. 'Did you and Florine have screaming rows? Hit each other? Indulge in long silences?'

He grimaced in distaste. 'Of course not.'

She breathed deeply again, trying to calm herself and the heart that was threatening to beat itself to a pulp against her chest wall. 'Then *someone* will be happy. Her name is Clémence. She'll be happy for several years, maybe right up until adulthood, because you'll be a wonderful dad and Florine will be a great mum and you're able to be civilised, polite and friendly to each other. That's all Clémence needs. Any . . . nuances will whoosh over her head because her wonderful parents will give her a great life.'

Then, despite her good intentions, her conviction that she was acting for the greater good, she couldn't resist giving herself a straw to cling to. 'If, in a year, you're not back with Florine and you still think you love me, contact me then.'

'A *year*?' he demanded, his eyebrows curling like incredulous question marks, his eyes boring into hers. 'You can't mean *a year*, Kat.'

She pulled away, putting several strides between them. The constriction of her throat made her voice emerge low and guttural, like something from a horror film. 'I don't think we should see each other before you leave, Noah. I'm not going to pretend that I don't care about you. I'm going to tell you the truth. I love you, too, and it would be agony to watch you tie up the loose ends of your life in Alsace and pack to leave. It would be like knowing I had to have dental treatment without anaesthetic, but not when the drill was going to start.'

'So, you're going to pull out the whole tooth?' He sounded incredulous and angry. '*Now?*'

She nodded. If she spoke again, sobs would tear themselves from her throat and leave bloody wounds behind.

He breathed heavily for several moments. But when he spoke again, he was calm, the measured tone that she'd come to know. 'Then I'll see you in year.'

She closed her eyes so she didn't have to see him stride across the room and out through the small hall, where he belied the calm of his final few words by slamming the door behind him so hard that Angelique erupted in a volley of barking. Kat heard her hurling herself desperately at the kitchen door, shriller by the instant. '*Kat, Kat,*' she seemed to be yelling. '*Let me out. Something's happening. Let me at them and I'll protect you.*'

As if in a nightmare, tears pouring down her cheeks, Kat stumbled to the door to open it. Angelique launched herself from the room, racing into the salon, the bedroom, the bathroom, hunting frantically for the threat, barking so hard her front paws lifted from the floor. 'It's OK,' Kat said hoarsely, with what remained of her voice. 'He's gone.' She got herself a glass of water and half fell into a kitchen chair.

Angelique returned, panting, tail at a confused half-mast, gazing at Kat. Kat opened her arms and Angelique leapt up onto her lap, almost oversetting them both on the small chair. When Kat buried her face in the dog's fur to cry out her hopelessness and pain, Angelique accepted the role as stoic comforter, snuggling up on the cramped quarters.

Kat wept for how much it hurt to do the right thing. She sobbed because, contrary to what Noah said, hers and Clémence's situations were not the same. Both father and stepfather wanted Clémence, whereas neither had wanted Kat.

Twenty minutes later, the pity party over, she gave Angelique a last hug and let her down onto the floor. She drank more water, washed her face, and then picked up the lead. 'Come on, you deserve an extra-long walk,' she said, to the now tail-wagging dog. 'I think that when you became "Kat's dog" you rescued me, not the other way around. You deserve a treat.'

She picked up her house key and let herself out into the balmy night. Kat wouldn't be able to sleep and Angelique wouldn't mind a good old trek. Dogs could sleep any time. It was only humans who lay in bed staring fruitlessly into the dark and waiting for dawn.

Chapter Twenty

Kat must have slept eventually because she was awoken at eight a.m. by a knock at her front door.

Her heart leapt. Noah? Had he somehow found a route out of this maze of misery? She'd told him not to try but a hopeful heart was an irrational thing.

After grabbing a robe and stumbling to the door, she found her early morning caller was Solly. It was the first time she'd felt a stab of disappointment at seeing him.

'Hey,' he said, brushing past her after a quick hug then ruffling Angelique's ears. 'I thought you'd be up.'

She yawned. 'I should be. What's happening?' She took in the fact that he wasn't in park uniform and that his crash helmet dangled over one arm.

Solly followed her into the kitchen and glanced at her coffee machine as if disappointed that it wasn't on. She plugged in the kettle instead. 'News,' he said, dropping into a kitchen chair. 'I've formally accepted an offer to train in IT support to work for Dad and Phillipe.'

She took in his beaming smile. 'You look happy about it so good, congratulations!'

'Thanks.' His grin only grew wider. 'But first me and Ola are going travelling on our scooters. My boss at the park is pissed at me for not seeing out the summer and Mum and Dad are because I don't want to start work with them quite yet but we're a bit "in lurve".' He laughed self-consciously.

Kat halted, almost dropping the clean mugs she'd just picked up. 'You're what?'

He laughed again. 'You heard me. I'm taking a leaf out of your book, sis, and going travelling. Me and Ola have saved enough to have a few weeks off before she goes back to uni and I start work.' He glanced at the time and rose without even waiting for the kettle to boil. 'I'm here to say goodbye for now. I packed my stuff yesterday while Noah was working and he went out too early this morning for me to catch him. Will you say bye to him for me? I'll text him, too. He helped me a lot when I first arrived.'

Kat's conscience twinged. 'I was too taken up with Jakey to pay you as much attention as I should have.'

He pulled her into another giant hug. 'Rubbish. You've been fantastic. It's been great to spend the summer with you. Now Ola and me are headed south through France to Switzerland. See you in the autumn.'

And then he left. Kat sank into the chair he'd just vacated. She'd known Solly had fallen for Ola but hadn't anticipated him heading off across the continent with her. It was great that they were a bit 'in lurve', despite her own heart feeling like a rock.

Angelique padded in to lay her head on Kat's lap, flattening her ears and wagging her tail. Kat stroked the soft, smooth fur and wondered how Howard and Irina felt about Solly taking off.

She didn't have long to wonder because, almost

immediately, her phone rang. 'Solly's just texted to say he's told you,' said her dad, without preamble. 'I'm shocked and Irina's disappointed because she was trying to talk him into starting his training with us straight away.'

Kat bet she was. Irina had been keen to tie Solly in. Perhaps she'd seen how out of touch Howard had become with Kat and didn't want that with her own child. 'Solly's an adult, Dad,' she murmured. 'But he's also young and a bit starry-eyed.'

'That's true, I suppose,' Howard agreed. 'And he should be back in a few weeks.'

After the call ended, Kat dragged herself off to the shower, her thoughts returning to Noah's bombshell last night, filled with fruitless yearning. Why couldn't Florine be the kind of woman who would just say 'No' to Yohan's demand for a child and mean it? Or say 'Yes' and be happy? Couldn't she have stayed in love with Yohan? Or moved back to Castillon without taking Noah?

Impatient with herself, she snatched up the soap. If Florine moved back to Castillon then Noah *had* to. He'd made it perfectly plain when he followed Clémence to Alsace that living the breadth of France away from her was not acceptable.

And to think that she'd once been sure that all she had to do was stop the cyber-attacks on Livres et Café and her life would be OK . . .

After her shower, she dressed in shorts and polo shirt, plaited her hair and then put Angelique in the car and drove along the lanes to Muntsheim between farm fields of golden stubble, turning off before she reached Muntsheim's business park and driving under the black metal 'Parc Lemmel' sign. She left the car in the shade and let a dancing Angelique out, up on her paw tips in delight.

Kat paused, dog lead in hand. She shrank from walking down to the lake, or along the wild trail, because either might bring her in proximity to Noah. Her eyes boiled at the idea of facing him now, when her hurt was so raw and new.

A deep breath and she turned along the top of the park, away from the staff accommodation, up behind the huge wavy slide. They'd walk towards the gate and circle back. She was only halfway to the gate, though, when she heard a high, excited young voice. 'Angelique! Kat!'

Her heart sank.

Pinning on a smile, she turned. Clémence was running towards her, and Angelique immediately strained at the end of the lead, keen to meet her little friend. In the background, a smiling Florine was locking up her sleek car, parked beneath a stand of trees.

Clémence arrived in a breathless rush. '*Bonjour* Kat, *bonjour* Angelique. Papa's getting me a wristband today and I'm going on all the rides.'

Florine arrived at a more sedate pace, her well-cut shorts and beautifully fitting espadrilles looking as if they'd been handmade for her. She seemed more relaxed than at any time in the short time Kat had known her – presumably because she'd made her decision and was confident that Noah was about to whisk her off to her old life, Kat thought. Florine said, 'She's too excited to be at home so I brought her here, where she can run around and burn some energy.'

'Can we help you walk Angelique, please?' Clémence demanded, her eyes alight. 'I like walking her very much.'

Kat smiled. Apart from not having a hard enough heart to disappoint Noah's daughter, she could hardly refuse when she'd been intercepted so plainly heading away from Livres et Café. 'Of course,' she murmured, handed over the lead, and watched the pair run off together. Florine and Kat fell into step. Nearby, someone in park uniform was sweeping the paths. Kat felt a pang that it wasn't Solly and she wouldn't be seeing him for weeks.

Florine tucked her hands in her pockets. 'She loves your dog. Maybe I should get her one of her own.'

'If it suits your lifestyle, I'm sure she'd adore it,' Kat replied. And, with a masochistic urge to bring things into the open, 'Does Yohan like dogs?'

Florine hesitated. Then, she said, 'Clémence and I are going home to the Dordogne.'

'Oh,' said Kat hollowly. 'Just . . . just you and Clémence? For good?'

'Things haven't worked out with Yohan as I'd hoped.' Florine sounded a shade too light and happy for someone talking about the end of her marriage.

'I'm sorry,' Kat answered mechanically. She cast around for the polite sort of something you said to friendly acquaintances. 'We'll miss you at book club.'

Florine held her hands palm up in just the same way Kat had seen Clémence do. 'It's sad. But it will be good to have my old life back.'

A wave of grief swept over Kat at the thought that Florine getting her old life back meant Kat couldn't have a new one. She wished fervently that she'd walked Angelique in Kirchhoffen this morning and so avoided this chance meeting. Probably she'd adopt that strategy now, at least until she knew Noah had left. 'Do I assume you're getting back together with Noah?' She couldn't help the question popping out and was surprised at how even she was able to keep her voice.

Florine did the palms-up shrug again, which told Kat that the other woman wasn't ruling it out. 'That's not the reason I'm leaving,' she said guardedly. Then she added in obvious alarm, 'Clémence doesn't know we're going yet.'

That gave Kat the perfect excuse to say, 'Then let's not talk about it anymore.' She made her walk as short as was politely possible, silently promising Angelique a longer one later to make up for it, and said goodbye to the pretty mother and daughter outside the book café. They turned in the direction of the staff accommodation gate and Clémence took out her phone, Kat apparently instantly forgotten as she yelled excitedly into it, 'Papa, Papa, we're here!'

For the rest of the morning, Kat served tourists with refreshments and books, dealt with calls and checked her orders for next week. The chatty British ladies Kat had mentally christened Currant Bun and Friendly Pony turned up yet again and showed just as much interest – or nosiness – as last time. Kat almost melted in the sun as she tried to remain as friendly and polite as customers deserved while bearing in mind her earlier suspicion that they were picking her brains so they could open their own similar business.

It seemed less important, though, than the painful knowledge that somewhere in the park Clémence was gaily enjoying rides while her parents arranged to move the little family back across France to where they'd all lived good lives before.

She wished she could have had another day off.

Or a week.

A month.

At least until there was no danger that Noah would enter Livres et Café and Kat would have to watch Florine look to him for protection, a beautiful, elegant woman who seemed incomplete without a man.

By Saturday, Kat's nerves were in shreds.

Not a single word had come from Noah, which hurt no less for being exactly what she'd demanded of him.

Solly had kept in touch, latterly via a text to say he and Ola had bought a tent, were camping at a site at Sursee Waldheim in Lucerne, Switzerland and had swum in the lake.

Even Howard and Irina had been quiet, and Kat hadn't bothered discovering whether this was because they were busy settling happily into their new life, or because they saw no point contacting Kat if Solly wasn't around to be included in any arrangements. Or both.

Her thoughts frequently strayed to whether Florine would face – or had already faced – Yohan to tell him she and Clémence were returning to the Dordogne, or just pack and go. For the first time ever, she felt some sympathy with Yohan. If he felt anywhere near as gutted as Kat felt . . . well, maybe they should both learn not get in too deeply with people. The fun and superficial relationship she'd shared with Jakey may not have ended well but at least she'd been able to shuck it off. She hadn't carried the loss around with her like a cannon ball lodged in her chest.

Luckily, by the time Kat had worked twelve-hour shifts and given Angelique her daily walks she was tired enough to sleep for at least some of each night. If she lay awake for the rest, wondering whether Noah and family were back in Castillon-la-Bataille yet or still winding up their lives in Alsace, that was something she bore silently and alone. She emerged heavy-eyed in the morning, tormented by the temptation to run down the slope over the dusty summer grass to the lake to see if the man she'd fallen stupidly in love with was still on the kayak station.

She never gave in to it.

Like the well-worn ripping-off-a-sticking-plaster analogy, it was better to get it over with in one painful rush.

Danielle obviously picked up on the fact that things weren't going well because her brown eyes were full of sympathy whenever she gazed at Kat and she took to throwing out her arms for silent hugs, making hot tears prickle in Kat's eyes. None of the assistants asked Kat why she was going round with a face like a wet Sunday so she could only assume Danielle had given them the nod that their manager was in need of some understanding. Kat developed the habit of ducking into the office to occupy herself on the computer or phone when she needed a break from wearing her brave face, allowing her the bonus of Angelique's undemanding, loving company.

She was serving at the outdoor café seating when Graham turned up on Saturday evening. It was coming up to eight p.m. and Justine and Romain were cleaning down the tables and then bringing them indoors. Kat summoned a smile when she saw her boss, his grey hair on end and a face full of fatigue. 'Hello, stranger. Great to see you. How's Reeny? I've been waiting for the OK to start calling her again.' A glance through the window told her that no one had yet begun on cleaning the espresso machine. 'Coffee?'

Graham gave her a quick, distracted hug. 'Reeny's doing better. I don't want to jinx anything but there's a plan to move her out of intensive care soon.'

Gladly, Kat hugged him back. 'That's the best news I've heard all year.'

'Let's both have that coffee over a chat in the office,' he suggested.

After asking Danielle to take over closing up, Kat arrived in the office to find him behind the desk in the spot she'd grown used to occupying herself, his fingers steepled. She put down the coffee cups and took the seat on the other side of the desk.

Graham took up his drink. 'I want to thank you for the job you've been doing here. You've been a star.'

'You're welcome,' Kat said. 'Danielle's fantastic and we've had really good assistants this summer. We've been exceptionally busy and Park Lemmel should continue to attract a good tourist trade through September, tailing off through October. The park has some winter events planned so we'll gear up to take advantage of those.'

Graham's answering nod was vague, as if he wasn't really listening. 'Yeah. Course.' He sipped his coffee, swivelling gently on the office chair. He took a breath and looked Kat in the eye. 'I've got some news, gal.'

'Oh?' Kat waited, wondering what it could be as he'd issued Reeny's health bulletin and there was no reason she knew of for him to bellyache about Livres et Café.

Graham swivelled the chair a little harder. 'We're going back to the UK,' he said in a rush. 'When Reeny's well enough to transfer to UK medical care, I mean. Her having been so ill, Mum suffering in her old age, well, it's all made us realise we want to be nearer our family. We want to see the grandkids grow up and I owe Mum more than the occasional flying visit when she ends up in hospital. We miss our daughters. It was all very nice when things were going well and family could come out here to see us, but this year's taught us that things sometimes go badly.'

'Oh,' Kat said again, mind racing and heart sinking. It would be a wrench if her friends left, especially Reeny, who called herself Kat's family 'from love'. She swallowed. 'That's a bombshell, but if it's best for you and Reeny . . .' She had to swallow again before adding huskily, 'But don't worry. If I can manage Livres et Café for you while you're looking after Reeny, I can manage it for you while you're living in the UK.' She wasn't distressed enough to think that this was Graham's only option, though. She wasn't even certain it was lawful for a non-resident to own a business in France. Her lips were suddenly dry as she realised this might not just be about being parted from those who'd treated her like their own.

When Graham only frowned up at a corner of the ceiling without speaking, she gave him a nudge. 'Or do you plan to sell?' The last sentence hung in the air, thin and wobbly. Emotional. Exactly how you weren't supposed to negotiate with one of your bosses – but Reeny and Graham were so much more. Kat picked up her coffee cup and was shocked to see it tremble in her hand.

In the silence, Angelique yawned and stretched, left her bed and padded over to lodge her warm head on Kat's thigh.

Graham rubbed his jaw, flicking a glance at Kat and then away. 'It's already sold,' he said baldly. Then, as Kat just stared at him, dumbfounded, he added defensively, 'Needs must, I'm afraid. The opportunity came up.'

It seemed as if the *whump, whump, whump* of Kat's heartbeat filled her ears. Her chest and throat. Even her arms and legs pulsed along with it. 'What does that mean for the staff?' she whispered.

313

Graham took a long swig of coffee. 'Well,' he said awkwardly. 'The new people are going to manage it themselves.' A bead of sweat popped on one side of his forehead as he admitted, 'I'm afraid they don't need you, Kat. They're buying it as a going concern and intend to keep Danielle on as under-manager to cover when they take their days off. They don't need a manager as well. We're heartbroken to do this to you, of course, and so grateful for everything you've done.' His manner changed from grave formality to forced positivity. 'When the sale goes through there will be a nice bonus for you, don't you worry about that. Enough to see you through finding a fab new job. You're so dynamic and effective, you'll sort something out in no time.'

'And when is the sale?' Kat asked almost conversationally, stroking Angelique's ears while her eyes burned with shocked tears, taking comfort from the silkiness passing through her stiff fingers.

Graham examined his empty coffee cup. 'September 1st,' he muttered.

Though she trembled at this fresh shock, Kat managed, 'Two-and-a-half weeks' time?'

He nodded.

Mechanically, her hand passed over and over Angelique's furry head as she calculated numbly, the truth rearing up in her face like a monster . . . the sale must have been agreed ages ago. Months, maybe.

Graham blustered on that Kat mustn't think her work hadn't been appreciated, while she noted absently that the shock hadn't stopped the whirring of her brain. She must confront the monster. 'Just to clarify . . . you've scraped together the time to market the business and sell it, yet you've been too busy and upset to work a single shift at the book café or handle any ordering or emailing. And you have also been too busy to warn me what was in the wind? I've gone above and beyond, and you've kept me in the dark,' she added for emphasis, though her voice shook.

At the note of accusation in her voice, Graham stuck out his chin. 'If you want to put it like that,' he agreed abruptly. 'The most negative view, like.'

'The most accurate,' Kat rejoined, her voice stronger now. 'Just out of curiosity, how? Don't buyers normally want multiple viewings of a business?'

Graham rasped his jaw again, looking more sweatily uncomfortable by the second. 'Their accountant's seen the annual accounts and I showed them round the premises a couple of times.'

Kat stared at Graham, the man she'd long considered her friend. Whether he was acting out of character *in extremis* or whether she'd never known him as she'd thought, she felt an urge to hold him accountable, just as she'd called Jakey out when he'd treated her as if she was of no value. She was so freaking *sick* of being pushed aside. 'You brought them round when I wasn't here?'

'We were closed,' he agreed shortly, not meeting her eyes. 'And they've visited a few times as customers.'

Understanding broke over Kat in a hot, sickening wave, a vision of the women she'd mentally christened Friendly Pony and Currant Bun swimming before her eyes. 'Two British women have been visiting, asking me twenty questions every time. I guess that was them? I thought they were unusually nosey but, in their way, they were doing their due diligence.' Her throat tried to dry up on her and she took another drink to ease it. 'And to think I suspected they were considering setting up in competition and protected your interests by guarding what I said.'

He cleared his throat. 'Yes. Well. I'm afraid we need to give you your month's notice. The new people think it will work very well if that starts 31 August and it's the 13th today, so you get more than a month's notice, really, if you leave at the end of September, after you've handed over.'

Kat let out a crack of laughter that made Angelique jump and give her a look of deep reproach. 'You can go to hell,' she said in her most pleasant voice. Slowly, she rose, untying her apron and dropping it on the floor. 'I'm off.'

'Your contract says a month's notice,' Graham spluttered, jumping to his feet.

'Take me to a tribunal,' Kat suggested. 'But I think you're going to find it tricky to embark on a tussle from the UK, especially as the French Labour Code says that if I work more than a thirty-five-hour week you must pay me overtime – something you somehow overlooked – so I've no doubt worked my notice in advance.'

'But, but . . .' Graham stuttered. 'There's things Danielle doesn't know.'

'Then you'd better teach her.' Kat snatched up her bag, making Graham leap aside as if he feared she was about to beat him around the head with it. Ignoring his nervous flinch, she swung around his side of the desk, sliding out the drawers in order to retrieve the few possessions she kept there. 'C'mon, Angelique.' Angelique's ears and tail flew up as Kat swiftly picked up her lead and tucked the soft 'Kat's Dog' dog bed beneath her arm.

'Kat!' Graham protested as she yanked open the door. 'The new people are expecting you to hand over.'

She spun in the doorway. 'What did you do? Give them my word on it?' she challenged.

Graham had the grace to look shamefaced. 'All right, I can see why you're upset. I haven't communicated with you well enough. I'm sorry. But if you walk out, you're going to leave me in a very awkward situation.'

Slowly, Kat stepped back into the room, Angelique pattering at her side. She leaned on the desk and skewered her erstwhile boss with her gaze. 'You haven't "communicated" with me at all, and you've done it deliberately. You've taken all my loyalty and extra work and then dumped me. When I first came to Alsace, you and Reeny helped me out with accommodation and friendship. Consider the favour thoroughly repaid . . . and the friendship at an end.'

She whirled and stalked from the office out into the café area, which was strictly off-limits to Angelique, even when, like now, it was closed. Danielle looked up from the till in surprise.

Graham puffed after Kat. 'If you work your month's notice, we'll see if we can increase that bonus.'

Shock rippled over Danielle's face.

Kat eyed Danielle, for the first time feeling compunction for throwing in her apron so impulsively. She stepped slowly over to her friend and colleague and pulled her into a huge hug, Angelique's bed tumbling out from under her arm. 'I'm really sorry,' she said, against Danielle's hair. 'Graham's just told me he's sold the book café and I won't be needed. You'll be kept on. And with me gone you'll be in a good position to negotiate extra money from the new people.'

Danielle pulled back, her eyebrows flying up. 'He has sacked you from today?'

'No,' Kat admitted, 'he wants me to stay until the end of September. I'm walking out because I can't work even a minute more for someone who treats me as I've just been treated. Sorry,' she repeated, squeezing Danielle's hands.

Danielle's brows clanged down again. 'I'm not sure I want to work for him either. Or his new people.'

'Eh, here,' Graham protested, grey brows drawn down in a ferocious vee. 'It wasn't up to you to talk to Danielle, Kat. Danielle, that's a conversation for you and me.'

Danielle tilted her nose in the air. 'But my working hours are over for tonight so I'm going home.'

Graham looked aghast. 'Then . . . then we'll talk tomorrow.'

Danielle removed her apron. 'I'm not on duty tomorrow. It's the confirmation of my niece in the local church. I am not on the roster again until Tuesday.'

'So, what am I supposed to do for a manager on Sunday and Monday?' Graham snapped.

Danielle gave a marvellous French shrug, so Kat followed suit, though she was beginning to ache with sorrow more than anger.

In a few moments, the two women had flopped on a bench outside in the arcade, gazing at each other, Angelique sitting at Kat's feet and looking puzzled. Kat blotted her eyes on a tissue. 'I was wrong to spill the news to you like that. I'd better tell you the whole story.' She recounted the meeting with Graham, wondering whether Danielle would think she'd overreacted and return indoors to calm the situation down.

But Danielle only squeezed Kat's hand in sympathy. 'We have worked incredibly hard this summer, especially you. We deserve respect and respect is not there. I will go home and consider, and maybe meet with Graham next week. But maybe not. I could find a job where I arrive home by five or six. Graham is not the only one to want to see more of his family.'

After chatting a little longer, they hugged again and Kat walked Angelique around the building to her car, feet dragging, trying to absorb the astonishing fact that her time at Livres et Café had ended. If only she could talk it over with Noah . . . Her resolve not to see him wavered.

What if he hadn't left yet? Impetuously, she turned and began running over the grass to the staff gate, Angelique a happily lolloping escort, stabbing in the key code and hurrying along the left fork to where the old, green park home stood.

Her steps slowed as it came into view, looking shut up and abandoned.

She forced her reluctant feet to take her to the lounge window to peer in. All was neat. No sign of Noah's messenger bag hanging by the front door. She circled the caravan, peeping forlornly into window after window. Stripped beds. No coats, bags, shoes, books or anything that made a place look lived in.

Achingly slowly, she turned away. Noah had taken her at her word and left without saying goodbye. Somehow, she had expected him to at least try.

Angelique looked up at her and whined, as if puzzled as to why they hadn't gone indoors.

'Nobody there,' Kat whispered, trying to smile, and then she turned to trudge back up the dusty track and over summer-dry grass to her car.

When she arrived home ten minutes later, she checked her phone and discovered a text from Reeny. *Darling, we need* to talk. *I'm sure we can sort things out. Can you come and see me next week? xx*

Kat returned a chilly: *Oh, you're suddenly well enough to talk, are you? How convenient.*

She wasn't surprised when silence met her snark. Some of Reeny and Graham's recent lack of availability must have been political, designed to make it easy for them to keep Kat in the dark until the time came to jettison her. That knowledge made their entire relationship a mockery.

Kat was in no mood to talk.

They might as well know it.

Noah gazed around the new home he'd occupied for a week. It was nice. Recently painted and neatly furnished, the upstairs held a modest bedroom for Clémence and a larger master with an en suite shower room. He smiled to remember Clémence's puzzlement when he explained that *en suite* might be a French phrase but that the French didn't use it as the British did, to describe a bath or shower room directly off a bedroom.

The rooms were airy and bright and there was much more space than in the caravan, yet he found himself missing its worn and cramped charms. He missed his work at the park. He missed Solly coming in tipsy in the early hours.

He missed Kat. He missed her so much that every time he thought of her, he suffered from what he assumed was meant by the phrase 'a sinking feeling' – his heavy heart wanting to sink down into his hollow stomach.

He plodded down the open-tread wooden stairs and through the kitchen to the garden. Though small, it boasted a neat lawn. Florine and Clémence were seated around a green table on the patio and they looked up from the phone they were poring over. 'May I have a bookcase for my new room?' Clémence called excitedly. 'I like this white one, but Maman says you would have to put it together.'

He managed a smile for his daughter as he sat on the seat next to her and tilted the screen so that he could see the object of her desire. 'That sounds within my capabilities. A bookcase for your room is a great idea. Let's get it.'

'Now? *Oui, oui!*' Clémence leapt up and capered off towards the house.

Florine looked awkwardly at Noah. 'Shall I pay? We hadn't talked about this purchase.'

'No.' All they seemed to have done for the last week was talk. He curved his lips in the semblance of a smile to make up for the shortness of his reply. 'But thank you. Are you coming to the furniture store?' he added politely. It was strange now to spend as much time as he was in her company.

She flicked back her hair, looking equally unsure. 'If you don't mind.'

'Not in the least.' He gestured for her to go ahead of him, locking the patio doors, picking up his wallet and car keys, answering Clémence's excited chatter about whereabouts in the new room her bookcase would stand, getting into his car with Florine in the front passenger seat and their daughter strapping herself into the rear.

He didn't think he'd ever felt so lonely.

He'd left his heart in Kirchhoffen with a vibrant woman with springy dark curls. He'd thought he'd one day be making his home with her.

Chapter Twenty-One

Kat spent the next week feeling lost. Stalking out of Livres et Café had afforded her momentary satisfaction but her eyes kept leaking hot tears that she could do nothing to halt. No amount of feeling herself on the moral high ground prevented her from mourning the loss of the job she'd loved, despite the long hours.

No doubt the bonus Graham mentioned would not now be forthcoming and Kat would soon need a new way to make her living. At least in the short term, she could write features freelance again . . . if her present frame of mind didn't leave her totally bereft of inspiration.

Maybe what she needed was a whole new life. If she gave a month's notice on her apartment, she could sell or give away the furniture and go travelling again. She tried the idea out on Angelique, saying, 'Me and my dawg on the open road.' Angelique looked willing, if the speed of her tail wag was anything to go by, but Kat would probably have got the same reaction to 'I'd better do my laundry.' Angelique was reliably on Kat's side no matter the topic.

Or she could stay in the apartment she loved and get another job locally. There must be loads. Or she could try something entirely new, like decorating charity shop furniture, as she had for her own place.

In the end, the only decision she made was not to make a decision. She read, walked Angelique and trimmed shrubs in the garden, slathering on factor fifty because the sun made her feel as if someone had put her in a giant toaster.

And she remembered how it had felt when Noah had been beside her, laughing as they tackled the shrubs together, or said to hell with the gardening and went to bed instead. She spent a lot of time wondering whether, in sending Noah away, she'd been guilty of making a decision about their future alone when it should have been made jointly.

When the knocker sounded three weeks after she left the book café, Angelique raced to the door, as usual. When Kat caught up with her, she found on the doorstep a small, frail-looking female figure wearing a red cotton hat that only drew attention to the creamy pallor of her skin. 'Reeny!' she gasped, grabbing Angelique's collar to prevent her from leaping up. Reeny looked as if a puff of wind would bowl her over, let alone an exuberant canine.

'Hello, Kat.' A small tremor threaded Reeny's voice but her smile was exactly as Kat remembered: wide and twinkly.

Kat almost pulled her into a big hug, so glad was she to see her up and about. Then the reality of why Kat was hanging around at home instead of racing through her day at Livres et Café hit her like a cold shower. Still, she couldn't leave any twig-like human standing about. She beckoned her in. 'Come and sit in the shade. I'll make you a drink.'

She led Reeny to the outdoor table and settled her on the only chair with a cushion. Angelique gently laid her muzzle on Reeny's lap while Kat returned indoors for iced orange juice.

'Well,' she said, when she'd brought out the non-matching glasses and taken the chair opposite Reeny's. 'You don't look well enough to drive yourself so did Graham drop you off?' She saw no point in following the normal courtesies of asking after Reeny's health. What lay between them was too big and painful to add a polite gloss to.

Reeny smiled, her eyes crinkling. 'I sent him down to the tearoom. He galumphs into conversations like an elephant in Doc Martens.'

'True,' said Kat candidly. 'But is there much left for us to say to each other?'

Stroking Angelique's head, Reeny's lips turned down. 'I think so because we – you and me – haven't talked at all. To be honest, I shouldn't be here because I'm on immunosuppressants, but I was just so shocked at your reaction to our news, Kat.'

Kat was shocked in her turn. She'd assumed that if Reeny had anything to say, it would be an apology. The disappointed tone stung her into retorting, 'You should have stayed at home if you can't appreciate my grievance. How would you have felt, in my place? I worked my arse off for you guys when you needed me and you rewarded that by deliberately keeping me out of the loop, to the extent that Graham skulked about showing the buyers around the premises after hours, and I only met them when they visited Livres et Café posing as customers and pumping me for information.' She moistened her throat with a sip of orange.

After several moments, Reeny said, 'I apologise if that's how it seemed to you.'

Kat didn't suppress a snort. 'Seemed? Those are the facts.'

Bees droned around the rose that had swallowed up a nearby trellis. Angelique yawned and left the humans in favour of a spot of sunbathing on the lawn. A window of the apartment above opened with a screech and faint piano music wafted out onto the breeze. 'All right,' conceded Reeny, eventually. 'Those are the facts. But there are others.' She sighed, leaning forward to support herself on her elbows on the tabletop. 'I'm sorry, Kat. We have put our own interests first and, in retrospect, we didn't consider you and took your support for granted.'

'I can sympathise with you selling. But not the cloak-and-dagger way you've chosen to do it,' Kat put in.

Reeny inclined her head in acknowledgement. 'When life-threatening illness strikes,' she murmured, 'one becomes prone to looking inward. Your life becomes unrecognisable. It's taken up with appointments and treatments and waiting. Your future's under threat. Your priorities change. Your loved ones, too, face a different life and a different future. You have such a limited amount of energy and focus that perhaps you apply it selfishly.' She laid her hand over Kat's and it felt like a collection of sticks held together with tepid skin. 'If we had told you the business was up for sale you could have left at any time. We protected an asset – you – but we forgot that you're a person.'

'I thought I was a friend, too,' Kat murmured, her voice husky.

'Yes.' Reeny's voice was just as thready. 'One who's given us unstinting support and didn't deserve to be used.' Her smile wavered. 'Initially, we hoped they'd keep you on as manager, but we have known for a while that that wouldn't fly. I can only repeat our apology.'

'Thanks,' said Kat bleakly, watching the way the breeze ruffled Angelique's fox-coloured fur.

'Is there any way,' Reeny asked earnestly, leaning still closer, 'that you would consider coming back to do the handover?'

Kat wavered. She *could*. She could help her old friends out one last time and part on good terms, with big-hearted understanding for their traumas over the last year and generosity of spirit. It was on the tip of her tongue to say, 'Yes, OK.' Instead, when she opened her mouth she said, 'Sorry. You let me down too badly. Danielle and Graham can do the handover between them. Danielle's told me she's staying on, at least in the short term.'

Reeny looked shocked. She'd obviously anticipated Kat capitulating. 'Graham has to organise our return to the UK . . .' She halted when she saw Kat's lifted eyebrow. For the first time, a smudge of colour tinged her cheeks. 'Ah. Self-interest on our part again. And taking you for granted. I'm beginning to see your side of things.'

For several minutes they sipped their drinks in silence. A child laughed in a nearby garden, a pure and musical sound. It made Kat think of Clémence and wonder if she was happy, now she was back in Castillon, on the banks of the Dordogne. She and Noah were maybe even now cleaving through the water on kayaks or paddle boards. Florine, too, perhaps.

Reeny broke into her wistful thoughts. 'You know, Kat, people will always let you down – but usually with cause. We failed you but we had our reasons, even if you don't judge them as good reasons. If you're going to lead your life expecting everyone to act perfectly, you'll receive nothing but disappointments. And then there's the matter

326

of whether you always behave perfectly. Are you really always your best self?'

Another silence but for buzzing insects and singing birds. Kat's throat had filled with tears. She couldn't speak. She couldn't look at Reeny. She could only look inside and wonder what her best self looked like.

After a few minutes, Reeny took out her phone. 'I'll call Graham to pick me up. I hope everything works out for you, Kat.'

'And for you,' Kat managed to choke.

They sat on together until they heard a car on the gravel, then Reeny walked slowly and heavily back through the apartment, declining Kat's offer of an arm to lean on, and let herself out with a quiet, 'Bye.'

'Bye,' whispered Kat, already missing their friendship, or what she'd *thought* it had been. 'I wish you a long and happy future.' Kat would only know if Reeny got that if word reached her through the grapevine, she supposed, trailing back to the patio alone. On the grass, Angelique's paws were twitching as she raced through her dreams. Reeny's words reverberated around Kat's mind. *Are you really always your best self?*

Guiltily, she remembered again how she hadn't spent enough time with Solly in his first week in France because she was deep in her infatuation with Jakey. If Solly had felt let down, he hadn't ever betrayed it, despite it being his first time living outside the UK and his French not being very good.

And Noah? There had been an ocean of disappointment in his eyes at her abrupt departure from his life.

After staring into space for more than an hour, she took out her phone and called Solly.

'Kat!' he cried, his voice warm and happy.

'Just thought I'd check you were OK.' She felt unexpectedly wobbly at his obvious pleasure in hearing from her. 'The tent hasn't blown away or anything?'

'No, I lost it in a game of cards,' Solly answered irrepressibly. Then he roared with laughter. 'Joking. It's fine, we're fine. Once we've decided whether to head east into Austria or south into Italy, we'll be off again.'

'Italy,' called Ola's voice in the background.

He laughed again. 'Ola wants to head right down south and maybe cross to Sicily.'

'Sounds great,' Kat said huskily, making up her mind not to tell him about the many disasters in her life for fear of infecting him with her desolation. 'Well, you know where I am if you need me. Don't overtax that scruffy old scooter. See you in a few weeks when you come back to put your nose to the grindstone.'

Then she went indoors to where her laptop sat on the kitchen table and began an email to Danielle.

Hi Danielle. Hope everything's going OK. If there are any questions you want to ask me about Livres et Café, do. I've calmed down a bit now and want to smooth your path if I can. Let me know if you want to meet up.

The next message went to Ulrica, the book café's web designer. *Just to mention, the hacker who gave all the trouble before is once again angry at her boyfriend. I HOPE I've scared her off, but I thought I'd let you know so you can look out for anomalies. I told her I wouldn't reveal her identity if she left Livres et Café alone but if you do encounter more problems let me know and I'll pass you her details. I'm sorry we won't be working together in the future.* In both cases, she copied Reeny into the messages so she'd know that Kat was making some effort, however small, at being her best self.

In the cool of the late afternoon, she took Angelique for a long walk, through the village park and woodland and deep into the countryside, pausing to sit beside a stream so Angelique could wade in and drink. Kat took Angelique her own bottle of clean water but she always enjoyed a stream or, even better, a good muddy puddle.

All the time, Kat's mind was working.

It was hard to examine your own actions and trying to guesstimate how those you cared about perceived them. Scales were meant to fall from your eyes to enable that, weren't they? But who in the hell had scaly eyes in the first place? She sighed and Angelique bounded out of the stream to bestow a doggy kiss and shake water all over Kat's legs.

'Thanks,' said Kat, not bothering to dry herself because the cold shower was quite pleasant on a baking hot day. 'Am I my best self today?'

Angelique wagged her tail, so probably thought her owner was her best self *every* day.

They set course for home, Kat wrestling with her conscience. Was she inclined to canter off on her high horse sometimes? Had it become a prickly habit to see herself as Ms Overlooked? To indulge in self-pity? OK, things had been tricky in her childhood, but she was an adult now.

Thoughts of her childhood led her to just one person. Slowly, she took out her phone and hit the name *Dad* in her contacts.

'Hello, darling,' he boomed when the call connected.

'How's everything?' she asked. 'Anything you need help with? I haven't asked lately.'

Howard hesitated. 'Irina's in a tizzy about something to do with our euro account and when we can apply for the *Carte de Sejour*. Any help you can give there would be welcome.' He chuckled. 'We were trying to work it out on our own because you've got such a busy job.'

Guilt lanced through her. She hadn't told her dad her job was no more, but just moped about on her own instead. 'I could pop over tomorrow,' she offered.

Howard's voice boomed again. 'Marvellous! Fancy Sunday brunch at about eleven? The bakery near here opens on weekend mornings so we can get some delicious croissants and rolls.'

'That will be lovely,' said Kat, meaning it.

When Kat arrived at the timbered and balconied house Howard and Irina had rented at Lingolsheim at eleven the next day, she was surprised to find Howard in charge of brunch and Irina nowhere to be seen.

'She's gone furniture shopping,' Howard explained gruffly, peering anxiously into a small saucepan on the hob. 'Glad you're punctual because I've started eggs benedict.'

'Right,' Kat answered, looking from the kitchen to the well-appointed living room and wondering where more furniture was to fit. She wouldn't have left Angelique at home if she'd known Irina would be absent.

Howard gently whisked the hollandaise sauce, at the same time scrutinising four poached eggs bobbing in another pan. 'But I need to concentrate. Can you check the bacon's not overcooking? And split the seedy rolls that are warming and butter one side of each. And put two plates in to heat. And make coffee with the machine thing.'

Kat found herself laughing. '*Who's* supposed to be making this brunch?'

Howard's grin lifted his luxuriant sideburns. 'I'm the chef, doing the artistic part. You're the kitchen porter doing as you're told.'

In just a few minutes they were sitting down at the gleaming white breakfast bar to eggs benedict, little steaming rafts of perfection on white plates, coffee in fine green china and croissants already warming 'for afters', as Howard put it.

'I doubt I'll be able to eat croissants as well,' Kat protested. But, in the end, she found that she did, probably as a reaction to having had little appetite lately. She spread delicious flakiness liberally with Nutella and observed, 'I thought I was coming to help Irina with French bureaucracy. Has she handed it over to you?'

Howard suddenly made himself extremely busy dabbing at the last flakes of pastry on his plate. 'To be honest, darling, I wanted to talk to you alone.'

Kat's stomach turned over. 'Why? Are you ill or something?'

'Best of health, thanks. It's just . . . well, I want to talk to you again about coming to work for Phillipe and me.' He grinned boyishly. 'I don't think Irina quite approaches you in the most helpful way sometimes, so I suggested that she find something else to do this morning while we talked.'

'Oh,' said Kat, wrong-footed. She hadn't anticipated this subject coming up again, witness the fact it hadn't occurred to her to look in the direction of Howard and Irina when considering her next career move.

Howard held up a hand as if expecting Kat to leap in with a refusal. 'I know you love your current job and I understand that you feel loyalty to the owners in their times of trouble—'

'I've left Livres et Café,' Kat blurted, flushing when Howard's jaw dropped in surprise. 'Half let go; half walked out. They've sold the business out from under me because they're returning to the UK.'

Howard stared at her for a full ten seconds. Then he cleared his throat. 'You didn't tell me.' There was an obvious note of hurt in his voice.

Kat shifted uncomfortably on the white leather bar stool that went so well with the rest of the clinically fashionable kitchen. 'Sorry. I only realised that yesterday. It wasn't a conscious decision. I just . . . well, it hasn't been a nice time. I suppose I've been indulging in a pity party and keeping to myself.' Then, because once upon a time she'd taken every little worry and woe to her dad, it all came pouring out, not just the shock of finding herself without a job but the empty, awful, heart-searing reality of Noah returning to his old life.

Awkwardly, Howard took her hand. 'Oh, darling. When I saw you and Noah together, I could tell you'd finally found someone to fall in love with. I was so pleased for you. I said to Irina, "He's the one." I wish you'd confided earlier.'

She swallowed, his wistful tone sending little darts into her conscience. 'Sorry. I just . . .' Her voice cracked. 'I'm used to dealing with things alone.'

The laughter lines around Howard's eyes drooped. 'I know we haven't seen much of each other in the last few years but I'm your dad, Kat. You can always talk to me, especially now we're only a ten-minute drive apart.'

A mirthless half-laugh forced its way past the lump in Kat's throat. 'Sorry,' she said again. Then tears boiled suddenly down her cheeks and she slapped her hands over her eyes, mortified.

332

'Kat,' Howard murmured, and his arm slid tentatively around her shoulders. 'I feel as if there's a whole lot you're not saying. It's like a wall between us.'

She snatched up her bag to hunt out tissues. 'Some things are better left unsaid.'

'Those are usually the very things that should come out,' he answered heavily.

His voice was so filled with longing and sorrow that it was as if he'd stamped on a trap door inside Kat marked 'pain' and it all came tumbling out. 'OK, then. The reason I didn't come to you with my unhappiness is that Noah put his daughter first. But you didn't. You dumped Mum and me and moved in with Irina. Solly arrived and you were all set up with your new family. Oh, I know I was there at weekends,' she hurried on, when she heard Howard make a horrified protest. 'But only on the fringe of your new family. Irina treated me like a nuisance, and you focused on Solly. So, no, I didn't come to you about Noah. I didn't think you'd understand.'

Howard's face flushed plum red, then almost as quickly drained of all colour. 'Oh, Kat.' He sounded stunned.

It was Kat's turn to pat his hand. 'I didn't put that very diplomatically. Sorry.' She found a clean tissue on which to wipe her eyes. 'And, to be truthful, although I said Noah chose his daughter, I told him he *had* no other choice. He had to go and give Clémence the chance of a whole family again. He was . . . angry. He suggested I was attempting to make up for what had happened to me.'

Wordlessly, Howard rose and pulled out a whisky bottle from a cupboard and two glasses from another. He half filled one of the glasses but Kat shook her head when he hovered the bottle over the other. He took a big gulp from the glass he'd poured himself and then coughed. 'I didn't know you felt so badly.' His voice was hoarse with dismay. He used his shirt to wipe the corner of his eye. 'But as for dumping you and Joanne . . .' He peered down into the whisky, which the light, through the crystal, turned into a hundred amber fragments. 'I did behave badly, but it didn't go quite as you seem to think.' He took another sustaining sip of whisky. 'It was a particularly difficult subject to discuss with a twelve-year-old girl.'

'I'm all grown up now,' Kat observed, feeling a churning mixture of sympathy and anger towards the balding, greying man looking so shocked and unhappy before her. 'Tell me your side of things.'

'It does sound as if the conversation's long overdue.' Howard wiped his eyes again and lifted his grey gaze to Kat's. 'It's incredibly hard to admit to your little girl that not only have you had an affair, but you've got a woman pregnant. I felt about this big.' He indicated half an inch between finger and thumb. 'But as for dumping your mother . . .! Joanne gave me no option. They say confession's good for the soul, but it certainly isn't for your marriage.' He gave a ghastly smile. 'The instant I told her the truth, she told me to get out. We were over. There was no shifting her from that stance. I can't blame her, looking back on it, but then I was horrified and panicky.'

Kat gaped at him. 'You mean you'd hoped to stay with Mum?'

He flushed, dropping his gaze. 'Yes. I had a bit of a pash on Irina, it's true, but when she told me she was expecting, I nearly had a heart attack. There's nothing like a risk to your marriage to make you value it. I couldn't believe I'd been so stupid, how carelessly I'd hurt your mum and you by acting on a crush.'

'Right,' Kat said slowly. Absently, she unscrewed the

whisky bottle and poured herself a tot after all, though she topped hers off with a dash of orange juice. 'This must have all gone on before you and Mum sat me down and told me you were leaving?'

He nodded despondently. 'After a particularly painful heart-to-heart, we agreed not to burden you with the sordid stuff. But your mum told you I'd dumped you both?' He sounded incensed.

Guiltily, Kat thought back. 'Maybe she never said as much,' she acknowledged eventually. 'But that's what I saw. You went off with Irina.'

'Yeah.' Howard wiped his eyes, leaving tear tracks on his ruddy, leathery skin. 'She wanted me. There was a baby on the way so the idea of living on my own somewhere only felt like compounding my awful error. I probably saw her as a bit of a consolation prize.'

'And she conveniently gave you a home,' Kat pointed out candidly.

After a moment, Howard nodded. 'True. My parents made a similar point.'

Kat decided that if they were getting things out in the open, it was going to be everything. 'Do you think Irina got pregnant on purpose?'

His gaze was bleak. 'I always suspected so, yes.'

Kat felt fresh rage at Irina but ploughed on without expressing it. 'She was possessive of you, always chiming in if I got your attention. And Solly – she acted as if I'd infect him with rabies if I touched him too much.'

Howard dropped his head, running his hand over his bald patch. 'I'm sorry I didn't stop that.' He screwed his eyes shut and groaned. 'She's a forceful woman. I've come to love her and appreciate her better points but in the early days I didn't manage her very well. Your mother was so much easier to live with that I suppose I was a bit of a wimp, modifying my behaviour to keep Irina happy. If I gave lots of attention to Solly then she was less sharp with you.'

'That stinks,' breathed Kat.

He gave a laugh that was almost a sob. 'Doesn't it? What a weakling you must think me.'

A vice closed around Kat's heart at his bitter disgust with himself. Her dad was trying to be honest and she was being judgy in return. She poured him another generous measure of whisky and a tiny drop more for herself. Then she laid her head on his shoulder. 'I think you made some mistakes, Dad. But you're human, just like the rest of us.'

He slid his arm around her so that her head fit more easily on his shoulder. 'I need to learn from my mistakes, don't I? I should be able to show my daughter that I love her without my wife being difficult. I suppose her possessive ways spring from insecurity. She came from an underprivileged family so when she gets her hands on something she wants, she hangs on.'

Kat was silent. She didn't think they'd ever discussed Irina's background. It was quite a surprise to think of her as having a reason for her self-serving ways. Reeny's words came back to her: *People will always let you down – but usually with cause. We failed you but we had reasons, even if you don't judge them as good reasons. If you're going to lead your life expecting everyone to act perfectly, you'll receive nothing but disappointments.*

Howard gave her a squeeze. 'Do you mind if I say something?'

She straightened, wondering if more home truths were coming her way. 'It's only fair you should have a turn.'

He paused to gently stroke her hair back from her face. 'Having an affair and getting Irina pregnant – those were failings on my part. But from then on, it seemed as if Joanne and Irina decided everything. They chose for me. From what you've told me, it's made me wonder: have you decided for Noah? Have you taken his options away, just like Joanne – if understandably – took mine?'

The vice around Kat's heart tightened. 'I didn't mean to. But I so didn't want to be Irina; the unwanted stepmum, the obstacle to Clémence's parents being together.'

Howard regarded her keenly. 'You're not Irina. You're Kat. You're not breaking up a marriage.'

'Noah kept saying that, but I think Noah and Florine might get back together without me on the scene.'

'Bullshit,' Howard snorted rudely. 'That man's in love with you or my name's not Howard Jenson.'

Wonder tingled through Kat. 'He did say he was,' she admitted uncertainly. She was beginning to see that she'd never given Noah what he deserved: believing what he said. Never believed *in* him.

Howard clucked in exasperation, giving Kat a reproving look. 'And you sent him away? I have a certain sympathy with him being angry.'

Kat laughed and sobbed all at once so that her eyes, nose and throat all burned. 'Thanks, Dad,' she whispered, throwing herself at him and giving him a tight hug, one that she hoped expressed all the love she'd always felt for him, despite his human frailties and poor decisions.

He gave a theatrical sigh. 'But I suppose you'll be clearing off to live in the Dordogne now, so I've talked myself out of getting you to join the firm.'

Shakily, she laughed. 'Probably. I need to talk to Noah. He might have closed the door behind him when he left.'

'Pshaw,' grunted Howard. 'He's not the kind to fall out of love in a few weeks.'

Driving home later – when the whisky had had a chance to dissipate – Kat hoped her dad was right about Noah. She'd been able to say: 'I'm not Irina. My situation's different.' But even Irina, though she'd acted badly, had gone after what she'd wanted rather than just give her man up.

Part of her was dying to get home and call Noah.

The other part had decidedly chilly feet at the prospect of moving her life to Castillon and then finding that things didn't work out with Noah.

But . . . there was only one way to find out if that would happen.

She had to be her best self.

She wouldn't assume that Noah would be like Howard, using someone as a fallback plan because what he wanted had been withheld.

Noah had never given her any sign that he was the kind of man who'd do the easiest thing.

He'd do the *right* thing.

And so would she.

Chapter Twenty-Two

Noah leaned in the doorway to Clémence's room and watched her rearranging the contents of her new bookcase for the umpteenth time. The books made him think of Kat – not that he needed anything to jog his memory – and he wondered if she was working at Livres et Café today. He checked the time and was surprised to see it was after closing. He was enjoying having his daughter with him all the time and somehow the days just flowed together.

'Are you sorting alphabetically by author today? Or title?' he asked idly.

His little girl twinkled up at him impishly, blonde pony-tail streaming down her back. 'By colour, in order of the rainbow – red, orange, yellow, green, blue, indigo, violet.'

He smiled as she turned back to her task, wondering at the satisfaction she got from creating patterns and order. It made sense. Randomness or the unexpected made her somewhere between uneasy and hysterical.

Clémence paused to survey her stack of indigo books, a smaller pile than any of the other colours. 'Will we go to Kat's book café soon?' She gave him a sidelong look. 'I do like new books.'

He shifted uneasily but made his tone casual, taking advantage of the adult's default evasion phrase. 'We'll see. It's time for you to get ready for bed now.'

As he'd anticipated, Clémence's eyes widened in protest. 'But I haven't put my books back.'

'OK, then,' he said, pretending to give in. 'I should think that will take you twenty minutes, then it's bath and bed.'

The distraction technique worked like a charm and Clémence turned her attention back to her coloured book stacks. If she were ten years older, she'd make a fantastic bookstagrammer on Instagram, setting books into artistic displays and following favourite authors.

Noah stepped softly away and went to his own bedroom to flop on the king-sized bed and flick uninterestedly through the TV channels. Adult lives were complex and hard for an eight-year-old child to get to grips with. Noah was taking care to present a serene exterior to Clémence, but he was in an emotional tumult, and had been since Florine's pronouncement that she wanted to return to Castillon, and then Kat's extreme response. He might want to cast himself on the floor and drum his heels, but he had resisted.

It was taking even more self-control not to take out his phone and call Kat, just to hear her voice. That would be wrong of him because it wasn't what she'd said she wanted. He'd even resisted calling Solly to check Kat was OK, helped by the fact that Solly and Ola were travelling and he was likely buzzing around Europe, blithely unaware of his sister's emotional well-being.

*   *   *

340

It was an hour later, when Clémence was safely in bed, that Noah's phone vibrated and lit up. He checked the screen.

Kat

His stomach gave a shocked bounce. Kat? His finger – was it *shaking?* – hovered over the green 'accept' icon and his heart took up an uncomfortably irregular rhythm.

Good news or bad? Happy or sad?

Drawing in a long, slow breath, and then another for luck – which also shook – he accepted the call. He was pleased that his voice didn't waver as he said, 'Either I've left something at your place . . . or you're eleven months and a few days early.' It had been a long and empty three weeks and four days since she'd told him not to contact her for a year.

Silence.

His heart sank. Was this going to turn out to be a pocket dial? Would he be condemned to listening to the sounds of Kat's evening while she carried on unaware that some random pressure on her phone screen had connected them?

Then he heard her breathe a laugh. 'I'm . . .'

He waited, as if teetering right on the edge of something and not sure which way he'd fall.

She cleared her throat. 'I'm calling to say I should have listened to you and tried to figure things out between us instead of making assumptions and calling the shots. I had a long conversation with my dad about it.'

Surprise rippled through him. 'Your dad?'

'He told me I'd tried to make your decision for you, which is unfair, obviously. I've been thinking hard, and maybe my clearing the way for Clémence to have her parents together was really a way for me to protect myself.'

341

She was speaking slowly as if puzzling it out as she talked. 'I was trying to make up for my own past, in some muddled way, but also getting the pain over with in case you *did* return to Florine for Clémence's sake. And,' she added doggedly, when he tried to speak, 'I projected what I felt had happened with Dad onto you. I set you up to fail me.'

He envisioned her having a mental tussle with herself as she meandered through the French countryside, her fox-like dog faithfully at her side, and his heart swelled. 'I haven't failed you,' he said huskily. 'Clémence is with me temporarily, but Florine isn't here. In fact, she's with her husband. They've gone away to try and sort things out. She saw quite quickly that running away wasn't the answer. The answer is to show Yohan she has a voice in their marriage.'

She made a noise that could have been a sob. 'Then . . . I *am* eleven months and a few days early,' she whispered.

All the disappointment and anxiety of the past couple of weeks fled Noah's body in a hot rush, leaving him weak. He had to swallow before he could speak. 'I've so missed you.'

'Me, too. Me, missing you, I mean. Very much.' She sounded hoarse and uncertain. 'I can join you in the Dordogne. The reasons I gave for not leaving Alsace were barriers I erected. At least,' she added, 'I could have left the book café in Danielle's hands if I'd just put a few weeks into the handover. As it is, Reeny and Graham are selling up anyway, and there's no job for me.'

'I'm sorry,' he murmured, knowing she'd put her heart and soul into the book café. 'That's a lot for you to lose, all at once – your job and your friends.'

She drew in a long breath and puffed it out again. 'Turns out the friendship wasn't all I thought. Anyway,' she hurried on, obviously not wanting to go into that right then, 'Dad's pressed me to take on the role of business manager with his new company, but I'll find something near Castillon. If you still want me to,' she added shyly.

He laughed aloud, his heart beginning the slow jump of impending joy. 'Why would I move back to the Dordogne if Florine and Yohan are going to try and make a go of things?'

Kat hesitated. 'So where are you? I went to the van and it's all shut up and empty.'

'I'm in Muntsheim, in the house I'd already agreed to rent,' he told her softly. Then added, 'Kat, I told Florine about you and me. I said I'd help her, but I had my own life to live. She was mortified that she'd presumed too much. I've done everything I promised you . . . though I'm not sure I'd actually have been able to wait a year to tell you,' he added conscientiously. 'Now, as we're only ten minutes apart, is there any chance you could come over? Clé's in bed. We could continue this conversation in person.' He held his breath, a tiny, pessimistic part of him expecting that she'd find new obstacles to cast in their path.

But though she sounded slightly dazed, she said, 'Oh, yes! Oh, *yes*, Noah. I'll come now.' The phone line went dead. She rang straight back. 'You'd better remind me of the address.'

Kat drove the familiar route to Muntsheim still in a daze. Or a dream. A lovely, beautiful, dream-come-true dream. Her hands trembled on the steering wheel and she had to force herself to concentrate at junctions so she didn't bumble out and crash into somebody. She even had her sat nav on to make sure she got to the right place. She'd visited the little rental twice with Noah, but she was so shocked and nervous – yet deliriously happy – she might end up upside down in the river if she relied on her memory.

Noah hadn't left Alsace.

He hadn't returned to his old life. He'd kept all his promises.

Noah hadn't left Alsace.

She indicated to turn into La Place de la Liberté and then again into Rue des Roses. She paused at the junction to take several deep breaths before turning right into Rue des Oiseaux and pulling up outside a modest house with a lawn and a twining honeysuckle. She switched off the engine and took off her seatbelt, then a blur of movement caught her eye and she just had enough time to draw breath before the driver's door was wrenched open and she was pulled bodily out and into a pair of warm arms and crushed against a man's chest.

'What took you so long?' Noah's voice was muffled by her hair.

Shakily, she laughed. 'I drove straight here.'

'I was talking about the three weeks and four days. Come inside.' He slackened his hold in order to tow her up the path and through the front door, closing it softly behind them and plunging back into the conversation they'd begun on the phone. His blue eyes fixed unwinkingly on hers, fierce and compelling. 'Even if Florine hadn't gone back to Yohan, I wouldn't have picked things up with her. I wouldn't have been able to prevent her returning to Castillon, but I would have tried with everything I had to convince you there were ways for us to be together.' He began pressing hot kisses on her face, grazing his lips across her eyelids, her forehead, her mouth. He paused. 'I do hope she returns next week, as she plans, because I was able to put back my two-day interview for the Rhine river cruise people but I can't delay forever. They'll just give the job to the other candidate.'

Kat tried to kiss him back, but he was acting as if she'd vanish if he didn't kiss every inch of visible skin – which was going to get quite interesting around the shorts department – so instead she said shyly, 'I could look after Clémence, if you think she'd be OK with me. I'm currently unemployed.'

That got his attention. 'You've left Livres et Café already?'

She grimaced. 'Stormed out in a huff. I've sort of half-made things up with Reeny, but Graham and I aren't speaking.'

His brows drew down and he looped his arm loosely about her rather than continuing to squeeze her so hard she could scarcely breathe. 'Why on earth not?'

She found, suddenly, that that problem wasn't as important as it had been. She shrugged. 'They sold the business furtively and left me high and dry. I didn't care for it. The job Dad's already offered me sounds OK but I'm not sure about working with Irina.'

He wrinkled his nose. 'Ahem. Maybe not.' Then he laughed. 'We're both off work because I've had to take unpaid leave to look after Clémence. How very convenient for everything I want to do—'

'Papa, who are you talking to?' said a sleepy voice from the top of the stairs. Then, 'Oh, Kat! Have you brought Angelique?'

As Noah's arms remained firmly around her, Kat didn't pull away, but smiled at the rumpled girl in yellow pyjamas.

'I'm afraid not, sweetie. But maybe'—she sent a sidelong look at Noah—'we could take her out tomorrow.'

'Thank you,' said Clémence, rubbing her eye. 'Which park?'

'You can choose tomorrow,' Kat said huskily, her heart warming at the easy way Clémence had accepted that she was cuddling Noah.

The sleepy girl sank down on the top step and yawned. 'Thank you,' she said gravely. Her mouth curved into a small smile. 'Papa told me that one day you're going to be his girlfriend and we'd all be happy together. Is that day now?'

Kat felt Noah jump, as if the words had physically touched him, and her eyes flooded with tears. Pulling free, then taking Noah's hand, she towed him with her as she climbed the stairs to perch just below Clémence, Noah crouching alongside. 'If you don't mind,' Kat murmured, putting out a tentative hand to stroke Clémence's blonde, bed-mussed hair.

But Clémence just beamed. 'No. Because if we're a family then I am part-owner of Angelique.'

The childish simplicity made Kat want to laugh and cry all at once. Instead, she gave Clémence a big hug. 'You are. And I think Angelique will love it.'

Clémence pulled Noah into the hug. 'Will you carry me back to bed?'

'Yes, little one,' he murmured. With an easy movement he scooped his daughter up and took a few steps along the landing.

Kat followed to hover diffidently in the doorway of a room that shouted 'little girl's bedroom' with dawn-pink walls and a duvet covered with princess castles and rainbows. She watched as Noah made a performance of posting

Clémence under the sheet, making her giggle. She wondered if there was anything more heart-melting than the way he checked she was OK and kissed her goodnight, so tall and strong next to her delicate frame.

'Kat?' Clémence called sleepily.

Kat took a step nearer, wondering whether she was expected to kiss Clémence goodnight, too.

But Clémence was pointing at the foot of the bed. 'Look at my new bookcase,' she said proudly. 'It's my best thing.'

Eyes stinging again, Kat moved close enough to admire the piece of furniture, already nearly full of books. 'How pretty to arrange them by colour,' she said admiringly. 'I never thought of that.'

Clémence regarded her seriously. 'No, but it would be silly in a bookshop, wouldn't it? Your customers need the alphabet to help them find their favourite authors.'

'That's right. You're very clever,' Kat said sincerely, deciding not to break the news that she no longer worked at Livres et Café quite yet. It would keep until tomorrow.

'And it's time you went to sleep. You'll see Kat tomorrow. And Angelique,' Noah added as Clémence opened her mouth as if to remind him.

Kat and Noah tiptoed down the stairs together, only speaking again once they were safely in the salon and could talk without keeping Clémence awake. Kat stepped into Noah's arms again. 'You really told Clémence we'd be together?'

He stroked down her back and settled his hands comfortably on her buttocks. 'I . . . did . . . everything . . . I . . . promised.' He planted kisses on her lips between words, for emphasis.

347

'You did,' she agreed with pleasure, kissing him back. 'Now – how long before we can go to bed?'

He grinned. 'The time it takes to drink one glass of wine, I think. And don't worry. There's a lock on my bedroom door.'

Chapter Twenty-Three

One week later, Kat, Clémence and Angelique returned from a walk by the river in Muntsheim. Kat had told Clémence that she wanted to explore new areas, so Angelique didn't get bored, but really, she'd been avoiding Parc Lemmel. It was too painful to return to the place she loved so much after her abrupt departure from Café et Livre.

It was the second day of Noah's two-day interview and though Florine and Yohan were now back in Kirchhoffen, Clémence had asked to be allowed to stay with Kat at Papa's house this afternoon to be there when he arrived home. They'd even made a cake to welcome him, though it worried Clémence that the top sloped. Kat said reassuringly, 'But they're the hardest kind to make. We can cover it with white icing and then it will look like a ski slope. We can make a person out of icing, too, and pretend they're skiing.'

Clémence accepted this feeble attempt to head off her objections, though she made several remarks about it being summer and Papa liking water skiing, not snow skiing, making Kat make a mental note to ensure that she levelled cakes on the oven shelves in future.

It was late afternoon and they were helpless with giggles at the portly, ungainly skier they'd created out of balls of icing, when the front door flew open and Noah shouted, 'I've got the job!'

They shoved the cake into the fridge and flew into the hall to meet him, icing sugar sprinkled down their clothes. Kat made certain of letting Clémence have the first embrace with her father, remembering how Irina had always pushed ahead of Kat, but Noah picked Clémence up then reached out and pulled Kat in, too, making it a three-way hug. 'Fantastic,' she breathed, cuddling his broad shoulders with one arm and Clémence's narrow ones with the other. 'I couldn't be happier for you, you clever thing.'

'I am,' he said immodestly. 'I'll begin halfway through October so Marcel can have me back at the park till then, if he wants.'

Kat felt a pang at the thought that she wouldn't be going back there herself, though she said loyally, 'I'll bet he will.'

Then, in the kitchen, her phone sounded the alert for a FaceTime call and she slid out of the group hug to hurry up the hall and rescue it from the counter. She hesitated when she saw Reeny's name flashing up. To give herself a moment to compose herself, she rinsed the icing off her fingers at the sink and dried her hands. Then she picked up. 'Hello, Reeny. This is an unexpected pleasure.'

'Hmm,' said Reeny. She looked bright of eye, and less fatigued and waxen than she had for months. Her hair looked freshly trimmed, too. 'I expect you're being ironic, but you might be downright rude when you hear what I have to say.'

Kat's attention was piqued. She propped the phone up against the biscuit tin and leant her elbows on the counter. 'Oh?' Noah and Clémence entered the room, Noah with questions in his eyes, probably having heard Kat say Reeny's name. He looked handsome in his dark suit and white shirt, but his tie was already stuffed in his pocket. When she sent him a smile, his expression cleared, then he ushered Clémence and Angelique through the kitchen door to the garden.

On screen, Reeny's brow puckered. 'Oh, Kat, we do regret what happened. And I'm just going to come right out with what I've called to say, and you can slam the phone down if you want – though it's not very easy to slam a mobile, is it?' Her smile flashed, reminding Kat sharply of the old relationship, when Reeny had been dear to her. 'Will you come back and manage the business for us? The sale's fallen through and we're at our wits' end. Danielle's got in such a muddle with the orders and the banking, and Graham's ready to have a breakdown.'

Despite everything that had happened, Kat's heart leapt. With an effort, she kept her expression sceptical. 'What about you going back to the UK?'

Reeny sighed. 'We're still going, but also keeping a little holiday home here, too. Now I'm doing better, we realise that we don't want to lose Alsace altogether.'

'No, I can understand that,' Kat nodded. She'd made her own home in the beautiful region after all. 'Well, go on,' she prodded. 'How do you envisage me working for you when Graham and I aren't speaking?'

Reeny glanced to one side and the picture shifted. Graham appeared alongside his wife, red-faced. 'I'm going to apologise, beg forgiveness and make amends,' he said, with an almost comical hang-dog expression. Then the pair went on, offering olive branch after olive branch, pressing, urging, while Kat listened, and questioned, then listened again.

Finally, she straightened, taking the phone with her as she slipped on her flip-flops and stepped through the back door, out into the September sunshine, grinning as Clémence and Angelique gambolled up to meet her. 'I need to think,' she told the figures on the screen. 'I'll give you my answer in a few days.'

'Oh,' Reeny sighed wistfully. 'We're really longing for it to be "yes".'

On that hopeful note, Kat said her farewells and tucked the phone in the pocket of her shorts as she hugged Clémence, a hug into which Angelique seemed to consider herself automatically invited. Then they joined Noah where he waited on the garden bench, jacket discarded negligently over the clothesline.

'Do I take it that they want you back in your old job?' he demanded incredulously, cocking a surprised eyebrow.

'They do,' she confirmed with a laugh. 'The sale's fallen through. Apparently, when I run the business, it's so profitable that they can augment their pensions nicely. They'll pay me more, because of the responsibility, make it a minimum two-year contract, and Graham has grovelled his apologies.'

'As he damned-well should.' Noah slipped an arm around her. 'What do you think?'

'The book café is very nice,' Clémence reminded her, eyes hopeful.

Kat smoothed Clémence's hair, warm and silky beneath her fingers. 'That's true. I reminded them of the shock and disappointment at the furtive way they sold the business out from under me, of course. But . . .' She shrugged.

'What I remember more is loving every day at work, choosing books I knew would please the customers, organising kids' events, even laying out the pastries attractively and chatting with tourists. It's such a joy to step out of Livres et Café and into Parc Lemmel, whether it's heaving with tourists in summer, looking as if it's made of gingerbread in autumn, or even under a layer of snow like the icing on our cake.'

'The cake is supposed to be a surprise,' Clémence hissed, darting a look at her father.

Kat clapped an apologetic hand over her mouth. 'Sorry!' The three of them laughed and Angelique wagged her tail and grinned a doggy grin. Kat took Noah's hand. 'I haven't given them my answer, but I think I'm going to say yes.'

Clémence's gave a loud cheer. 'Hooray! We'll have children's events again.'

'Definitely,' Kat agreed. 'I told them that one thing we'd need to get straight is my hours. I'm not going to work twelve-hour days during the summer anymore.' She flushed. 'I'll want to spend time with you two.' Half shyly, she added, 'My family.'

And when a smile blazed over Noah's face, happy tears prickled into her eyes.

Clémence slipped her arms around Kat's waist. 'Your family is us and Solly and Angelique and your dad. And Irina,' she added as an obvious afterthought.

Kat hugged Clémence tight, revelling in the precious relationship she already had with Noah's daughter. Mixed with it was the familiar grief that she'd never felt love for her own stepmother. But, for the first time, it was Irina she felt sorry for because she'd never been big-hearted enough to want Kat's affection, when a child's love was such a wonderful thing. 'That's right,' she said softly.

'I have all my family living near me in France now. I'm richer than I've ever been.'

This confused Clémence's literal mind. 'Because Reeny and Graham are going to pay you more euros?'

Kat pressed a kiss on Clemence's forehead and then one on Noah's cheek. 'No. Because I have love. And that's worth *loads* more than money.'

Loved

Summer at the French Café?

**Then why not try one of Sue's
other sizzling summer reads
or cosy Christmas stories?**

**The perfect way to escape
the everyday.**

Grab your sun hat, a cool glass of wine, and escape with these gloriously uplifting summer reads . . .

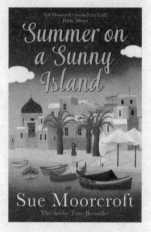

Dive into the summer holiday
that you'll never want to end . . .

Curl up with these feel-good festive romances . . .

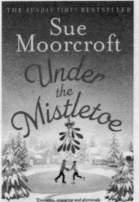